The
Girl Without
A Name

SUZANNE GOLDRING

The
Girl Without
A Name

bookouture

Published by Bookouture in 2020

An imprint of Storyfire Ltd.
Carmelite House
50 Victoria Embankment
London EC4Y 0DZ

www.bookouture.com

ISBN: 978-1-83888-841-1
eBook ISBN: 978-1-83888-840-4

In memory of my late father,
George James Goldring.
A good father and friend to many.

When I was a child, I spake as a child, I understood
as a child, I thought as a child: but when I became a man
I put away childish things.
I Corinthians ch.13, v.11

I was a child and she was a child,
In this kingdom by the sea;
But we loved with a love which was more than love –
I and my Annabel Lee.
'Annabel Lee' – Edgar Allan Poe, 1849

Chapter 1

16 August 2004

Not Again

Dick Stevens, widower, father-of-three and grandfather of more than he can remember, doesn't normally watch daytime television, but the rain today has driven him indoors. Since he lost Maureen three years ago, his daily routine has revolved around golf or fishing, gardening or the pub. Her death from lung cancer was the trigger he needed to finally give up smoking. Maureen only ever had a ciggie to be 'sociable' so it doesn't seem fair she succumbed to what's called passive smoking, when he's puffed away twenty a day for sixty years, ever since he was fourteen. Was it his fault she got a bad chest or was it their love of pub lunches? Every pub he's ever been to has a welcoming fug of blue smoke and yellowed ceilings. Should be banned, then he wouldn't sit there with his *Daily Mail*, trying to breathe in the tempting but now forbidden scent of tobacco when he has his pint.

So these days he's replaced his filthy habit with other vices. When he walks to the nearby Tesco Express for his daily newspaper, he is always tempted by the newly baked croissants and pains au chocolat, his favourite. Lovely with a fresh cup of coffee. And when his eldest daughter Billie calls in as she does every day, with ready meals or easy-to-cook chops, she nearly always stays for a cuppa and offers him a piece of home-baked lemon drizzle or an iced yum-yum. Him and Billie, they've both got a sweet tooth. Hasn't done either of them any favours. At least the fags helped him keep his weight down. Maureen always told him he'd balloon once he gave them up. He must have put on at least a stone since she went.

Placing a fresh cup of tea on the coffee table next to a new pack of plain chocolate digestives, he settles himself with an indulgent sigh into his most recent purchase, an immensely comfortable, easy-rise reclining armchair, upholstered in brown jumbo cord. A sensible choice, he decided, since he planned to take most of his meals in the chair. Always been a messy eater, he has.

'Ugly thing,' Billie said when it was delivered. 'You won't catch me letting Kevin have one of those, no matter how relaxing they are. He'd be dozing off in no time.' But that's the point, Dick tells himself, thinking of Billie's stiff leather sofas, so slippery he always fears sliding off and onto her shagpile carpet. If you can't indulge in a few bad habits by the time you reach your seventies, when can you? He presses the chair's switch, stretches his legs out on the cushioned extension and sighs with pleasure.

Dick takes a bite of his biscuit and switches on the television, expecting to find a gardening programme, though he'd prefer *Homes Under the Hammer*, reminding him what a good investment his house is. He keeps the garden tidy, but his expertise is limited to mowing the lawn and clearing leaves from the paths. Maureen was always the one for potting on seedlings in the greenhouse and filling the gaps in the borders with bedding plants. She was so patient and pinched out her sweet peas to achieve long-stemmed flowers that won second place in the Garden Club show the year before she became ill. Dick might not have his late wife's green fingers, but he enjoys watching others working hard and sometimes thinks he might transform his suburban garden with smart decking or a water feature. That would be soothing, sitting in the sun, when there is any sun, listening to the sound of harmonious trickling.

But the scenes bursting into his sitting room are not calming or inspiring, there is no transformed garden with a cheery Alan

Titchmarsh or buxom Charlie Dimmock, no cosy antiques auction, no smug property expert trying to persuade reluctant buyers to make a decision. Instead, the screen is filled with cars floating like corks, a turbulent river tossing a van like a tin toy, a helicopter hovering over roofs and lowering a winch. Dick hears the roar of crashing water and the thunder of heavy rain, the underlying accompaniment to the newscaster's dramatic commentary:

> *Scenes like this have not been seen since the Lynmouth flood of 1952. Today in north Cornwall the River Valency burst its banks and emergency services have been summoned to the village of Boscastle. Persistent rain over a period of a few hours has caused a flash flood and created a state of emergency. Officials say sixteen millimetres of rain fell in fifteen minutes this afternoon. Rescue crews from all over the West Country are attending the scene and helicopters have been alerted all over the south of England.*

'No, it can't be,' Dick moans. His heart turns over, his breath is rapid. 'Not again, how can it…?' He tries to reach the remote control to turn off the droning voice and the rolling news coverage that's stirring up memories, reminding him of that time, of all he has tried to forget and put behind him. The drone of the helicopter blades sounds like the bomb convoys, the crash of rocks and cars like broken homes, the urgent commentator like the air raid wardens shouting at them to take cover and the slap of the water like the thwack of the beatings.

As he stretches out to grab the remote control, he gasps. A fierce pain stabs his head, he feels faint and he senses all strength draining from his muscles. He is feeble and helpless, unable to move. He slumps back in his chair and the control drops from his weakened hand to the floor.

But the commentary on the newscast rolls on, the water rages and the cars are thrown against the bridge. Dick cannot halt it, nor can he prevent himself from watching it. If a punishment could be prescribed to suit the person, to match the crime, this would be it. Like Prometheus, Dick is fated to watch the doom-laden rolling coverage of the disaster now occurring in Cornwall forever. And if he closes his eyes, he can still hear that urgent voice and the thunder of the circling helicopters and the hurtling river. On and on it goes, repeating the highlights of the incident in dramatic, excited tones:

All roads to Boscastle are closed. A ten-foot-high wall of floodwater surged through the car park at forty miles an hour, crashing into the visitor centre, which collapsed shortly afterwards. Helicopters have begun winching residents and visitors to safety…

'No, no,' Dick mumbles, his mouth drooping, saliva seeping from his lips. 'Roo, ere are oo…' And his eyes well with tears, which slowly trickle down his lined cheeks to meet the drool that is dripping onto his checked shirt, till his chin, his neck and his clothing are damp and stained with the sticky mush of the chewed chocolate digestive. But still he stares with wet, glistening eyes at the flickering screen, at the graphic images, at the roaring water, and still he moans.

Chapter 2

16 August 2004

On the Stroke of Five

Billie knows he'll be at home. Dad is always home at the end of the afternoon. Ever since Mum died three years ago, Billie Mayhew, trained librarian and mother-of-two, keen baker but lapsed Zumba enthusiast, has made a point of calling on her father at 5 p.m. every day, whether she is working or not. She is the eldest and the nearest of his three children, but even if Keith and Pam did live closer she knows they wouldn't be as attentive. She delegated her duty to them at Easter so she and Kevin could go to Bournemouth for a break, but her brother and sister didn't bother going to see him every day. Keith said he could only manage to pop in once and Pam said he had plenty in the fridge so she didn't see the need.

'But it's not just about what food he's got in, is it? It's company,' she told them, 'as well as checking he's okay. Oh, I'll do it myself.' And she does. Every day, week after week. She doesn't really mind. He's her lovely dad and she can't bear to think he might be lonely. Besides, she's been on her feet all day, sorting returned books and helping people use the internet. She's dying for a cuppa and one of the chocolate brownies she picked up at the Women's Institute stall in the civic centre. She got a jar of this year's strawberry jam too, but she might keep that for herself.

The lights in the house are already on, although it's early. Drizzly rain has hidden the sun all day and gloom is descending over the street. She can hear the TV (or is it the radio?) burbling in the sitting room as soon as she lets herself in through the back door.

'Dad,' she calls out, 'I'm here. I got you some lamb chops and broccoli in Tesco.'

She puts the meat in the fridge, checking he's eaten the ham she left for his lunchtime sandwich. So he must have stayed home instead of lunching at the golf club or the pub. Billie approves of both, as it's good for him to get out every day, now he's on his own in the house. When Mum was alive they had lunch at the garden centre or a bistro pub at least once a week. Mum loved her plants and was always finding room for something new. Pelargoniums were her favourite, overwintered in the heated greenhouse and planted out all summer. Mum was talented like that.

Then Billie calls again, thinking he must be engrossed in a programme. 'Dad, I'll make us a cup of tea now. I'll bring you a cake as well.' But as the kettle begins to boil and there is still no answer, she feels her heart give a sudden flip. Mum had given them all fair warning with her cancer, all that awful treatment and relapses spread across four years before she couldn't hold on any longer, but surely not Dad without any warning? He was right as rain yesterday.

She rushes through the kitchen door. He's there alright; he's watching the news on TV, stretched out on that horrible new chair that he loves so much. But what's wrong with him? He isn't taking his eyes from the screen. He isn't acknowledging her, he's slumped to one side, his face drooping, his mouth drooling.

'Dad, what's happened? Are you ill?'

He can't tell her, but his right hand is trying to point. It wobbles and shakes as he holds it out, but he's definitely pointing at the television screen. And at the same time he's attempting to speak. His lips are twisted, his mouth has fallen to one side, the sound is distorted and Billie can't make out what he's trying to say.

She kneels down beside him, holding his shaking hand, desperate to understand what he is saying. 'Dad, what is it? What's happened?'

'Roo… ey,' he seems to be saying, in a trembling gasp. 'Roo, rooey…'

'What do you mean, Dad? What are you trying to say?' Her chest is fluttering with anxiety, but she tries to keep her voice steady and calm.

He takes a deep breath, as if he is summoning up all the strength he has left. He pulls his hand away from hers and his finger straightens and jabs in the direction of the screen, then falls to his side.

Billie turns to find out what is making him so agitated and sees a picture of chaos and devastation. Helicopters hovering, a river raging, cars tossed like rubber ducks, buildings crumbling. She catches fragments of words from the commentary… flash flood… torrential rain… winching to safety… And the ticker tape caption rolling across the bottom of the screen… Boscastle… destruction… danger…

And her father is still trying to articulate words and pointing, but Billie knows she has to act fast. 'Don't try to talk, Dad. I'm calling an ambulance. I think you've had a stroke. We have to get help right now.'

Chapter 3

16 August 2004

Snapshot From the Past

'You don't know how relieved I am, Dad. I thought I was going to lose you there.' Billie sits beside her father's bed in the hospital room, holding his hand. The air is stifling and warm, scented with hand sanitiser and the biscuity smell of starched clean laundry. She longs to open a window to breathe the cool evening breeze and she strokes his hand as she speaks. 'Thank goodness they could give you that injection so quickly. They're sure you're going to be alright now.'

Dick doesn't open his eyes. He lies back on the stiff plumped pillows, looking exhausted in a blue and white hospital gown, a crisp white sheet and a drip binding him like a straitjacket to the bed. His lopsided mouth trembles and for a second Billie thinks he might have something he wants to say, but no words or sounds emerge from his dry lips. She wonders if she should offer him cool sips of water or dab his mouth with a wet cloth, but she knows he has to stay on a drip until the consultant is sure he can drink and swallow without choking.

Billie fans herself with a folded newspaper, bought in the hospital's shop. It does little to cool her flushed face. Menopausal women don't thrive in hothouse conditions like this. 'I'm going to have to go home in a bit, Dad, but I'm sure you'll want to sleep soon.' It was a little after five when she found him slumped and mumbling in his new armchair and it's now nearly ten. The emergency responders said it was just as well she had rung for help promptly, so they could treat him within the key window of time for strokes.

'You gave me such a shock, Dad, finding you there like that. When we get you home, we're going to have to look after you properly. I've told Keith and Pam, and they agree with me, we'll all just have to pitch in till you're back on your feet again.' Billie only mentions her younger brother and sister to reassure her father that they know what has happened to him and that they care, but she knows they won't come rushing to help. They will expect their big sister to look after him as she always has, ever since her mother died.

Billie dabs her eyes with a crumpled tissue. She's always thought of her father as so strong and invincible. And now he's a deflated figure, unable to help himself. When she was a little girl he lifted her up, right over his head. He thrilled her with drives in the bucket seats of his many fast cars (don't tell your mother we touched 90 just then) and offered her the first cigarettes from his own pack of Player's (I'll be the one getting in trouble for this, not you). Now he's a shell of the man he was, weak and helpless. He was mowing the lawn only the day before, after a game of golf. How quickly he's been felled.

'I'll just put the TV on for a moment and catch the news while I'm waiting for Kevin to get here.' She'd ridden in the ambulance with her father, holding his hand and talking to him all the way, then paced the corridor with a scalding coffee and a packet of crisps from the vending machine while he was being assessed. She should have brought those chocolate brownies with her. They would have kept her going.

Billie aims the control at the TV and flicks through the channels. The ten o'clock news is just beginning, with aerial film coverage of the devastation in Boscastle. She's transfixed by scenes of the river breaking its banks and roaring through the picturesque village, tearing the shops and homes apart, gathering rocks, trees and vehicles as it raced through the narrow valley to the sea. She is so engrossed by the news coverage and the voiceover that at first she doesn't notice her father has become wildly agitated. While she gazes at the screen, he is shaking and tossing behind her, trying to attract her attention. It is only when she hears his moans that she realises he's become terribly distressed and then understands that he is reacting to the images and words on the screen.

He is trying to lift himself up with his good arm, then begins tugging at the tight sheet stretched across the bed. His eyes are bulging, his forehead is beaded with sweat and creased with anxiety. He looks terrified.

'Stop it, Dad,' Billie cries. 'You've got to stay in bed.' But he slips to one side of the mattress, crashing against the bedside cabinet, knocking over the jug and spilling water across the sheets and the floor.

She rushes round the bed and hauls him back before he can slip any further. 'You can't get up, Dad. You've got to stay put. You'll pull the drip out if you fall off the bed.'

He groans, alternately clutching at her arm and feebly pointing to the television. 'Okay, I'll turn it off, if that helps. It looks awful, doesn't it? But they're saying there's been no loss of life. Everyone's been picked up. You wouldn't believe such a dreadful flood could happen in the middle of summer, would you?'

She settles him back on the starched pillows and tucks the sheet around him again. He plucks at her sleeve, staring at her and making unintelligible sounds. 'Dad, I'm really sorry, I wish I could understand you but I can't right now. But never mind. You'll soon be your old self again and then we'll be chatting away like old times. Don't you worry.'

Her phone buzzes and she takes a quick look. 'That's Kevin, Dad. He's waiting for me outside in the car park. I'll have to go right away. He doesn't want to pay for a space. They charge a ridiculous amount. Kev says it's such a rip-off.'

She walks around the room, collecting her father's belongings. 'Now, I'm going to take all your clothes back home with me. I'll be back in the morning with some clean pyjamas and your sponge bag. If they haven't managed to clean you up, then I'll do it somehow. You'll feel so much better once you're freshened up and I expect before long you'll be able to come off that drip and catheter and have a shower.'

She folds the garments and packs them in her bag, then opens the drawer of the bedside cabinet. 'I'm taking your wallet with me as well. I know you always like to keep it with you, but you never know what might happen in hospitals. I think it'll be far safer coming home with me.'

But before she tucks the wallet away in her handbag, she thinks she should take a quick look at the contents. As well as two ten-pound notes, it holds his library ticket, a bus pass, a debit card and a driving licence. Billie looks at the tiny blurred photograph on the licence and laughs. 'This is the worst photo of you I've ever seen. It looks nothing like you! And that reminds me, I'll put the MG in the garage tomorrow. I know you don't usually, but I think it'll be safest in there until you can drive it again.' She knows how her father loves his blue car, which she suspects was bought with the insurance payout after her mother went. She didn't approve, but it wasn't her money, so she kept her mouth shut.

As she slips the licence back into the wallet, she sees a folded raffle ticket, left over from the church summer fair. 'And you don't need this either. That was all over ages ago.' She pulls out the folded ticket and something else tucked behind it falls on the floor. She bends down to pick it up. A little black and white photo of a young woman. The snap is crumpled, as if it has been handled many times, the corners are dog-eared. She stares at it for a moment. The hairstyle is quite old-fashioned and the face is smiling. Could it be Mum, or Dad's older sister, Auntie Joan? She doesn't recognise the girl but then she hasn't seen early photos of either of them in a long while, though there are some in a box back at the house. She is about to ask her father who it is, but when she looks back at him she sees he is finally sleeping, so she tiptoes from the room, thinking she will show him the picture in the morning.

No more pencils, no more books,
No more teacher's ugly looks,
No more things that bring us sorrow
Cos we won't be here tomorrow.

Chapter 4

1 September 1939

An Awfully Big Adventure

'I don't want to wear that hat today,' Ruby said as her mother tucked her long plaits back behind her ears and tied the knitted blue pixie hood under her chin. 'It's not cold. And it makes my ears all itchy.'

'You'll be glad of it in a few days' time when it's not so warm. And it might be much colder out in the country. Now let me think. Have you got everything?' Her mother frowned and consulted the Ministry of Health leaflet listing the essential items every child should take with them. Christchurch School, which Ruby had attended since she was five years old, was being evacuated to a village near Barnstaple in Devon, where Mrs Morrison hoped and prayed kind, generous families would take care of all the children, especially her precious Ruby. She didn't really want to send her only child so far away, but everyone was urging parents to dispatch their children while they had the chance, before the Germans started bombing the whole of London. But at least she'd be going with all her school friends. That should help to stop her getting too homesick. And since Frank had been lost at sea two years ago, she felt she had no choice but to send her daughter off to live with strangers. An accident before the ship left Hong Kong, the telegram said. Drunk and beaten up in the stewpots of Stanley, more like. Still, she got his pension and that went further without him spending all his pay down the pub. He always came home from his stints at sea with extravagant presents, all smiles and charm, and then he'd be off drinking again. He was enough to put her off men for life. But at least she and Ruby were better off than some families, with him inheriting his parents' house and leaving it to her.

'Now let's see… It says gas-mask, underwear, night things, plimsolls, socks… Oh dear, I do hope I've given you enough… toothbrush, comb, towel… Honestly, you'd think they could give you all a clean towel… Oh well, soap, facecloth, hankies… That's everything then.'

She clicked the little case shut, then checked that her daughter's coat was buttoned up and the label with her name written on it in capital letters was securely pinned to the lapel. Then she hung Ruby's gas-mask in its cardboard box round her neck on a piece of thick string. 'There now, you're all set. And I've made you ham sandwiches for the journey, with a bit of fruit cake. They said just to give you chocolate, raisins and an orange for the train, but I can't see that keeping you going all day on a long journey.'

Ruby took the paper bag of food. She didn't like fruit cake, but she could swap it later with Joyce or Grace or one of her other school friends. She was looking forward to the train and going away with her class. It was going to be a big adventure. Getting away from home, where Mum fussed so over every smudge on her dresses and every graze on her knees. She'd never been far from home before. Mum only liked going on the train as far as Epping and the bus to Romford market.

If Dad was still here, Mum wouldn't be so bothered and maybe there'd be brothers and sisters. But Dad had hardly ever been home, he was almost a stranger, and now he was drowned he'd never come back. Ruby last saw him two Christmases ago, when he brought her a wind-up tin monkey, clashing cymbals in its paws. He said it was a toy from China, but she didn't think it looked a bit Chinese, not like the dark-eyed family at the laundry that Mum used for their sheets and blankets.

Ruby was sure she was going to have a grand time, like when the school had its annual seaside outing to Southend and she got her socks and knickers wet, paddling at the beach. She'd been sick on the way home too, after eating all Joyce's pink rock as well as her own, but she hadn't told Mum that. Miss Harris, her class teacher, had mopped her down with a damp hankie, so nothing showed up when she arrived home tired but happy.

'Come on, Mum,' Ruby said. 'Miss Harris said we've got to get to school early this morning. She said it's really important we're on time for the bus to the station.'

Mrs Morrison looked at herself in the hall mirror, patting her hair and touching up her lipstick. She put a clean handkerchief in her jacket pocket, then opened the front door. Ruby skipped down the path, turned and called to her mother, 'Race you there,' and she was off down the street lined with dusty lime trees, their leaves just beginning to turn colour after the first chilly night as summer ended.

All the pupils at Christchurch School were lining up in the playground when Ruby ran in. She knew exactly what to do, because this was how the classes assembled every morning. Their parents stayed outside, while they all lined up in their forms, so the teachers could see at a glance that everyone was there. Usually they checked the register in the classroom, but today they stood outside in the cool sunshine on this first day of autumn. But at that moment, as the names were called one by one and each child answered 'Yes, Miss Harris,' Ruby realised that this was not going to be quite the big adventure she had been expecting. She had been looking forward to going away with her two very best friends, playing games of hopscotch and skipping, giggling about the boys in the class and singing 'Ten Green Bottles'. But now it was all wrong. Joyce didn't answer to her name when it was called; nor did Grace. Ruby twisted her head and looked up and down the column of other ten-year-olds. Her friends weren't at the front of the class line and they weren't behind her either. Nor were they racing across the playground, apologetic latecomers.

'Right now, children,' said Miss Harris, 'I was expecting a few more of you this morning, but it seems perhaps some families have changed their minds at the last minute. But all of you here will be travelling together and as our bus is waiting for us, we can all set off. Single file now and no pushing. We want to show the people of Barnstaple what well-behaved guests they'll have staying with them.'

Ruby clutched her little brown cardboard case and the paper bag of sandwiches. The class turned round and filed towards the school entrance, where the bus was waiting with a small group of parents. She saw her mother's fixed smile. Was she glad to see her daughter leaving? But then all the parents looked happy, smiling and waving as their children approached the bus. Ruby felt her bottom lip quivering, but was determined not to cry. She had been so looking forward to this, ever since Miss Harris had told the whole class that they would all be going away together. So why weren't Grace and Joyce here? Maybe they'd been sick in the night, maybe they'd been cheeky and told they couldn't go as a punishment.

She climbed into the bus and Miss Harris took her case and put it in the luggage rack. The air in the coach was already stuffy on this warm autumn day, and heavy with the cloying scent of mothballs seeping from winter coats brought out of storage. Still, the smell of camphor was better than the stink of some of the children from the poorer families, who wore hand-me-downs darned and patched, stained with the grubbiness of their previous owners. Ruby was glad her clothes were always so clean and well-ironed, even if her mother did make a fuss over the tiniest speck of dirt or a lost button.

The coach was so full, Ruby had to sit down next to an older boy, Stevie, who was two classes above her. She knew that wasn't his real name, but everyone called him Stevie. His big sister, Joan, was helping some of the younger children with their bags. At fourteen, she was old enough to leave school, but she seemed to have been recruited as an assistant teacher now. 'Don't cry,' she was saying to one of the littler ones. 'It's going to be lots of fun. You'll see.'

But was it going to be fun? Ruby thought. It wouldn't be the same without Joyce and Grace, she was sure of that. Who was going to play clapping games with her now? Who else was good at turning the rope at the right pace so they could take turns skipping in and out?

She looked out of the bus window and saw her mother dabbing at her eyes with a handkerchief. She wasn't the only one. As the bus began pulling away, all the parents waved their children off, several applied the hankies that had been waving them away to their weeping eyes and some even collapsed in each other's arms.

At this sorry sight, Ruby felt the enormity of the parting and fat tears began rolling down her cheeks. She wished she had a hankie ready. But all her hankies were folded and packed in her little case, high above her in the rack. Then, as her tears dripped onto her paper food bag and she began to sob, Stevie, beside her, said, 'Here, have this. You don't want your tuck getting soggy.' He handed her a clean handkerchief and smiled at her. His nails were etched with grime, but the hankie was clean. 'Don't cry. Me and Joan will look out for you.'

Ruby stopped her crying and managed to smile at him, noticing how very blue his eyes were. Then Miss Harris called out to the whole bus, 'Come on, class, let's have a sing-song. How about "Ten Green Bottles"?' And as everyone began to sing, Ruby thought being evacuated might not be so bad after all.

Chapter 5

1 September 1939

The Chosen Few

'You're going to live with some nice people,' Ruby's mother had said. But what nice people? And where were they?

'Who will I have to stay with?' she asked Miss Harris, as the train steamed through the unfamiliar countryside towards Devon.

'A nice family,' her teacher said. 'A pretty little girl like you, all neat and tidy, why, everyone will want to have you. Don't you worry about it.'

Did that mean that if you weren't pretty, neat and tidy, no one would want to have you to live with them? Ruby's long dark hair was washed regularly at home and brushed and plaited every day by her mother. Her clothes were always clean and her nails were trimmed. But Mavis Riddle had short, lank hair, a thick coating of freckles and a permanently runny nose. Rosemary McGee's teeth were bad, she smelt sour and her dresses were always stained. Did that mean that they wouldn't be chosen by anyone? And then where would they sleep and have their meals if no one wanted to offer them a home?

Ruby was anxious for the whole journey, trying not to crumple her coat and dress, not to scuff her polished shoes, and she shook her head when Miss Harris offered them all a warm drink from the Thermos flasks she'd brought. There was no toilet on the train and Ruby didn't want to be caught short. Better to be thirsty than have wet knickers.

As the train wound across Somerset and into Devon, the late afternoon sun gleamed through the grimy windows, making the carriage hot and stuffy. And it was still light when the train finally reached Barnstaple after several hours. The carriages emptied out one at a time, so Ruby and the other children could line up in their usual forms. They were told to use the station toilets first, then they were all marched across the track to metal pens, where each class had to stand together. Ruby knew what the pens were for straight away. It was just like Romford market, where her mother sometimes liked to shop for a change and buy dress fabric. This was a cattle market, normally filled with beasts, now packed with tired and grubby, fractious children. Some had never seen something like this before and thought they were being taken to a prison, so they began crying. 'Shh now,' Joan said, going round and hugging them. 'It won't be long now. It's just so we all stay in our groups.' But for Ruby it felt like they were all on show, waiting to be sold to the highest bidder, like the bull with a ring in his nose in Romford High Street.

When several buses arrived at the market entrance, each class filed on, led by their teacher. 'This way, children,' Miss Harris called. 'You'll soon be going to your new lodgings.'

Ruby hung on to Joan's hand and Stevie followed close behind. Their bus wound through country lanes for about fifteen minutes, then stopped outside a village school. All the children got out and were marched to the toilets again, then directed to sit in the classrooms. 'Now if any of you want to pair up, go and sit with the person you want to be with,' Miss Harris said. Ruby looked around and then clung again to Joan, who smiled and let her sit next to her. Stevie sat alongside with Will, another boy from his class.

And then it seemed that the school really did turn into a version of the cattle market. Local women who had agreed to take in London children filed in and began to choose, pointing at a girl here, a boy there. The children had no say in the selection whatsoever. 'I won't let you go on your own,' Joan whispered in Ruby's ear. 'Don't you worry. You're staying with me. I'll say you're my cousin.'

Ruby was holding her breath, tight with fear that she would be parted from Joan and be sent off with someone she didn't like. A large red-faced woman with a pork-pie hat sporting a feather pointed at Stevie and then at Will next to him. 'Those two,' she snapped, then folded her arms across her large bosom. 'They look strong and healthy.'

Joan gasped and turned round. 'But he's my little brother. I want him to stay with me.'

Miss Harris stepped forward. 'Joan dear, people can only take two lodgers each. Stevie will enjoy going with his friend. It'll be an adventure for them, won't it, Stevie?'

He grinned as he stood up, clutching his rucksack and his gas-mask. 'Don't worry, sis, I'll see you in school, won't I?' And the boys followed the broad-hipped woman out of the classroom.

Ruby and Joan were chosen by Mrs Honey, a widow who lived nearby. She looked like a kindly granny, with her neat white hair. 'It's only a short walk to my cottage, my dears. And I've a lovely stew ready and waiting for your supper. There's apple turnovers too. You must be so hungry and tired after your long journey.'

As they left the school, they saw Stevie and his friend climbing into the back of a farm truck, together with a black and white collie dog. Alongside the red-faced woman was a very large man with a bushy white moustache and side-whiskers. A bit like Father Christmas, Ruby thought.

She watched the truck splutter down to the end of the lane and out of the village, heading towards the streak of red sun setting beyond the hills. The boys each had an arm around the dog and they were laughing and waving to her and Joan. It looked like they were going to have a grand old time.

Chapter 6

17 September 1939

Hair Today, Gone Tomorrow

Ruby tried telling herself she could be brave and that she wouldn't cry. After all, being evacuated wasn't so bad. She shared a lovely bedroom with Joan, overlooking the garden. The pink and blue floral curtains were faded but clean and the walls gleamed with fresh whitewash. They had speckled brown eggs for breakfast every day, because Mrs Honey, their landlady, had plenty of chickens in coops in her large back garden on the edge of the village. There were vegetable plots and fruit trees as well, providing all they needed.

Their first day, when they arrived at the village school, had been long and tiring and many of the children were both tearful and afraid. She hadn't liked the look of some of the plump rosy farmers' wives and their big-handed husbands, who she heard saying they could only afford to take older boys who could be 'useful' around the farm, even though they'd eat more than the smaller girls.

But at night she felt she was a long way from home. She missed her cat Sooty and to her surprise she missed Mum too. At home they always had a mug of cocoa together before bedtime. Then Mum brushed her long dark hair till it shone and put it in a single plait for the night. In the morning, she brushed Ruby's hair all over again and divided it into two neat long braids that reached almost to her waist, tied with elastic bands and topped with dark blue ribbons. 'You're just like Rapunzel, you are,' Mum would say, admiring Ruby's thick hair. And although Ruby knew that the character in the fairy tale had golden hair, while hers was dark, she liked the comparison, liked to think she was just like the princess in the tower, waiting for a prince to come one day and rescue her.

But now there was no chance she would ever be a princess, now that she was about to lose her lovely long hair. The village families blamed the new arrivals from London and everyone from Christchurch School blamed the local children for the infestation of nits. Two weeks ago they had started classes in various locations: the village hall, the church hall and in the local school itself. London children sat next to country children; heads from the smog and the slums brushed close to heads from the haystacks and hedgerows.

Nitty Nora, as the nit nurse was commonly called by the children, had been called in to the school a week after they'd arrived. She had inspected every head and made a note of her findings, tutting over live and dead discoveries and cleaning her comb after every investigation.

Miss Harris broke the news to her charges after the nurse's visit. 'I'm sorry to say that we have a bad outbreak of nits this term. No one's to blame, but you are all going to have to have your hair cut next week. And then, just to be absolutely sure we don't have any little problems lurking still, you will all have treatment, which will be washed out afterwards.'

Ruby didn't think she had ever had her hair cut. Now and then her mother would trim the ends of her long plaits, just to even them up, but she couldn't remember ever sitting in a chair with an apron around her neck, having her hair cut all over.

'Will you have to have your hair cut too?' she asked Joan, who had begun to curl her hair at the front like many of the young women did. 'I jolly well hope not,' Joan said. She was sitting on her bed in front of the mirror on the chest of drawers they shared. 'I'll put my foot down if they try. Anyway, I know how to keep my hair clean. I use this all the time and I add vinegar when I wash my hair.' She held up the fine-toothed comb she dragged through her hair as well as brushing it. 'Here, undo those plaits and I'll comb your hair through too.'

It was soothing having her hair combed. Joan was gentle, unlike Mum, who brushed with vigorous strokes that tugged at the roots and made Ruby's neck ache. She thought she could almost fall asleep with Joan combing and humming at the same time. 'I think you're in the clear,' Joan said, 'but you may still have to have it cut tomorrow. They won't want any more nits turning up. And long hair like yours needs such regular combing. I think they'll insist on it being cut short.'

It all happened in the school hall. The boys on one side, girls on the other. Villagers and Londoners all mixed together, all ashamed, some tearful. The boys didn't cry, of course, although their haircuts were the worst. After snipping any floppy hair away, the barber took a clipper to their heads, so they looked bald, as if they were newly sentenced prisoners.

When it was Ruby's turn, she climbed into the chair, the gown was tucked into the neck of her dress and then her lovely long plaits were chopped off, without even being unwound from their braiding. One clean snip with big scissors, just below her ears. That's all it took. They were never unravelled, never brushed through, they were just hacked off and fell to the floor, like two long lengths of twisted rope. Ruby's head immediately felt lighter. She looked down at the plaits, so long a part of her, as the barber combed her remaining hair and snipped around the edges. 'All done,' he said. 'Down you jump.'

And then, as she walked away, she took a look at herself. She shouldn't have done, she thought later. But then they shouldn't have put a mirror there for the newly shorn to see their new selves. She looked at her reflection and saw that she was definitely no longer a princess. Her lovely plaits were gone forever. She looked like a boy, with a bowl of hair clipped to just above her ears and straight across her forehead. And then she began to howl. 'Come on, it's not so bad,' Joan said, putting an arm around her and taking her hand. 'It'll soon grow again, anyway.'

'I don't like it,' Ruby sobbed. 'I don't look like me any more.'

And then she heard another voice at her side and another arm fell around her shoulders. 'But you'll always look like Ruby,' Joan's younger brother Stevie said, grinning even though his soft brown fringe had disappeared and he was newly shorn, his head looking smaller and more vulnerable. 'You'll always look lovely to me.'

And through her tears, Ruby managed to smile at these words from this kind boy, who seemed to really like her.

Chapter 7

26 November 1939

All Stirred Up

'I pity folks in the cities,' Mrs Honey said, throwing finely chopped suet into the enormous glazed basin in which she was mixing the ingredients for Christmas puddings. 'Those who don't have their own gardens or the countryside on their doorsteps will go short this winter, no matter what the government says.'

After attending a church service early that morning, Mrs Honey told the girls to put on their aprons and help her in the kitchen. Today was Stir-Up Sunday, the last Sunday in November before Advent, and there was cooking to be done.

Ruby sat on a stool, chopping the apples that Joan had already peeled and cored into tiny pieces. Huge quantities of apples, picked from the trees in the garden early in the autumn, to go into the puddings and also to make mincemeat. 'We learnt our lesson in the last war,' Mrs Honey said as she tossed in handfuls of currants and sultanas. 'I said to my Harry after that, I'll never be caught short again. And as soon as things started looking iffy, I said to myself, I'm not waiting to be told, I'm going to be pickling, bottling and stashing away till that pantry's full to bursting.'

She nodded towards the large walk-in larder that the girls knew contained rows of tinned fruit and meat, jar upon jar of plum and raspberry jam, bottled pears and pickled onions, a whole wheel of cheese and a smoked side of bacon, wrapped in muslin. Enamel bins and stone tubs contained flour, sugar and dried fruits, safe from the nibbling and droppings of mice but prone to the odd weevil. And that was not all the smallholding had stored away for the winter. In a cool outhouse, set above the ground on what Ruby thought were stone mushrooms, but was told were called staddle stones, were trays and trays of apples and sackfuls of potatoes grown over the summer and harvested just before the first frost. Ruby knew she would never go hungry in this well-organised household and wondered if her mother had laid in stores at home or thought of digging up the dusty hydrangeas that bordered their narrow strip of London garden to grow cabbages and carrots. She hadn't said anything about such preparations in her last letter, but had written, '*I'm beginning to wonder what all the fuss was about when we had to send you all off to Devon. You might as well have stayed home after all.*' And Ruby read those words and thought however much she might sometimes miss Sooty and Mum, she really didn't think drab London would be preferable to the comforts she was enjoying in Devon.

'Why is it called mincemeat, if it's not meat?' Joan said, peeling yet another apple for Ruby to chop with a little vegetable knife.

'Because in the olden days it was made with real meat,' Mrs Honey replied. 'All the spices kept the meat from going bad and if it was a bit past it, then the fruit and sugar hid the smell and the taste. Nowadays, the nearest thing to meat in it is the suet, which is the fat from cows. I get it from the butcher in the village and chop it into tiny crumbs.'

'When will we eat it?' Ruby asked.

'When it's good and ready, Missy. I'll add a drop or two of brandy and that helps it to keep well and brings out all the flavour. You can help me make the mince pies on Christmas Eve and I'll let you have one as soon as they're out the oven.'

'How will I help make them?'

'I'll make the pastry, then get you to cut out the cases with a pastry cutter. And when we've put their lids on, I'll let you make three little holes in the tops with a skewer.'

Ruby paused in her chopping and looked puzzled. 'Why holes?'

Mrs Honey laughed. 'To let the steam out, as they cook, of course. But some say, and I believe it myself, that the mincemeat is like the gifts the Three Kings brought for the baby Jesus and the three holes are therefore the kings themselves.' She turned to the shelves in her scullery and came back with a tower of white pudding basins and a stack of white cloths.

'Goodness me,' Joan said. 'How many puddings are we going to eat at Christmas?'

'Oh, these aren't for this year,' Mrs Honey said, lining the basins up on the well-scrubbed kitchen table. 'We're eating last year's pudding this Christmas. I usually make two every November and keep one back for the following year. They always taste better when they've matured.'

'But there are six basins here. Do you think you'll need six puddings next Christmas?'

'No, ducky. No one could eat six of my puddings in one Christmas dinner, though my Harry, when he was still here, could eat a fair portion.' Mrs Honey's smile faded and she said, 'His chest never was right after the last war, but he always did have a good appetite.' She shook her head to chase away the memories. Ruby had seen a framed photograph of their wedding and another of him as a young man in uniform, but when 'my Harry' had last sat at the table to eat his wife's cooking, she couldn't be sure. Then Mrs Honey said, 'But if we make six this year, while we've got the makings of a pudding, we might have enough to see this war through.'

Ruby watched their faces as Joan frowned with realisation and Mrs Honey wiped a tear away with a floury hand. Did she mean eating puddings would make everyone strong and fit while the war lasted? Ruby wasn't sure and then Mrs Honey said, 'Come on, girls. Time to have a stir and make a wish. You can't make the most of Stir-Up Sunday without making a wish.'

She passed the wooden spoon to Ruby first, and Ruby stood on a wobbly milking-stool and tried to stir. It was so hard to push the large spoon through the stiff mixture of spices and fruit, thickened with flour, suet and eggs, that Joan had to help her. 'I wish…' Ruby began to say aloud, but Joan stopped her. 'No, you mustn't let us hear. It has to be a secret wish.' So she wished in silence and no one ever heard the last Christmas wish she breathed into a home-made pudding, but she wished she could stay living there forever.

After both the girls had stirred enough, Mrs Honey began filling the basins and when they were more than half-full, she said, 'Now you can each put a piece of silver into every pudding and whoever gets it when they get their share will have good luck all the following year.' Ruby's eyes widened as Mrs Honey gave them each a silver threepenny bit to drop into their puddings, while she put coins in the remaining four. Three whole pence! That could buy half a loaf of bread, she knew from when Mum sent her to the baker, or three bags of penny sweets. Such extravagance in a pudding!

Then she watched Joan and Mrs Honey spread butter papers over the top of the basins and wrap them in muslin cloths tied on top like the ears of a white rabbit. 'How long do they take to cook?' Ruby asked, as each basin was lowered into a pan of simmering water on the top of the black kitchen range.

'They'll take the rest of the day,' Mrs Honey said. 'And Joan, it's your job to keep checking they don't boil dry. These puddings are precious. If our ships can't keep us in supplies, we won't see the like again in a long time.'

And Ruby wondered why she sounded so concerned, when the pantry and the storeroom were full and the kitchen filled with steam scented with the sweet spice of Christmas puddings.

Chapter 8

4 December 1939

Real Pea Soup

As the days shortened and the leaves finished falling, Ruby became glad of the knitted pixie hood her mother had insisted on packing for her. Now the mornings were frosty and the air chilly, it kept her ears warm and when the wind blew she didn't get the earache she'd had so much the previous winter in London, along with the nagging chesty cough that tired her. She'd caught a cold a week or so ago, but Mrs Honey had given her spoonfuls of rum sweetened with honey, night and morning, and it soon went. Mum would have fussed terribly and made her stay in bed for a week with a hot-water bottle, getting bored and irritable. There were still no reports of bombs from London, so Ruby hoped Mum wouldn't say any more about her going back home.

'You're looking quite perky again,' Mrs Honey said one morning. 'You've got roses back in your cheeks.'

Ruby smiled at her as she was handed her usual winter breakfast, a bowl of porridge, which she was allowed to drizzle with honey and cream. 'I don't always have roses, Mummy says. Last winter I was very poorly. She said I must wear my thick vest in winter, so I don't get a bad chest again.'

Mrs Honey looked concerned. 'Do you often get a bad chest then, deary?'

Ruby shook her head. 'Only when it's foggy, I do.' She looked towards the window. A thick white mist hovered over the fields just beyond the end of the garden, surrounding the cottage so it felt like an island in the sea. Country fog was always white or grey, not yellowy brown like the London fogs that stifled breath and crept in from the streets and into the very kitchens and sitting rooms of city houses, coating clothes, chairs and lungs with a clammy film of smut. She remembered how her mother always made her cover her nose and mouth with a scarf when the fog was so thick she couldn't see the far side of the road. Then she'd make her blow her nose when they reached home and the handkerchief would be sprayed with black snot.

Mrs Honey looked out at the mist enveloping the cottage. 'I've heard about those dreadful London fogs,' she said. 'Nasty things they are, full of dirty smoke from all the chimneys and fumes from the traffic. No wonder you got such a bad chest in London, poor little love.'

'But I might get a bad chest here, mightn't I? Cos it's foggy today. Look, there's lots of fog outside this morning. Mummy said next time the fog was bad, I'd have to stay indoors until it cleared up.'

'Well, you won't have to do that now you're here. Country fog is just cold air rising from the ground, a bit like steam from a kettle, only cold not hot.' And as if to demonstrate, she put the kettle back on the hob, till it began to boil and whistle.

Ruby loved the sound of the kettle whistling. It always meant good things were on their way, like a hot cup of tea, or a boiled egg or sometimes a steamed pudding with syrup. 'I put my thick vest on today though. Just in case.'

'Good for you. It's really nash out there today. You wrap up warm. That woolly hood your mam knitted will help.'

Ruby wondered what nash was all the way to school, then asked one of the local boys. He roared with laughter, and said, 'It's right nash. It's chilly!' So nash meant cold. But could you say your toes and fingers were nash, Ruby wondered. So many unfamiliar words in this part of the world, so far from home and yet part of the same country. Mrs Honey was always saying strange things, like when she said, 'Be sure to be home before dimmet,' when she went out to play after school and it was a while before Ruby understood that she meant before dusk.

That winter afternoon when Ruby and Joan returned from school, Joan with a pile of exercise books under her arm to mark and Ruby with *Black Beauty* borrowed from the school library, there was a savoury smell as they entered the kitchen. 'Ooh, what are we having for tea today?' Joan said appreciatively, looking at Mrs Honey, who was slicing thick chunks of crusty bread. She always had a strange way of cutting the bread, Ruby thought, standing the loaf up on end and cutting across the top towards her plump, aproned middle, with a large serrated knife.

'I thought seeing as it was getting foggy again, I'd make sure you girls had a nice filling bowl of thick soup to come home to. Young Ruby here put me in mind of it this morning, with all her talk of bad chests in the winter.' She turned to stir the large pan simmering on the hob, then put bowls to warm next to the range. 'Sit yourselves down and I'll bring it over.'

They shed their coats and boots and sat expectantly at the table, covered as always with two layers, a pale green oilcloth then a clean checked tablecloth over the top. The brown teapot was warmly wrapped in its cosy of red and green stripes, crocheted from remnants of sweaters past.

'Shall I pour?' Joan said, reaching for the mismatched teacups and saucers. Mrs Honey had a complete matching set in the parlour dresser, kept for best, but day-to-day they used various patterns and shapes. Ruby liked her special cup with its bright daffodils, the cup Mrs Honey had said would be hers from the day she arrived, even though it sat on a plain blue saucer.

'Here you are,' Mrs Honey said, placing full bowls of yellowy brown soup in front of them both. Ruby thought she could see flecks of carrot and ham in the liquid, thick as her morning porridge. 'All that talk of fog made me think this was just what we needed tonight. They call them pea-soupers in London, don't they, Ruby? Well, this is the only kind of pea soup we have out here in the country. It won't give you a bad chest, it'll build you up and ward off coughs and colds. Split pea soup. Took me all day to make it, but there's enough here for tonight and tomorrow as well, I reckon.'

Ruby took a mouthful. It was delicious. The texture was smoother than porridge, but thicker than the thickest cream. She didn't say a word, she just ate spoonful after spoonful, wiped her bowl clean with her crust of bread and thought how lovely it was that out here in the country, pea soup was something to be enjoyed and not feared.

Chapter 9

23 August 2004

Picturing the Past

'Do they think his memory's going to recover?' Dick's older sister Joan asks Billie, as they agree to have a quick cup of tea after visiting the ward.

'He hasn't actually lost his memory, they've told me it's fine. It's more about his speech and trying to find the right words. I tell you, Joan, he's so much better than he was. If you'd seen him when I found him the other week, you'd have been shocked too.' Billie puts a pack of shortbread on the tray. Lunch had only been a snatched cheese sandwich and a custard tart so she could get to the hospital in time for afternoon visiting.

'Oh, love, I'm so sorry I wasn't here to help you.' Joan puts an arm around her niece's shoulders. Her tiny frame means she has to stretch to accommodate Billie's plump figure.

'Oh, there wasn't much point in you rushing back from your holiday. There was nothing you could do. They said he'd survive and now it's just going to take time.'

'I would have rushed back, you know I would. If it could have made any difference, that is. He is my little brother, after all. But I brought some Kendal Mint Cake back from the Lake District for you. I know you've always liked it.' Joan is two years older than her brother, but regular walks, hiking holidays and a lifetime's dislike of alcohol and smoking mean she looks and acts ten years younger.

'Ooh, thanks. I shouldn't like sweet things like that, but I do.' Billie looks rueful. She is trying out another diet. She and her husband Kevin have both agreed to give the 5:2 diet a go. Five days eating sensibly, two days fasting. Maybe if it was the other way round, she'd see some results. She could eat some of the syrupy-sweet mint cake on her non-fast days. Or maybe nibble it on the fast days, to cheer herself up; she's finding it tedious as well as difficult.

'So what's the next step for him?' Joan asks as they both sip scalding cups of tea in the hospital café. 'Have they said when he can come home?'

'Soon, they hope, but he'll need a lot of care for a few months. And he gets upset very easily. I suppose it's having your whole life turned upside down like this, not being able to communicate clearly. He'll have therapy sessions as well, so I expect I'll have to drive him backwards and forwards for quite a while.'

'I can help with that. I'd like to help.'

'That would be wonderful, Joan. And we've also got to keep encouraging him to talk as much as possible. He's struggling to find the right words, but it will come eventually, they say.' Billie reaches down for her roomy handbag. 'I've got some photos here. The therapist said that might be helpful. Get him talking about the family.'

'Let me see. Recent photos or old ones?'

'Recent mostly, but there's also some of your parents and ones from when Dad was a child. He looked like a right little monkey,' she says, offering Joan a picture of her father when he was six years old, in a cowboy outfit with toy guns. 'Here, take a look.'

Joan studies the pictures one by one, then stops. 'Ah, you've got our old school photo here as well. It was taken when we were all evacuated.' She holds up a large black and white print of a group of children standing in two lines, taller ones at the back, facing the camera. Most are smiling, some look solemn and a couple of the younger ones have gaps in their teeth. 'I was due to leave school that year, but they let me go with them, because I was his big sister and I could help in class. That's when I decided I wanted to be a teacher.' Billie has great respect for her aunt, training once her own children were at school. Joan had taught in primary schools for the rest of her working life and still helped out, long after retirement, as a volunteer reading support assistant.

'What year was that?'

'Soon after the war started. In the September of 1939, I guess. Yes, that would be it, because I remember us making Christmas cards in the first term. The whole school was sent off to Devon, apart from those few whose parents didn't like the idea. This must have been taken in our first week down there.'

Billie stares at the picture, then points. 'That's Dad, isn't it?'

'Yes, that's him and I'm one of the taller ones at the back.' She laughs. 'I remember they all had to have their hair cut right off, soon after this was taken. There was an outbreak of nits. The London kids got the blame for it, of course. Not very flattering pudding basins they gave them. So if this picture had been taken a week later they'd all be looking like criminals. I was lucky. I was old enough to skip the chop. My hair was just above my shoulders then and I'd have been very upset if I'd had to have it cut short. Pixie cuts weren't the fashion then. Different now though.' She pats her neat white cropped hair. 'It was just the younger kids who had their hair cut. They'd have got me too if I hadn't looked older and been helping one of the teachers.'

'What, even this little girl, with her lovely long hair?' Billie touches the heart-shaped face of a small girl with long dark plaits in the front row.

'Oh yes, even her. She wasn't at all happy about it. Cried her eyes out, she did.'

'Dad got upset all over again when I showed him this picture, but I couldn't understand why. He kept pointing to that little girl. Who was she?'

Joan takes no time at all to answer. 'Oh, that's Ruby. Ruby Morrison. Sweet little thing, she was. And sweet on your dad too for a long time.' She smiles at the memory. 'When we were evacuated I shared a lovely billet with her for the first year, then she got taken back to London by her aunt. We were staying in a cottage in a village near Barnstaple and we shared a bedroom. It was like she was my little sister. We were the lucky ones. We lodged with a wonderful lady who taught us to cook and fed us really well, considering there was a war on. Your dad wasn't so lucky, unfortunately. Got placed with a dreadful farming family.'

'Ruby,' murmurs Billie. 'I wonder if that's what he was trying to say when I first found him and later when I showed him this photo. I couldn't really understand him. It sounded like *Rooey*. And he seemed to be saying that when I asked him about this as well.' She looks in the pocket of her handbag and brings out a much-handled leather wallet. 'I had to take this from him for safe keeping, while he's in hospital. And look what I found inside.' She holds out the crumpled snapshot, a little Brownie camera snap, old and creased but obviously viewed many times over the years.

Joan takes the little photograph and stares at it. 'Well, blow me. That's Ruby as well. I think she'd be about sixteen there.'

'What, the same Ruby as in the school photo? The one you said was sweet on Dad?'

'The very same.' Joan looks up. 'I remember they had quite a thing going on after the war, when they were a little bit older. That was before your dad did his National Service. She always was sweet on him.'

Billie takes the picture back and looks at it again, then sighs and looks at her aunt. 'Dad got really upset when I took this out of his wallet and asked him who it was. Do you know what happened to her?'

Joan frowns as if she's trying hard to remember all the people from her life, years and years before. 'Well, she was living with her aunt and uncle, both during and after the war. They ran the Victoria and Albert. The Vic, everyone called it. You know, the pub near the park? It's an Indian restaurant now. She got sent back to them after her mum's place was bombed out. She'd lost both her parents by then, poor thing.'

'Do you know what happened to her? Did she get married or move away?'

'I'm not sure. I have a feeling I heard she'd left London and lost touch with them and other people round here. But I don't know where she went. Funny, that. We were so close when we were younger. I saw her from time to time when I first had the children, but you know how it is. I had my hands full with the kids and running the house, so there was no time to see old friends.'

'Dad must think this is important,' Billie says. 'He was trying so hard to say something when I showed it to him. I wonder if he wants to see her again. Now Mum's gone and he's been on his own for three years, that could be just what he needs, to see an old girlfriend. And even if she's married now, wouldn't it be lovely for him to hear from her? I'd do anything to help him get better.'

Joan is lost in thought for a moment, then perks up and says, 'I've just remembered. Ruby's aunt's still alive. I don't know where she's living now, but I'm sure I've seen her at the Clockhouse Day Centre, when I've gone in with the choir. You might want to have a chat with her. Ida Cherry, her name is. She used to have a bit of a reputation for being a right old dragon. But I suppose she had to be, running a pub round there. It was a rough area in those days, after the war.'

Glory glory Alleluiah,
Teacher hit me with a ruler.

Chapter 10

Christmas 1939

While Shepherds Washed

Ruby hopped up and down on the cold station platform. It was the afternoon of Christmas Eve. The steaming engine was coming to a halt with a wheeze and a chug and she was eager to see her mother again. Mrs Honey had said it was only fair Mrs Morrison should share the festivities with them, since she was on her own, while Joan's family were still all together and would have company for Christmas.

Ruby looked up and down the throbbing train, looking for her mother. Would she bring presents, more warm clothes or the dolls she had asked her to fetch from home? But when she stepped off the train, carrying a tiny case and wearing a faded headscarf tightly tied under her chin, Ruby realised this thin pale woman with her quiet trembling voice was not going to contribute much to the occasion. She gave Ruby a quick kiss on the cheek, but didn't seem particularly excited to see her, although she commented on how much she'd grown already.

While they waited for the bus back to the village, Mrs Morrison responded to Mrs Honey's questions about life in London with the briefest of answers. Then she said, 'And as we haven't had any bombs so far, I've been thinking it might be best if Ruby comes back with me after Christmas. After all, quite a few families have brought their children home again.'

'No,' screamed a voice in Ruby's head. 'I don't want to go home. Please don't make me. I like it here.'

And she was utterly relieved when she heard Mrs Honey say in her slow, comforting way, 'Well, why don't we see how you feel later on? She's no trouble and she's thriving on the fresh air here. She hasn't had any more than the slightest bit of a cold so far this winter. And you'd never forgive yourself if the bombing started the minute you went back, now would you?'

Mrs Morrison nodded in agreement and the matter seemed to rest there. Ruby was slightly reassured. But what if Mum mentioned it again? What if she insisted that her daughter should come home? Ruby didn't want to live in smoggy, dirty London any more. She loved the clean countryside. There were little things she sometimes remembered about life at home that she missed for the briefest of moments, like stroking Sooty as he purred by the gas fire or playing with the dolls she'd had to leave behind, but on the whole, life with Mrs Honey and Joan was far more enjoyable than the sad quiet house with Mum.

When they arrived at the cottage, where Joan had warmed the teapot and a fire was blazing, Mrs Morrison murmured, 'This is all very nice, I must say. What a lucky girl you are.' Then Ruby was glad her mother had joined them just so she could see how Christmas could be so much jollier than the last couple of years at home. Last year they'd only had a sad little fake tree with scratched baubles and dinner was a small piece of roast beef on the table. But was it any better when her father was still alive? She couldn't remember him ever being home for Christmas. All her life he had been at sea more than at home, so she didn't miss him any more now he was gone forever.

The cottage was decorated with paper chains she and Joan had made over the past few evenings by the fire. And a green holly wreath, brightened with clusters of red berries, hung on the front door. A freshly cut tree was stood in a pot and decorated with rows of paper angels holding hands and stars Ruby had cut out of old newspaper. A very ancient wonky fairy that Mrs Honey said had been hers as a girl was brought out of its bed of tissue to stand on the very top of the tree. This was a proper Christmas.

The following day, preparations were well under way after they had all been to church. Smells of roasting and steaming filled the household. Ruby was folding napkins, her mother was polishing glasses, Joan was checking the water level on the pudding and Mrs Honey was fanning herself with her apron. Everyone was helping in one way or another to prepare the feast when there was a knock at the back door.

'Goodness, Stevie. Just look at the state of you!' Joan stared at her brother with an expression of distaste as she let him in. He was muddy, wet and cold. The first snow of the winter had fallen overnight on Christmas Eve and Stevie had walked three miles from his lodgings on the Barfords' farm to join his sister for Christmas dinner. He had bright pink ears and cheeks from the bitter chill, and a black eye.

'Whatever's happened to you? How'd you get that nasty shiner?'

'It's not so bad.' Stevie grinned. 'Tom Barford's got one as well. And I give him a bloody nose.'

'You've been fighting? Whatever for?'

'I said his mum weren't being fair on me and Will. He always gets the best helpings. And he doesn't have to do all the mucking out the cows and horses we're both made to do every day.'

'Oh, Stevie, what are we going to do with you?' Joan put her arms around her younger brother and pulled him into the warm kitchen, where Mrs Honey was stirring the gravy to serve with the roast goose. Ruby's mother gave him a timid glance and carried on laying the table for dinner.

Joan pulled off Stevie's wet jacket and sweater and as she did so his grubby shirt and vest rose up his back and she gasped at the sight of the livid red welts on his skin.

'Oh my goodness. However did you get those marks? Whoever did that to you?'

Stevie pulled away from her and tugged at his shirt, tucking it back into his muddy shorts. 'It's nothing. Old Barford gets a bit narked sometimes. Don't like me answering back. Will says I'd be alright if I didn't give him so much lip.'

Mrs Honey frowned in disapproval. 'Heavy-handed, they are, those Barfords. I'll have to have words with Martha. If my Harry was still here, he'd speak to Ted himself. Harry never was one to hold back and wouldn't have stood for a boy getting such a beating.'

'No, please don't.' Stevie sniffed and wiped his nose on his shirtsleeve. He was shivering, despite the warmth radiating from the kitchen range. 'It won't happen again.'

'Like it won't snow in January, it won't. He's a hard man, Ted Barford is.' Mrs Honey glanced at Stevie. 'You had your breakfast today?'

He shook his head. 'Weren't time. I had jobs to do before I could leave. They weren't happy about me coming over at all as Will's gone home for Christmas. Said they want me back before milking time an' all.'

'We'll see about that. Now sit yourself down and get stuck into these, while I finish off here. Won't be long now, but if you're that empty inside, you won't go spoiling your dinner.' She put a plate with two warm mince pies in front of him and he wolfed them down in seconds with a couple of bites apiece.

Ruby sat quietly watching the whole scene from start to finish. She'd had thick, hot porridge as usual that morning, made with creamy milk and topped with more cream and brown sugar. She couldn't imagine not having any breakfast at all, particularly on such a cold day. 'What do you get for breakfast other days?' she asked, as Stevie licked his finger and wiped it round the plate to gather every crumb of sugar.

'Bread and dripping if we're lucky, if we've done our jobs.' He looked up. 'It's alright when we're in school, cos then we get school dinners. But now it's holidays, me an' Will, we're hungry all the time.'

Ruby considered this. She'd never thought the dinners at the village school were as good as the meals cooked by Mrs Honey, but she supposed that if you weren't being given much to eat, then a hot dinner of stew, swede and mashed potato, followed by rice pudding and jam, would be more than welcome.

'I don't like it when they give us beetroot at school,' she said. 'It tastes like earth.'

'We sometimes get beetroot sandwiches for our tea. They're alright if you're really hungry. Better than nothing.'

'We have boiled eggs for our tea most days. And bread and jam.'

'Wish I was here and not stuck out there on that horrible farm.'

'Is it really awful?'

He gave her a huge smile. 'Nah, it's a bit rough, but at least they don't make us have a bath every week.'

Ruby suspected he hadn't had many baths at all since he'd been taken away in Farmer Barford's old truck the day they arrived in the village from Barnstaple. His light brown hair was lank and greasy, there was grime in and behind his ears as well as round his neck and a sour smell hovered about his person. 'We have a proper bath here every Saturday. Hot water from a boiler. Joan goes in first, then me so she can wash my hair.'

He laughed, 'Yeah, you don't want nits again.'

'I never had any nits in the first place. They just cut my hair because everyone was made to get their hair cut.' Ruby shook her hair at him. It had grown a lot since that awful day and was now just below her jaw, but it was nowhere near the length it had once been, when she could almost sit on her lovely long plaits.

'Come a bit closer then. If I've got some nits, they can be my Christmas present to you.' Stevie leant across and made to hug her and let his head touch hers, but Ruby squealed and jumped down from the table, making the adults turn round with raised eyebrows as the two younger children ran from the kitchen shrieking.

'We'll keep him here tonight,' Mrs Honey said, 'and give him a good scrub in the bath before bedtime. We don't want any unwanted visitors now, do we?'

She picked up Stevie's jumper and jacket with her fingertips, holding them out at arm's length. 'And we'll see what we can do about these, an' all.' She threw them in the laundry basket in the scullery. 'Something of my Harry's might do him, though he's skinny as anything and needs feeding up.'

She glanced back at him, sizing him up. 'I'll have a word with Martha and tell her he's coming over here for his tea once a week. She won't care as long as she gets her rations and he can still help out. We'll soon put some meat on his bones.'

Chapter 11

25 December 1939

Away in a Manger

'Did you get a stocking when you woke up this morning?' Ruby whispered from the bed she shared with Joan, who was tired out after helping Mrs Honey with all the cooking of the Christmas dinner and full to bursting with goose and pudding.

Bedded down on a camp bed, squeezed into the girls' bedroom, Stevie turned over beneath the blankets and eiderdown Mrs Honey had found for this extra visitor. She had also given him an old flannel nightshirt of her Harry's, saying, 'Good thing I never threw any of his things away after he'd gone. I must've known I'd have a houseful again, one of these days.'

'Nah,' said Stevie. 'Bet Tom Barford got a stocking though. Spoilt pig. I'm sure his mum's given him the jumper my mum sent for me. Mrs Barford grabbed the parcel off me and said she'd keep it safe for now. Mean old bitch.'

Ruby gasped at his use of this shocking word and it was a moment before she could speak. 'We got stockings, me and Joan. Nuts and sweets and a toy. Do you want to see?' She didn't add that she knew her mother hadn't added to the bulging stocking, nor that she was disappointed with the grey hand-knitted beret she'd been given that morning.

By the flickering of the candle they were allowed to keep alight as they fell asleep, he could see the knitted rabbit Ruby held out for him to touch. He stroked it, then said, 'It's nice here. I wish I lived with you and Joan.'

'Can't you come and stay here with us? If you write and ask your parents?'

'Nah. Don't wanna worry them. Anyway, it's all got to be official. There's ration books and stuff. That's why people take us in. They get extra. It's not as if they really want more kids to feed. Most of them only do it for the rations and cos we can do their jobs for them.'

'Don't say that. Mrs Honey is lovely. She's ever so kind to us.'

'Yeah, she's alright. But others aren't. People like the Barfords just want us so we can work for them.' He sniffed.

'Do you want my walnuts? I got them in my stocking, but I don't like them.'

'Yeah, alright. Hand 'em over.'

Ruby passed him a handful of nuts, then said, 'Can you open them carefully? I want to make cradles from the shells. Mrs Honey showed me one she made for her niece's doll's house. I'm going to make some too.'

He sat up in his bed and slid a long hard thumbnail into the crevices where the shells split and eased them apart into two halves, then picked out the kernels and popped the pieces in his mouth. 'Here you are,' he said, handing back the shells. 'Will you show me when you've made the cradle?'

'I've made a chest of drawers out of matchboxes too. Would you like to see?' Ruby sat up in bed and reached into the bedside table. She pulled out a little set of drawers made from three boxes glued together and covered with patterned paper. Small beads formed the handles and she showed Stevie how the drawers slid open smoothly.

'Where's your doll's house then?'

'I haven't got one yet. My dad was going to make one for me. He promised a long time ago, before he went away. But I won't ever get one now, because he was drowned. My mum says she'll see if Uncle Reg will help, but I don't think he will, cos Aunt Ida keeps him busy in their pub all the time.' Losing Dad was sad, she knew, but she hadn't felt it deeply, even though her mother looked sad and cried, because he'd always been away so much all her life. She felt the loss of the promised doll's house more than the loss of a father.

'Never mind, Ruby. Maybe I can make one for you. We're doing woodwork at school next term and I'm good at stuff like that. Even Old Barford says I'm handy with a hammer and saw.'

'Would you, Stevie? Oh, thank you so much. That would be wonderful.' Ruby felt wide awake with excitement. Today had been the best Christmas ever, from the moment she had woken up and felt the weight of the lumpy stocking at the bottom of the bed, then the joyous carolling church service, which had warmed the grey solemnity of the place, through to the delights of the dinner with goose (which she had never before tasted and had loved, with its apple sauce and rich stuffing), crisp roast potatoes and parsnips, then the fruitiness of the pudding and mince pies with cream and brandy sauce. And now this as well, the boy she so admired, offering to give her what she most wanted in the whole wide world. Her very own doll's house. How happy she was and how she loved Stevie for his cheekiness, his kindness and even his grubbiness, now soaped and scrubbed into rosy cleanliness.

Stevie finished eating the nuts and managed to prise most of them cleanly apart into matching halves, then handed all the shells back to Ruby. 'Watch this,' he whispered, so as not to wake Joan. He sat upright in his bed and began cupping his hands and wiggling his fingers so animal shadows danced in the candlelight on the opposite wall. As a deer followed a rabbit, a dog, a duck and a bird, she stifled her giggles but still nearly choked with laughter as she tried so hard not to disturb his exhausted big sister, on the happiest day of her life so far, on this, the happiest of Christmases.

Chapter 12

23 January 1940

Getting What For

It was an icy grey morning, but Ted Barford's crimson face was sweating. He threw his heavy gaberdine mac onto the barn floor and the thick leather belt swung again with a whistling thwack, the sharp buckle ripping into the flesh of Stevie's back, already striped with blood. Will cowered behind the stacked straw bales. He'd done his best to stop it happening. 'He didn't mean it, Mr Barford,' he shouted. 'Please don't hit Stevie.'

Now and then Ted stood back to catch his breath, rolling his shirtsleeves up, arms thick with muscle from years of hefting bales and rolling sheep onto their backs. A well-built, well-fed man of fifty years and more, he could have felled the skinny twelve-year-old boy with one blow, but he was enjoying the punishment too much to walk away.

Then Martha came running from the house, waving her plump arms and nearly slipping over in the iced yard. 'You stop that right now, Ted Barford,' she screamed at her husband. 'Carry on like that and you'll end up killing him. That's enough, I say.' And this time he'd listened to her. He hadn't listened to Stevie's excuses, nor to Will's protests that his friend was sorry. He'd listened only to his wife.

Ted stepped back, mopping his brow with a rag from his pocket, and Stevie slumped down on the floor of the barn. 'That'll teach him to cheek me. Crafty bugger.' He spat on the ground near the fallen boy, picked up his coat and cap, then strode off, refastening the belt around his corduroy trousers.

Martha wasn't normally kind to the two boys lodging with her, but she helped Stevie up and held him as he staggered into the farmhouse, leaning against her sturdy figure in its uniform of wraparound apron and gumboots. Will slipped out from his hiding place and ran after them, his grubby face streaked with tears. 'Hope you've learned your lesson now,' she said as she stripped Stevie of his bloodied, ripped clothes and bathed the wounds with fierce iodine. She sent him to bed in clean pyjamas for once, while her smug, red-faced son lurked nearby, sniggering at the belting his father had delivered with his huge shovel hands and heavy belt. And before she sent Will back outside to finish sweeping out the stable, she took pity on his pale, shocked face and gave him the end of the cob loaf with dripping. He was taller and thinner than Stevie and needed feeding up if he was to cope with extra work while his friend was laid up.

That was a week ago and now Stevie was hiding. Will crept into the hay barn and called out, 'Where are you? I've got bread and cheese for you.'

Stevie peered out from between the towers of straw and hay. He'd wrapped a sack around his shoulders and he was shivering. He grabbed the food and began tearing at it with urgent, ravenous bites.

'It's ever so cold out here. They shouldn't make you sleep in the barn again tonight.' Will pulled his jacket close and wrapped his arms across his chest.

Through chattering teeth, Stevie said, 'She won't let me back in. Not till I've apologised to that lazy pig. Her Tom should be doing his share of the work. He's older than us, but he's lazy so I'm not going to apologise. He should take a turn mucking out the stables and the cow barn. Not just us.'

'I know, it's not fair. But we have to put up with it. Why don't you come back in and get it over with?'

Stevie had his mouth full. He shook his head.

'You'll freeze to death out here on a night like this.'

'Nah. It's not so bad. Besides, if I come indoors, old Barford might belt me again. I'd rather take my chances out here. I'll creep out later on and get Jess to come in here with me.' The friendly collie dog's thick coat kept her warm in her kennel and she'd kept Stevie warm on more than one night out in the barn.

'He gave you a right whacking last week. He used the buckle end again.'

'Yeah, he's enjoying that. Think he likes seeing blood.'

Will turned towards the farmhouse. He thought he'd heard a shout. 'She doesn't know I've sneaked out with this. I'd better get back inside.'

'Yeah, you go. No point in both of us freezing to death out here. Thanks.'

Will ran back to the house and Stevie heard shouts and the slamming of a door. He hoped his friend wasn't in trouble as well and wouldn't get beaten. So far, the most Will had suffered was a badly aimed cuff to his ear. Most of the time his willing smile and his big brown eyes helped him escape any worse.

I don't mind them being strict, Stevie thought. That's fair enough. I know I'm a cheeky beggar, but they're too hard on us, even Ma Barford can see that.

It had seemed like an adventure at first, climbing into the farm truck with his friend Will and Jess the dog, then getting to know all about the sheep, cows and horses, but now it was more like a nightmare. He wasn't used to luxuries and he wasn't afraid of hard work, but he was beginning to think he couldn't take much more of the thrashings on top of the mean rations of food. He knew he and Will could survive on bread and dripping if they had to, but the farmer's son, Tom, was given thick slices of ham and fried eggs.

Ruby's landlady had said he should go to her for tea once a week, but if he came back late after school, it only made matters worse.

I can't risk another thrashing, Stevie told himself. And I can't rely on Will to bring me food all the time or he'll cop it an' all. Barford's getting worse. He's out to break me. The more I refuse to be cowed by him, the more he goes for me.

He tunnelled between the scratchy bales and huddled down in the straw. It felt as warm as the attic bedroom the boys had been given, if not warmer. He thought of the Barfords sitting close to the glowing kitchen range or in the sitting room with a blazing fire. Once the two boys had completed their jobs around the farm and had whatever Mrs Barford deigned to feed them, they were usually kicked outside or sent up to their room. It hadn't been so bad to begin with, while the evenings were still light enough to kick a ball around the yard or run across the fields, but in the depths of winter, the hay barn was the only refuge they had. That or the stables, leaning against the flanks of the two carthorses, Brandy and Whisky, named after Ted Barford's favourite tipples.

With a thick mattress of straw beneath him and layers of sacking as covers, Stevie felt the barn was almost better than the thin blankets and cold beds indoors, and he curled his arms around Jess, as a canine hot-water bottle. The barn door was open slightly and he could see the star-sprinkled sky and the moon shining on the frosty yard. All was still and quiet apart from the rustling of rats and mice searching through the bales for lost grains of wheat. Jess cocked her ears at the sounds and made little whimpers until she too fell asleep.

Before first light, he was awake. The cockerel was calling from the henhouse, impatient to strut in the yard, and he heard the back door clank open. He crept out from his bed of straw and threw the sacks back into the cavern between the bales. They might be needed to keep him warm again tonight. Then he brushed down his shabby clothes and slipped out into the farmyard, shooing Jess towards her kennel. He was very hungry. Maybe Mrs Barford would let him in and he could have some breakfast. He opened the heavy oak kitchen door and peered into the warm room. She was stirring a pot on the range and looked up as he entered. 'Come to say sorry, have you? Well, there's nothing here for you till you've done your jobs.'

Tom Barford was sat at the kitchen table, eating a plate of eggs and bacon with thick fried bread. His red cheeks and chin were shiny with grease and he smirked at his mother's words. Ted Barford had nearly finished his meal and was wiping his plate clean with a crust of bread. 'You heard her. Get out there or I'll be after you.'

Stevie slipped straight back outside. He ran to the stables, skidding on the icy cobbles. Sometimes the horses had hot mash. That was like porridge. He could have a handful of that to keep him going. But no such luck. Both the carthorses had empty pails. Either they'd been fed early, or, more likely, they had yet to receive their breakfast too. He hugged them both, their solid warm bodies giving some relief from the bitter cold of the morning as clouds of steamy breath drifted from their soft noses.

Knowing what might happen if he didn't start work immediately, Stevie began clearing away the clods of droppings on the stable floor. He shovelled it all into a barrow and wheeled it out to the pile beyond the stable yard. That too was steaming in the bright chill of day. It seemed that everything was warm, apart from him in his thin jersey, threadbare jacket and shorts. After spreading clean straw in the stables he cleared the mess in the cow barn, where some of them were stamping their feet, eager for milking time. Looking around to check no one was watching, he grabbed a pail and quickly pulled at the teats of the nearest cow, then gulped the frothy milk. He didn't dare take much, but it helped to warm him. He wiped his mouth on his sleeve, then cleaned out the bucket with straw. He daren't give old Barford an excuse to wallop him again.

When he was finished, he saw Will leaving the house and heading towards the track into the village. It must be time to go to school now. Stevie ran to the farmhouse and opened the door to the kitchen. Mrs Barford was stacking dishes in the sink. 'You're too late,' she said. 'Get off to school and take this to the hens on your way out.' She pushed a chipped enamel bowl into his hands. There, among the crushed eggshells and bran mash, were potato peelings, carrot tops, bread crusts and mouldy cheese. Breakfast, he thought.

'Wait for me,' Stevie called out to Will. The boy turned as his friend came running down the hard, rutted track, laced with frozen puddles.

'You missed out on breakfast again,' Will said. 'But I managed to steal this for you.' He pulled a chunk of bread out from under his jumper.

'Ta. I had bits out the hens' mash, but I'm still hungry.' He chewed on the crust as they walked.

'I reckon we should have a word with Miss Harris,' Will said with a frown. 'About how bad it is here. I don't want to write home. It'll only worry my mum, with Dad away. But Miss Harris might get us moved somewhere better.'

'Maybe,' Stevie mumbled. 'But if she lets on and old Barford gets to hear we've been complaining behind his back, we'll both be for it.'

'You reckon? So we should keep quiet?'

'I've got a better idea. I say we don't have to put up with it any longer. I say we clear off right now.'

'What, run away?' Will thought for a moment. 'I heard the Barfords saying really bad weather's coming in. Could be the worst winter ever, they said. So maybe we should wait, till spring perhaps?'

'You can if you like. I'm not staying here another minute. If I put a foot wrong, he'll go for me. Slightest excuse and I've had it, so I'm off out of here.'

'You mean you're going today?'

'Yeah. You coming with me?'

'Maybe after school dinner? It's Friday, fish and chips.'

'I know, but I can't risk getting stuck here. He might finish me off next time. No, I'm not hanging around any longer.'

They had reached the junction in the road. Right to the village and school, left to the highway. 'Right, that's it, I'm off then,' Stevie said, heading for the main road.

'Where are you going?'

'Home. Back to London. I'd rather face Jerry's bombs than Barford's belt, any day.'

'All the way to London? How you gonna do that?'

Stevie turned to face his friend, but continued taking backward steps. 'I'm not gonna walk all the way. I'll hitch. Lots of lorries from the farms round here take stuff up to town every day.'

'But what should I tell them?'

'Nothing. Say you never saw me this morning. Say I never turned up. You don't know nuffin'.'

'Good luck then.' Will watched him run towards the main road, then he turned and ran to the school. There'd be more chips to go round today, with Stevie gone.

Chapter 13

25 January 1940

Not Present But Correct

Mrs Honey looked anxious when Ruby and Joan returned from school. 'I met Martha Barford in the market today. She told me Stevie never turned up at the farm after school yesterday. Do you know where he might be?'

The girls had just walked back through the icy lanes at the end of the afternoon. They had both noticed that Stevie wasn't present in class, but thought he could have been kept behind at the farm to work. 'I've no idea,' Joan said. 'But he wasn't in school yesterday either. What do you think has happened to him?'

'There's bad weather on the way tonight. But he should have been able to walk back there alright yesterday afternoon, even though it would've been dark by the time he got to the farm.'

Mrs Honey took the steaming kettle off the range, poured boiling water into the glossy brown teapot and wrapped it in the striped crocheted tea cosy that kept it warm while they had their tea.

'Oh dear. I do hope he hasn't been fighting again.' Joan helped Ruby out of her coat and stood both their pairs of boots near the range to dry out. 'He hasn't seemed at all happy, the days he has been able to get into school. He's been late more than a couple of times and he always says he's been held back at the farm to finish his jobs.' She frowned as she helped to lay the table for their tea. 'Do you think Mr Barford's been beating him again? I know Stevie can be a bit cheeky, but he's only young, after all.'

Mrs Honey cut slices of bread to toast. 'I had words with Martha after he was here at Christmas. She said she'd keep a close eye on him. It's a pity he ever got picked by that family. They'd have been better off asking for land girls, but Ted wouldn't have it. He don't believe in women doing a man's work. And I expect they thought youngsters wouldn't need so much feeding. But there we are. Not everyone wanted children from London in the first place. And it weren't like none of you could pick and choose where you went.'

Ruby began to cry and sobbed, 'They've all been horrid to him. It wasn't fair he had to stay with them. I wish he'd been here, with us, right from the start. We'd have looked after him.'

Joan put her arms around her and stroked her bobbed hair, now grown to well below her chin. 'Don't worry, he'll turn up very soon, I'm sure.' But then she turned to Mrs Honey and said, 'But what if they've harmed him? I mean, really harmed him this time?'

'Now, Joan, don't go giving the girl ideas. I'm sure there's nothing to worry about. Martha didn't give me the impression she was making up a story about him. I think she just wanted him back to save her lad Tom from going out in the cold. Now eat and drink while it's hot.' Cups of tea, buttered toast and boiled eggs were set before the girls and they sat down to eat.

Joan cracked open her egg, then stopped and said, 'I should've written home. After Christmas, when we knew he was having such a hard time. Loads of other children have gone back home. But he never wanted me to say anything to Mum and Dad.'

Ruby kept quiet. She was worried about Stevie, but she didn't want the subject of going home to pop up again. Mum had mentioned it a couple more times in her letters, but had always followed it with something like 'seeing as you looked so well in the country, perhaps it's best you stay put for the time being, now rationing has come in. I can see you were being fed well down there.' And Ruby would feel relieved and put the thought out of her mind. She'd be sure to tell Mum every little detail of every nourishing meal she had this week when she wrote her weekly letter home on Sunday. Breakfast porridge, rabbit pie, meaty stews and steamed puddings.

Mrs Honey sipped her tea and nibbled a corner of toast, then stood up and went into the hallway. She came back wrapped in her thick coat and fur-lined boots, wearing her broad-brimmed velvet hat, with a fur tippet tucked around her neck. 'I'm just popping out for a few minutes to the phone box. You girls eat up and when you've cleared away, you can settle down with your knitting by the fire.' Joan was making herself a sweater from dark green wool unravelled from one of the late Mr Honey's old jumpers. She was teaching Ruby to knit, but so far the simple scarf Ruby was attempting had more purl than knit and many dropped stitches.

The girls washed their plates in the deep sink when they'd finished eating. Joan was silent, but Ruby said, 'Do you think Stevie is hiding from Mr Barford? Then maybe he'll come here?'

Joan hung the tea towel to dry on the wooden airing rack that hung above the range. 'I don't like to think of him out in the cold, but I'd rather he was anywhere now than on that blessed farm. I wish I'd said something before.' The fierce look on her face told Ruby that tears weren't far away, so she went off to study her uneven knitting and Joan soon joined her.

It seemed like an age before Mrs Honey returned, but when she came back she was smiling. 'You can both stop fretting. He's safe and sound, thank goodness.'

'Well, where is he?' Joan jumped up from her chair and her knitting fell to the floor, the ball of wool rolling across the fireside rug.

'He's at home with your parents. I thought to myself I'd best telephone them first, in case he'd come to mischief, and blow me, it turned out he was there all along. He walked in early this morning and has been eating them out of house and home ever since. They won't be sending him back, they said. Not after the way he's been treated. At first your father tore him off a strip for worrying us so, but once he heard the full story, he decided he's going to make an official complaint and make sure that other boy at the farm, Will, gets taken away as well.'

'But how on earth did Stevie manage to get all the way home?'

'Hitched a ride on a lorry taking cabbages and potatoes from round here up to market in London. Says he told the driver he'd had a letter from home saying his mother was at death's door and there was no other way of getting back in time.' Mrs Honey shook her head, smiling. 'He certainly knows how to spin a yarn, that one does. Then he walked all the way across the city to your dad's garage and then on home. He says he's sorry for not letting you know first, but he happened to see the lorry parked off the main road when he should have been heading to school and decided he had to make a run for it, as things hadn't been too good at the farm the night before. Just as well he took the chance when he did, with this bad weather coming in.' Mrs Honey looked grim as she hung up her hat and coat.

'But he was going to make me a doll's house this term, he said.' Ruby's chin quivered and she was near to tears.

'Never mind, darling. Me and Joan will make you one. We'll find a clean box and you'll see, you'll soon have your doll's house, won't she, Joan?' Mrs Honey went off to the scullery and came back with a wooden box with a panel down the centre. She upended it on the floor with the division running horizontally across and it looked just like a narrow terraced house with a ground floor and an upstairs. 'There, see. And we'll find you some material to make a curtain across the front.'

Ruby managed a weak smile. It did look a bit like a house. It didn't have a front door and windows, but it did have an upstairs and a downstairs and it was better than nothing.

'Now, me and Joan need to get on, so why don't you take this up to your bedroom and see if the furniture you've already made will fit inside? And then best get ready for bed. It's going to be very cold tonight and I want you tucked up for the night in the warm.'

Ruby carried the heavy box up to the bedroom, where the chill was warmed by a small electric fire. She set the box on the floor and began to place her few bits of home-made furniture inside. The slats were rough and uneven and the delicate pieces wobbled as she tried to stand them up. It didn't work. Stevie would have made a better job of it. She sobbed. But was she missing him, or just the doll's house he'd promised to make?

She put her face in her hands and tried to picture him. His eyes were blue, weren't they? And he had dark eyelashes although his hair was light brown She liked the sprinkling of freckles scattered across his nose and, best of all, his cheeky smile. She was going to miss him and wondered if he'd miss her. Of course he wouldn't miss the farm where he'd been so badly treated, and now he was home, welcomed back by his parents, he might not think about her any more. After all, she didn't think about home very much at all because living here was so much nicer.

After a moment or two she tiptoed out of her bedroom to the top of the staircase. She could hear murmuring and crept a little further down the stairs to hear worrying fragments of what was being said.

'Black and blue… may have a cracked rib as well. Your father's furious. Wanted to come up here… tackle Barford himself… Used a belt, your brother said.' And she heard Joan sobbing and saying, 'Should've got him away from there before… should've helped him…' Mrs Honey's soothing tones drifted up the stairs. 'There, there, he's safe and sound now, even if he did frighten the life out of us all.'

Then she heard Joan's voice very clearly. 'Oh, I don't know what to do. Maybe I should go home as well now.'

'And what good would that do, deary? You've been saying how much you're learning by working with the children in school, helping you learn how to be a teacher.'

'I know. It's really good experience. And then there's Ruby. I wouldn't want to leave her on her own. Oh, what should I do?'

'Sleep on it, I would. See how you feel in the morning. At least you know he's all in one piece. Get a good night's sleep and think about it tomorrow.'

Ruby heard doors opening and closing, so she crept back upstairs and undressed. She crawled into the bed, already partly warmed by the stone bottle Mrs Honey always put between the sheets and blankets before bedtime. She curled up in the small patch of warmth and slowly pushed the bottle down the bed with feet wrapped in thick socks. Then she pulled the eiderdown up over her ears, closed her eyes and tried to picture the house Stevie was going to make for her. She was going to miss him and wished he could have stayed longer so she'd have a proper doll's house, not just a wooden box with a curtain.

The North wind doth blow,
And we shall have snow,
And what will poor robin do then?
Poor thing.

Chapter 14

26 January 1940

Let it Snow

'Well, they were right. They said the weather was going to be bad.' Mrs Honey was busy in the kitchen when the girls came down to breakfast. Snow was steadily falling, shrouding the whole garden, the hedges, the paths and the road in a padded feathery eiderdown. Ruby was quite excited, even though it was very cold. She'd never seen this much snow before. Maybe they wouldn't be able to go to school today and could stay here to build a snowman.

But Mrs Honey had her own priorities. 'Joan, dear, we need to be prepared. So before you even have your breakfast, I want you to take food out to the hens and give them a fresh bed of straw. They'll be quite safe in their house for a few days, but I doubt you'll find they've laid any eggs in this weather.'

Joan began pulling on her wellingtons over an extra pair of thick socks, then, once she was wrapped in her coat and scarf, opened the back door. 'The snow's piling up already. I'd better shovel some out of the way right now.'

Ruby peered out. The fallen snow was several inches thick. Pure white pillows rested on the box bushes lining the path and more fat flakes were drifting down fast. She held out her hand and caught one, watching it melt on her skin. Last winter snow had fallen in London, but it was only as clean as this in the garden at home. The streets were soon churned with dirt and soot.

'Shut that door now,' Mrs Honey called, 'we need to keep the warm inside. And you can go fetch me some more kindling from the back scullery.'

Ruby knew exactly what to do. She took the log basket into the icy scullery off the kitchen and collected bundles of sticks that Mrs Honey had collected earlier in the autumn and winter. 'You have to get dry wood when you can,' she had said, instructing them never to go for a walk in the surrounding woods without bringing home an armful of sticks to keep the fires going. Larger logs were brought in by a neighbour, who split and stacked them for Mrs Honey. 'My Harry used to do it all himself. But Fred's been very good to me since Harry's been gone.'

Ruby returned to the kitchen with the wood, expecting to be told she could now have her breakfast, but Mrs Honey said, 'And the next job is making sure the pipes don't freeze up. Here, you watch the porridge while I light the oil stoves. The kitchen should be alright with the range going full pelt, but we need to think about the water coming into the house.'

Ruby stirred the pot while Mrs Honey bustled about, turning off stopcocks, wrapping pipes and lighting stoves. When she had finished, she wiped her hands on her apron, saying, 'There, all done. With luck, we'll see this cold snap through without burst pipes.'

Then Joan rushed back through the door, stamping her feet and complaining of being frozen through. Bits of straw were stuck to the curls emerging from her scarf and a dusting of flakes sparkled on the shoulders of her coat. As she eased her feet out of her boots, a crust of snow fell onto the doormat. 'There were only two eggs and they're all snuggled up in there now. I've shut their door again so they won't be tempted to go out. Their water was frozen over, so I broke the ice for them.'

'If you can do that every day for me, I'd be most grateful,' Mrs Honey said. 'Winters can get right bad up on Exmoor and this one feels like it's just starting.'

'When can I go outside?' Ruby said. 'I want to play in the snow.'

'Have your breakfast first, then I'll come out with you and we'll make a snowman.' Joan smiled at her. She might be a young woman now, but she could still share a child's delight in this heavy fall of pristine snow.

'You stay close by, mind,' Mrs Honey said, bringing their bowls to the table. 'It looks like we'll have a right storm soon. And when that happens you can't tell where you are or where you're going. If it starts drifting, I've known grown men lose their way even though they know their bearings like the back of their hand. If it's bad, we could be snowed in till yawning.'

'What's yawning?' Ruby asked, her spoon hovering above her steaming bowl.

'That's lambing time, deary. We don't want that now, do we? So you eat up and then you can go out.'

After breakfast, wrapped in thick woollens and boots, Ruby and Joan ventured out of the front gate to the lane. Not a single footstep could they see, just the delicate tracery of birds' feet, veiled with the still-falling snow. 'No one's come out today,' Joan said, looking up and down the lane, usually a regular thoroughfare into the village. 'It's so quiet, you'd think we were the only ones here.' The girls listened, but there was nothing for them to hear; everything was muffled by the thick snow. The birds had retreated to dense hedges and sheltering eaves, while all around them hidden wildlife was watching and waiting, just as they were.

'It's hard to believe there's a war on, when it's as peaceful as this,' Joan said. 'In Mum's last letter she said loads of evacuees have gone back home. Lots of people think there won't be any bombs now. And long may it last.'

Ruby didn't want to think about returning to London and her mother's fretful whine after the comforting calm here in the countryside. She remembered her mother's last words when she caught the train home: 'You do seem to be thriving here, Ruby. I can see it's doing you good to stay, bombs or no bombs.'

'Do you think the war has finished then?' She watched their clouds of breath floating in the chilly air, among the gently falling flakes. 'Has the snow stopped all the fighting? And has it stopped the Germans sending us bombs?'

'Maybe for a while,' Joan said. Then she scooped up a handful of snow and threw it at Ruby's back. 'But it's not going to stop a snowball fight!'

Ruby shrieked and threw a handful back at Joan, then the girls set to making their snowman right at the front of the cottage, so they could see him from indoors. The freshly fallen snow was soft and powdery, making it difficult to sculpt.

'Look,' Ruby said, pointing to where the garden path lay hidden. 'Our footprints have gone already.' There was no sign that they'd walked through the garden only half an hour earlier and the snow was still falling.

'Five more minutes,' Joan said. 'Then indoors for hot cocoa.'

'Do you think it's snowing in London?'

'Expect so. I think it is everywhere. But it won't be as beautiful as here. All those buses and trams will spoil it and make it dirty. Here it's like heaven. All pure and unspoilt.'

'Then I wish Stevie was still here to see it,' Ruby said.

'I'm just glad he got home safely. Imagine if he'd run away once the snow had started. He might never have made it back. And Will's moved on now as well. They're both safe.' Joan gave Ruby a hug as they both thought how lucky they were to be with Mrs Honey in her warm, well-stocked cottage.

Four days of snow they had. The worst winter on record. Snow drifted round the cottage, round the henhouse, the school and the whole village. No one went to school, no one went into Barnstaple, no milk could be delivered and the hens ceased laying altogether. By the second morning, the snow around them was three feet deep; by the time it stopped, it was over seven feet. Joan gave up trying to dig a channel to the henhouse and they all hoped the hens would survive. 'Will they really be alright?' Ruby asked, peering out of the bedroom window and looking down on the buried coop.

Mrs Honey wiped the hoar frost from the windowpane. 'They've got thick feathers, deary. They'll huddle up together to keep warm.'

'I can't see our snowman any more. He's hidden by all the snow.'

'He'll be alright too. He's got a nice thick blanket round him. And you gave him a warm scarf too, didn't you?' Ruby's botched attempt at knitting had been deemed suitable for the snowman, but all signs of the red scarf had been obliterated. 'Now come with me and we'll see what we can make for our tea today.'

'Are there enough potatoes for jacket potatoes again?'

'Course there are. Enough to last us the whole winter. And if we need any more vegetables, I'll send you outside to find that carrot you took for your snowman.'

Chapter 15

16 September 2004

Happy Memories

Billie makes sure she gets to the Clockhouse Day Centre at the right time. 'Go mid-morning, around eleven,' Joan had said. 'They give them lunch at twelve and then half of them fall asleep, so no point in going later.'

She's early and once she's parked the car she sits for a moment, asking herself if she really should be doing this. Her father is making very little progress. His speech is still very difficult to understand. 'Hello' is 'ay-oh' and Billie's name sounds like 'ee – ee'. The only expression she is confident she can interpret correctly is 'Rooey', which he often repeats, staring at her with his watery eyes and pawing at her with his feeble hands. *She must mean something to him if he keeps saying her name,* she thinks. *He is asking for her, I'm sure of it. I don't know what news I can bring him, but I've got to try and do anything I can to help him feel more at ease.*

'I've come to see Mrs Cherry,' Billie tells the woman on the reception desk, as a man shuffles past with his walking frame. She can hear loud music and singing coming from the large meeting room. It sounds like something Mum used to sing to her when she was small. Something about a pink toothbrush and a blue toothbrush. She can hear Mum singing it now, usually at bathtime when all three children took turns in the bath. Max Bygraves, wasn't it? Mum loved his songs.

'Is she expecting you?' the woman says. 'Morning music will be over any minute. You can take a seat here for now. Mrs Cherry doesn't like being disturbed during our music sessions. She loves them.'

Billie sits on one of the plastic chairs lined up in the waiting area. The walls are full of bright photographs, labelled to boast of the variety of activities available to all the elderly people attending the centre. 'Our Day Out at Southend', proclaims one, beneath a photo of two white-haired ladies in wheelchairs holding sticks of candy floss, while another labelled 'The Clockhouse Summer Fete' shows an old couple smiling as a little girl tries to hook a duck in a paddling pool.

The music comes to a stop and is followed by clapping and an announcement from the pianist, then the receptionist says, 'You should be alright to go in now. She's over on the far side.'

'Which one is she?' Billie says, 'We've not met before, but an old friend suggested I visit.'

'That's her.' The woman points. 'The one with the blue rinse and the purple trouser suit. She usually dresses smart like that. We always compliment her on her outfits.'

Ida Cherry is studying her bright red nails. Her lips are bright red too, but the lipstick has been applied with a shaking hand and is smudged over her lip line.

'Hello, Mrs Cherry,' Billie says in a bright, cheerful tone, 'May I sit down here and have a chat with you?'

'What do you want?' the old lady says with a suspicious look. 'I said I didn't want one of those scooter chair things. Or a stairlift. I'm not wasting any of my precious money.'

'I haven't come to sell you anything. I'm hoping you can help me. I've got a couple of old photos I'm trying to identify and my sister thinks you might know the people in the pictures. It would be very helpful, if you wouldn't mind.'

'I used to know everyone round here in the old days. You do when you run a pub. Heart of the community, it was back then. Everyone said the Victoria and Albert was a home from home.' She sniffs. 'Certainly was for some of them. Some of them never went to their own homes. And you can't say that now it's run by Pakis. Stinks of onions and curry. Can't stand the stuff.'

Billie ignores this and pulls an envelope from her handbag. 'It won't take a minute. There's only a couple of pictures. But it would be great if you can tell me a bit about them.'

'Show me then,' Ida says, adjusting the bridge of her purple-winged spectacles so the sweep of the frames echoes her thickly pencilled eyebrows.

Billie holds out the old school photograph first. 'I've been told this was taken in the autumn of 1939, when the local school was evacuated. I wondered if you knew this little girl.' She points to the face her father has touched with his quivering finger, the heart-shaped face framed by two dark plaits.

Ida sniffs again, and says, 'Huh, I might do.'

'Well, what about this one?' And Billie passes her the crumpled snapshot she found in her father's wallet, of the young dark-haired woman with the sweet smile.

Ida stares at it for a couple of minutes before she speaks. 'Ungrateful little madam. Always did think she was better than the likes of us.' She hands the photo back to Billie.

'So you did know her then?'

'Know her? I was a second mother to her after my sister – her mum, Hilda – went in the Blitz. Her father drowned out in the Far East before the war even started. So we were her nearest and dearest, weren't we, and it was up to us to take her in. We did right by that girl. And did she show us any thanks? Did she hell! I never heard a word of gratitude from her, all the time she was under our roof.'

'What was her name?'

'Ruby. I ask you, what sort of a name is that? Daft, Hilda was. She said I've always hated my name. I'm not going to give my daughter a boring name like mine, I want her to have a name that makes her feel precious and pretty. Silly cow. Always did have daft ideas.'

'And what was Ruby's last name?'

'Morrison. Kids at school teased her. Called her Ruby Murray. Curry, you know? Served her right.'

Billie gives a faint smile in recognition of the rhyming slang, but inside she was thinking how prejudiced the old woman was. Surely not all of her generation were so judgemental? 'So she had to come and live with you after her parents died?'

'That's right. I had to go all the way to Devon, to this village near Barnstaple, to fetch her back. October 1940. Sick on the train, she was. Right old mess. Still, she was only eleven.' Ida's laden charm bracelet rattled on her wrist as she took a lace-edged hankie from her sleeve to dab her nose. It seemed as if she was remembering how she'd tidied up the child she had reluctantly had to foster. 'And we couldn't even go straight home that night. We got caught in a raid and had to shelter down the Tilbury. Terrible night, that was. I wasn't half glad to get out of there, I tell you, the morning after.'

'Did Ruby stay with you very long?'

'Long enough, I'd say. About ten years. I reckon she left the year she was twenty-one. Me and Reg gave that girl everything she needed. She had her own room. Ate at the same table as us. All she ever had to do was help out now and then. We never asked for any reward. Ungrateful little hussy.'

'Was she still living with you after she left school?'

'Oh yes. We never threw her out. She left of her own accord. Just upped and left one day. She had a lovely job in Bodgers. You know, the old department store in Ilford. And all we ever asked was for her to help in the snug when we were busy and sweep up before she left in the mornings. But oh no, that wasn't good enough for Miss Ruby Morrison.'

'And did she never tell you where she was going?'

'All she said was she was going away to visit friends in the place where she'd stayed during the war, when she and the rest of her school went off. As evacuees, you know.' Ida looked indignant. 'Well, if she thought being with them was better than being with her own flesh and blood, all I can say is good riddance to her.'

'And where did these people live?'

'Barnstaple. Like I told you before. Well, near Barnstaple. She was always going on about how she missed the countryside and the lovely fresh eggs and that. La di da. She ate well enough with us. There was always fish and chips for our tea, even if she did have to go an' fetch it. I mean, I'd got a pub to run. I'd got no time to do fancy cooking.'

'So you never heard from her, after she left?'

'Not a bloody word. And I wrote to that woman she'd stayed with before too. Never heard back. I expect Miss High and Mighty tore it up herself.'

'Do you really think she stayed there in Devon and never wanted to come back?'

Ida Cherry stemmed her venom for a moment, pursing her smudged scarlet lips, then said, 'She had a little vanity case. Blue it was, with a little mirror and hairbrush inside, just big enough for a weekend away. That was all she took with her. She didn't even take the photo of her parents on their wedding day. Now you'd think that would be the first thing anyone would take if they were going for good. Just shows how little she cared for her own family. No, I reckon she had a fancy man.'

'A boyfriend, you mean?'

'No, a fancy man. Someone she couldn't decently bring back home. Married, probably. I expect she was getting desperate she was gonna be left on the shelf. She always was secretive. Never told us what she was up to.'

'And can you think when this might have been? When she left?'

'It was the summer of 1952. I remember it because we had a dreadful summer that year. Pissed down with rain every day in August. No one went away on holiday, everyone round here was right fed up so they came to the pub all the time. We was run off our feet.' Ida scoffed. 'She picked a right old time to bugger off. After that, me and Reg wouldn't have wanted her back again if you'd paid us to.'

Billie was taken aback as much by the old lady's clear recollections as she was by her vitriol. Life with Ida Cherry could not have been pleasurable. A young girl, orphaned, living with this woman's hard face and attitude… she could not have felt loved. Her expression must have betrayed her feelings, for Ida slapped the photos on Billie's lap and said, 'Whatcher wanna know for, anyways? Fortune-hunting, are you? There's nothing there, I can tell you.'

'No, I just… she may have been a friend of the family, that's all.' *I can't say she may have been my father's girlfriend, not when she's already accused her of having a fancy man.* 'A relative of mine wants to meet up with old friends.'

'Well, if you do find her, tell her she owes me. Ran off without paying for her keep that summer, she did. I don't call that gratitude after all we did for her.' The old woman tutted, her lips twisted, and then she said, 'But maybe she was in trouble, see. Her and her fella. Maybe she couldn't stay with us no more. We ran a respectable establishment in those days, we did,' and she topped her summary of the situation with a harsh cackle.

Postman, Postman, do your duty,
Take this to my loving beauty

Chapter 16

5 February 1940

Knock, Knock, Who's There?

After they'd had their tea of jacket potatoes and cheese, Ruby and Joan cleared the table and then settled by the fire. They had their knitting and Mrs Honey was reading the parish magazine when there was a sudden knock at the front door. 'Whoever can that be?' Mrs Honey said, heaving herself out of the armchair. She answered the door and all was quiet for a moment, then she came back into the parlour shaking her head and saying, 'There's no one out there.'

A minute or two later, they all heard the door knocker rattle again. This time, Mrs Honey started to shift in her seat, then she said, 'Oh, of course, I know what's going on. Tomorrow's Shrove Tuesday, isn't it? It'll be those lads from down the road. Little monkeys.' She heaved herself up again, waddled into the hall and opened the door, then shouted out, 'Be off with you. That's enough for one night.'

'What's up?' Joan asked as she returned to her seat, sighing and tutting over the inconvenience.

'Round here we call it "dappy-door night". It's an old tradition, the night before Shrove Tuesday, just before the start of Lent. Gives them an excuse to make mischief, I suppose, before giving up for Lent. Everyone puts up with it just for the one night. But you wait till tomorrow night.'

'Why, will they do it again?'

'No, they won't come knocking, they'll throw shards of pots into our doorways. "Lent-sherd night", we call it. Harry did it when he was a boy an' all. All the boys do. As long as they don't make too much mess I don't mind. I sweep up the crocks and use them for potting up in the garden.'

'Are they naughty the night after that, as well?' Ruby asked, her eyes wide at the sheer unruliness of it all.

'Not if I can help it, they aren't. There's traditions and then there's sheer bloody-mindedness, as my Harry used to say. We let them have their fun on two nights, but no more. Enough's enough.'

'We didn't do anything like that in the East End,' Joan said. 'Things are very different out here in the country.'

'But you had pancakes, surely? On Shrove Tuesday? Don't everyone have pancakes then?'

'Sometimes,' Joan said. 'If Mum remembered and wasn't too busy.'

'I don't remember ever having them,' said Ruby. Mum didn't cook puddings. Sometimes she offered Ruby tinned peaches with a drizzle of evaporated milk, or a bought jam tart with Bird's custard. But as far as Ruby could remember, Mum had never made pancakes.

'Well, you're getting them for your tea tomorrow, come what may,' Mrs Honey said. 'What's the world coming to if we don't have Pancake Day? We might not be able to have them with a squeeze of lemon though, more's the pity. I haven't seen a lemon since before Christmas, nor an orange, come to that. We'll have to make do.' She looked a little sad, Ruby thought.

The following day when she and Joan returned from school, Mrs Honey invited them into the kitchen, where she had a large bowl of batter already beaten and ready to cook. 'The trick is to get the pan really hot,' she said, demonstrating by holding the blackened iron frying pan over the hotplate. 'Then a little touch of lard. You don't want the batter swimming in grease, just enough to catch it right away.'

She transferred the batter from the biscuit-coloured bowl into a chipped white jug, then poured a trickle into the greased pan and swirled it over the surface with a steady turn of her wrist. It immediately appeared to thicken and crimp at the edges. 'Now don't make the mistake of trying to turn it before it's ready,' Mrs Honey said in a serious voice. 'You'll go breaking it if it's not cooked underneath.' She took hold of the handle and shook the pan. 'See, it's not shifting yet.' She put it back on the hob for a few more seconds, then gave the pan another shake, and this time the pancake slid towards her with a sound like the rustle of dry brown parcel paper.

'Now it's ready.' Mrs Honey deftly jerked the pan and the pancake flew up up in the air and came back down for the underside to be cooked.

Ruby giggled in delight. The cream-coloured pancake was laced with a pattern of brown spots. After another minute Mrs Honey slid it onto a warm plate. Then Joan had a go, failing at first to catch the pancake on its downward journey, making all of them laugh as she tried to push it back into the pan the right way up. She succeeded with her second turn and Mrs Honey said she was a 'natural' and could finish cooking all the batter, as they should eat their fill before Lent truly started.

'Can I have a go as well?' Ruby asked, hopping up and down in her excitement at this method of cooking, which was also a game of skill. Mum would never have allowed her to handle a hot, sizzling frying pan. The thought of letting her little Ruby near a hotplate would have had her in a nervous tizz.

'Of course you can, deary, but that big old pan is awful heavy for your small hands. You put your pinny on and I'll fetch a little'un.' Ruby tied the strings of the apron Joan had helped her make while Mrs Honey bustled into her scullery and returned with another pan, just as black and well-worn but half the size of the original. She set it on the hob to warm and greased it with a smear of lard. 'And seeing as Joan's pan is twice as large, you must make two pancakes for every one of hers, mustn't you?'

So with Joan and Mrs Honey helping, Ruby poured, waited, shook and tossed so she succeeded in making four evenly cooked pancakes with lace edges. And when they sat down to eat them with a selection of accompaniments from the well-stocked larder, deciding that honey and sharp, bottled apples went well together, Ruby thought she'd never enjoyed a tea so much in her life. If Mum had left London and come to live here with them, maybe she wouldn't be a sad, anxious widow and life with her might have been so much better.

That was one of many times when the customs of this Devon town touched Ruby's heart and helped her not to miss her home in London. At Whitsun, the girls wore white dresses to church and then there was Morris dancing in the town square in Barnstaple. The men were also dressed in white then, with black hats jangling with bells and ribbons. They waved sticks adorned with bells and as they stamped and circled each other, more bells jingled on garters below their knees.

How strange it all was compared to London and how little she missed her old school friends and her mother. Country schoolgirls were just as good as Joyce and Grace at the clapping games they played at breaktime. But there was one occasion when she missed a dear friend and that was at haymaking. Mrs Honey announced they should all go along because the local farmers had said if they didn't gather in the hay soon the crop would be spoiled and there'd be little fodder for the winter. The previous winter, Ruby's first winter in Devon, had been very hard with all the deep snow, frost and ice, so everyone was anxious to ensure a good store of supplies for families and livestock in the dark months later in the year.

But late July, with school holidays started, was hot and balmy for a few days and there was a feverish feeling in the countryside as everyone worked to turn the drying hay in the sunshine. Mrs

Honey didn't stoop over the field; she sat in the shade, offering cool drinks from her basket and sweet turnovers of apple and pear. Both girls flopped down beside her after helping with the hay and Mrs Honey said, 'You don't want to sit here with an old lady like me, go back out in the field and the boys will come after you soon. Look, some of them are already making the hay sweet.' Then Ruby saw Will and the other boys chasing the girls with rings of hay twisted into garlands, throwing them over the girls' heads to hold them tight and sometimes leaning in for a kiss, crying 'Sweeten the hay, why don't you?' Joan leapt up and raced off to join the throng, but Ruby stayed at Mrs Honey's side.

There was no one out there she wanted to catch her. No one she'd like to kiss her. For the only boy she liked was back in London now.

Chapter 17

14 February 1940

Roses are Red

Ruby saw how Joan sneaked the card out of sight that morning. It was lying on the doormat as they came downstairs, dressed and ready for breakfast. She noticed straight away that there wasn't a stamp, so that meant it must have been delivered by hand. And although Ruby was only ten, even she understood the significance of 14 February. All the girls at school had talked about it through the previous week. And when she had accompanied Joan to Pride's the butcher's shop on Saturday, Stan the delivery boy, in his striped apron with his straw hat, stood by his bicycle with its great big basket and blushed when he saw Joan.

Stevie's big sister was very grown-up now. She curled her hair and Ruby noticed that lots of men in the village, not just the butcher's boy, followed her slim curves with their eyes. The green sweater she'd knitted for herself clung to her bosom and Ruby hoped that she would be as pretty as Joan when she grew up, even if she couldn't knit half as well as her.

She saw Joan put the card into her coat pocket. Maybe she could take a peek later and find out who had sent it. But Valentines shouldn't be signed – they were meant to be sent in secret, weren't they? How would Joan know who had sent it if she had lots of admirers? If she'd never seen their writing before, she wouldn't have any idea at all. And Ruby thought then that if Stevie sent one to her, she'd know right away it was him, because he'd written to her soon after he'd run away.

'*Dear Ruby,*' he wrote, *I'm sorry I couldn't stay and make you a doll's house after all, like I promised. But now I'm back in London it would be too heavy to pack up and send on to you. Anyway, my dad has got me polishing cars in the garage now. I tell you, that's more my cup of tea than mucking out the stinky cow stalls and stables at that smelly old farm. I'm glad I got away when I did. And if you see Tom Barford at school, tell him from me that I hope he has to do all the jobs on his own now, every morning and every evening. Will got away as well, I heard. He didn't cop it as much as I did, but he was still hard done by, so I'm glad he's been moved on to a better family in the village.*

Well, cheerio for now, Ruby. I hope you get your doll's house one day.

Your friend, Stevie

She cherished that letter, written in pencil on lined paper. He wasn't much of a scholar, but at least it was legible, unlike some of the essays she'd seen him write in class, strewn with ink blots and crossings-out. She'd written back right away, but hadn't heard from him again. Perhaps letter-writing wasn't something he was fond of doing. She hadn't written to him any more. If she had, she would have wanted to say, *I wish you were still here with us. I wish you were here to make me a doll's house. I miss you.*

As Ruby sat at the table in the warm kitchen, eating her creamy porridge, she noticed Joan had curled her hair even more carefully than usual. And if she wasn't mistaken, there was an unusual touch of pink to her lips and her eyebrows were smoothed with Vaseline.

Mrs Honey was making the hens' morning mash from boiled-up vegetable scraps and bran. Most had survived being snowed in the month before and the two that had died were gutted and plucked, then boiled up for stock and soup. 'Joan, dear,' Mrs Honey said, giving the mash a final stir, 'do you think you could pop out at dinner time and see what Mr Pride can give us today? Wednesday's early closing as you know and he promised me some kidneys the other day, but I need to stay here and finish the wash this morning.' Mrs Honey was a woman of habit and liked to do her laundry regularly. Large items, like sheets and tablecloths, all went off to the laundry, marked with an indelible HH for Harriet Honey, but smaller things were washed at home.

Ruby noticed how Joan blushed, making her look prettier than ever, as she said she'd be happy to call round to the butcher's shop. 'I'll make sure you don't go hungry,' Mrs Honey said. 'There'll be a big bowl of my thick pea soup waiting for you here and you'll easily get back to school in time for the afternoon classes.'

Joan was practically a proper teacher now herself. She read to the little ones and heard the slightly older ones read their books to her. She took the smallest to the toilets and hugged them when they grazed their knees in the playground. Everyone loved Joan, so why shouldn't Stan Pride love her too?

Later that day, when they were walking back from school, Ruby said, 'Do you like Stan Pride?'

'Who?' Joan said.

'The delivery boy at the butcher's shop.'

'Oh, him? That skinny, spotty boy? Why would I like him?' Joan laughed, a little unkindly, Ruby thought, and she didn't ask any more questions, but she did still wonder who had sent Joan that card.

When they got back to the house, Mrs Honey was smiling. She pointed to an envelope on the kitchen table. 'Came in the second post,' she said. 'Go on, open it.'

Joan leant towards it, then said, 'Oh, it's not for me, it's for you, Ruby. Here you are.' She handed Ruby the envelope with its London postmark and to her delight, Ruby recognised the handwriting instantly. Joan clearly did too, for she was smiling. Inside was a card decked with roses and violets, unsigned, just saying '*From an Admirer*', and there were three large X's beneath these words.

Ruby beamed with delight. There was no name, no flowery message, but all the same, she could tell it was from Stevie and she hugged it to herself and hoped that every year from now on, there would be a card in the post for her from a secret admirer.

Salute the King,
Salute the Queen
Salute the German submarine

Chapter 18

12 October 1940

A Black Hat Day

'I've had a letter this morning from your aunt, Mrs Cherry, dear,' Mrs Honey said. 'She'll be arriving today so you're to stay here with me while Joan goes into school.'

Aunt Ida? Why? Ruby had settled well into her new life. The fresh air, away from the smogs of a London winter, had cleared her chest and the abundance of fresh food and a summer running through the fields had given her a colour no strolls through London parks ever could.

It wasn't long since she'd had her last letter from home. Early on, soon after the school was evacuated, her mother had begun to say she wondered if she might bring Ruby back home, as London hadn't been bombed after all, and she'd nervously pondered the question again at Christmas. But once the summer was over, Mum wrote saying she thought Ruby was better off staying in the country.

We've had a few bombs go off round here, but you're not to worry. If I'm home, I run down to the Anderson shelter and if I'm out then I make for the nearest Underground station. Lots of people go down there and it's like one big party. Mind you, some are better than others and I got caught out running for my train at Liverpool Street station recently and had to go in a dreadful place called the Tilbury. It was filthy, so I'll avoid that one in future.

*

'We'll give your aunt a special tea when she comes,' Mrs Honey said. 'You can help me make a cake.'

Ruby couldn't understand why her aunt was coming and not her mother, but maybe Mum was unwell, maybe she was busy or maybe she couldn't afford the train fare. It was a long journey, after all. But she liked helping Mrs Honey in the kitchen, so she put these questions aside, washed her hands and tied her apron around her waist. Ingredients were laid out on the kitchen table that Mrs Honey scrubbed every evening after preparing the day's meals. Ruby read the lettering on the storage tins – flour, sugar and sultanas. There was a small block of margarine and a bunch of carrots.

'First, we need to scrub, then grate the carrots,' Mrs Honey said. 'They're sweet, so that means we won't use so much of our sugar ration. And luckily, we've got our own eggs, so we don't have to use that awful dried egg.'

There weren't a lot of sultanas in the tin, so only a handful went into the mix, along with a handful of sugar. Ruby was allowed to do a little of every stage of the cooking. She beat the eggs in a cup, grated a small mountain of orange carrot, rubbed the margarine into the flour and stirred the mixture with a big wooden spoon. Mrs Honey showed her how to line the baking tin with greasy butter papers and lastly added a pinch of precious cinnamon and nutmeg from her dwindling store of spices.

While the cake was in the oven, filling the kitchen with the fragrant smell of good home baking, Mrs Honey set a tray for tea. 'Fetch me the rose plates from the dresser, will you? And the matching teacups and saucers. We want to show your aunt we can do things properly here in Devon. She might be used to grand London shops and theatres, but we'll show her.'

Ruby couldn't remember how grand her aunt was. She only ever met her at Christmas and birthdays. Once, before the war started, her mother had taken her on the train into London from Ilford, then by Underground train to Stepney, where Aunt Ida lived above a public house. Ruby had never been into a place like that before. It smelt sour, like vinegar, but she liked the mirrors, doors and windows with their glittering glass, etched with words and flowers. The 'bar', as her mother called it, was much more attractive, with its shining brass and sparkling glass, than the pokey rooms upstairs where her aunt and uncle lived. Mum had been cross with Aunt Ida, saying things like, 'You've no right,' and 'It's not your place...' Quite why they had to go visiting there, Ruby wasn't sure, but when they left, Mum slammed the main door with its polished brass handles, saying, 'That's the last time I come all the way over here.'

So Ruby was feeling a little wary at the thought of Aunt Ida's imminent arrival, but she went to her room to brush her hair, which, though longer now than when it was cut a year ago, still wasn't long enough to plait. Joan said she shouldn't grow it any more, to save time in the mornings. Ruby found a clean jumper and pulled up her knitted knee-length socks. She washed her hands and face and was, she thought, quite presentable when they finally heard a knock at the door. She peered into the hall as Mrs Honey answered, and heard murmured greetings before her aunt was brought into the parlour, where the tea tray was set out. She couldn't quite hear all that was said as her aunt removed her hat and coat in the hall; she just caught the words, 'No, I thought it best coming from you,' and 'I promised if anything happened...'.

Then Aunt Ida entered the room, dressed all in black, with a sparkling black necklace looped in two strands across her bosom. She was wearing a little black hat, velvet with a black feather and a tuft of netting, perched on the back of her head, contrasting with her deep red hair. A waft of stale scent and cigarette smoke from her journey hovered around her. 'Well, there she is. Haven't you grown since I last saw you? Come on, give your auntie a kiss, why don't you?'

Ruby felt obliged to give her aunt's thickly powdered cheek a quick peck, then retreated, her hands behind her back. The smoky smell was more bearable if she kept her distance. Aunt Ida regarded her with her head tipped to one side, her small dark eyes and thin scarlet mouth reminding Ruby of the hens inspecting grubs they had scratched from the soil in their run. 'Hmm,' she said. 'You don't half remind me of Hilda.'

That's Mum's name, Ruby thought. Then Mrs Honey said, 'Why don't we all sit down and have some tea first.' She pulled out a chair for Ida and one for herself and indicated that Ruby should also take a seat.

The tea was hot and the cake was good, although Aunt Ida broke it into little pieces and inspected it, saying, 'Well I never! Carrots, eh? Who would've thought?' But all the time, Ruby's stomach was tight, her breathing shallow, because she was wondering what was going to happen next. Why was her aunt here and not her mother?

And then it did happen. Aunt Ida took a deep breath, put down her teacup and folded her hands in her lap. 'Well, I'd better get right to the point, I suppose. I haven't come all the way here to be sociable. I've come to take you back to London with me, Ruby.'

Ruby's head filled with questions, but she couldn't find the words to speak.

'You're probably wondering why I'm dressed all in black. It's not my colour and doesn't suit me, but I like to do things proper. We had a funeral yesterday, Ruby. It's your mum. A bomb hit the house.' Ida shook her head as if she was astonished this could have happened, when everyone knew how many bombs had been falling all over London since 7 September. 'That means I'm your nearest living relative now, so you're going to have to come and live with me from now on.'

The speed of this revelation and the harshness of its delivery dazed Ruby. She sat in silence, her mouth gaping, then finally managed to say, 'Mummy? I don't have a mummy?' And she looked, not at her aunt but at Mrs Honey, who slid from her chair and knelt beside Ruby, holding her hands, saying, 'There, there, dear. I'm so sorry.'

Then Ruby felt the true impact of this news and her tense stomach churned and she vomited all the carrot cake and the tea, directly into Mrs Honey's lap. 'I'm sorry,' Ruby whispered through her tears. 'I didn't mean to.'

'Never mind,' Mrs Honey said. 'I was still wearing my apron. It'll wash.'

But Aunt Ida said, 'Well, that's the last time we give you carrot cake, young lady. And we've got to get a move on. We've got a train to catch.'

'You're not going right away, surely?' Mrs Honey stood, bundling up the soiled apron and looking bewildered.

'We're catching the four thirty train. We should get back just in time for last orders.'

'But she's no trouble. I'd be happy to have her stay a while longer. And Joan will be sorry to see her go too.'

Ida shook her head and the feather on her hat quivered. 'No, my mind's made up. I can't go traipsing round the country on trains every five minutes. Anyway, I promised Hilda when her Frank went that if anything ever happened to her, we'd always take Ruby in.' She sniffed. 'It's only right she's with her own family now.'

'But there's been a lot of bombs recently. Don't you think she'd be safer here?'

Ida's back stiffened. 'She's coming home with me and that's that.'

'Come along then, dear,' Mrs Honey said, taking Ruby's hand. 'Let's go upstairs and I'll pack your case for you.'

'Make sure you pack all her things, mind,' called Aunt Ida as they left the room. 'I've nothing ready for her and every blessed thing that family ever had went up in smoke.'

Chapter 19

12 October 1940

Into the Fray

Ruby barely said a word on the train. She felt numb, unable to speak or cry. But Aunt Ida had plenty to say. 'Your mother, she thought she was well out of it in her lovely house near the park. All the way over there, out of the city. We've had it non-stop since the beginning of last month. Night after night and daylight raids too, some of the time. I expect she thought they wouldn't bother with bombing Ilford. But no one's safe these days. Don't matter where you are.'

Her voice droned on and on, weaving in and out of the rattling of the train as it chugged back to London. Ruby couldn't keep her eyes open all the time and she must have drifted off and slept for part of the journey. At one point, she woke and Aunt Ida was saying, 'Here, have a sandwich to keep you going. We won't have a chance to eat before we're home.' She offered the pack of sandwiches and cake Mrs Honey had pressed into her hands before leaving. Ruby took a triangle of folded bread and tried to nibble it. Normally, coming back from school, she'd have been so hungry she'd have eaten it in two bites, but her stomach still felt tense and uncertain. And she wished she'd seen Joan before she left. She hadn't had a chance to say goodbye. She wondered what Joan would say when she came back after school and whether she'd miss her.

Aunt Ida offered her a sip of sweet tea from the Thermos flask that Mrs Honey had refilled before they left. That was more palatable and Ruby drank from the little cup that screwed over the top. She looked out of the window at the countryside flashing past, thinking how little she wanted to return to London, especially now bombs were falling, killing people and destroying buildings. What happened when a bomb hit a house, she wondered. Did Mum know she was going to die? Was Sooty killed too? She felt sorry for her mother and was sad she was dead, but since she'd left home she'd never longed to go back there.

When she had first been evacuated with all the other children a year ago, the fields and hills of Devon had seemed alien, so vast, so green, so full of large animals that strolled towards you and made loud noises. But she'd become used to her new environment and grown to love the changes in the seasons that she'd never been aware of in London. In the spring, Mrs Honey had shown her clumps of pale yellow primroses sprouting in the banks along the lanes, then seas of bluebells under the trees in the woods. Over the summer she'd helped to pick raspberries and strawberries, gather peas bursting in their pods and long green beans that hung from tented poles in the garden. At home she remembered the park with its boating lake, tennis courts and wide expanses of grass, but that was near her old home, the home that Aunt Ida said had been destroyed. And she didn't know if there were any open green spaces or parks with trees near Aunt Ida's home in the pub.

When the train finally arrived at Paddington, it was late in the evening. Aunt Ida grabbed her hand and dragged her to the Underground station to catch a train to Aldgate. But they'd only got as far as Liverpool Street when the train stopped and everyone was told it would go no further that night. 'We'll just have to walk the rest,' Aunt Ida said. 'Not long now.' She yanked Ruby with her up the steps and out into the street. But they hadn't gone far when shafts of light split the sky and the screech of a siren wailed. 'That's all we need,' Aunt Ida complained, starting to hurry. 'There's nothing for it now. We'll have to dive into the Tilbury and put up with it till the all-clear. It's the nearest shelter.'

Ruby could barely keep up. Her legs were running as fast as they could and soon they were joining a swarm of people pushing and shoving their way through gigantic gates and down a slope into a dim cavern. So much noise, the screams of little children, the scolding of their mothers telling them to hurry and above all that clamour, the shrieks of sirens, the drone of planes and the first boom of the bombs. She couldn't understand where they were going, but Aunt Ida seemed to know what she was doing as she dragged Ruby past great bales of paper and dark arches where trucks waited in railway sidings.

When they had gone some way, past families spreading blankets out on the stone floor and hawkers peddling cold fried fish, Aunt Ida stopped and pushed Ruby into a wooden bay between the pallets and barrels. 'This'll have to do,' she said. 'At least we're near the privies down this end. Better use them now, before they get to overflowing like last time I had to spend a night here.'

They had no bedding, nothing soft to make a mattress, but with the mass of bodies crowded into the shelter and the lamps being lit in the tunnels, Ruby didn't feel cold. Nor was she frightened down here in this crypt, because although she could hear thudding above their heads she couldn't see the danger in the skies or the aftermath of the bombs. All around her Ruby could hear babies wailing, the murmur of those trying to calm themselves and settle down to sleep and now and then, some raucous singing and cries of 'Shuddup!' The air was clammy and stale, a mix of bodies, engine grease and filth, overlaid with something rancid.

'It doesn't smell nice down here,' Ruby said, sniffing and holding a fresh hankie to her nose.

'Could be a darn sight worse by morning,' Aunt Ida said with a toss of her head. 'That sour smell's the margarine they keep stored down here. Don't fancy having that on me bread after this rabble's messed the place up. And there's horses further down so that's not helping neither.' She examined her stockings, then said, 'Dammit, there's another ladder. When I'll get new ones, I don't know. You won't catch me in wrinkly lisle or ankle socks, like some. Got to keep up appearances in my business.'

She sighed and patted her black hat. 'And I expect I'll be grey by the time this war's over, I will.' Ruby had noticed her aunt's red hair wasn't as vibrant as she remembered. 'If it goes on as long as the last one I'll have to start adding veils to all my hats to hide my roots. Can't get my dye for love nor money right now.'

Ruby had noticed a border of mousey hairs among the red when they were on the train. She stared at her aunt removing her hat and tucking her hair behind her ears, then taking out a compact mirror from her handbag to examine her reflection in the dim light. It was hard to see clearly, but there was an undyed streak down the middle parting. Like a rusty badger, Ruby thought. Mrs Honey had neat white hair she wore in a tight bun. She had no need of dye.

Ruby managed to fall asleep on the damp sacks in the shelter, despite her dreams being haunted by the cries of babies and the hoarse shouts of drunkards. When she woke, Aunt Ida said, 'Well, that's a night I never want to repeat.' She'd already replenished her lipstick and powdered her nose. 'If you need to do a wee before we go, you'll have to squat down behind that truck. The lavs are overflowing, so you can't go in there.' She pointed to a dark corner.

Ruby crouched down, trying not to wet her shoes and socks. Aunt Ida stood guard. Just as well, since a shabby man came shuffling nearby, fumbling with the buttons on his trousers. 'Not here, you don't,' Aunt Ida said, waving him away with her gloved hand.

When Ruby had finished and straightened her clothes, Aunt Ida grabbed her by the wrist and started marching towards the entrance.

'With a bit of luck, the WVS ladies will have set up their tea stall outside. Let's get there before everyone else does.'

They passed mothers feeding babies, little children sleeping naked on blankets, like grubby cherubs, people rubbing their eyes and clearly wondering how they would face the day. And everywhere stank of sweat and human waste, as there were no facilities.

Outside, the air was grey with smoke and dust, but there was a mobile canteen manned by two women in bottle-green and beetroot-red WVS uniforms, looking like cheerful human robins. There was already a shuffling, dishevelled queue of about twenty or so. Aunt Ida grumbled, but said, 'Suppose we'd better get something here. Gawd knows what's happened at home.'

She bought two cups of tea and two currant buns and as she took her change, she asked the WVS lady how bad the bombing had been last night. 'We got off lightly this time,' the lady said. 'They reckon there was about thirty. At least it wasn't as bad as last week. We had nearly seven hundred on the ninth. We're hoping they're running out of bombs now.'

'There's a chance my old man's still in the land of the living then,' Aunt Ida replied and the two of them laughed.

The tea was hot, sweet and strong, and the bun was stale but welcome all the same. When they'd finished, Aunt Ida grabbed Ruby's hand again and set off. 'We'll see if there's a bus. If not, we'll have to go on the Underground again.'

After they'd waited for some twenty minutes, a double-decker bus arrived. It was painted grey, not the usual bright red that Ruby remembered from before she left London for the countryside. Some of the windows were boarded up with wood and there was a lady conductor selling the tickets. Once they'd sat down, Aunt Ida heaved a sigh. 'If I find Reg hasn't swept the floor in the bar when I get in, I'll murder him.'

Ruby had only a faint memory of Uncle Reg. He had a bristly moustache that had tickled her cheek when he'd kissed her when she'd visited with Mum. He'd seemed kind, kinder than his wife, and he'd given her pennies to buy sweets from the corner shop. She'd chosen her favourite, Jelly Babies. But she hadn't had money for sweets in a long time and anyway, sweets were in short supply as well because of the war.

When they reached a stop fairly near the pub, Ruby looked back at the bus as it left them. 'Why aren't buses red any more?' she asked.

'Oh, for goodness' sake, all your questions. I don't know. Some just aren't, that's all.' Aunt Ida dragged Ruby along the street until she could see the pub still standing on the crossroads. 'Thank Gawd. It's still there. And no more broken windows this time.' Some of the pub's etched windows were boarded up, making it a dark cavern when they stepped inside, even though the lights were switched on. 'I've told him before,' Aunt Ida said, flicking the lights off. 'Only when we've got customers. What's he thinking? We're not made of money.'

Ruby followed her through the sour-smelling, darkened bar and up a flight of stairs to a dingy sitting room furnished with a dining table and two armchairs upholstered in worn maroon moquette, the arms and back shiny with dark greasy patches. A gas fire flickered in the grate and Uncle Reg was fast asleep and snoring, his paper spread across his lap. Aunt Ida thumped Ruby's case down on the floor and slapped her husband on the shoulder. He woke with a start. 'You're back then?'

'Course I'm back. Weren't you worried last night?'

'I did wonder. But you're here now. Have you picked up any bread?'

'Heaven help me. I've travelled all the way back from Devon with your niece being sick, spent the night without a wink of sleep in the Tilbury and all you can say is, where's the bread? Go and get it yourself. I need a wash and a lie-down.'

Ruby watched all this, wide-eyed. Mum and Dad had never argued. They called each other 'love' and 'dear' all the time, even though Mum often rolled her eyes when Dad came back smelling of beer and being very jolly.

'You come with me,' Aunt Ida said after hanging her coat on the back of the door. She was still wearing her hat as she carried Ruby's case up another flight of stairs. 'You're in here,' she said, pushing open the door to a small, dreary room with a bed, wardrobe, chest of drawers and a little sink in one corner. The striped wallpaper was red and cream, peeling in a corner near the window, which looked out on a walled backyard and tiled roofs. It was very different to the clean whitewashed bedroom she had shared with Joan, with a view of the fruit trees in the garden, and nowhere near as nice as her bedroom at home, with its rose-patterned wallpaper. She remembered Mum struggling to hang the paper on her own. But she was so proud that she had managed to make Ruby's room so pretty. 'It's like a bower in a country garden,' she'd said when she'd shown Ruby the decorated room with rosy curtains. And the memory brought tears to Ruby's eyes. She knew she had been loved then.

'Bathroom's on the floor below, but be quiet. I need to shut my eyes for a bit.' Ida left Ruby sitting on the bed and as she went back down the stairs, she called, 'Tea's at five. Come down then. There won't be anything later on.'

Ruby was already hungry, but she didn't dare ask if she might eat earlier. She clicked open the latches on her case and began to take out the few clothes she possessed. This was all she had. They smelt of lavender from the little muslin bag Mrs Honey had packed in the case. Ruby held it to her nose, remembering how she and Joan had picked the flowers in the summer. 'They must be gathered on a fine day,' Mrs Honey told them. 'Then we'll hang them to dry out near the range.' She'd been so happy stripping the dried stalks of their scented flowers to fill the little bags she and Joan had stitched. She missed Joan and wondered if the girl who had been like an older, wiser sister missed her too.

She removed her folded nightdress and placed it under the thin, hard pillow, so unlike the feather pillows Mrs Honey had put on her bed. One by one, she hung her two dresses, her cardigans and skirts on hangers in the wardrobe. When she opened the chest of drawers, she saw it was lined with newspaper and had a musty smell so she laid the lavender bag among her socks, vests and knickers.

And when she had nearly emptied her case, she found that Mrs Honey really had thought of everything. At the bottom of the case were the little pieces of doll's house furniture they had made together. She arranged them on top of the chest of drawers. It wasn't a doll's house, but she could imagine. And then she opened the small tin Mrs Honey had also packed. Two plain scones, still fresh. She nibbled the slightly sweet pastry, tasting Devon, the village and the home she had so loved for the past year. And as she ate, the dry blandness of the scones, devoid of cream and jam, was salted with her tears.

Chapter 20

29 October 1940

One Last Time

'Alright, I'll take you down there. But just this once, mind. Then maybe you'll believe me that house is no longer fit to live in and shut up your pestering.' Aunt Ida threw Ruby's coat at her and turned to the oval etched mirror above the fireplace to paint her lips with a shrunken stub of red lipstick. Her eyes swerved to take in Ruby's reflection, standing there stunned, her coat in her hands. 'Get a move on then. I haven't got all day. I've got a pub to run and customers to keep happy.'

Ruby's fingers fumbled with her coat buttons. Two weeks had passed and she was slowly getting used to the new routine of living above a public house. Every morning she had to sweep the floors downstairs in the bars, which were littered with sawdust sticky with spilt beer and gobbets of phlegmy spit. It was not a pleasant task, but the first time she found a penny in the filth she looked over her shoulder, then put it in her pocket. Once she'd scattered fresh sawdust, she had to polish the rinsed glasses, wrinkling her nose at the smell of beer slops and stale tobacco.

After that, as long as the nearby school was open, she went to her class. That was the part of life that felt almost normal, but the school day could finish quickly if there was suddenly an air raid, though the bombs mostly came over at night. It wasn't quite what it was before, however. She didn't know the children who'd stayed behind. And if it had been her old school, that wouldn't have been the same either. Joyce and Grace were no longer there. Her two best friends, who hadn't joined her and the other evacuees the year before and fled to the safety of Devon, had perished in the raid that had killed her mother. Poor Joyce, poor Grace, her friends since she first started at Christchurch School when she was five. She missed them and was sorry they were no longer there to play clapping games and skipping in the school playground. Joyce was very good at doing the 'bumps' when Ruby and another girl whipped the skipping rope faster and faster. And Grace was the best at sewing and patiently showed Ruby how to do a nearly invisible hemstitch on the sample of fabric they were each given to mount in their needlework books, along with examples of buttonholes and blanket stitch.

At midday, when the pub opened for a couple of hours, Ruby was expected to keep out of the way if there was no school, washing up in the kitchen in the pub's living quarters or running down the street to the corner shop to fetch bread and milk. In the afternoon, Aunt Ida and Uncle Reg put their feet up, meaning they both had a nap, in preparation for the long evening ahead, which started around half past five. Ruby was sent out for fish and chips just before they opened. That was all they ate. Fish and chips or bread and cheese. No more fresh vegetables from Mrs Honey's gardens, no more apple pies, no more rabbit, no more new-laid eggs.

She often thought with longing of that rabbit pie. The succulent meat swam in a thin golden gravy, surrounded by chunks of carrot, covered with Mrs Honey's very crumbly, melt-in-the-mouth pastry, the whole crust decorated with scored leaves and supported by a blackbird piping steam. At first some of the other London children had struggled to eat the food of the country folk. They weren't used to having meals cooked at home with fresh ingredients. 'Why can't we go down the chip shop?' they'd say, staring at a plate of stewed beef with turnips. And 'We always go down the pie and mash shop for our tea,' when faced with a home-made steak and kidney pie or a golden toad-in-the-hole with meaty sausages. Ruby wanted to have good memories of her life back home with Mum, but when she compared Mrs Honey's cooking with her mother's tasteless offerings of bland boiled fish or watery cottage pie, she realised how much she had enjoyed every country mouthful after running back from the village school. And now there was no home cooking, good or bad, just the chip shop.

The evenings at the pub dragged, although she could read or listen to the radio. She was allowed to borrow from the library once a week, running there while her guardians had their afternoon rest, enjoying the peace there as much as the books. 'You're lucky your school's still open,' her aunt said, when her school day was cut short yet again. 'Why the Jerries have to bomb the schools, I don't know. But you're reading and you know your numbers, so you know enough to get by.' And long after she had gone to bed, in that little thin bed at the very top of the building, she was woken by the ringing of the bell and a distant voice shouting, 'Time, gentlemen, please.'

All the way to Hampton Road in Ilford to see the bombed-out family house, Ruby thought about the library book she had been reading last night. *Lorna Doone*, a tale of romance and brigands, set in the wild north Devon countryside that she had come to love. She wished she was back there now, among the heathery moors, woods and clear streams, not rattling through dark tunnels on the Underground train.

They walked from Gants Hill station across Valentines Park, its once-smooth lawns now scarred with trenches and bordered by allotments dotted with rows of swelling cabbages. Cadets were training on the boating lake where Ruby had once sailed on a fine summer's day, an ice cream cornet in her hand, her mother nervously grabbing the sides of the boat as her father rowed them around. But that was before. That was before the war started, before her father went away, before she went to Devon and before her parents were both dead.

After walking across the park, they passed through the grand wrought-iron entrance gates on the far side. 'Well, here we are,' Aunt Ida said, coming to a halt a few minutes later in the rubble-strewn street. Ruby could hardly recognise it. 'Now will you believe there's no way you could come back here?'

That wasn't entirely true. Ruby's childhood home wasn't quite a pile of smashed bricks. One corner of the house was still standing. Part of an upper floor still clung to the walls. A ragged curtain hung limply by a broken window, beneath which Ruby could see the bathroom sink, where she had brushed her teeth every night before going to bed. I remember Mummy making those curtains, she thought. Blue curtains with seagulls.

'There, you see,' Aunt Ida said. 'Nothing's left. Anything that survived that bomb will have been nicked by now.'

Ruby was silent. Her bedroom, walls papered with pale blue stripes intertwined with roses, the sitting room with its radio and plush chairs, where they would sit before a fire, Mum knitting and Ruby playing with her dolls, it was all gone. All that remained was a torn mattress, soaked and stained by the fire hoses. And where was Sooty? Did he die too or had he run away to live in the park?

And then she stepped off the pavement, despite her aunt's cries and attempts to drag her back. She stepped over the fallen bricks, the burnt carpet and the shards of crockery and bent down. She turned back towards her aunt and held up a photograph in a silvered metal frame. The glass was smashed, but she could still see the image. Her mother and father on their wedding day. Him in a dark suit, her in a slim white dress that skimmed her ankles, with a circlet holding the veil just above her eyebrows.

'I want to keep this,' Ruby said, stepping with great care back over the bricks.

'Well, I suppose it can't hurt,' Aunt Ida said, her voice a little softer than usual. 'At least you'll have something to remember them by.' She took the picture from Ruby and tapped it on the pavement so the sharp slivers of glass fell, like fragments of ice. Then she shoved the broken glass to one side with the toe of her shoe and wrapped the picture in her scarf, before putting it away in her handbag. 'It'll be quite safe in there till we get back. Don't want you cutting yourself now, do we?' And she turned away from the bombsite to walk back through the park.

Ruby took one last look at the remains of her home. All she had in the world was the clothes Mum had packed for her when she was evacuated, and now this photo. She had so little of her own. And before Aunt Ida could call to her and before she had gone too far away, Ruby bent and picked up a fragment of china. It was all that remained of her mother's favourite tea service. Perhaps this scalloped, gilded edge was from a teacup that had once touched her lips, Ruby thought, as she hid it in her pocket and ran towards the park and her aunt's stiff back.

Underneath the spreading chestnut tree
Mr Chamberlain said to me,
If you want to get your gas-mask free,
Join the blinking A.R.P.

Chapter 21

March 1941

Hop It, Son

Stevie was only fourteen; he should never have been allowed onto the freshly bombed site. Boys his age, too young for conscription, were only meant to carry messages, racing from place to place on their bikes across tarmac showered with a hailstorm of glassy splinters. He was supposed to hand over the note from one of the Air Raid Precautions wardens, lumped together as the ARP, requesting the attendance of the fire service or asking for a rescue squad, then move on. But in the drama, in the excitement, he sometimes lingered. Maybe this time he'd be the one to find the rolls of fivers stuffed inside a split mattress, or it would be his lucky day and there'd be a cracked gas meter spilling coins into the debris. The meters got emptied out quickly by looters; one time one of the boys said there wasn't a penny left by the time the gasman came along, only hours after the flats were bombed.

He laid his bike down at the side of the road where he could keep an eye on it. Bikes had been known to disappear and he needed wheels for his night-time volunteering as well as running errands at home during the day. He was lucky he'd had it with him when their house was bombed, before he and his parents moved to Nan's. He wouldn't have got another one too easily. They were all in the Anderson shelter at the bottom of the garden when the bomb hit their street. When it calmed down they could see that their house wasn't as bad as the rest of the terrace, but Dad said it had been deemed unstable, so they couldn't stay. And just before all three of them traipsed out of the shattered house with their cases, he saw Dad jemmy open the meter. 'What do you think you're doing, Jim?' his mum called out. 'Keeping it safe,' he replied, with a wink to his son. 'Some bugger'll get it sooner or later, so I'd better look after it, hadn't I?'

Stevie saw just how easy it was and how many handfuls of silver coins he shovelled into his pockets. Dad was sharp like that, never one to miss an opportunity. 'You've gotta look out for Number One,' he was always saying. 'How else d'you think I can keep the garage going?' Stevie knew that he dealt in engine parts salvaged from the streets as well as giving various unsavoury characters his mother called 'spivs' storage space in his lock-up. 'Just because I'm too old to serve in this war, don't mean I can't still serve my country,' he'd tell her with a grin, slipping her a pack of tea (fallen off the back of a lorry) as he hugged her.

Stevie squeezed through the crowd milling in the street. ARP wardens were yelling at people to stand clear, but it was so chaotic, and he was tall and in uniform, so they must have thought he was one of them. Everyone was shouting and then someone called for quiet, so they could listen out for anguished cries below the rubble.

He stumbled over the collapsed building with the rest of them, charred timbers glistening and still dripping with the spray from the firemen's hoses. With everyone busy looking the other way, he might be lucky this time. An extra bob or two was always handy with fags, tobacco and a ticket for the flicks to pay for. And he needed his visits to the cinema. Takes you out of yourself it does, looking at the screen. You can forget what's going on every day when you're in there.

He began poking around the smashed houses and while most of the men were in a huddle, pulling away slabs of brickwork, he noticed a child's shoe peeping out from under a chunk of collapsed wall, a blue shoe with a button strap. It looked so lost, that little blue shoe, and as he bent down to wipe away the brick dust on the toe he realised the shoe wasn't empty. A crumpled white sock covered a little foot and he could see the start of an ankle under the bricks.

He called to the rescuers, but they were busy at their work and no one seemed to hear him above the shouts, the rumble of trucks and the distant sound of sirens, so he got on with it on his own, lifting the pieces of rubble carefully, so carefully but quickly all the same, hoping to find a little girl breathing and alive. He'd come hoping to find rich pickings, but now he was intent on being the hero of the hour, rescuing an injured child. But he didn't find a girl. He only uncovered the stump of her leg, cut off just above the knee, looking like a joint of lamb on the butcher's slab. There was no little girl and no matching shoe. There was just the one he'd found.

He stared at the leg for what seemed like an age. She must have fallen recently, playing hopscotch or skipping maybe, as there was a scabbed graze on her knee. Then he began scrabbling through the debris again. Where was she? Where was the rest of her? You could lose a leg and still live, couldn't you? She might be alive under there. He kept on digging, tearing his nails, his fingers bleeding from cuts caused by slivers of glass and fragments of brick. Then he felt a hand on his shoulder. 'Come on, son,' a voice said. 'We'll take over now. You've done enough.'

Stevie stood up, breathing deeply. He wanted to stay and see if they'd find her. He so wanted her to be alive. But he felt his legs trembling and his hands began to shake. He held himself together just long enough to scurry off to the other side of the road where his bike was still waiting. And as he grabbed the handlebars, he heaved the fried-egg sandwich his nan had made him have for his tea before he left, all over the pavement.

He was ashamed as he walked away. Think yourself so clever, trying to see what you could pinch. Yeah, but if I hadn't been on the lookout, I wouldn't have seen that shoe. That's right, if you hadn't been on the lookout, you wouldn't have seen a sight that's gonna haunt you for the rest of your days. Think about it. He could never forget that shoe, that little girl's leg. He had nightmares that the rest of her was under the rubble, calling out for him to carry on digging.

Chapter 22

March 1941

Friends Reunited

Ruby wasn't sure it was him at first, when she saw the tall boy poking the rubble on the bombsite near Bethnal Green market. But when he looked up, he saw her and smiled. 'Wondered when I might see you again,' Stevie said. 'I heard you'd been sent off back to your aunt's place. Stepney, isn't it?'

'That's right. The Victoria and Albert. I've been back a while now.' She felt shy, suddenly seeing him again after nearly eighteen months. He was taller now, his voice had deepened and the first shadowy signs of a moustache darkened his upper lip. 'I was sorry you couldn't stay in Devon,' she said. 'We were worried about you at first.'

'Yeah, well, I had to get away from there.' He shrugged, as if shaking off uncomfortable memories of his time at the farm. 'You'd have been more worried if I'd stayed. Old Barford had a temper on him, he did.'

Ruby thought about the livid welts revealed on his back that Christmas. But now he looked well fed and much healthier than when she'd seen him last. 'What are you doing here now?'

'I'm on my way to the ARP post. Look, see, I'm authorised.' He leant towards her so she could see the badge stitched on to his jersey. It was a gold crown embroidered on a red rectangle, with the letters 'NS' in gold thread on one side. 'That's my National Service badge and now I'm working towards my Scout War Service badge. I have to do stuff like unarmed combat and weapons for that.'

'What's ARP stand for?'

He lifted his chin and straightened his shoulders with pride. 'It stands for Air Raid Precautions. Making sure everyone gets to a shelter when there's a raid and other stuff.'

'And you don't have to go to school as well?'

'Nah. There ain't no school now. Our old school got bombed, same time as our house. We've moved in with my nan in Hackney. It's alright there. Near Victoria Park and I can cycle up to Hackney Marshes. Anyhow, I don't need school no more. I'm fourteen now and I've learnt enough to get by. The boys say I'm learning on the job.' He fumbled in his pocket, brought out a tobacco tin and began to roll a cigarette. 'Want one?'

Ruby shook her head. 'So what do you have to do?'

'Deliver messages from ARP to the police and fire services, bit of fire watching, reporting incidents, that sort of thing. I'm working in my dad's garage an' all, polishing cars an' that.'

She was impressed. He seemed so grown up and important. 'And were you doing a job for them just now?'

'Nah. Just checking over the site, seeing if there's any pickings.' He frowned, then his face brightened. 'I've only found a few pennies so far, but you should hear the stories some of the boys tell. One fella said there was rolls of pound notes stuffed inside a mattress. And another place, all the gas and electric meters had been broken into. Every single one was empty. Cleaned out. All those shillings. Makes you think, eh?'

It made Ruby think of her mother and her old home, of how nothing of any value was left there. Was it all destroyed in the blast or pilfered once her mother's body had been taken away for burial? 'I went back to see my old house,' she said. 'It was horrible, but I got this.' She held out the fragment of china she had salvaged from the rubble, kept in her coat pocket so she could touch it and remember the house as it once was. 'And I found a photo of my mum and dad on their wedding day, but that's in my bedroom, my room at my aunt and uncle's, that is.'

'They run a pub, don't they? What a great life, eh? Living on the premises.'

'It's alright, I suppose.' Ruby thought it wasn't homely, not like a real home, not like her old house or Mrs Honey's cottage. The living quarters were cramped, mean little rooms steeped in the smells of stale beer and cigarette smoke from the bars below. 'I wish Joan was here. She's staying in Devon still, isn't she?'

'Yeah, she wrote and said as she's learning to be a teacher, she's better off staying there till the war's over. She's got a boyfriend though. Trevor, he's in France now. My mum reckons they're getting married when he gets back.'

Ruby thought how quickly Joan had grown up, become a real adult since they had their snowball fight in the hard winter of the previous year. Sixteen, maybe seventeen now, and already there was talk of marriage.

'You going back to the pub now?'

'Yes, I only came out to get our rations, but I had to go a bit further than usual to find everything. I don't usually come all the way over to Bethnal Green, but Aunt said she'd heard the market here was better.' She showed him her string bag of meagre groceries. 'I have to help them, as it's very busy all the time.'

'I'll walk you back. I was going in that direction anyway. Here, let me,' and he took her string shopping bag, hung it on the bars of his bike and they started walking side by side. 'So, they let you go out on your own then?'

'I do some of the shopping most days and I go to the library every Thursday. I can go out in the afternoon when the pub's closed, if there's no school, after I've done all my jobs, but there's no one to go with and nothing to do.'

'What about those school friends of yours? The ones who didn't come away with us? What were their names?'

'Oh, you mean Joyce and Grace. It would be nice if they were still here. But they aren't. Their houses got bombed.'

'Bad luck them. So you've got no one to walk with or take you to the pictures?'

'No. Aunt Ida says she hasn't got the time or the energy to entertain me. She says I've got to learn to stand on my own two feet.'

She felt him looking closely at her. 'What time do you usually go to the library?'

'About three o'clock. Why?'

'I could meet you outside. You get your books changed and then we'll go to the Regal. They're showing *The Ghost of St. Michael's*.'

'I'd really like that. I can't stay out too long though. They need me back before opening time. Aunt Ida usually sends me out to fetch the fish and chips just before they start in the evening so I'd have to be back by five.'

'Okey dokey. We should get to see the feature at any rate. It'd do me good to have a bit of fun.'

It was then that Ruby noticed a cloud pass across his face, wiping away the mask of bravado to reveal the frightened young boy he really was. 'You alright?'

'Yeah, course I am. It's just that… sometimes you need something to help you forget. Like the other day. Us scouts are only meant to run messages and the like, but sometimes you can't help seeing things you'd rather not see.'

He drew on his wizened roll-up with a trembling hand and after he'd exhaled the smoke, said, 'You think when the bombs go off, people just fall down dead, but they don't, Ruby, they don't. People are blown apart, they end up in pieces. And one place I had to cycle to, they were having to pull bodies off the walls of the house. You don't know how terrible it is, what a bomb can do to a person. It blasts a body right into the wall, pushes it into the plaster and as the men pull it away, the flesh and clothes get left there… stuck to the wall. They have to hose it off in the end.' He shook his head, trying to dispel the hideous images, his voice quavering, and she could tell he was holding back tears. 'And the worst part is the stray dogs, sniffing around in all that dust and rubble. I throw something at 'em if I see 'em.'

Ruby took his hand in hers and just held it. He was older than her, but not so very much. She wondered if her mother had been killed outright or had been retrieved in pieces. She hoped Mum hadn't been crushed into the wall of the sitting room, with its rich floral wallpaper.

'That's why I'd like to go to the pictures, Ruby. To think about good things.' And he managed a weak smile as they continued walking towards the pub, still holding hands, the rhythmic ticking of the bike's wheels the only sound to accompany their shy silence.

Chapter 23

March 1941

Just Friends

'You took your time changing your book,' Aunt Ida sneered when Ruby returned after her first visit to the cinema with Stevie. 'Got your nose stuck in *Encyclopaedia Britannica* now, have you?'

Ruby hesitated. She was holding a book, but it wasn't new, it was one she'd borrowed last week, the same one she'd tucked under her arm when she'd left the pub early that afternoon. She hadn't changed her book because she'd wanted to be sure she met Stevie on time, and suddenly she wasn't sure she wanted to let her aunt know that she'd had a lovely afternoon, sitting next to Stevie, laughing at Will Hay as the schoolmaster and shivering at the scenes set in a spooky Scottish castle. She hugged the memory of their time together inside herself and thought she didn't want to let Aunt Ida spoil it.

He was waiting for her when she arrived, smart in his uniform, buffing his badge with his cuff. 'They've got ices,' he said, once he'd bought their tickets. 'You can have one if you like.'

'But I can't pay for one,' she said. 'Mum used to give me pocket money, but Aunt Ida only gives me enough for the shopping and getting our tea at the chip shop.'

'That's alright. My treat. Dad pays me for helping out at the garage. Threepence a bumper and a whole shilling when I wash a car. And I found two bob when I was poking around a bombsite yesterday.'

Ruby was impressed. He was rich. 'Do you think it came from one of the gas meters?'

'Could be. Maybe someone got there before me and nicked the rest. Better luck next time, eh?' He laughed as he paid for their ice creams and they found their seats.

In the warm fug of the darkened cinema, Ruby could forget the meanness of her aunt's pub. Uncle Reg wasn't so bad; he'd even told Aunt Ida the other day she was too hard on her niece. But her aunt seemed to have great difficulty uttering even the smallest kind words, preferring brusque orders and jibes to expressions of gratitude. So here, before the flickering screen wreathed in cigarette smoke, seated in plush comfort, despite the smells of unwashed hair, socks and other garments, Ruby ate her ice, laughed and was delivered from her everyday life of drabness and the fear of another air raid. The film wasn't all that scary, although when she first heard the eerie sound of the bagpipes, signalling that death was coming to the creepy castle, she screwed her eyes shut tight and cringed into her seat. But then the laughs began and she turned to see Stevie guffawing and was glad that the nightmares he tried to hide from all but her were banished for the time being.

'That weren't half bad,' he said as they made their way out when the film finished. 'Do you want to come again next week?'

Over the road, the church clock was chiming the half-hour and she knew she had to dash. 'I've got to go. Aunt Ida will never forgive me if I'm late with the fish and chips.' She clutched her library book to her chest. 'But thanks ever so. And yes, I'd love to go again.'

'I'll wait here then,' he called after her as she began to run. 'Same time next week.' And he gave her a mock salute as she waved to him.

From then on, most weeks followed the same pattern. As soon as her aunt and uncle went to their bedroom to lie down after lunchtime service, Ruby ran past the library and straight to the cinema. She'd realised that Aunt Ida never took any notice of what she was reading, so if she finished her book she often changed it earlier in the week, and her aunt never commented. Sometimes she reached the Regal ahead of Stevie and waited nervously on the steps, wondering if he would still turn up. There were days when he came but held out empty hands, saying, 'Sorry, Rube, I'm skint this week. Dad's still doing his repairs, but he hasn't had much for me to do lately.' Ruby knew he spent some of his earnings on tobacco and Rizla papers, but how could she mind that when she couldn't contribute a single penny?

And yet she knew that although she was penniless, she offered him something no one else could. She didn't have to pay for their outings, their ice creams or their sweets, for she could let him reveal his fears while she held his hand and listened. When Stevie couldn't afford the pictures, they walked in the park, sat on a bench and he'd tell her whatever was troubling him. It sounded awful and she tried not to picture the details, otherwise she'd have nightmares too, but at least she only heard about it second-hand from him and never saw the gore and bloody flesh for herself.

'Me and the boys were checking around these bombed-out flats yesterday. The chief ARP warden there's the local vicar, Reverend something or other, and he was insisting he didn't think the rescue parties had accounted for everyone the night before. So we all said alright, we'll do another check then. They didn't think they'd find anyone, so that's probably why they let me stay this time. They don't really like us younger ones seeing the worst. Anyway, we all poked around the fallen bricks, calling and listening out and then I heard a little mewing sound. I shouted to the boys, over here, I think there's a cat. And the others came and listened and the rescue squad started digging.'

'And did you find the cat?' Ruby thought of her lost Sooty, the black cat she'd last stroked the day she left to go to Barnstaple.

'It weren't no cat. It was a girl. She could barely speak, her throat was so filled with mortar dust. A little squeak was all she could do. She was still sat in a chair and her mum was dead under the kitchen table.'

'Oh no, poor girl. But she was still alive?'

'She weren't too bad. Broken leg, bit of bruising, that's nothing. But what gets me is, if I hadn't heard that little sound, or if I'd thought it really was just a cat and we'd moved on, she wouldn't have got out. She'd have been buried alive, Rube.'

And every story like this finished with shaking hands that struggled to fashion, then light, a wizened roll-up that he held to his trembling lips, while Ruby listened, encouraged him to talk and held his hand in hers.

Their hand-holding continued in the dark of the cinema when they did go. Like brother and sister really, considering Joan was big sister to both of them.

Then about a year after they'd first started the habit of meeting to go to the pictures when she was meant to be at the library, Ruby spotted one of the pub's regulars on the back row canoodling with a girl. She knew he was married, so what was he doing with her? She tried not to look round at them, but couldn't help thinking about this large florid man with his big moustache, over six feet tall.

'Filling out nicely,' he'd said to Aunt Ida, nodding when Ruby squeezed past with a tray of glasses in the bar the other day. And her aunt hadn't reproached him, she'd just slapped his meaty shoulder and said, 'And she does alright by us.' But then Ida relied on customers like him, not just to push their sweaty coins across the bar in exchange for the watery beer, but to find her 'extras' like stockings, lipstick and hair dye. And Arthur Cox as he was, wharf master at one of Bethnal Green's many wharves, was just the man.

Later that same day, after she'd returned to the pub, after she'd fetched their tea, after she'd gulped the greasy chips and soggy batter, Aunt Ida came through into the tiny kitchen while Ruby was washing up. There wasn't much to do till some beer glasses needed rinsing out later, as they ate their meal straight out of the newspaper wrapping. Waving a pack of nylons, Aunt Ida said, 'Friend of yours wants to say hello. Says he saw you down by the Regal today. Hope you weren't meeting a fella. You're far too young for that sort of thing.'

Ruby blushed, wiped her hands and slipped downstairs to the bar. Peering from the doorway, she saw him. Mountainous Arthur Cox in his shirtsleeves, swigging from a tankard. Was that who was asking after her? She couldn't see Stevie anywhere. She stayed where she was, wondering if she could slip back upstairs, but Arthur caught her eye. He tapped the side of his nose and said, 'Our little secret, eh?' And he winked.

She turned and ran up the stairs and then up the last two flights too, all the way up to her bedroom. Breathless, she sat on her bed. Why did his remark make her feel so uncomfortable? What was wrong with seeing Stevie and why did that man make her feel so ashamed? They were only friends, weren't they?

Chapter 24

10 October 2004

David Who?

'You off to the home again, love?' Billie's husband Kevin lets the lawnmower crawl to a halt. The lawn doesn't really need another trim, but he's obsessed with the stripes. Billie tuts to herself. Still, he's slowing down a bit now. He mowed the grass twice a week during the summer months, creating a carnage of fur and feathers churned with grass cuttings the time the cat left its kills on the lawn.

'I've got a meeting with the therapist first. I'll go and see Dad after that, but I'm worried about how long it's taking. He just doesn't seem to be getting any better.'

'I expect these things take time, don't they?'

'I know. I just wish there'd been more progress.'

Nearly two months after his collapse, Billie's father is still unable to wash, dress or feed himself properly. He can use one hand to nibble toast, biscuits and the corner of a sandwich, but can't yet manage cutlery. His hands tremble too much for a cup and Billie hates seeing him given the degrading come-down of a beaker with a spout, even though she knows perfectly well that keeping him hydrated is important and that a degree of independence is necessary in a nursing home with staff too overworked to feed and water everyone by hand.

Chigwell Care had seemed to be the best step after he was discharged from hospital. He needed time to recover and in time he surely would. Billie tells herself that whenever she arrives at the spacious home, surrounded by well-kept gardens. She glances into the lounge and sees him dozing in an armchair facing the patio windows. He likes to look out onto the terrace where residents can sit on warmer days, where a range of bird feeders holding seeds and peanuts attracts a flutter of blue tits, finches and robins.

She decides not to disturb him until she's had her meeting with Fiona, the young therapist who has been caring for her father ever since he arrived here. Dad likes her, Billie can tell. Fiona is slim and dark-haired, casually dressed, but still with an air of authority about her.

'I've brought some more old photos from the house,' Billie says. 'I thought they might encourage him to talk.'

'That's always a good idea,' Fiona says, reaching out for the album. 'How nice to see them all displayed like this. Hardly anyone ever does that, these days.'

'I know. Not the same having them on a computer, is it? Though most of my old photos are still in their envelopes. But my mum was really good at sticking pictures in albums. And this volume is one of the oldest we've got. Goes right back to when my dad did his National Service.'

'Gosh, that must go back a bit,' Fiona says, turning to the early pages. 'Nineteen forty-five and 1946, it says here.'

'I didn't know they knew each other then. I always thought they met after he came back. But maybe Mum thought the pictures were important and should be saved.'

'Palestine,' murmurs Fiona. 'And there's some labelled Jerusalem and Haifa. That must have been quite an experience, being out there then.'

Billie looks again at the photos of her father standing, arms folded, alongside other young men. The uniforms appear light grey in these black and white pictures, but presumably were khaki or sandy beige. Such young men, sunburnt faces smiling and squinting in the bright sun. It looks hot and dusty. 'D'you know, he's never really talked about his time out there. I just knew that's where Dad went when he was in the army, but I've never heard any details.'

'Which one is your father?' And Billie points to the tanned man in the middle of the group. 'What a handsome chap he was,' Fiona says with a broad smile.

'Me and my brother and sister used to look through these old photos on rainy days sometimes. They were all jumbled up in a box, before Mum mounted them in this album. And when me and Kevin decided to go to Sharm El Sheikh, we wanted to do a trip to see the Pyramids and Dad said he'd been to Egypt too.'

'Quite the traveller in those days, wasn't he? Well, maybe these pictures will help prompt his memory and speech. As I've said before, his inability to summon up the names of things isn't memory loss as such. Names and information are still stored in the memory, but the mind is having trouble locating it. We call it anomic aphasia or anomia, but it isn't permanent memory loss.'

'Happens to me all the time.' Billie laughs. 'Can't remember what I went upstairs for half the time. And I completely forget what I'm meant to be buying when I'm shopping, if I don't write a list and remember to take it with me.'

'It's bit like that. It's a matter of summoning the memory and bringing up the right word.' Fiona closes the album. 'Why don't we try him on these this afternoon? He'll probably be waking up now.'

Billie follows Fiona into the lounge. Her father is staring straight ahead at the garden. 'Hello Dad, we've brought some old photos from home. Thought you might like to look at them with us.'

They pull up a chair either side of him and place the album on his knees. Billie skips past the first few pages and opens it on a picture of her parents' wedding. 'Look, Dad. Isn't this a lovely one of you and Mum?' Both figures smile at the camera, her mother angled to hide her swelling figure. 'And here's me, Dad. Only a few months later! You saucy pair. I never realised, till I was old enough to put two and two together, that you'd had to get married. You were ahead of your time, you were. All the kids live together nowadays before they get hitched.' Billie glances at her father's face. She could swear she's getting a hint of a smile from him.

'Keep going,' Fiona says. 'You're doing really well.'

So she flicks back to the beginning of the book. 'But these are the ones I don't know much about,' she said. 'You out in Palestine. You must have taken all these while you were out there with the army.' She turns the pages slowly, reading out the captions written in white ink underneath the tiny snaps secured with triangular mounts onto the black paper. 'It's like doing a Grand Tour here. Bethlehem, Jerusalem, such exotic places you went, Dad. And here you are with these chaps you must have served with.'

She turns over another page and then stares. None of the photos on this page have captions. And they appear to be showing rubble and ruins. 'I don't remember these pictures,' she says. 'It's ages since I looked at this. Mum must have rearranged the album at some point. Did you go to some archaeological site? It looks like a dig out in the desert.'

Her hand, touching his at the side of the album, feels him stiffen. She looks at him. His eyes are bulging and his mouth is trembling. 'Dad, whatever's the matter?'

Fiona leans forward, looking concerned. 'He's trying to speak. I think he's reacting to these particular pictures.'

'Tell me, Dad, tell me what's troubling you.'

Billie clasps his hand and begins to slide the album away, but Fiona stops her. 'No, wait a minute. I'm sure those photos have stirred something in his memory. Let's see what he might have to say.'

'Dad, do these pictures mean something? Do you want to tell me what happened?'

And then he takes a sharp intake of breath that rattles in his throat, and he makes a gasping sound: 'Ayid...'

Both women crane to hear him and interpret this fractured word or words. 'Do you know anyone called David?' Fiona says, after a second or two.

'I think there's a cousin, but how that would relate to this, I don't know.' Billie stares at her father's contorted face, his lips trying to work, his slack mouth lacing his sweater with a thread of saliva. 'Atell... atell...' he repeats. '...ill hoot... ill heet...'

'I'm not sure we should show him any more today. This doesn't seem good for him.' Billie can't bear seeing him upset.

'No, don't worry. I know it looks distressing, but it's not doing him any harm. It's just that it's a struggle for him to find the right information. But I feel sure he wants to say something important and that these photos are helping.'

'Maybe he's trying to tell us about one of the men in that group photo?' Billie says, sliding the album towards her lap and turning the pages. 'They're all named.' She runs her finger over the silvery letters underneath the picture of the four men, standing in front of the rubble, holding spades. 'But there's no David here.'

She turns to look at her father, who visibly relaxes as she closes the album. 'Oh, Dad, what are you trying to tell us? How on earth are we going to help you, if we don't know?'

Chapter 25

July 1943

On the Rag

When Ruby was fourteen she woke one morning to find blood on her nightdress and sheets. Her stomach ached and she felt slightly sick. She knew what it was, luckily, because Joan had explained the workings of the female body to her when they shared a bedroom earlier in the war. 'It will happen to you as well one day when you're older,' she said. 'It's a sign you're a real woman and will be able to have babies when you're married.'

But Aunt Ida wasn't so understanding when she asked for help. 'Oh, you've started, have you? Better get yourself down to Doreen's shop and get her to sort you out then.' She gave Ruby a few coins, but didn't hold her hand and take her there, didn't explain how Ruby was meant to cope with this surprising flow of blood, didn't take pity on her with her shocked face or ask if she was in pain. Ruby was sure if Joan had come back to London and hadn't decided to stay in Devon to help in the school, she'd have given her a warm hug and told her not to worry. She might even have dashed to the shop herself to buy the necessary. Even Mum would have been kinder than Aunt Ida. She might have been a worrier, always expecting the worst to happen, but she would have told Ruby to go back to bed, made her a sweet cup of tea and put her sheets and nightie in to soak.

Ruby walked on her own to the corner shop with a pair of dark socks tucked inside her knickers, hoping blood wouldn't start running down her legs till she had the things she needed. She'd already rinsed her nightdress in cold water in her little bedroom sink and tried to clean herself with her flannel.

She lingered in the shop, waiting for it to empty so she could ask for sanitary towels in private. It was busy that morning, with customers picking up rations and gossip, but finally Doreen turned to her with a smile and asked her what she wanted. And at that point, feeling so alone, so unsupported, Ruby's eyes filled with tears.

'Come here, ducky,' Doreen said. 'Come into the backroom and we'll have a cup of tea.' She turned round the sign on the shop door, so they wouldn't be disturbed, and took Ruby's arm to lead her into the little sitting room behind the shop. 'Sit yourself down and when I've made the tea, you can tell me all about it.'

She offered broken biscuits she couldn't sell in the shop, hot sweet tea and sympathy. Doreen was a good sort. She was more of an aunt or substitute mother to Ruby than Aunt Ida would ever be.

'You might get a bit of a bellyache sometimes,' Doreen said, once Ruby had told her what she needed. 'So I'm going to give you some aspirin as well, just in case.' Then she told Ruby to pop in her bathroom to sort herself out and gave her a sheet of newspaper so she could take her blood-soaked socks home to wash.

And from that moment, Ruby felt that here was someone she could tell all her troubles to. Someone kind and never dismissive, cheerful and optimistic. Doreen had been widowed early on in the war, when the first bombs fell. Her Fred didn't make it home one night. 'He got caught after one of the raids,' Doreen said. 'They got the all-clear, then a wall fell into the street, right on top of him. But I'm luckier than some. My Val does her bit and she's still here.'

Doreen's daughter moved out when she got married, but still sometimes helped out in the corner shop. Her son Alan was over in France and although Doreen worried about him, she sent regular parcels of biscuits, jam and puddings, along with home-knitted socks. 'He says all the boys can't wait for my parcels and reckon he's spoilt rotten. He'll be alright, he will, as long as he keeps his feet dry and his belly full.'

From then on, when she wasn't sweeping floors, washing glasses or sitting in the cinema with Stevie holding her hand, Ruby escaped to Doreen's. Sometimes, if the shop was busy, she helped out, weighing the minimal rations of margarine, bacon, butter, cheese, cooking fat, sugar and tea. Doreen didn't sell eggs herself, but visited her cousin in Woodford once a week, returning with a couple of dozen eggs that she reserved for special customers, to supplement the sole fresh egg allowed with rationing.

'Here you are, dear,' she said when Ruby was ready to leave after visiting her that memorable morning. She handed her a paper bag containing two brown eggs. 'Have them while they're still fresh. And if your aunt asks where they've come from, you can tell her from me, they're to help with your Auntie Flo.' And she winked as if to say of course Ruby understood this joke between women, for that was what she was now.

Ruby felt so comforted as she walked back to the pub. *I'm going to have those eggs right away*, she decided, *with hot buttered toast and a big mug of tea*. She daren't leave them in the kitchen. Aunt Ida would crack them open for her husband's egg and milk breakfast. No, she was going to eat them as soon as she could.

She found a chipped enamel pan in the kitchen and set it to boil on the stove, then searched the cupboard for egg cups. She'd never seen them used in all the time she'd lived here, but there were two dusty glass ones at the back of the cobwebbed shelf, behind an abandoned celery vase and a cracked Toby jug.

'Bit late for breakfast, ain't it?' Aunt Ida said, swishing past her. 'I need you out there, sweeping the floor.'

'Doreen gave me two eggs this morning and I didn't have any breakfast before I went out.'

'Sorted you out, did she? Where's the change then? And I hope you didn't pay for them eggs.'

'No, she gave them to me.' Ruby fumbled in her skirt pocket for the remaining coins and handed them over.

Aunt Ida looked at the money and pursed her lips. 'Keep it. Hang on to it for next month.' It was the only concession she ever made to acknowledging that Ruby would require money of her own from now on. She'd never given her niece cash for sweets or ice creams, and on rare occasions when she clothed her, it was with finds off the market. 'And take what you need from the tin when you have to. Only what you need, mind.' And she nodded at the tea caddy on the kitchen shelf where she put cash for shopping and trips to the chip shop. 'I'll be keeping an eye on it.'

She poured herself a cup from the fresh pot of tea Ruby had just made and took it through to the sitting room. Almost as an afterthought, before she sat at the table to read her magazine, she added, 'And you watch yourself with that lad now. Last thing we need is you getting yourself up the duff now you've started.'

Ruby was shocked by these blunt words. Her mother had never explained how babies were made, but dear Joan had told her the facts of life after they'd seen a farmer's ram mount a complacent ewe in the field near the cottage. 'See that big bag between his back legs? That's where he keeps his balls and they make the seed that goes into the female sheep to give her lambs.' Procreation seemed to be everywhere in the countryside, cockerels pouncing on indignant hens, dogs jumping on bitches, stallions presenting to willing mares. 'It's the same with men and women,' Joan said. 'But only when they're married.' But that wasn't true, Ruby knew, because she'd heard Aunt Ida talking to a neighbour about a girl across the road. 'Should be ashamed of herself,' she'd said. 'He'll get the shock of his life when he comes back from France.' 'If he comes back,' the neighbour added and they both looked with stern disapproval at the young woman heaving her bulk into her mother's house.

But it won't happen to me, Ruby thought. The only person I'd ever do it with is Stevie. And that won't be for ages. Not till we're married.

First you hear the engine,
Then you hear it stop,
Dive and count to thirty,
Then you can get up.

Chapter 26

July 1944

No Betty Grable

Now Ruby was nearly fifteen, there was no more school for her. Aunt Ida told her she'd really be able to earn her keep soon. 'Your Uncle Reg is getting on and I can't do everything by myself,' she said. 'We're relying on you, girl.' Her words made Ruby feel guilty and ungrateful; she had been given a home here, even though it wasn't a comforting one. And her uncle was much older than his fearsome energetic wife, who dealt with the brewery and ticked off the customers.

Ruby really wanted to get a job away from the pub, but since the air raids had started up again she was afraid to go far from this place she had to call home, with its cobwebbed cellars where they sheltered among the beer barrels. One time she and Stevie had gone to the cinema and the sirens had wailed halfway through the film. They'd dashed to the nearest Underground station and ended up staying there all night. That must have been January, she thought, when the Germans came back to try to finish London off. Aunt Ida wasn't a bit pleased Ruby hadn't come back in time to help clear up that evening. She hadn't seemed concerned for her safety, just annoyed that she hadn't done her usual jobs. And the bombing continued, making her jump every time it started up again, even if most of it was further away, hitting important landmarks and buildings of state.

Then in June, a new terror swept across London. The 'doodle-bug', a flying bomb, began appearing. No German pilots to shoot down, just a deadly bomb designed to batter Britain into submission. Ruby soon came to recognise and fear the buzzing of its dreaded engine. 'I'm scared to go out for our tea,' she told Stevie. 'There's no shelter between the pub and the chip shop, but Aunt says I have to go every evening or we won't eat.'

'Just count to thirty,' he said. 'As long as you can hear them, you're quite safe. But when it cuts out, that's when you have to start worrying. You've got to either hide or throw yourself down on the ground right away. When the engine stops, count to thirty and by then it will have crashed and exploded somewhere else.'

'And then can I get up again?' Stevie seemed to know so much about keeping safe and she felt calmer when she was with him. And he seemed calmer when she held his hand too. His trembling and need to roll yet another fag ceased when she was soothing him with her hand-holding. 'I feel I can keep going, if I talk to you,' he said. 'Mum don't want to know and Dad's only interested if I've seen some scrap he can use.'

Sheltering in the pub cellar was another matter entirely. If it was cold, Aunt Ida insisted they had to have a flowerpot heater, made of two earthenware pots, and a candle. 'It's in the official handout,' she said, swearing as the pots tipped over with the slightest vibration. Uncle Reg smoked his pipe till the cramped space filled with choking fumes, making Ruby think she'd rather take her chances outside.

Aunt Ida smoked a cigarette now and then, for her 'nerves' she said, but it only seemed to fuel her non-stop complaints if the pub was empty when the siren started screaming. 'For Gawd's sake, another early raid and we'll go out of business. Why can't they start when the regulars are already in the bar? Then we can keep them down here for the night.' But Ruby felt those nights were the worst, with extra bodies crammed into the damp cellar, all smoking, drinking and pissing in a drain in the corner.

But the worst job of all in the pub was cleaning the toilets. The Ladies wasn't so very bad, apart from the used bloodied rags, screwed up and tucked behind the pipes if the bins were full. And who would have thought that ladies would scratch such crude messages on the insides of the toilet doors and on the walls? It was worse than the girls' toilet block at school.

But the Gents was awful, reeking of urine, beer and fags. She had to rinse around the stained urinals as well as the lavatory itself. Could they not see where they were aiming or had they had so much to drink they had no chance of pissing where they were meant to? It made her feel sick. Every day she was meant to go in there and clean up after them. They weren't no gents, they were animals.

Then one morning she was a bit behind with her jobs. She was tired as they'd spent half the night down in the cellar and she hadn't been able to get to sleep again in her bed when they got the all-clear. So she was still cleaning in the Gents, her last job, just before lunchtime opening. Aunt Ida wasn't too happy, as she liked Ruby to help out the back, washing glasses, once the customers started coming in.

So she was still mopping the floor in the toilet when Arthur Cox burst through, his flies already undone. ''Ello, 'ello, what have we here?' he grinned, but didn't let her stop him doing what he'd come in to do. His mountainous bulk blocked her way to the door. He pissed quickly, then didn't make himself decent, but began fondling himself. 'You're a big girl. Old enough to feel one of these now, aren't you?' he said, pulling her towards him with one of his shovel hands, with the other offering her his erection.

Ruby was horrified. She tried to push him away with her mop, but it fell. Then he grabbed her hand and made her hold him. 'See, it likes you. Pretty girl like you needs one of these inside her. Bet your lover boy would like to do it to you too.'

It was revolting. Ruby screamed as loudly as she could and luckily Uncle Reg barged through the door. 'Get your hands off her, you dirty bugger,' he shouted. 'Clear off.' He tried aiming a blow at Arthur's head as he shot out of the toilets, but his hand merely brushed the tall man's shoulder. 'And don't ever come back.'

As her assailant disappeared, Ruby heard Arthur's parting shot: 'Won't bother. She's not worth it.'

'Here,' Uncle Reg said. 'Take my hankie. Better wash your hands quick. Your aunt wants you.'

Ruby rinsed her hands, dried them on the handkerchief and handed the sodden rag back to him. Sniffing, she picked up her mop and bucket and went to the scullery. Uncle Reg followed her. 'I'll tell your aunt what happened,' he said. 'Tell her that filthy bastard's banned from here.'

Next minute, Aunt Ida stormed in. 'Right, for a start, go upstairs and take off that tight sweater. Wear something respectable and you won't have no more trouble. You're no Betty Grable but some of these fellas can't keep their hands to themselves.' Then she turned to her husband. 'You've just got to keep an eye on him. He's too useful. If you didn't spend every minute studying racing tips in your bloody paper…'

Ruby went up to her room. True, the sweater was tight, at least tighter than when she'd first knitted it. She must have grown over the winter. She pulled a loose blouse and cardigan out of her wardrobe. They skimmed her figure from shoulder to hip. No one could see her delicate curves now. She looked at herself in the mirror hanging over her chest of drawers and tucked her dark hair behind her ears. None of the pub's customers would look at her or want to touch her, nor did she want that. She wanted to go unnoticed by them, with no one remarking on how she looked.

But with Stevie it was different. She felt safe with him. He would never make her do anything she didn't want. And she knew that she could comfort him the way no one else could. When she was younger, they had just held hands, especially when he was upset; then he had begun to kiss her on the cheek when they met and when they parted. And now he was nearly seventeen, so they kissed on the lips, lots of kisses, and he said she made him 'excited'. They didn't join the courting couples in the back row of the cinema – they were too shy for that and besides the seats were more expensive. But there was a secluded alleyway leading to the shell of a bombed-out house where they sometimes sheltered. Stevie's wet kisses bruised her lips and he gave her a love bite on her neck one time, which she had to hide from Aunt Ida. 'I love you, Ruby,' he'd murmur, kissing her again, then moving her hand to cup the bulge in his trousers. But at least he never tried to do anything so disgusting as that awful Arthur Cox in the Gents.

Chapter 27

8 May 1945

VE Day

'Bless 'im, bless 'is little old lovely bald head,' cried the drunken man, clutching the edge of the bar as he tried hard to stay upright. Aunt Ida rang the bell and called for quiet, then turned up the radio so the gathered throng could hear Winston Churchill's broadcast confirming the end of the war.

The singing and laughing hushed while the Prime Minister spoke of the 'toil and efforts that lie ahead', then rose again to a crescendo when his speech finished. All were drunk on relief and happiness as well as beer; some had started their celebrations the night before, when the BBC made an announcement late in the day that the war in Europe was finally over and that the following day, 8 May, would be a national holiday.

Stevie had rushed into the pub last night, after they'd heard the news, just before closing time. 'Have you heard? It's all over. Ain't it grand, Ruby? You've got to come with me first thing tomorrow morning. We're all going up West. There'll be singing and dancing in the streets. The biggest party ever. You've got to come with me.'

But Aunt Ida interrupted. 'No, she's not, young man. She's needed here. Pub hours are extended. We'll be run off our feet all day tomorrow.'

'But I'll look after her, Mrs Cherry. Promise I will. Scout's honour.'

Ida sniffed with disapproval. 'The streets'll be full of drunks. I know the sort. She'll be far safer here. Besides, she's too young to go wandering the streets at all hours. I know you lot, you'll be staying out all night.'

But was she safer at the pub, Ruby wondered, as she felt hands squeeze her hips as she pushed through the bar of rowdy, singing drunks, collecting empty glasses. She tried to avoid the leering gaze of Arthur Cox, leaning on the bar, pint pot in his hand topped up by Aunt Ida, who was in a good mood on account of the nylons he'd brought her.

Ruby had tried to argue with her aunt last night, seeing the disappointment on Stevie's face. 'But I'm nearly sixteen. And I want to go. Everyone will be there.'

'Don't I know it. So that's why you're staying right here, young lady.' Aunt Ida pulled her away from Stevie as he tried to hold her hand. 'I'll let you go to the party down our street for a bit in the afternoon.'

'But that's for the children. I'm too old for that.'

'Well, you can go along and help then. I'm sure Doreen and the other ladies round here will be glad of a hand.' She pushed Stevie out of the pub's front door. 'Now you clear off and don't come back putting any more ideas in her head. She's not going and that's final.' Then she'd slammed and locked the door. 'Get on up to bed now. Tomorrow's going to be a long day.' And as Ruby started to climb the stairs she could hear her aunt shouting at her uncle, 'And as for you, you can make yourself useful an' all. We need the business after all we've been through these last few years.'

And now the war really was over and there really was cause for celebration. The sun shone, everyone smiled and flags and bright bunting hung from the lamp posts across the road. Ruby helped the local housewives bring out every table and chair, setting them out in a long line that ran right down the street. The women called themselves the 'tea committee' and they'd been planning this day for a long time, knowing that it would come eventually.

'We've been round all the neighbours for contributions, even the hospitality ladies, and we struck gold there,' Ruby heard Doreen say. 'Those girls gave us a huge tin of corned beef, butter and several tins of peaches. And all of it's from our American friends! Wonder what kind of hospitality they had to offer to get hold of all that, eh?' And there was coarse laughter, with one or two saying they weren't happy benefiting from the wages of sin. Nobody else commented; they looked away, although laughing openly, and flapped clean tablecloths over the borrowed tables set with jugs of lemonade and vases of flowers. They were only too happy to see the piles of sandwiches, pies and tarts emerging from all the houses and pinned patriotic rosettes and flags at every place.

Then the children were led out, squealing, laughing, wearing paper hats, the girls with red, white and blue ribbons in their hair. Everyone is happy, Ruby thought. Everyone but me. I should be running down the Mall with Stevie and dancing in Trafalgar Square. And then beyond the smiles, she noticed others whose faces weren't so full of joy, wearing smiles that weren't reflected in their eyes. The widows whose husbands would never return, the women whose men were still serving abroad, the parents who'd lost a much-loved son. And me as well, she thought, although she tried to join in the merriment. Mum and Dad both gone, so long ago now, and no Stevie to comfort me today. I wish I was with him. Even being back in Devon would be better than being stuck here. Mrs Honey would put on a feast and join in the village celebrations. And I wonder if Joan is back home and gone up West with Stevie, or is she meeting her boyfriend Trevor now it's all over? Joan's last letter had been brief, making it clear that she expected to be married as soon as Trevor was demobbed.

And that night it was even harder for Ruby to pretend to be cheerful. After the children were all in bed, tired and well fed, the party continued in the pub and spilled over into the street outside, where people whooped at the showers of fireworks framed by the searchlights criss-crossing the sky. They no longer picked out bombers intent on destruction; now they set the stage for the nationwide celebrations. Uncle Reg worked harder than he had for years, running up and down the cellar stairs to set up yet another beer barrel to quench the non-stop thirst of the merrymakers.

Aunt Ida trimmed her black hat with red, white and blue ribbons and had called on the services of one of their regulars to be the pub's potman that night and help on the bar, but he was no better than the main crowd, as nearly every order he served included the phrase, 'And have one yourself, why don't you?', which he honoured by taking another tot of whisky. Beer would have meant leaving the bar too often, but little nips of whisky kept him at his post, pulling pints for the customers and getting increasingly drunk himself. 'Here, you have one an' all, Ruby,' he kept saying. 'It might put a smile on your face.'

Ruby felt tears sting her eyes and she dashed into the Ladies. She didn't normally use the toilet there during opening hours, but she needed to get away from him quickly. And as she burst through the door she was confronted by a lady in a shimmering jacket and skirt, wearing a large hat decked with mother-of-pearl buttons and ostrich feathers. It was Hackney's Pearly Queen, who was doing the rounds of all the pubs with her Pearly King husband that night, collecting for the war orphans of the East End and being treated to free drinks by all the happy customers. She turned from the mirror where she'd been reapplying her lipstick and Ruby's tears vanished, replaced with a watery smile.

'Sorry,' Ruby said, 'didn't mean to disturb you.'

'That's alright, ducky. Bedlam out there tonight, innit?' She laughed and as she did so her bosom shook, so the hundreds of buttons on her suit shivered and caught the light. She noticed Ruby gazing at the sight and said, 'It was me mum's. She were one of the first Pearlies.'

'It's just beautiful,' Ruby said. 'Can I touch it?'

'Course you can, darlin'. They're all sewn on by hand. Every single one of 'em.'

She held out her arm and Ruby stroked her sleeve. The tiny gleaming buttons weren't just white or cream, they were shot with little shafts of rainbow colours, purple, green and blue, sewn onto the finest black needlecord that had faded to charcoal grey.

'Fifty years old now, it is,' the Pearly Queen said proudly. 'Went everywhere with me in the Blitz, it did. I said there's no way those Jerries are getting my mum's suit, no matter how heavy it is. Dragged it all over with me, I did.' She lifted the corner of her jacket and placed it in Ruby's hands. 'Here, feel it.'

Ruby thought she'd never felt such a weighty piece of clothing. 'Oh, it's really heavy, isn't it? But it is just lovely.'

And then she could sense the Queen's gaze upon her, seeing her true feelings beyond her words, and the grand lady said, 'I can tell tonight's not a happy time for you, dear. Not everyone's able to celebrate tonight, I know. But your time will come, I can tell. I got a bit of the sight from my old mum and I can see it in your face. You'll have a journey, but you will find where you belong one day. With your special one.' She ducked to kiss Ruby's cheek, her curling feather tickling her neck. 'Look after yourself, deary, and try giving that lovely smile an airing more often.'

She left in a haze of perfume and mothballs and Ruby gave her face a splash of cold water, then dried herself with the bar tea towel, which was tucked into her waistband. My special one, she thought. She must mean Stevie, of course she does – but how could she know? She wondered if he was missing her as much as she missed him, thinking of her as he danced in the centre of London. She should have been with him tonight, not clearing up after all those drunkards in the smoky bar. And she consoled herself by imagining she was dancing down the street with him, his arms around her and his lips kissing the cheek that bore the stamp of the Pearly Queen's red lipstick.

Now the war is over Hitler will be dead,
He hopes to go to Heaven with a crown upon his head.
But the Lord said No! You'll have to go below,
There's only room for Churchill so cheery-cheery-oh.

Chapter 28

Promise to Write

'You will be careful, won't you?' Ruby pleaded as she clutched
Stevie's hand. 'And I promise I'll write to you every week, at least.'

'You mustn't worry about me. The war's all over now, everywhere.
I won't be doing anything dangerous like I was when the war was
on. And you know how fit and strong I am. I got Grade I in my
medical exam. I'll be fine, you'll see.' The scars on his back from
the heavy-handed beatings in Devon had provoked questions from
the medic, but he put the thought from his mind and draped his
arm around her shoulders for the last time while they waited for
the train from Waterloo to Brookwood. Now Stevie was eighteen,
he'd been called up to do his National Service, which all healthy
young men were obliged to do.

Ruby leant her head against his shoulder as she had done so
often in the last few months. They had become close, very close,
kissing in the dark of the Regal and in their favourite alleyway,
his hands wandering under her sweater. She wondered how she
could manage with him away for eighteen months. His jokes,
his sensitivity and their trips to the cinema were all she lived for,
although she had started full-time work that summer, sweeping the
floors of the ladieswear section in Bodgers, the department store in
Ilford High Street. She had to travel by train, an expense that Aunt
Ida had complained about at first, until she began to appreciate
the shop-soiled items Ruby was allowed to purchase at a greatly

reduced cost. Once nylon stockings found a regular path to the pub, Aunt Ida decided she was fully in favour of Ruby's position at Bodgers. She even said, 'Hilda, your mother, she'd have been pleased. She never did like getting her hands dirty. She'd have said the ladies' department was just the ticket for her precious daughter.' Ruby hoped she'd soon progress from the sweeping to folding undergarments, but she agreed it was better than the kind of work many girls had to accept, like Plesseys factory or on the market.

'And the army'll give me a training I wouldn't get anywhere else,' Stevie said. 'With the Royal Engineers you can learn lots about construction as well as mechanical stuff like engines and electrics. Once I've done my bit, I'll have skills, Ruby. I'll be qualified for a good job as a surveyor or an engineer maybe.'

'I know that,' Ruby said, 'but I do worry they might send you abroad, somewhere that's not very safe.'

'I don't know what's going to happen yet, but I'm really excited about it. Dad says the Royal Engineers played a big part in ending the war. They built and repaired bridges and mended roads too. Without them, vital supplies and convoys of men couldn't have got through to keep our boys advancing on the Jerries. Important work. Makes you think, don't it, eh?'

Ruby was silent. Although she admired the bravado and camaraderie of soldiers, she was thinking about all the weeks and months that lay ahead. No one to share a trip to the pictures, no one to walk with her and hold her hand in the park after work and on Sunday afternoons. No one to hold her tight and kiss her, slip a hand under her sweater and tell her she was beautiful. She'd be all alone. The other girls in the shop were always giggling about their boyfriends, but they weren't particularly friendly and didn't include Ruby in their gossipy chats.

'It'll be an adventure, eh? And if I do get an overseas posting, then I'll be seeing the world at the state's expense. That can't be bad. Dad reckons I've joined the best regiment alright. He says I've got the knack for mechanics. And I must say it'll be a darn sight more satisfying than mucking about with dipsticks and buffing up bumpers, like I've been doing the past couple of years.'

Now Stevie was going to leave home properly at last. Not like the last time, when he'd been evacuated with the whole school on a bus full of little kids all clutching sandwich bags and clean hankies, watched by their grief-stricken parents. Now he was leaving with the prospect of a future ahead of him, a real man's future.

'And you'll write back often as well, won't you?' Ruby begged him, holding his hand tight. 'I'll be looking out for your letters every day.'

She hoped she would be able to collect the post before Aunt Ida saw it. Ruby could well imagine how her aunt would hold up the envelope to the light and joke about reading the contents. The postman usually came before Ruby left for work, but she would not be back in time to prevent her aunt sniffing at the afternoon post.

'Course I will. It'll be just like soldiers going off to France, writing to their sweethearts back home. You never know, you might end up getting letters with foreign stamps from me. Could be Germany, but they're sending lads out to the Middle East, Malaya and India, so who knows where I might end up.'

He looked a bit worried, Ruby thought. His hand trembled a little as he dragged on his cigarette. And that little nerve at the side of his cheek twitched. 'I don't fancy Germany much, not after all we're heard about the camps over there. Bastards.'

Ruby knew how to banish the dark clouds that often crept across his face. She smiled and said, 'Now where would you like to be sent if you could go anywhere in the world? I'd love to go to Paris to see all the fashions and eat all that lovely food.' Ruby longed for beautiful clothes and a chance to wear something other than her plain black dress every day for work, or the unflattering thick knitted twinsets with an old pleated grey skirt Aunt Ida had said she could have. Uncle Reg had given her a pair of his old flannel trousers to alter, but the cut wasn't quite right for her slim figure, not at all like those worn by Katharine Hepburn in *The Philadelphia Story*. And anyway, slacks tended to attract rowdy comments from the drinkers in the public bar.

'I'd like to go somewhere really exotic,' Stevie said. 'Egypt perhaps to see the Pyramids or India because of the temples.' Then he turned to look at her and hugged her tight, saying, 'But really, I'd like to go back to Devon, with you. I know I had some bad luck there, but it would be nice to enjoy that countryside properly, wouldn't it?'

Ruby glowed with pleasure as she snuggled her cheek against his jacket. 'When you're back, when you're demobbed, let's go there. We could walk across the moors and never see a single soul, just the ponies and sheep.'

'You're on. But now I've got to go. My train's waiting and I mustn't miss it.' The thunder of the pulsing engines, the squawking of the tannoy, made it hard to hear his last words, which drifted away on the steam bellowing from trains impatient for the guard's whistle. Stevie bent to kiss her and then he strode towards the platform for the Aldershot train calling at Brookwood. She noticed a handful of other young men headed in the same direction, all carrying small cases or kitbags with the few personal items they were allowed to take. And she noticed too how Stevie threw back his shoulders, puffed out his chest and marched as if he was not the slightest bit apprehensive, setting off on his new adventure.

She watched until he passed through the ticket barrier, she watched him stride down the platform and she watched as he opened a carriage door, leant out of the window and gave her one last wave. She knew she wouldn't see him for weeks, maybe months, and she couldn't stop the tears welling and then spilling down her cheeks. How she was going to miss him.

Corps of Royal Engineers
Aldershot

15 October 1945

Dear Ruby,

Life here is not so bad. Some of the boys here have never been away from home before and are finding it hard, but I reckon my time with that farmer and his wife in Devon really tuffed me up, so I'm not complaining. It's much better here than that. At least we get decent grub and lots of it.

But I can't wait for our training here to be over and get sent off to see some action, as we do a lot of drilling and hanging about. I'm in a barrack hut with everyone – twenty of us in all. We've each got an iron bed (see, told you it was better than the Barfords'!), a footlocker and a steel wardrobe.

Our day starts at 6.00 a.m. and we have a washroom off our hut. After breakfast we have drill on the parade ground, then field and rifle training. Dinner is at 5.30 so the evening seems awful long. Then they try to keep us busy, cleaning the barracks and preparing kit. Serves me right for griping about polishing cars for Dad! That's nothing compared to what they make us do to our kit! Just about every little bit has to be done just so.

And as for our beds, well, you've never heard the like, Ruby. Every day the mattress and blankets have to be piled neatly on the frame. And then once a week we have to lay out every single bit of kit and uniform on the bed for inspection.

I swear they do it just to drive us mad, honestly, I do. And if it's not laid out in the right order we never hear the last of it.

I've got the hang of it now, but a couple of the boys have been having trouble so I've helped them out. If you put your gloves where your boot brushes should be or any little thing out of order our corporal knocks it all off the bed and makes them start again. One of the boys decided he'd rather sleep on the floor, with his kit laid out on the bed so he was ready for inspection in the morning! Can you believe it!

Send me all your news, won't you? And I'll write again very soon.

With love from your Stevie xxx

Chapter 29

15 October 1945

Blanco and Brasso

Brasso perfumed the air in the barracks. Up their nostrils, under their nails. Kit inspection demanded Brasso on buttons, badges and buckles, and Stevie was nervous. It should have been a doddle after all that motor car buffing he'd done, but that was a piece of cake compared to preparing for the weekly inspection.

Like most of the new recruits, he'd thought he was prepared for any hardship. It couldn't be worse than his time at the Barfords' farm, surely? Some of the boys had never been away from home before and were struggling. 'It's better than when we were evacuated,' Stevie said more than once to Bill, who he'd palled up with on the train. 'We get our grub regular here. If I put a foot wrong on the farm, I sometimes didn't get to eat all day and I got a right belting if I complained.'

'We ate alright in Hitchin,' Will said. 'My dad was a fireman on the railways, so life was pretty normal, apart from the rationing. Hardly saw any bombing neither. I reckon we had it lucky.'

'Bugger,' Stevie swore as a minute drop of Brasso spilled on his belt and spread out on the freshly treated webbing. Every new recruit had to treat the belt fabric with a damp green paste, known as blanco. 'What the hell, it's getting bigger.' He tried to remove the drip, but the stain was indelible. 'I'll get what for from our corp.'

Bill laughed. 'Yeah, but you won't get starved. Could be worse.'

'I won't get thrashed, like on the farm.'

'That bad, eh?'

'You lot don't know the half of it. All these buggers moping about missing home' – Stevie looked around the barracks at the boys polishing furiously and laying out their kit – 'I bet none of them have been thrashed to within an inch of their life. Taught me how to survive, it did.'

Stevie had quickly cottoned on to the exacting standards required for inspection. Every piece of kit, including bedding, had to be laid out in an approved pattern. Anyone deviating from this strict order risked having the bed overturned and the kit knocked to the floor. In the first week, he had been so anxious he'd laid out his kit the night before the inspection was due and slept on the floor. It was an uncomfortable night with his pullover for a thin pillow. He wasn't the only one, but now he'd memorised the order. It was like remembering the parts of an engine or the workings of a clock. He was good at the patterns and workings of mechanics.

'And didn't some of them blub up, getting their hair cut, too?' Stevie said.

'Reckon some of them usually got their mums to cut their hair,' Bill said. 'One lad told me he's never been to the barbers.'

'We got worse when we was evacuated. Everyone got nits so they took the whole lot off.' All the new recruits were shorn on arrival. Nothing left on the back and sides, just a short tuft on top. Some lads mourned their quiffs, but Stevie wasn't dismayed by his haircut: 'Save on Brylcreem, at any rate,' he said.

On arrival, they'd also been allocated their uniforms. The young men filed past the trestle tables piled with khaki battledress. Quartermasters sized them up in seconds and shoved each recruit a set that was a near-enough fit. 'Blimey,' Bill said when they changed into their new clothes. 'Fits where it touches, is all I can say.'

The berets weren't much better. Black and shapeless, sitting on the back of the head like a burnt pancake. 'You've got to steam it and iron it. Knock it into shape,' said the hut's corporal. 'You can't wear it looking like that, like a bleedin' black scab.'

Stevie set to work, till his beret was broken in and sat on his shaved head at just the right angle. Mum had always wielded the iron at home, but he'd often pressed a collar or sharpened his trouser creases before seeing Ruby, so he could cope, but some boys had never handled or even seen an iron before.

Bill struggled with his new boots. Not only did boots have to shine like mirrors for inspection, but new ones had to be broken in. 'How d'you get a shine on these bastards?' he complained, rubbing away at the pimpled surface.

'They said use a candle, melted boot polish and the back of a spoon,' Stevie said. One of the recruits had been sent to the NAAFI to fetch tins of Brasso, Kiwi boot polish and blanco for everyone. Twenty packs of each, one for each lad. 'Beats me why we can't have regular leather for our boots.'

'It's to break us,' Bill said. 'Turn us into soldiers, not civilians. It's the army way. Blind obedience, doing any darn stupid thing they can think of. Like square-bashing.'

'I don't mind that so much. I'm not going to complain like that lad did the other day. He got sent to weed the garden with his knife and fork.' Stevie snorted at the thought of it.

'Or that one whose locker got emptied out. All his stuff thrown outside in the wet. He was pissed off, I tell you.'

'We'd better keep our noses clean then.'

Corps of Royal Engineers
Aldershot
30 November 1945

Dearest Ruby,

Thank you very much for your last letter. I'm glad you are keeping well and that your aunt hasn't managed to read any of my letters yet. Maybe I should let her know what I think of her in this one, just in case she takes a sneaky look, nosy old cow!

Not long to go now till our passing-out parade. You can come along if you like, but I know you probably can't get a day off work and your aunt and uncle won't want to spare you neither. My mum and dad are coming and Joan says she'll try, but she's being sick every morning and doesn't fancy the train journey. Told her she could have waited till I'd passed out before getting a bun in the oven.

We've practised our drill for weeks now. Like clockwork toys, we are. And we've got to have haircuts again, as if it weren't short enough already. We'll all look like convicts again so don't be shocked if you come and see me nearly bald! When they do our hair it's nearly as bad as when we were kids and Nitty Nora sent us off for haircuts.

But the best bit is that after the parade, we get ten days' leave. And that means I'll be home this Christmas. What luck, eh? If you can wangle some days off, we can go to the pictures, go dancing or maybe even go into town to see a show. Think what you would like to do and we'll make the most of it.

All my love, Stevie xxx

Corps of Royal Engineers
Aldershot
2 January 1946

My dearest Ruby,

That was the best Christmas ever and I am missing you already, my darling. You are my loveliest sweetest girl, waiting for me when you could have your pick. I know you always say there's no one else, but I've shown the boys your photo and they all think you look wonderful, just like Vivien Leigh with your dark hair.

I wish I could tell you now what is going to happen next, but I've got to do six more weeks special training because they think I can handle electronics as well as the mechanical stuff we've done already. I won't know till all that's over where I'll be posted and it looks like I won't get any more leave before I go either, though some of the chaps say you get embarkation leave if you're going far away.

Now it's so blasted cold and our hut is freezing, I'm beginning to think I'd really like to be sent off somewhere hot for a change. I wasn't sure when we were first asked where we'd like to serve, apart from wanting to avoid Germany. I rather thought I'd opt to stay home and be nearer to you, but if the chance arises I wouldn't mind somewhere exotic. But whatever happens next, I'll always have my memories of our time this Christmas, my darling.

All my love, your Stevie xxx

Chapter 30

15 January 1946

How to Smoke

Ruby read his letters over and over. He always made it sound as if he was having fun. Playing soldiers with a crowd of other lads the same age. It wasn't like the war, when they were at risk, she told herself. This time they weren't being shot at or blown up. It was like the Boy Scouts. All boys together, running, marching, waving their guns about but never using them.

But some of them will want to use them. Some of them are going to want to fire real bullets, kill real people. Not Stevie though, surely? She remembered the look on his face every time he talked about some of his dreadful experiences back in the Blitz. 'Have respect for the dead,' he'd said. 'I try, but it's hard when we're shovelling them up in bits and pieces. We go in with a rake and a stiff broom. Like when we had to peel 'em off the walls.' She'd watched him go pale and sweaty, then fumble for his fags and matches, trembling till he'd had a few puffs. When he'd calmed, he'd offer it to her and she'd take it just to be friendly and to taste the paper that had touched his lips, but she never smoked properly.

Stevie smoked a lot, all the time. 'We all did in the war,' he said. 'That's how you got through it all. The stench gets right up your nose. Stays with you, but the fags help.' Once he'd signed up with the Royal Engineers, he told her, 'We get a fag ration. But it's not enough for the likes of me. Twenty a day. Still, some lads don't smoke so the rest of us buy 'em off 'em.'

Sometimes Ruby wished she did smoke. She imagined Stevie lighting her cigarette like in the films with a cigarette lighter. She'd lean towards his Zippo, her head nearly touching his arm. Then she'd take a little intake of breath and elegantly exhale a misty plume of smoke, while holding the cigarette between her index and middle fingers. The rough men who came in the pub often sucked at their wrinkled roll-ups between a yellowed finger and thumb. She didn't like that. And some of the women who lived near the pub talked with a fag dangling from a corner of the mouth while they hung out their washing. That wasn't elegant either.

The staffroom at Bodgers was always full of smoke during breaks. Most of the women there smoked. Not Miss Perkins, the department manager, of course. She only entered the staffroom to reprimand girls for taking too long on their tea break or to ask them to be quiet. She didn't even take her own breaks in the staffroom, she had her own office where she checked the orders.

One day, one of the girls produced a silver cigarette case containing slim coloured cigarettes, like little bright crayons. 'It's a present from my Frank,' she said, lighting one and posing with the smoke curling prettily from her fingers. 'What d'you have to do to get a present like that, eh?' another girl said and they both shrieked, drawing Miss Perkins out of her lair, a stern frown lining her face.

Ruby thought that was a lovely present. She'd like to smoke such pretty cigarettes. 'Sobranie, they are,' she was told. But when the girls left the shop at the end of the day, she saw them giggling with two older men, who took their arms and walked them to the pub near the station. Maybe Sobranie were expensive and only older men with good jobs could afford to buy them for their girlfriends.

She mentioned them when she got back to the pub later that day. Aunt Ida scoffed and said, 'Don't you go getting any ideas, missy. Hoity toity, fancy fags. Cocktail cigarettes, they call them.' She gave a coarse laugh, more a cackle than a laugh. 'Tart's fags, more like. Cock and tail. Suits those sluts, don't it?' And she shrieked some more, repeating her joke to herself, 'Cock and tail, ha ha ha!'

Later, after washing up glasses and clearing the plates from their usual fish and chip supper, Ruby took a cup of tea up to her sparse, cold bedroom. It was warmer downstairs, but she wanted to write her daily letter to Stevie and if she stayed in the little sitting room above the bar, Aunt Ida was bound to comment. 'Writing to lover boy again, are we?' she'd said the other day. 'You're wasting your time with that one. Girl your age should be looking out a fella with money in his pocket, before you're past it.' That was about the only indication she ever gave that Ruby might be attractive and desirable. Aunt Ida was only interested in men who were useful to her, like Arthur Cox, who still leered at Ruby and brought boxes of fags to the back door of the pub. Maybe Aunt Ida had only married Uncle Reg for the livelihood offered by the pub; he certainly hadn't ever been a looker or a high roller, but he gave her a home and a decent enough living.

Ruby sat on her hard bed, wondering what to tell Stevie. She couldn't just say she was missing him, was lonely now he was gone. He might be homesick, though his letters always sounded cheerful, as if he was having a really exciting time. And she loved him calling her his 'dearest' and 'darling' and signing off with all his love and a line of kisses. But what was she doing? Every day was the same. Each morning she swept the bar before she left to catch her train to the shop and then when she got to Bodgers, she had to sweep another floor. Lunch was a ham or cheese sandwich that she took with her if there was anything to make it in the pub's grubby, ill-stocked kitchen. One day she had to dampen the bread so she could cut it, and wrapped it around a few chips left from the previous night. Aunt Ida never ate much breakfast. Her aunt and uncle were like Jack Sprat and his wife, only the other way round. She was thin and pecked at her food, only having a slice of toast in the morning. Then she took Uncle Reg, who had a big cushion of a beer belly, a mug of warm milk with an egg beaten into it. 'For his indigestion,' she always said.

Ruby thought of telling Stevie about the Sobranie, but she didn't really understand the girls giggling or Aunt Ida's joke. She sat there with the sounds of the bar drifting up the stairs, getting colder until she had to wrap herself in her dressing gown and get under the bedcovers. Her little electric fire didn't give out much heat. Aunt Ida said they couldn't afford more for the electric.

Maybe I'll tell him what I'm reading, she decided. Life's not an adventure for me, like it is for him, but with the library there's so much to explore and imagine. So she told him about her latest book. She usually managed to read a whole book every two weeks and she had just started reading *Rebecca*, a tale of love and mystery. I'm a bit like the main character, she thought. Shy, uncertain, in awe of a handsome man of the world. You could hardly call Stevie a man of the world, but he seemed very grown up before he went away and now that he was abroad, well, he was bound to have new experiences and come back with a mature, manly attitude to life.

Chapter 31

October 2004

A Parent's Past

Billie looks at the old photos again once she is home. Is it Dad's condition that is making him so upset? She can't remember anything ever being said about these particular pictures from his time in the army when she was young.

But then what do any of us really know about our parents? Is it just me, she thinks, or is it like this for everyone? No child, however old they are, likes to think about Mum and Dad having sex. They're our parents, but we don't know them in the way we do our partners or our closest friends. Parents have lived another life before us, particularly if they've lived through challenging times, like the war. We've only lived in peacetime. There's been nothing to really upset my life so far, she thinks, and sighs. Apart from losing Mum and now this.

Billie unpacks the little bit of shopping she'd managed to do on the way home. It still seemed odd not popping in to see Dad in the house at the end of every afternoon, sitting down with him and chatting about the non-events of the day over cups of tea and something to nibble. She opens a new pack of Jaffa Cakes. She knows she shouldn't but after that upsetting visit, which had distressed her as much as it had her father, she needs sugar to boost her energy before she sorts out the washing she'd put on before leaving for the care home.

Even Fiona, her father's kindly therapist, who'd said she shouldn't worry about unsettling him, seemed bothered by the extent to which he'd been upset. 'I am beginning to wonder if there's more to this,' she said, as they walked towards the home's reception area, with its photos of residents on outings to local gardens 'Usually people with his condition exhibit frustration when they are struggling to find the right words, but I have to admit he does seem genuinely distressed by those photos. Are you sure he's never expressed any feelings about his time in the army? Never told you why these pictures were taken and what they meant to him?'

'Not a word. They were just more old photos to me. I didn't know anything about them.'

'And has he ever acted like this before, at any time?'

'Not that I'm aware of. Well, he was upset when my mother died, of course. But that was more like a sadness. She was ill for such a long time, so there was a bit of relief for all of us, when it was finally over.' Then Billie remembered the little snapshot from his wallet and retrieved it from her handbag. 'But he was also distressed by this. And I'd never seen this picture before, until I took his wallet home for safe keeping after his stroke. Every time I've shown it to him, he's got quite upset. I know who she is now, because his older sister, that's my Aunt Joan, recognised her. She was his very first girlfriend and I've been trying to find out where she is now, if she's still alive, that is.'

Fiona looked at the picture. 'How sweet. She's very pretty and very young. Do you think she broke his heart?'

'I don't know. He tries to say her name when he sees this.' She stared at the picture. 'It makes me think how little I know about him. Same with my mother really. They're just our parents to us, aren't they? And we're always the children, whatever age we are, just accepting them for what we see. To me he's just my dad, funny, kind, bit of a maniac with his cars, but I know nothing about *him*, the real person inside.' She laughed. 'I didn't even realise they'd had to get married until I was planning my own wedding. I was looking for my birth certificate to take to the register office and I was sorting through the envelope where my parents kept important documents. And that's when I noticed the date when they married. Barely six months before I was born! So what else don't I know about him? And now I can't even ask him.'

Fiona passed the photo back. 'I could be mistaken, but it seems to me that his behaviour is reminiscent of people I've known who've experienced trauma in the past. Do you know if anything deeply distressing has ever happened to him?'

Billie was taken aback. 'What sort of thing? I can't think. As I say, I'm realising now how little I really know about his life.'

'Maybe an accident or ill treatment in his childhood?'

'I don't think so. I can remember my grandparents. There was never a hint of any ill feeling there. I think he got his love of cars from his father. He said he'd helped out in his dad's garage business when he was young.'

'Then maybe something happened during the war or when he was doing his National Service. Remember how he reacted to those photos today. I'm just wondering if he's buried some memories and the experience of the stroke, of being helpless, is bringing it all to the surface.'

'Do you think I should try to find out more? I could ask his sister.'

'Only if you feel you want to. They're his memories after all, and we can't force him to face up to anything that is too painful for him. But I think it could be useful. It could help us understand his reactions and his feelings a lot better. And then maybe we'll be able to understand what he's trying to say. It's up to you.'

Fiona's words stayed with Billie on the drive home and while she dashed into Waitrose, and now, while she sits munching her third Jaffa Cake, she is still weighing up the idea. Should she pry into his past? And how would it help? What if she finds out that he did something dreadful? She's always thought he was respectable, hard-working and loving to his wife and children. Does she want to risk her view of him being destroyed?

She shakes her head and decides to sleep on it. But she wakes in the early hours of the morning before first light, knowing that if she doesn't ask more questions she will always wonder. Whatever she discovers, it cannot obliterate her love for him. And maybe, just maybe, it can help her ease his mind and bring him peace.

Corps of Royal Engineers
Aldershot
17 February 1946

Dearest Ruby,

I hope you didn't receive many Valentine cards, my darling, other than one that you may have guessed was from a not-so-very-secret admirer! And now I have one more special surprise for you, which I hope will make you very happy. I have been granted two weeks embarkation leave, starting this Friday!

I know you will regard that as good news and bad news in one. It means I will get to spend time with my Ruby, but it also means that I am going abroad, as home postings don't get leave. I am being posted to Palestine, which I am really very excited about. It will mean I have to have vaccinations before I see you, so be careful how you hug me when we meet, as I may be rather sore. But better safe than sorry, eh? Some of the boys say they don't fancy mixing with the Arabs, but I think it's going to be quite an adventure. I mean, it's the Holy Land, isn't it? And I know I'm not the church-going type, but all the same, it's a chance to think about what they tried to drum into us in school.

And here's a funny thing that will make you laugh. We call the youngest officers ARABS and can you guess why? It means Arrogant Regular Army Bastard! Sorry for the language, but that's what being in the army does for you. I won't repeat any more army slang though, don't you worry, as some of it isn't meant for young ladies' ears. It's just men's talk and keeps us cheerful when we're being slapped down over our kit or drilling.

Well, that's all for now, Ruby. I'll let you know as soon as I can when my leave comes up and we'll have a grand time so you can send me off with happy memories of you.

All my love,
Your Stevie xxx

Chapter 32

3 March 1946

More Than a Kiss

Ruby's heart sank when she read Stevie's letter. She had so hoped he wouldn't have to go far away. Germany would have been bad enough, but Palestine – why, that seemed like halfway round the world. Malaya would have been even worse though, with steamy jungles and the diseases that everyone had been hearing about ever since men had started returning from the horrors of Burma. She was glad he wasn't going to the Far East.

But other women had coped with their menfolk abroad. All through the war, some hadn't seen their husbands or sweethearts for months, years even. And Mum hardly ever had Dad at home. His tours of duty with the Merchant Navy lasted around eighteen months at a time and Mum seemed to cope. Or did she? When Ruby tried to remember her mother, who she'd last seen more than six years ago, she pictured a pale, sad-faced woman with no enthusiasm, no joy, her subdued voice always sounding worried. Of course she had been three years a widow by then, but Ruby couldn't ever remember her rolling with laughter or singing. Ruby hoped she wouldn't become like her, like a deflated, colourless balloon, when Stevie was gone or if he never came back.

Soon after she'd read his letter she asked Miss Perkins, her supervisor at work, for some days off. 'My boyfriend's got two weeks leave before he goes to Palestine. He's going to be away ages, so I'd really like to spend some time with him before he goes.'

'It's usual, Miss Morrison, to book annual leave three months in advance. Is this really necessary?' Miss Perkins was not known for her approval of female staff having boyfriends. She pursed her lips, then said, 'Well, as it's not our busiest time, I suppose you can have a few days. Not the whole two weeks, mind.'

The sniffy disdain of Miss Perkins could not dampen Ruby's excitement. She knew that her time with Stevie would be bittersweet and it would be followed by his long absence, but she was determined to make it the best time ever, a time he would remember while he was away.

When she told her aunt that Stevie would be back soon and that she might not be able to help in the pub as much as usual, Aunt Ida said, 'Oh, it's alright for some, isn't it? I have to keep this place going, day in, day out. I can't go swanning off with my fella.'

Ruby felt a little twinge of guilt. 'I expect I could manage to do a few jobs in the mornings, before I go out for the day.'

'Well, get lover boy to come round here and help. Tell him to keep his hands to himself, mind.'

'Your aunt's an old dragon, ain't she?' Stevie held Ruby close as they nestled in the hollow tree in Epping Forest. They couldn't afford the cinema or dancing every day, but the bus to the forest with a Thermos flask of tea and sandwiches cost hardly anything. Stevie told her he'd often cycled there when he was younger and recognised paths from years before as they walked hand in hand over the rustling leafy floor to a spot where they could shelter and make a small fire.

The day was cold but bright with a promise of spring. Ruby noticed catkins as they walked through the woods, reminding her of those happy days in Devon when she explored with Joan and Mrs Honey, finding such an abundance of beauty in the wild, with primroses followed by cowslips, followed by bluebells. London was so drab and grey by comparison, although nature tried to force its way into crumbling terraces and bombsites, with pink rosebay willow herb and purple buddleia.

Ruby giggled. 'We should run away and camp out here and never go back.'

'Oh yeah, and get me gaoled for desertion,' he said, nuzzling her neck. His voice, so close to her ear, was soft but deeper than it used to be.

'No, of course not. But just for now, we can pretend we're living here. It's so peaceful.' She hugged Stevie tight under his greatcoat, thinking how much firmer he felt than when he had first set off on his adventures. And she ran her fingers over the velvet fuzz of his newly cropped scalp, feeling the shape of his head.

'Shut up then and kiss me,' Stevie said, wrapping his coat around the two of them like a thick blanket while they lay on their bed of crackling leaves.

As their kisses grew deeper, his fingers found their way under Ruby's jacket and squirmed their way up her sweater and into her bra. She liked him stroking her breasts, even though they were swollen and tender as they always were when it was her time of the month. She felt his hardness pushing against her thigh, his hand guiding hers towards it. But when he began to lift her skirt and edge towards the elastic of her knickers, she stopped him. 'No, I don't want to.' But it wasn't that she didn't want to; she thought he would recoil in disgust if his fingers were smeared with blood. One day, she told herself. One day, when we're married, we'll do it.

And he didn't insist. 'Make me happy, Ruby,' he whispered. 'Hold me.' And she did make him happy and sticky, with her hand wrapped in a clean handkerchief.

Afterwards, they lay close together, him stroking her hair. 'You know I love you, don't you, Rube?' He kissed her forehead as she snuggled under his chin, smelling soap and sweat overlaid with the mushroomy scent of woodland.

'I love you too,' she whispered. And she did. She truly did. I always have, she thought, ever since I first sat next to him on the bus taking us all away to Devon.

She closed her eyes for a minute and thought they might fall asleep, but then he sat up and wriggled out of the cramped hollow space. 'Got a surprise for you,' he announced and he began making a fire with dry kindling from the forest floor. He added crisp leaves and sheltered the spark, blowing on the twigs until there was a small flame, to which he added more wood. Then he began emptying the knapsack he'd carried all the way from home.

Ruby laughed. 'What on earth have you got in there? Kitchen sink?'

'Almost,' he joked, bringing out a small saucepan, a frying pan, a tin of tomato soup and some sausages wrapped in greaseproof paper. 'Gotta keep my strength up. Especially if you're gonna exhaust me the way you do.'

'I've got sandwiches too. It's only meat paste, though. I was lucky to even find bread in the kitchen this morning. It's not very fresh.'

'Give 'em here then. We can fry 'em after I've done the sausages.'

They both crouched by the fire as the wood crackled and the bangers burst. They sipped sweet, tepid tea from Ruby's flask, taking turns with the little screwtop cup, then wiped it out to drink the hot soup. Fingers greasy from the burnt split sausages and the fried bread, Ruby thought she'd never been so happy. Everything they needed was here in this glade, where there were no sounds but the cooing of wood pigeons, the occasional squawk of a pheasant and a distant dog barking. When she needed to wee and change her sanitary towel, she crouched behind a thicket of brambles so Stevie wouldn't see her.

'We should have brought sweets,' she said, 'then it would be the perfect picnic.'

'We're sweet enough,' he said, kissing her. 'My sweet little Ruby.'

Chapter 33

10 March 1946

Stay Safe

Once Stevie had left for Palestine, Ruby thought about him all the time. On her morning walk to the station, sitting on the train, scurrying along the road to her job in Bodgers, she thought about the journey he was making. Would he be seasick on the voyage? She felt queasy just going on the swing boats at the fair. And what about the food? He might catch some horrible disease and be disfigured. But she'd still love him even if he was pockmarked or injured. He was her Stevie and she worried all the time about how he'd cope. And nothing, not the silly gossip of the girls in the shop, a stroke with a neighbour's tabby cat or even treating herself to a bag of violet creams from the sweetshop, could untangle the knot of anxiety that twisted in her stomach all the time and reminded her that he was far away from her, as she waited anxiously for a letter to say he'd arrived safely.

Don't be silly, he's grown up, she'd tell herself. Of course he'll cope. This'll really make a man of him. But then she'd remember all the times he shook, the times his trembling hands suddenly had an urgent need to find a cigarette. He'd fumble for matches or the Zippo she'd given him last Christmas. She'd been so pleased to find that for him in the market. It wasn't new and it was engraved with someone else's initials, but he was thrilled. Said it made the ciggies taste even better. She thought it made him look like a film star when he pulled out the shining lighter, then flicked the lid and spun the flint wheel in one fluid motion. A bit like a cowboy in a Western going for a quick draw in a shootout.

But the smoking didn't always calm him. Often the shakes only went when she'd sat with him for a while, stroking his hand, just sitting there quietly while he talked on and on about the terrible things he'd seen. She didn't dare close her eyes while he talked, but stared down at the floor all the while. If she shut her eyes, she'd see it too. See the man thrown against the wall of his home, splattered like squashed strawberry jam. Or the lady crushed beneath her bathtub, or the children buried in the cellar, one of them still holding a charred teddy bear. 'Such dreadful sights, Ruby,' he'd say, taking great gulps of smoke and shaking his head. 'I can't ever forget. It won't go away.'

When she thought about where he could be sent to do his National Service, she was glad he wasn't being posted to Germany, even though it was nearer. How dreadful would that be for someone like him? All those bombed towns and cities. Worse than London. Worse probably than anywhere in England. And with all those starving refugees as well, with their own horror stories, that wouldn't be a good place for him. He'd comforted her when they saw the newsreels about those awful concentration camps at the Odeon. She'd found it upsetting alright, but she'd kept her eyes shut for much of it, so she suspected that he had been more upset than her by the sight of the emaciated bodies, alive and dead. So maybe Palestine wouldn't be so bad for him. After all, it was going to be the Promised Land for the people who'd suffered, wasn't it? So it should be a happy place, full of people wanting to make a better future.

Every evening after work, after a quick fish and chip supper, after gathering up dirty glasses from the bar, she slipped up to her room before Aunt Ida could find any more jobs for her, to write her daily letter. 'Dear Stevie,' she'd start, then wonder what else she could say that wasn't the same as the day before and the day before that. 'Old Perkins was a bit sharp today.' And 'the girls in the staffroom were showing us how to jive today.' Maybe she should learn these modern dances to impress him when he was home again. She'd like to dance with him, but the jive only meant holding hands. She'd rather something old-fashioned, where he had to hold her in his arms, where she could rest her head on his shoulder, smell his freshly shaved skin and their cheeks could brush against each other as they floated around the dance floor.

Ruby sighed. She didn't know how to waltz either. Aunt Ida didn't give her much time off, so she hadn't ever been to regular dances at the Palais. But she could still learn, she told herself. She could learn so that when she and Stevie were together again, they could dance together. She promised herself she'd ask Uncle Reg to teach her. He'd been in the Great War. He must know how to waltz. And blow it if Aunt Ida didn't approve. They could just have a quick turn after tea some nights, before the pub reopened.

Sometimes she told Stevie about her latest letter from Mrs Honey. '*She says the hens hardly laid at all this winter, even though it weren't as bad as the one when I was there.*' And on Sundays she sometimes had time in the afternoon to pop over to see Joan, who'd had her first baby early in the year. 'Honeymoon baby, she is,' she told Ruby with a mischievous smile. 'I knew Trevor couldn't wait, but never thought it would be that quick.' Ruby counted on her fingers and thought maybe the wedding had been brought forward on account of baby Carol. It had been a very small, rushed affair at the register office and Ruby hadn't been present, although she left work in time to join the family in their local pub, The Feathers, afterwards.

So without any new and exciting news to tell Stevie, she often ended up writing letters about her dreams for when they'd be together again forever. After expressing her hope that he was safe and well, she would write:

> *I often think that when you are home, I should take you to one of the happiest places I ever lived. I know things didn't work out so well for you at that time, but I loved staying with Mrs Honey and she was fond of you too, wasn't she? We could get away from all the bombed-out places in London and see the green of the countryside. One day I'd like to live there, in a little cottage with a garden and chickens. We'd grow runner beans, potatoes and blackcurrants. We'd have an apple tree too, so I could make you apple pies, like Mrs Honey taught me. You'd like that, wouldn't you, as I know you do love a pie with custard and I don't suppose you get many of them out in the Holy Land. I'll make you one when you get home if I can get Aunt to let me clear up the kitchen properly.*
>
> *Well, that's all I can think of for today. I miss you terribly but will stay cheerful and look forward to your next letter.*
>
> *With love from your Ruby Xxx*

Chapter 34

October 2004

What Did You Do?

'Oh, how I wish Mum was still here,' Billie says. 'Dad might have talked to her about his time overseas doing National Service.'

'Show me again,' Joan says, reaching for the album on the coffee table. They are sitting in the lounge enjoying cups of tea and home-made flapjacks.

'She might have known something about these photos from Jerusalem.'

Joan shakes her head. 'Maybe, but I think she and your dad met quite some time after he came back.'

'So why did she put them in the album then? Was she just being organised, rounding up all the old photos to have a complete record of their lives?' Billie nibbles a corner of flapjack and brushes away the crumbs sticking to her sweater. 'She spent a lot of time resting at home in her last year or so and I think that was when she redid this album.'

'I do remember he was quite different when he came back,' Joan says, after a moment of quiet. 'It struck me he was much more cocky than he used to be. I mean, he always was a confident, cheeky kid, but he'd also been so considerate with it. And it seemed to me he was a right selfish show-off when he came home. He wasn't the only one who'd been sent abroad, was he? But he came back so full of what he'd seen and learnt. What the Holy Land was really like and so on and how he'd seen the Pyramids and what he thought of the Arabs.'

'I wonder why that was? He wasn't the only one who did National Service there after the war, was he? And it couldn't have been nowhere near as bad as actively serving during the conflict, surely? I'd have thought being posted to Malaya would have been far worse.'

'You don't know your history, girl. It was a very tricky time for the British out in Palestine. Our men were hated by the Arabs. From what I remember, they blamed us for giving Palestine to Israel. There was a lot of resentment and quite a few bombs as well.'

'I didn't know that.' Billie looks thoughtful, her hand stroking the photos that had so upset her father. 'I wonder what it was really like at that time. He talked about his experiences, you said?'

'Not half! Never mentioned the troubles there though, just went on about all of the exotic things he'd seen. Sounded like he'd had a whale of a time.'

'Did he ever write to you while he was out there?'

Joan laughs. 'What? My little brother, write? He just sent the odd postcard now and then. And it didn't say much neither. "*Dear Mum and Dad, Guess what, I'm in Bethlehem*", that sort of thing. They never got a long letter. Don't think he's ever written a proper letter in his life.'

'But maybe he was writing to my mum. Lots of soldiers wrote to their girls back home then, didn't they?'

Joan frowns. 'Mmm, they did, but as I said, I'm pretty sure he hadn't met your mother by then. When he was called up he'd been seeing a bit of Ruby, the girl I told you about. If I remember right, he met Maureen afterwards, well after he'd come back.'

She takes several sips of her tea, then says, 'We all thought he was living it up a bit, when he got home. He got a good job with his qualifications from being in the Royal Engineers and he started flashing money around, seeing lots of girls.'

'What, as well as Mum?'

'Yes, same time as, I reckon. And do you know, I can still remember the party we had at The Feathers for his homecoming. I was expecting again then, really heavy I was, and I couldn't really enjoy myself. Had to stay on lemon barley and I was in the Ladies about every half hour. And Ruby turned up at the pub and found him smooching with some blonde. Really upset, she was. I tell you, going away changed him. Ruby was a quiet little thing, devoted to him she was. And he broke her heart. But by then he was going for the livelier ones, the girls who liked a good time.'

'Like Mum, you mean? I'd never have put Mum down as a good-time girl!' Billie thinks of her sensible mother, her love of roses, her home cooking and her needlepoint.

'Oh, we were all young once, you know.' Joan gives Billie a playful slap on the arm. 'Sowing oats before settling down and all that. And your mum was a great dancer. Met your dad down the Royal. That's where he generally picked up the girls. We all used to go there. That's where I first met my Trevor.'

'Uncle Trev? Was he a good dancer as well?' Billie pictures her rotund uncle and tries to imagine him jiving or doing whatever was the dance of the day.

'No, not great. But he made me laugh.' Joan smiles. 'Still does most of the time.'

'I can't imagine Dad running around with lots of girls. He always seemed so devoted to Mum.'

'Well, that was then, in his younger days. He was a good-looking chap, always was. And when he first came home from abroad, he looked very handsome with his tan. Really suited him. And didn't he know it, an' all.'

'But he was faithful to Mum, wasn't he? You never had any suspicions, did you? Please tell me you didn't.'

'Don't you worry yourself.' Joan laughs and puts her arm around her niece. 'Your dad always had a bit of glamour about him, having been abroad to exotic places, having money to spend and a taste for fast cars. But I think he was true to her.'

'He's always liked his cars, hasn't he? Mum used to get a bit annoyed with him, forever changing his car. She had her own eventually, of course, but she always said what's the point of you and your fast cars? They're cramped and uncomfortable, give me a nice Cortina any day of the week.'

'Well, she wasn't just riled by the money he wasted on the cars, it was the way he drove them too. He had a few near misses, I think, and more than one got written off. Your mum was worried he was going to write himself off one day.'

'Poor Mum. I never thought of it like that. As kids, we were just excited when Dad came home with yet another shiny flash car. We'd get to sit in it and have a ride as well sometimes. Usually only one of us at a time, as the sporty numbers were so cramped. Just big enough for two, they were.'

'Yeah, that was him all over. Nothing practical for your dad.'

'Too right. Even the other year, when got his red MG Midget. And he only ever uses it to go to the golf course and back. We joked about it when he bought it. I said, "Dad, you're not going to attract a rich widow driving that tiny car. They're never going to be able to bend down and squeeze into the darned thing!" Mum would have laughed her head off, seeing him driving that ridiculous car around. He loves it of course, especially with the top down on a sunny day.'

'You'd better hope he doesn't pick up a younger woman and leave everything to her then.'

The two women laugh and then Billie says, 'But seriously, if these photos are really significant, if they mean he's been hiding something all these years, how on earth am I going to find out what it is?'

'Do you really need to?' Joan is standing, holding the two empty cups. 'Does it really matter?'

Billie thinks for a moment. 'Trouble is, I think it does. I feel he's trying to tell me something happened. And if he can't find the words himself, then I have to find a way of getting the answers for myself. I don't know what to do about that photo of Ruby either. Should I try to find her?'

She looks at Joan with tears in her eyes. 'I have to help him find peace, Joan, so I've got to keep asking why it matters.'

Palestine
1 June 1946

Dearest Rube,

*It ain't half hot here! Think of the hottest day you can ever
remember in Blighty and double it! And there's no sloping off
to Southend for a paddle or nipping down the pub for a pint
neither for any of us. We're on duty in full kit, like it or not.*

*No swanning about in white sheets for us, like the Arab
wallahs out here. Bet you'd like to see me wrapped up in a
bedsheet, eh, Rube – you and me between the sheets! Down,
Charlie, behave yourself. Rube don't want a mucky letter,
do she, and the censor won't like it neither.*

*Me and the boys are getting a break soon and we're going
to see a camel race. The Arab boys race them, just like at home
at the Derby, but with camels not horses. Perhaps I should
put a few bob on, eh? Wonder what they call them and how
we pick a winner? I'd have been alright if I'd backed the
winner in the Grand National this year. Me and Dad, we
were looking forward to it after no racing there for five years
while the war was on. Lovely Cottage, the winner was – out
here, they'd have to call it Lovely Pyramid or Horrible Hovel!*

*Their houses are worse than the worst East End slums.
You ought to see them. I mean, I know there we had bomb
damage, but these look like they were never proper houses
in the first place. Some of them are no better than shacks
made out of wooden crates with rusty tin sheets over the top.*

Right, must go. Duty beckons an' all.

All my love,
Stevie xxx
P.S. Reckon they have tic-tac men at the races, like back home?

Chapter 35

20 July, 1946

Hot and Bothered

'Scram you lot,' Stevie shouted, waving away the scrawny kids who pestered him and Bill every time they walked back to camp. 'Baksheesh, baksheesh,' the grubby urchins wailed, running alongside them, their bare feet kicking up dust on the scorched track. He felt one pluck at his sleeve and flicked the filthy hand with its blackened nails away from his pressed uniform. 'I said bugger off, didn't you hear me?'

Sarge said they should never give in to their pleas, however pitiful they might look. 'Give 'em an inch and they'll swarm all over you. Ignore 'em.'

Bill strode on, keeping his eyes straight ahead, but Stevie couldn't help looking at them. They were such little children, probably no more than five or six years old, a boy and a girl. Their smiles were framed by cracked, crusted lips, revealing broken and missing teeth; their eyes were rimmed with oozing yellow styes. Hair that should have been shining black was scorched orange and brown, tangled like a bird's nest and riddled with lice probably. No white sheets wrapped around their tiny frames either, these little rats of the street, just ragged shifts made of something rough and filthy, like they'd been stuffed into a couple of old sacks with holes for their arms.

'No have,' Stevie shouted, waving them away. But it felt bad, refusing to help these ill-fed kids when he knew he and Bill were both heading back to a good meal in camp. They met them everywhere, bony arms outstretched, begging for money, running through the dusty streets on dark skinny legs pocked with sores. It was worse than anything he'd ever seen in the East End, even in the most dilapidated streets and tenements, worse even than in the Blitz. He looked back over his shoulder. The smallest child, the little girl, was still there, but her brother was running back the way he'd come. She was crouched in the dust, rubbing her eyes as if she was crying, and then she looked up and saw he was watching her. With a listless gesture she held out her hand again and he felt his heart reaching out to her. He knew he shouldn't, he could hear Sarge's booming voice, but he found some coins and casually dropped them at his feet as if they had just then fallen through a hole in his pocket. She jumped up beaming and dashed towards him. He gave her a brief smile, knowing she'd expect the same the next time he passed by. And why not? He could spare the dosh. She was probably a sweet kid underneath all that filth. Then he turned and quickened his pace to keep up with Bill.

He'd keep this to himself. He wouldn't tell anyone, not Bill, not the rest of the boys and certainly not Ruby. But what could he really tell her when he wrote his regular letters? Why worry her when he was in good health, the platoon was well fed and the camp was safe? Rumours were rife that snipers were stalking their patrols, but he hadn't heard of anyone being shot yet and the whole camp had been told to be vigilant at all times.

That's a fine thing, he thought. Vigilant when we're being deployed to build bridges and take them down again. Bit hard to be looking over your shoulder when you're hauling a cross-beam, mate.

So many alien sights, so many experiences he wanted to share but felt unable to write about to Ruby. Like the Jewish girls they'd all seen wandering the streets of Jerusalem in their sleeveless summer dresses, their forearms permanently scarred with the blue tattoos that marked them out as survivors of Dachau and Belsen. They might be strolling in the sunshine now, but he could picture what they had endured only a year or so before; images of horror were seared on his brain. Those newsreels at the Odeon had shown everyone the shameful hell that had been hidden from the world. And Ruby couldn't bear to stay and watch the films. That one about the liberation of Belsen, she'd stumbled down the aisle of the cinema and he'd had to go after her, hold her tight, she was that upset. He'd been quite glad to get out of the cinema too that day. Those unforgettable pictures made him sick up his tea in the Gents. So, no, he couldn't tell her about the girls in a letter. She was trying her best to cope while he was gone. He couldn't upset her any more.

And he couldn't tell her what some of the other lads were getting up to neither. He reckoned they might come to regret their shenanigans when they got back home to their regular girls, but for now they were full of tales of 'doing it' with an exotic girl. 'You can't see much in there,' one lad said of the dark, smoky hovel he'd just emerged from with a big grin on his face. 'She don't undress, just lifts up her dress and gets on with it. Then she wafts some incense up her jacksie. They keep it burning in a metal holder all the time in there.'

Stevie didn't like to think about the bugs nor the unwashed fanny his mates were sticking their pricks into. The street with the brothel was running with sewage, soldiers lining up to wait their turn, then staggering out after just a few minutes, buttoning their flies. They were issued with johnnies, but some of the men had run out and said they'd take their chances. No, he'd stay away from that both in person and on the lined paper he used for his letters home. His Ruby was fresh, sweet and wholesome.

The sickly smell of incense crept everywhere the platoon went, from the curtained shops in the casbah to the crumbling homes, as well as the brothels. It seeped into every cranny they patrolled, but it did little to mask the underlying odours of perspiration and rotting rubbish and beneath those smells there was something more sinister he couldn't quite identify, something crawling from the dung, filth and dead dogs in the gutters.

'What d'you reckon they've cooked up for us today?' Bill said when they'd caught up with each other. 'Curry again, I bet.'

'Hope it's not goat this time,' Stevie said. Every day was some variation on goat, lamb or very tough beef. The street urchins would love to fill their empty bellies with any of those, but he was getting sick of it. The curries were hot enough to set you on fire. 'Why can't they cook us a decent shepherd's pie, eh? I've had enough bloody curry.'

'The cooks got the habit out in India. Covers the taste if it's off,' Bill said. 'But maybe spuds are in short ration.'

'I could murder a bit of roast lamb for a change. With mint sauce and some Yorkshires on the side.'

'Me too. Can't wait to get back to my old mum's stew and dumplings. She makes a lovely apple pie as well. Count the days, eh?'

'What, count the days till we're on meat duty again? The stink, eh?' Stevie and Bill were on a rota that meant every other week they had to drive to the abattoir at 5 a.m. to collect supplies. Freshly slaughtered carcasses were hung on iron supports in the back of the lorry, under the canvas covering. When they arrived back at camp, the meat was already covered in flies and had to be butchered and cooked right away because of the heat. As they unloaded the joints and took them into the cookhouse opposite the mess tent, flies dive-bombed their heads and their ears. Stevie hated that bit the most, not having a free hand to brush them away, the smell of the fatty raw meat clinging to him as he staggered with the carcass resting on his head and shoulders. And once it was cooked, kite hawks swooped down, trying to steal the meat as the meals were being carried from one tent to the other.

No, he could only tell Ruby a little of what he saw and smelt. But maybe he could make a joke about the meals. Tell her he loved a Ruby Murray. Cos he did, didn't he? He loved Ruby Morrison.

Chapter 36

22 July 1946

Sappers on Ops

'Right, lads, we're on. This is the big one.' Sarge looked grim, harrying his men to load the trucks with heavy lifting equipment, wheelbarrows and spades. 'We've got to get a move on, sharpish.'

'Where we going, Sarge?' someone called out.

'Jerusalem. You'll find out why when you get there, soon enough.'

And the trucks took to the bumpy road, dust flying in the heat, the men crammed into the cabin at the front and into the open rear, partly shaded by the flapping canvas. 'I reckon it's a bomb,' Bill said. 'We wouldn't need all this lifting gear if we were doing just another bridge.'

'The Arabs have been getting jumpy,' someone else said. 'And Sarge don't set this sort of pace when it's a bridge or more roadworks.'

Everyone was quiet for a moment in the creaking, jolting truck, then Bill said, 'I ain't never seen a dead body before.'

'There might not be any,' Stevie said, then sat in silence for a minute. He hadn't expected this when he joined up. Bridges, roads, endless bloody army drill yes, but not more bombs and bodies. He'd had enough of that for one lifetime.

'Yeah, but they're saying it could be a bomb. And if it's a bomb in the middle of the city, stands to reason there's sure to be lots of people around. And you saw how Sarge was acting. I reckon there's gonna be bodies.' Bill had a gleam in his eyes, a gleam of excitement, not fear. 'This is what we've been waiting for, isn't it? Better than mending bloody roads and bridges, I'd say.'

'Look, we don't know nothing yet.' It was all very well for Bill. He'd spent his war in leafy Hertfordshire, not picking over the bombsites of London. It was obvious he knew nothing of the horror a bomb could create. 'Keep your mouth shut and don't think about it,' Stevie said, shutting his eyes for a second, trying to shake the images of the Blitz branded on his memory, but they weren't going anywhere, they never would. He glanced around the truck at the rest of the squad. He guessed some of them had shared his experiences and maybe his nightmares too. They too had gathered severed limbs and scraped shattered flesh from walls. But they were the ones who looked as if this was a Scouts jamboree, laughing and joking. He knew what they were doing. They were stoking themselves up to face the horror of the job ahead. But some were pensive and silent, with no idea what they might face, anxious they might throw up at their first sight of a maimed corpse.

Stevie gave a deep sigh, trying to bury his memories. Useless, he was. But you could never tell anyone. You had to carry on, put a brave face on it, just like they were going to have to do today, out here in the searing heat of the Middle East. It must be 83°F at least. They'd have to move fast. And he couldn't brag to Bill that this would be nothing compared with what he'd seen in the past, that he could cope with any digging out of corpses because he'd already seen far worse. It wouldn't be fair, not while he could never forget that blue-buttoned shoe with its white sock, nor the others that came after that. No, he couldn't tell him any of that.

When the trucks screeched to a halt, they knew for sure it was a bomb by the broken glass and rubble littering the street. Stevie jumped out with his crew and began unloading equipment from the other trucks. Sarge went off to consult an officer talking to a group of men. All around them they could hear wailing, shouting and barking. Stevie looked up at the sky, shading his eyes. It was going to get hotter and they'd be working all day in the full glare of the sun. Overhead, a kite was flying in hopeful circles.

'Right, you lot, we've got a job to do.' Sarge strode back, looking purposeful. 'There's casualties buried inside, so get cracking.'

'What's this place then?' Bill said.

'See for yourself,' Sarge said, pointing to the buckled sign. 'The King David Hotel. British HQ is stationed here, so they're our people, our responsibility. You lot,' he pointed to Stevie's group, 'get stuck into the main building. And you lot,' he pointed to the second group of men, 'get this street cleared up as best you can, then we can move about a bit more. Careful where you step, the blast caught some of the shops and pedestrians out here too.'

Stevie hesitated and caught the sergeant's eye, then took a deep breath. 'It's alright, Sarge. It's just the civilians... you know... but the longer we leave it, the worse it'll get.'

'Too right, son. You're Royal Engineers. You sappers are here to clear up. Just get on with it.'

Three whole days it took. All of them working in shifts to clear the debris; heavy lifting gear to move the largest chunks of rubble, spades to clear the shattered walls, hands to pick out fragments of bodies from the remains of the hotel. They took to shooting the roaming dogs and the swooping birds competing with them for lone fingers and lumps of flesh. Every piece of what had been a living person early that morning was saved as they dug and dug, sweat pouring down their backs and into their eyes, in the hope of finding anyone still alive.

Stevie tried not to think who the dead could be, tried not to think of them as living people with names, jobs and families. Once the heaviest pieces of masonry were cleared, he and the others knelt in the rubble, mechanically sorting brick fragments from body parts, timber from torsos. He shut his mind to who they might once have been, refusing to let his brain piece together the whole person. Most of the time this trick worked; he could extract a bloody, dusty arm ripped from a body and not flinch. But then he found the little foot. A sick wave hit him in the guts. He stared at the coffee-coloured skin, powdered with brick dust. He turned it over and looked at the calloused sole that meant the child had never worn shoes to scamper through the streets. He fingered the tiny white toenails edged with black grime.

How did this child's foot land here, in the middle of the hotel? It was so small, so young. It had to be a child from the street, torn from a mother's hand, blasted from the road, away from the market stalls and into the doomed building. He held the foot in his hand. It barely covered his palm. It could be her, the little girl he'd pitied on the way back to camp. No, not her, not here in Jerusalem, but a girl just like her, no more than five or six years old, a girl who'd done no wrong, who'd been begging or shopping just to stay alive.

He gently brushed the dust from the skin with his finger, tracing the little toes. How long he stared at it he couldn't tell. But his sudden idleness must have been noted, for he felt a heavy hand on his shoulder and Sarge said, 'Leave it, lad. Take a break.' He struggled to stand and stumbled across the heap of rubble, then slumped in the shade of the truck, swigging water.

After a few minutes, Bill threw himself down beside him. He too gulped water, his hands shaking as he held the bottle to his lips. 'Poor bastards,' was all he managed to say. 'Think I'd rather go back to repairing bridges.'

His remark did the trick. Stevie nearly choked with laughter, water spraying from his mouth, tracing rivulets through the dust coating his hands and arms. Bill poured the rest of his water over his head, then snorted into his hand and wiped it on his trousers. 'We'd better get back,' he said. 'Sarge don't like slackers.' They both heaved themselves up and marched back to their work, Bill slapping his friend on the back before they parted in brief acknowledgement that they had maybe not had the worst of it yet.

'Sarge ain't half getting soft on us,' Bill said when they ended their shift. The squad had been divided into three groups, each doing an eight-hour stretch at a time.

'Reckon he's getting fond of us,' Stevie said. 'His boys, he calls us.' He took a drag of his roll-up and leant back in the truck. They'd just come off the site and were about to be driven to a temporary billet for the night to rest, then be ready to restart in the morning. Lights were being erected as they pulled away, so the next group could work through till dawn. 'Do we know why this hotel was picked on?'

'Because we're here, I think. Because the British are in Palestine. Dunno if they've found out yet who's done this one though. Could be connected to what a lot of our boys were doing last month, but that was Jewish terrorists.'

'But we're out here, trying to help them. Trying to help people who were persecuted and mediate so everyone can be happy.'

'Yeah, well, that's what you get for trying to help. No one likes us poking our nose in. That's the half of it.'

'Ain't it just. Ungrateful bastards.' And Stevie took another swig of warm, brackish water from his can to wash away the taste of dust and dead flesh.

Chapter 37

30 July 1946

Banish the Thought

It properly hit him a week later, after the second day. The futility of it all after those desperate hours of struggling to reach the last surviving casualty on the final shift.

Plastered with brick dust and sweat, Stevie directed the heavy lifting gear down towards the slab of stone. The southern wing of the hotel, where the British offices were located, was the worst hit. Everyone had been at their desks when the bomb exploded. There were dozens of casualties. And our boys could still be down there, he kept telling himself as he sweltered in the relentless sun. Got to keep going till we're sure everyone's out. Only five survivors had been found so far and the body count was rising steadily.

He guided the chain around the slab and slowly, slowly, it began to lift and as it swung away, he thought he heard something. Waving for quiet, he listened. Yes, a faint moan. There was someone still alive down there. Injured certainly, but alive for now. He signalled for the work to continue and knelt down, ignoring the pain of the shards of glass and brick grazing his knees through the serge of his trousers. He called for other sappers to join him and piece by piece they picked away at the shattered bricks, till there was a gap through which they could see a body, a living body. His eyes were closed, he was smothered in powdered debris, crusty blood smeared his face, but he was just about alive.

Stevie and the boys kept at it all day, despite the merciless beating of the sun on their backs, sweat and dust stinging their eyes. And finally, they'd reached him. He'd almost wept with relief to find someone alive in the destruction after all the dead they'd seen. But now he knew it had all been pointless.

'Thought you'd want to know,' Colonel Barton said, 'as you were the first one to find him. I'm afraid the British Assistant Secretary didn't make it after all.'

'Thank you, sir. For letting me know, that is. I could see he was in a bad way.'

'Yes, poor chap. Bad luck, but you did your best.'

That's how it is, Stevie told himself. You do your best. You pick up the body parts, bag them up, shovel up the rubble and go back to camp. Stiff upper lip and all that. How many casualties were there in the end? Ninety? A hundred? Not to mention the poor bastards out in the street, whose only crime had been to open up their shops so families could buy food for their table. Women and children, some of them. It was hard to know some of the time. Chunks of flesh, like lumps of meat, who could possibly tell? But the hands, the feet and what was left of the faces, that got to him, got to all of them. And then there were the shoes, the sandals still strapped to the remains of feet, the leather threaded between the blood-smeared toes. So many shoes and feet shuffling through his disturbed dreams, with the little bare brown foot hopping to meet the little blue shoe.

They were quiet at first in the trucks going back to camp. Tired, dirty, reflective as they lit their fags and studied their boots. Then someone started humming 'Kiss Me Goodnight Sergeant Major' and they all joined in and when they reached base, Sarge said, 'Right, you lot. Get yourselves cleaned up. You've all got a twenty-four-hour pass starting six o'clock tonight.'

'Thanks, Sarge,' they shouted back and one wag called out, 'Who's going to kiss you good night if we're all off out?'

'Behave yourselves. Twenty-four hours. That's your lot.'

As the men showered away the sweat and grime, still humming the tune of the song they'd been singing in the truck, Bill said, 'Reckon we deserve some fun now, don't you? Bugger kissing the sergeant major, I fancy being kissed myself tonight. You coming?'

Stevie hesitated, then thought, why not? Why shouldn't he try to relax and forget the horror of the last few days? He'd been able to push it all to one side till he'd heard about that last death, mechanically shovelling and keeping his mind on the job in hand. But now it was over. Now he wanted to wipe it from his memory. And Ruby would never know, just as he'd never tell her about the little foot that had sat in the palm of his hand. 'Yeah, alright, you're on. Lead the way.'

They weren't the only ones who wanted to get away from the camp near Balad esh-Sheikh, so half a dozen crammed themselves into a jeep and set off down the lower slopes of Mount Carmel and into town. 'Do we know where we're going?' Stevie asked, as the group meandered through narrow alleys, past churches, mosques and shops, in and out of the quarters that claimed to be Jewish, Christian, Muslim and Armenian.

After working up their courage in a bar on beer and wine, they set off again till they found themselves in an even narrower, darker alley. 'This is a good 'un,' Bill said.

'You been here before?'

'Yeah. Once. It's cleaner than most. And younger.' Most of the women in the villages near the camp were unveiled. They looked to be sixty or seventy years old, but were really only half that age, weathered and wizened by childbearing, hard work and poor nutrition.

Bill went in first, while Stevie waited outside, nervously smoking with the other lads. Up to now, he'd thought his first time would be with Ruby, probably once they were married. They'd petted and that had been satisfying, but when you've spent three days slaving in the sun, clearing up the mess caused by some bloody Arabs, you need more than a handjob. It's nothing to do with her, he told himself, it's about me and what I've been through. I need this and she'll never know a thing. The lads all whooped and joked about how their mate would be making a hash of it, to stop them thinking about the distant shots they could hear above the barking dogs in the dark of the night.

When it was Stevie's turn, a stooped elderly woman pulled back the beaded curtain to the dimly lit room. It smelt of incense and attar of roses and a very young woman was washing her hands in a silver bowl. Although the light was poor, her hair appeared to be long and glossy, her teeth were white and her skin was clear. There may have been the shadow of a moustache or sideburns, like he'd seen on many of the local women, but in the brothel's dimness he couldn't tell. She stood before him and parted her front-opening robe so he could see her full breasts and the dark shadow between her legs. She took his hand and pulled him towards her as she sank down onto the cushioned couch.

Was that when it started? Was that how he came to realise that here at last was something that could erase the memories of the horrors? Well, not totally erase, not wipe them away for eternity, but for the moment at least. As his body responded to her charms, as he dropped his shorts and lay on top of her, moving into her, he entered a world of pleasure where there were no bloodied body parts, no screaming casualties and no solitary blue-buttoned shoe or little brown foot.

Later, there would be more girls, some exotic, some back home willing to do it in an alleyway for a shandy. Then over the years, he discovered other thrills that could soothe the pain: revving cars and the thunder of the racecourse would all help chase away the darkness. But for now, there was this, a musty scent, silky thighs and a satisfying explosion of pleasure.

And as soon as it was over, he felt the urge to rush out of that stifling, heavily scented room as fast as he could, into the cooler air of the street. He straightened his clothes, then put some coins into her hand. 'Shukran,' she said and bowed her head. Her voice was high and childlike and he suddenly wondered how old she really was. Definitely younger than Ruby – but he shook the thought away.

'Well, how was it, eh?' Bill clapped his mate on the back as he rejoined him in the alleyway. 'Best medicine in the world, doncha think?'

'It did the trick, Bill. Now come on, we've got some serious drinking to do. I want to get blotto and forget everything.' Forget the foot, forget the fuck, forget Ruby. Just drink and then fuck some more till it's all gone.

Oh soldier, soldier, won't you marry me,
With your musket, fife and drum.
Oh no, sweet maid, I cannot marry thee,
For I have a wife at home.

Chapter 38

5 April 1947

When I Come Home

Ruby was sure Stevie must be home by now. His last letter had been weeks and weeks ago, but he'd said he'd be demobbed by Easter. Well, it was Easter now. Yesterday was Good Friday and tomorrow Easter Sunday.

Maybe his ship hadn't docked yet, she fretted. She'd never been on a long voyage. A paddle steamer at Southend was her lot. She imagined high seas battering the troopship sailing back from the Middle East. It was a long journey by sea. In his first letter when he'd been sent out, he said it was rough round the Bay of Biscay and then they stopped at Gibraltar. Bad weather could have delayed his return. Or maybe he was unwell. Yes, that could be it. All that heat, strange food and foreign people. He might have caught a terrible tropical disease. He'd sometimes mentioned bombs in his letters, but never said there were any near his camp and surely if he'd been badly injured his parents, as next of kin, would have let her know? She could go and ask Joan, who she hadn't seen for months, but she was so busy these days being a mother and housewife since she and Trevor had moved out to Barkingside, where new houses had been built.

Ruby's imagination swirled, feverishly sketching all kinds of possibilities, until she decided the best thing was to call on his parents as soon as she finished work that day. Aunt Ida and her urgent duties in the pub would just have to wait. Her concerns for Stevie had to take priority.

*

There was no answer when she knocked on his parents' door later that day. The house was obviously empty and she was walking away along the terrace in disappointment when a passing neighbour noticed her and said, 'You won't find anyone in, love. They're all down The Feathers, celebrating now their boy's home from overseas.'

Of course they were down their local, just a five-minute walk away near the station. Just fancy, she'd gone right past it on her way here from the train, she'd been in such a hurry to get to the house. Oh, but she wished she'd been able to go home to change out of her drab work dress and sensible shoes. She didn't want Stevie's first sight of her after all these months to be her in her work clothes. If only she was wearing her blue dress that matched her eyes. He'd always liked that one, but if she went back home she risked being caught by Aunt Ida and then she'd never be able to get away. And why hadn't he let her know he was back safely? Didn't he realise she'd be worried? She felt a little peeved, but vowed she wouldn't show it when she finally saw him.

Two scruffy schoolboys were crouched outside the pub, tipping a little blue bag of salt into the bag of crisps they were sharing. Ruby stopped for a moment, checking her lipstick in her compact mirror, took a deep breath, then pushed open the heavy oak door to the saloon bar. She'd heard the commotion from out in the street. Piano thumping out 'Roll Out the Barrel', lusty singing, shouts for more orders and raucous laughter.

Joan spotted her first. 'Ruby,' she called. 'Come and join us.' She was pregnant again, blooming and cheerful, sitting with a group of women including Stevie's mother. Two years now she'd been married, right after Trevor was demobbed, and now she was expecting her second baby already. Only twenty-two and already a married mother-of-two. 'I'm on barley water. It's best for me waterworks when I'm like this. But the others are all on port and lemon.'

'Don't get up, I'll get myself a drink then,' Ruby said. 'Where's Stevie?' She looked around the crowded bar but couldn't see him in the blue haze drifting up to the yellowed tobacco-stained ceiling.

'He's back there somewhere. But I'd better warn you, he's had a skinful already.'

'When did he get back?'

'Wednesday, I think. It was Wednesday, wasn't it, Mum?' Joan appealed to her mother, who nodded her head.

'Only I hadn't heard anything and I was getting worried. He wrote ages ago and said he'd be back for Easter. But I thought he'd let me know as soon as he got home.' Ruby couldn't help but show her irritation at his thoughtlessness.

'Oh well, you know men. First thing on their mind is where's the pub?'

Ruby pushed her way towards the bar through the forest of men. She didn't even want a drink, she just wanted to find Stevie and tell him how much she'd missed him. Maybe she'd tick him off a bit too, for not getting in touch as soon as he docked. She hadn't seen him since his last leave before he left for Palestine last spring. They'd had such a special time and she had memorised every wonderful moment, especially their picnic in Epping forest. He'd written every few days when he was first called up and doing his training. Even when he was first sent overseas, he wrote quite often. But since his spell in Jerusalem last summer, she'd felt him drifting further and further away from her. His letters were shorter, less frequent and he no longer added kisses or wrote 'all my love'. Was that significant? She told herself that he was kept busy, had to follow orders, was worried his squad might be the one next in line for an Arab bomb, but she weighed every word of his letters and couldn't help wondering why she hadn't heard in weeks.

She stood at the bar, purse in hand, waiting to be served. The bar was thick with men leaning forwards, arms outstretched to get attention, ten-bob notes clutched in their fists. The landlord was more interested in pulling pints for them than in serving a lone woman. And then, while she stood there, she glimpsed him through the bodies clamouring for orders. He was sat at a little corner table, tucked away, and he seemed to be busy talking to someone close by.

Ruby edged herself between the men waving their cigarettes and beer tankards till she reached the end of the bar and could see more clearly. Stevie had his arms around a bottle-blonde girl in a low-cut, dark red dress. Their heads were together, touching, whispering. Not just that, but kissing. Not deep, full-mouthed kisses, just permitted-in-public smooches on the lips, but kisses all the same, her lacquered hand stroking his cheek.

Ruby gripped the edge of the bar counter, puddled with spilt ale and littered with damp beer mats. This was her Stevie, who she'd been longing to see, longing to hold and kiss, snogging another woman! All the breath seemed to leave her body and she felt faint. And that was when he saw her. He stood up swaying, holding out a hand to her, trying to pull her towards the spare seat at the table. 'Ruby love, come and meet Trixie. I've been telling her all about you.' His words were slurred as he turned to the girl beside him. 'Trix, this is Ruby, like I was telling you about. My lovely Ruby. My little friend ever since our school was sent off to the country in the war. What you drinking, Ruby?'

She pulled away from him as the girl extended her hand with its long red nails. 'Ever so pleased to meet you. I'm Patricia, but everyone calls me Trixie.'

Trixie? His little friend? Whatever happened to being his sweetheart? Wasn't she his darling Ruby, not just a little friend? She had no words for either of them. Her mouth was dry and her heart was hollow. She felt small and shabby in her black work dress compared to this glamorous, confident woman.

'Ruby? Aren't you pleased to see me? You'll stay and have a drink with us, won't you?' he shouted after her as she turned away and plunged back into the dense crowd. She was nearly at the door to the street when she felt a hand on her shoulder, pulling her back. He leant towards her and attempted to kiss her, but she turned her head away. 'Come on, Ruby, I don't call that very friendly,' Stevie said, staring hard at her. 'Come and have a drink for old times' sake. Oh, come on. Surely you can stay for a bit and have a drink with an old friend.'

She stared at him for a moment, almost tempted to throw herself into his arms now he was so close to her. His eyes were bluer than ever in his sunburnt face, his hair tinted gold by the sun. He was so close she could smell the cigarettes and beer on his breath, enticing her – but then she caught the whisper of sickly-sweet perfume clinging to his skin, so she pulled away from him and pushed through the door. The cool air outside was good after the sour smoky atmosphere of the bar. She strode across the road towards the station, but hadn't gone far when she heard him shout, 'Oh, grow up, Ruby! You could at least say welcome home!' She bit her lip, willing back the tears, then ran all the way down the road.

Chapter 39

6 April 1947

A Changed Man

'You didn't have to come all the way over here,' Ruby said when Joan heaved the pushchair up the front steps and into the pub.

'Yes, I did. Anyway, I stayed over at Mum and Dad's last night, so I didn't have to come far.' Joan rubbed her back, then bent down to pick up the toddler strapped into the seat. 'I said to Mum, that poor girl, he's no right yelling at her like that. Honestly, Ruby, I don't know what's got into him.'

'You'd better come in. Come upstairs. We don't open again till seven. Aunt Ida's gone up for a lie-down and Uncle Reg is reading the paper. I'll make us a pot of tea.'

'I'd love a cup. But I'd better nip into the Ladies first. Can't last five minutes, I can't. Here, I'll take Carol with me while you put the kettle on.'

Upstairs, Uncle Reg had fallen asleep in his armchair with the *News of the World* spread out on his lap. The little parlour was stifling with the gas fire flickering, so Ruby turned it down. The weekends were tiring, but even though Sunday opening hours were shorter, Ruby never took the opportunity to have a nap during the day.

Joan came puffing up the stairs with Carol in her arms. 'Take the weight off your feet,' Ruby said, pointing to the armchair opposite Uncle Reg, the other side of the fireplace. This drab room, with its threadbare upholstery and antimacassars stained from her uncle's hair oil, wasn't the nicest place for them to meet, but she could hardly expect Joan to let Carol breathe the stale beery fumes downstairs in the bar.

'No, I'm better off sitting on one of these,' Joan said, plonking herself down on one of the Victorian spoon-back dining chairs beside the table. 'Put me in a low armchair in this state and I can't get meself out again.' She laughed at her ungainly shape as she patted her bulge.

'How much longer have you got to go?'

'Oof, only another month or so. Glad I'm not having it end of the summer though.' She stroked the golden curls of the child sitting on her knee. 'If you ever have a baby, make sure you're not carrying it all through a hot summer. Everyone says it's murder.' Then she pulled a wry face. 'Sorry, Ruby. With things the way they are with Stevie, I shouldn't have said that. Sorry.'

'No, don't worry about it.' Ruby poured the tea, then pulled the quilted, stained cosy back over the pot. 'I don't understand what's going on either. But there we are. I'm just trying to forget yesterday ever happened.' She swallowed hard to push back the tears and took a deep breath to will them away.

Joan shook her head in exasperation. 'I'm sorry to have to say this, Ruby, but he's not the lad he was before he went out there. He was always a bit cheeky and full of himself before, but not like this. He's only been back a short while and I honestly think he's been seen with a different girl every night. And not very nice girls either. Sorry, but it has to be said.'

Ruby stared at her. She didn't say a word, just stirred her tea, hoping the sick feeling in the top of her stomach didn't rush up her gullet.

'We all thought he was sweet on you. Well, he was, wasn't he? We all expected him to come home and be overjoyed to see you. I told Mum I was expecting wedding bells. Like me and Trev. When he got back, he couldn't wait to get me all to his self.'

Carol started grizzling, so Ruby took the lid off the biscuit tin shaped like a thatched cottage and, with a nod from Joan, gave the child a plain Rich Tea. 'That'll keep her quiet for a minute or two,' her mother said, then continued with her story. 'So, where was I…? Oh yes, so we're just as surprised as you are. I mean, when we were sent off to Mrs Honey's, all those years ago, I thought you was like my little sister. I never thought he'd have eyes for anyone else. I'm livid with him and these stupid tarts who seem to think he's the bee's knees with his film-star tan and all his tales of overseas.'

Ruby waited a minute while Joan fussed over Carol dropping soggy fragments of biscuit on her lap. 'But I suppose people can change, can't they? I mean, life's not changed for me. I'm still helping out in the pub and working at the shop, just like I was before he went away. But Stevie's seen life now, hasn't he? Travelling all that way, going to all these countries, seeing all sorts of places and different people. I suppose it must change a person and give them another outlook on life.'

'Didn't change Trev,' Joan said. 'Came home from France just wanting to get back to normal. Said the thought of marrying me and having a family was what kept him going through all the hard times out there.' She smiled and glowed at the thought of her dear loyal Trevor.

Ruby thought this was the last thing she needed to hear, but she just said, 'Well maybe, because it wasn't like the real war, Stevie didn't have the same feelings as Trevor. He never said it was dangerous all the time he was out there. In his letters he just said it was hot and that they kept repairing bridges and roads. They had a few bombs, but he never said they were in any danger. But maybe coming back home here just seems so dull after all the exotic things he's seen and done.'

Joan snorted into her tea. 'Ain't it just! We didn't go all the way through the war because we wanted excitement. All we wanted was peace and quiet. That's what normal everyday life is like, Ruby, and he's gonna have to get used to it. And so far, I don't like what I'm seeing. He's out of order, he really is. It's not just how he's treated you, it's him swanning around, thinking he's better than the rest of us. He's got skills now, he says, and he's got plans to be a chartered surveyor. Says he's half qualified already and he'll soon be earning good money. But I tell you, he won't have money for long if he does all the things he says he plans to do, like buying a car now he can drive.'

'He's learnt to drive, as well?'

'One of the perks of National Service, he says. Had to learn to drive their trucks right from the start. Well, it's useful, I suppose. Maybe I'll get him to teach me, when I've got rid of this.' She patted her bulging stomach. 'Wouldn't mind driving myself around instead of pushing a pram with all me shopping.'

Ruby looked down at the hankie she'd been twisting and turning in her hands while Joan had been talking. 'Perhaps he'll calm down in a day or two, after the excitement of coming home's worn off. But I'm not going to go running round after him, begging him to take me out.'

Joan pulled a face. 'Quite right. You show him. But he'll have to get himself sorted out pretty soon. He'll run out of money at this rate. Though Dad's been generous with him since he got back and there's always someone down The Feathers ready to buy him a pint and hear his stories about his foreign floozies.'

'Floozies? You mean girls? When he was abroad?'

Joan waved her hand. 'Oh, it's nothing. You know how men show off. They probably got dragged along to some filthy dive one night and saw some fancy strip show with feathers and fandangos. I'm sure there's nothing more to it than that.'

Ruby felt cold. Her tea was tepid. And she could hear steps overhead. Aunt Ida must be getting up after her lie-down. Uncle Reg must have been disturbed too, as he suddenly started from his nap, grabbing his paper as it slid to the floor.

Joan noticed Ruby glancing up at the ceiling. 'Right then, I'd best be going or I'll miss my bus back to Barkingside. Got to get this one bathed and in bed after tea.'

'Yes, I've got to get the tea here as well before we open again tonight.'

'I'll see myself out then. Thanks for the cuppa.' Joan kissed Ruby's cheek. 'I'll let you know if I hear anything,' she called as she went back downstairs.

Ruby heard her unbolt the pub door and leave. Floozies? That must be it. A beautiful dark-skinned girl with long black hair would seem much more exciting. No wonder Stevie was restless. How could she have ever expected him to want to come back to her, a skinny pale mousey English girl? It all made sense now. She'd thought she understood what he needed, holding his hand and calming him when he was disturbed by memories of his beating and those bloodied bodies, but now she knew she was no longer enough for him and she'd have to try to forget him.

Chapter 40

Christmas 1947

Give Me a Ring

'Cheer up, love. It might never happen.' The customer chucked Ruby under the chin as she squeezed through the crowd in the pub with a tray of dirty glasses. At least it was her chin this time, not her bottom.

'You want to try smiling a bit more, girl,' Aunt Ida said when she laid the tray down on the end of the bar. 'Might stick if you did it a bit more often. Then you might get yourself another boyfriend. Told you that Stevie was a waste of time. I hear he's racing around in a fast car with all sorts now.'

Ruby didn't want her aunt's advice. She didn't want to be told to cheer up by anyone. She knew how unhappy she looked, but she couldn't force herself to smile. This wasn't the kind of Christmas she'd thought she'd be having once Stevie returned from his stint abroad. She should have been blissfully happy, thrilled to have her man home again, enjoying his company and a kiss under the mistletoe. They'd be going to parties, the cinema and dances, or maybe saving up to get married. Yes, that was it, she'd been convinced that by now they'd at least be engaged. He was twenty now, nearly twenty-one, and earning good money. She'd be nineteen next summer and even though she didn't earn much at Bodgers, she was sure they could have got by. They were nearly old enough to marry and she was sure Uncle Reg would have given his consent.

She didn't think Aunt Ida would ever have approved, but then she only thought about herself and how she'd manage without

Ruby's unpaid help. They might have to employ a barmaid if she left. 'Me and your uncle have done a lot for you, young lady,' she was always saying. 'Put a roof over your head. We didn't have to, mind, and many wouldn't have wanted another mouth to feed. But family's family. We've done our duty by you and it ain't much to ask for some help in return.'

Ruby didn't begrudge helping her aunt and uncle in the pub. I know they've helped me, she told herself. I'm an orphan. It could have been the orphanage for me. Then she pictured the Dr Barnado's home in Gants Hill, which they often passed on the bus. The house was surrounded by dark trees, but from the top of the bus she could see a coloured Romany caravan in the grounds and she thought playing there, pretending to be an exotic gypsy with gold hoop earrings and a full embroidered skirt, might well have been preferable to sweeping the pub floor.

Sometimes in her dreams, she asked herself if she could leave and move elsewhere to break the endless cycle of sweeping floors, both in Bodgers and back in the pub's bars. But where would I go? I wouldn't know anyone if I moved away from east London. It's all I've ever known, apart from Barnstaple and Mrs Honey. I used to think I could go back there, work in a village shop or on a farm perhaps, but Mrs Honey's with her Harry now, long gone from there.

Her letter addressed to the cottage that summer had been returned marked 'deceased' and when she'd asked Joan if she'd known, Joan had clapped her hand to her forehead and said, 'Blimey. Didn't I tell you? Sorry, I think it was the week Bobby popped out.' She patted the baby's back and burped him. 'Completely forgot with all that going on. Couldn't have gone all that way on the train anyway, not with all my stitches.'

'Buck up, gel.' Aunt Ida's words stopped her daydreaming. 'Stop moping about and get those glasses dried up. They're no good to us on the draining board, are they?'

Ruby grabbed the tea towel her aunt threw at her and set to work. It was Christmas Eve and the pub was packed. Laughter, coarse and cackling, shouting, general hubbub and above it all the jangling of the pub piano. Doreen from the corner shop had taken over the keyboard as usual. She wasn't a trained pianist but she could thump out a tune and she was attempting a jaunty version of 'The Twelve Days of Christmas', with much bawdy laughter as the singers couldn't remember the sequence of gifts and were substituting their own versions.

Ruby smiled as she heard Doreen's attempts to rein in the raucous crowd in the pub, trying to make them sing the correct words to the well-known Christmas songs. 'Sing it properly,' she yelled as the men lapsed into 'Shepherds washed their socks by night', much as they had when they were schoolkids.

Ruby went back to the bar with tray after tray of dry, polished glasses. The crowd seemed denser and drunker, less inclined to make way for her as she went backwards and forwards, gathering dirty glasses and returning with clean ones. On one of her final trips, pushing through the mass of rowdy men, she felt a pinch on her bottom and as she squeezed past, her breasts brushed against Arthur Cox's jutting elbow and he turned to her with a leer. Then a group waved Christmas crackers under her nose and insisted she pull one. 'Come on, gel, get your hands round it. That's it, give it a good yank!'

The bawdy banter and coarse laughter bothered her, but she thought if she joined in, she could then escape. She pulled the cracker and its contents fell to the floor. A joke, a paper crown and something else. One of the men bent down to pick it up, then knelt on one knee, placed the hat on his head and, to the amusement of his sidekicks, in a loud voice said, 'Miss Ruby, will you marry me?' On the palm of his hand he had a ring, a sparkler fallen from the cracker. Ruby looked at the cheap ring and him with horror, then slapped his hand away, and his offering rolled across the dirty pub floor between the mud-and-plaster-encrusted boots of the drinking labourers. Oh, how the crowd loved that. They roared with laughter.

Her cheeks burned, her eyes filled with tears. She pushed her way through the bar and out to the backroom. But as she passed Aunt Ida, she heard her say, 'Well, well, a proposal of marriage at last. Aren't you the lucky one?' And as she tried to escape, she heard her shout, 'Maybe you should accept. Might be the only one you'll ever get!'

Chapter 41

Arabs and Arak

The crunch of pebbles announces her arrival as Billie slowly steers the car into the curved gravel drive fronting the bay-windowed Edwardian house. The drive to Bishop's Stortford down the M11 hasn't taken as long as she thought it would and she's a few minutes early.

It was Kevin's idea that had set her on the trail. 'There must be some kind of old boys' group,' he'd said after her conversation with Joan a few weeks ago. 'Dig around and see if there's any kind of set-up for men who served in Palestine at that time and maybe were in his regiment.' And he was right. She'd found it straight away. The Palestine Veterans Association. And it had a message board to help family members trace old soldiers.

She'd posted a public message asking if anyone had served with her father during the years 1946–47 and had received a response two weeks later: 'I remember your father well. Good chap to have on our side during those challenging times.' When he said he had photos from that period, she sent him her email address and now they are meeting face to face.

As she steps from the car with the old photo album under her arm, the front door swings open. A tall, upright gentleman with a small white moustache and neatly combed white hair smiles at her and holds out his hand. 'Mrs Mayhew? It's a pleasure to meet you.'

'Reginald Barton?' She shakes his hand and he ushers her inside the spacious hall, where a grandfather clock ticks with a soothing rhythm and walking sticks are bunched in a mirrored hallstand.

'Please call me Roger,' he said, 'everyone does, ever since I signed up. Army chaps always seem to like a nickname.' He waves her through into a sitting room where a gas fire glows and a small table is set out with biscuits and two cups. 'My wife's just brewing coffee. I take it you could do with a cup after your drive?'

He is an affable and courteous host, urging her to have another biscuit with the coffee his wife pours for them. His album contains similar photos to the ones she's already seen, the tanned young men in uniform, leaning against army trucks, the piles of brick and rubble, with the same men, sitting down, spades instead of guns laid at ease by their sides. Then he says, 'I expect you're wondering why these pictures were taken?' His are captioned, while hers aren't.

'Yes, I don't know what they mean, but it's more that I keep wondering why my father seems so upset to see them again. It's made me realise I know so little about his past. To me he's always just been Dad. He's a good father, he loves his fast cars and his golf, but more than that I just don't know.'

Roger seems to settle back into his armchair, looking thoughtful. 'When I answered your message on the veterans' site, saying I knew your father, I should have said he was under my command. That means I knew him as one of my men in the platoon, though not intimately as a person. But it does mean that I know what was going on at that time and what challenges he and the others faced. Has he never talked about his time in Palestine?'

'No, nothing at all. I suppose I always knew that was where he'd been sent during his National Service, but I can't ever remember hearing any details. I hadn't even really taken any particular notice of the photos before. And I know there were a couple of souvenirs from that time. One's a cigarette case made of aluminium, I think, with engravings of the Pyramids and the Sphinx. He once said the local Arabs made it out of metal from a crashed German plane.'

Roger smiles and nods. 'I think we all came home with one of those. The local people were very resourceful and looked to make a buck wherever possible. They were particularly keen to get their hands on parachute silk if they could.' Then he looks serious and says, 'But it wasn't exactly a holiday out there, you know, despite the keepsakes. They were very tense and volatile times. Our presence wasn't welcomed by everyone. Your father was there just as things started to get really nasty.'

Billie shakes her head. 'I know nothing about that period in history. But maybe if you can perhaps tell me more about what was happening, I might be able to understand what my father experienced and what it means to him.'

He sighs. 'I doubt you'll ever be able to fully understand, but I'll try to help you. Firstly, these photos of yours, well, they may look like rubble but they're not ancient ruins. It's not some romantic archaeological dig out in the desert. It's the destruction your father and others had to dig through after a serious bombing incident.'

Billie looks again at the pictures. Roger's album is labelled 'King David Hotel, July 1946'. But in his collection, as well as ones duplicating her pictures of rubble, there are also two shots showing stretchers being carried out of the debris.

'In 1946, a terrorist bomb killed ninety-one people at this hotel in Jerusalem. Your father and other chaps serving in the Royal Engineers had to dig out the bodies. They dug in the hope of finding anyone alive, but the carnage was horrendous. Everyone who was involved in that operation was badly affected by it. We were out there in Palestine to help and this was the thanks we got.' Roger looks less composed than he had a few minutes ago and takes a deep breath.

'I'm so sorry. How dreadful.' Billie considers his words for a moment. 'But if you feel you could bear to, can you tell me a bit more about the entire incident so I can get a clearer idea of the impact this may have had on my father?'

And then, almost as if he is reciting from an official report that he has committed to memory and can never forget, Roger slowly begins to speak. 'The British HQ for administering Palestine had offices in the southern wing of the King David Hotel in Jerusalem. Early on Monday, 22 July 1946, the Irgun, a militant right-wing Zionist organisation, carried out a terrorist attack on our section, during the Jewish insurgency in Mandatory Palestine. The bomb caused ninety-one deaths and badly injured forty-six people of various nationalities. Most of the casualties were in the hotel, but some were also civilians outside in the road and in neighbouring buildings. Hot countries like that, everyone's out and about very early. The street was lined with shops and stalls. The place must have been buzzing just before the explosion. It was a cruel and cynical time and place to detonate a bomb.'

He pauses to sip his cooling coffee and gather his thoughts. Billie is transfixed and doesn't drink or eat during his detailed explanation.

'Members of the Irgun disguised themselves as Arab workmen and hotel waiters. They planted the bomb in the basement of the main part of the hotel. The southern wing housed the mandate secretariat and offices for the British military headquarters.' He pulls a wry face. 'I'd actually been called in to that division a couple of times myself. Luckily, not on that particular day.'

Billie remembers news reports she's seen on TV of bombings in marketplaces in Afghanistan and Iraq, imagining devastation similar to what he describes. She realises she'd been picturing her father's time in Palestine as a post-war sweaty jaunt through the Holy Land, rather than a bitter fight between sniping factions. 'It sounds quite terrible.'

'It wasn't pretty, I tell you. The Royal Engineers were summoned to the scene soon after it happened and we brought in heavy lifting equipment. I directed the sappers to form three groups, each one doing an eight-hour shift. We worked for three whole days and removed around 2,000 lorryloads of rubble. Our men worked day and night, trying to find survivors. And many of those killed were unidentifiable. It was a dreadful mess.'

'And was my father one of these men, digging through the rubble?'

'He was one of the best. Wouldn't stop till we'd found the last person alive. That was the British Assistant Secretary. He was badly injured and died a week later.' Roger throws his head back and looks at the ceiling. Billie thinks his eyes are glistening but she can't be sure.

After a moment of silence punctuated by the sounds of the hall clock ticking and Roger's wife bustling in the kitchen, he gives a small cough, then says, 'I've never forgotten our time out there, and I'm sure your father hasn't been able to either. As commanding officer, it was my job to direct the men, but standing on the sidelines is not quite the same as digging through the remains of buildings and bodies.'

'Thank you so much for telling me all this,' Billie says. 'Do you remember how my father reacted at the time? I'm sorry to ask, but I'm just trying to understand what all this means to him.'

'Of course.' Roger sighs. 'I can't really say how he felt in himself, of course. We were all pretty shaken up by it. Ghastly business, picking up bits of flesh and bone and not knowing who it belongs to.' He shakes his head. 'The worst bit was that there were children too. Not in the hotel or the offices. Probably the street or one of the nearby shops. That hit some of the chaps hard. Maybe your father was one of them. Bad enough dealing with adult fatalities, but children…' he shakes his head, 'even the toughest of soldiers can crack then…' He pauses. 'They were only young lads, mostly. Trained, of course, but young all the same. Nineteen, twenty, some of them, no more than youngsters. It's the army way.'

Billie is silent for a moment. He is obviously deeply affected by the memory. 'I can see that's not something easily forgotten. Poor old Dad. And he never talked about it.'

'Battle fatigue, we used to call it. Post-Traumatic Stress Disorder nowadays. But all the same, it goes deeper with some than others. You can't blame a man if it eats away at them. It's not their fault. Just the way a chap's made, you see.'

Roger slaps both hands on his knees and Billie senses this is him drawing an end to his revelations. But then he continues. 'It wasn't all bad though. Some of the time the Arabs were friendly. Off duty, we drank arak in little Arab bars.' He shakes his head again and gives her a weary smile. 'Never did really like the stuff, but sometimes it was all we could get.'

'Shouldn't have had that coffee,' Billie tells herself as she begins the drive home. 'Need the loo already.' She knows there are no services on the motorway, so she stops while she's only still on the outskirts of Bishop's Stortford. Then, back in her car, nibbling the healthy granola snack bar she's just bought in WHSmith (with chocolate chips, but who's checking?), she can't help thinking about the decent, reserved man who has just told her the most shocking story in such a civilised and so very middle-class manner. When he'd finished telling her all about what her father must have experienced, it was clear that he too had been badly affected by that particular incident. She'd wanted to throw her arms around him, tell him it was alright to feel upset, even though it had happened years before. Did his wife know how he felt? Had he ever told her that the sight of his men digging for hours in the heat, picking out shattered pieces of bodies from the dust, could never leave him? That the sight had been seared with a red-hot branding iron on his eyes and brain?

Oh, Dad, Billie curses herself. What was I doing to you, making you remember sights you wanted to forget? How could I do that to you?

She tucks the screwed-up snack bar wrapper in the pocket of the car door. Better whip that out when I get home, or Kev'll tick me off. And she drives off, Radio 2 blaring to wipe away the scenes that are now haunting her too.

Lottie Collins has no drawers.
Will you kindly lend her yours?
She is going far away
To sing Ta-ra-ra-boom-de-ay!

Chapter 42

I Know You

That morning, time seemed to drag so. Ruby folded and refolded the camiknickers, then checked that all the bloomers were in order of size and colour, white, peach, pink and black. The corsets and girdles were fiddly with their suspenders dangling and catching and had to be tucked away in their compartments.

She made sure she closed the cabinet drawers with a sliding whisper when she'd finished so Miss Perkins wouldn't tick her off again. 'This is ladies' lingerie, you know, Miss Morrison,' she'd snapped yesterday, when Ruby had shut the satin slip closet with a bit of a bang. 'You're not at home in a public house now, you know.' Her manageress couldn't resist reminding Ruby of her inferior status. Miss Perkins' father was a councillor and had won a medal in the Great War, so she considered herself to be vastly superior to all the girls under her supervision and especially Ruby.

She glanced across the department floor to where Miss Perkins was rearranging the folds of a peach satin housecoat on a mannequin. Every aspect of her being was tightly pinned and belted. Her thin flat-chested figure was wrapped in a calf-length black dress buttoned right up to her neck and her steel-grey hair was scraped back so fiercely that her white scalp was visible between the strands knotted into a mean bun.

Had any man ever held that angular frame, ever kissed those tight lips, Ruby wondered. She dressed in black like a widow, but

Ruby knew she had always been a 'Miss'. And she would never dare ask if there had ever been a sweetheart or a fiancé, as so many middle-aged women of Miss Perkins' generation had lost their true loves in the first war, the war to end all wars; so many had not been able to find a suitable match among the few eligible men who returned.

And am I any luckier? Ruby thought. Will it be my fate to carry on living with Aunt Ida and Uncle Reg till I'm past it too? Does my future lie here, with the knickers in Bodgers? She was sorely tempted to slam a few drawers when she thought about it and to hell with a ticking-off from Miss Perkins, who had by now marched across to the stockings counter, where the new girl was having a problem with the pneumatic tube that delivered payments to the department's cashier.

Thank goodness it's not me this time, Ruby told herself, watching how the manageress wagged her finger at the red-faced assistant. She could remember how she had struggled to operate the payment system herself, when she had first been promoted from a lowly cleaner in the store to junior sales assistant. She knew very well what the whizzing canisters were for, but she couldn't understand how on earth they operated when she was first allowed to take up her position behind the counter instead of beneath it, sweeping up dust and mud from the street, stray threads from price tags and the occasional bead or sequin dropped from a customer's hat. 'Just screw it back firmly, after placing the notes and the receipt inside,' she'd been told. But the first few times she either forgot the cash or the bill or didn't fasten it tightly enough.

But other than the stern Miss Perkins, Ruby loved working in Bodgers. She'd loved it when she first started at the age of fifteen and she loved it now – well, most of the time she did. With its scents of fresh linen, lavender and sandalwood, its polite murmurings and clear assignment of duties, it was a haven of calm compared to her aunt's public house.

Sometimes, when she had finished work for the day, even in the early days when she might be called on to dust yet another counter or sweep under a deep cupboard, she would linger, not wanting to return to the beer, the sawdust, the coarse language and the insinuations. And as soon as she walked through the door marked 'Saloon' in frosted letters on the glass, Aunt Ida would be there issuing orders, demanding she collect glasses in the public bar, thick with cigarette and pipe smoke. Ruby might have been on her feet all day and in need of a cup of tea and a rest in the armchair by the fire, but she would be expected to 'jump to it, gel,' and earn her keep, while Uncle Reg rested his elbows on the bar, checking tips in the paper with his cronies, and Aunt Ida displayed her newest gaudy brooch while she sipped port and lemon.

'Daydreaming again, Miss Morrison?' that piercing voice snapped. Miss Perkins ran her finger along the top of the counter. She inspected her fingertip and sniffed. 'Get this polished right now. I'm opening the store in two minutes precisely.'

Every day, every surface had to be spotless and every item for sale had to be in its correct position before the managers unlocked the doors to admit customers. Ruby quickly dusted the counter and checked her section was all in order. Nightgowns hung from padded hangers, brassieres were folded in trays, although a couple were discreetly displayed on armless models like the *Venus de Milo*, petticoats were laid in drawers and knickers of all shapes, sizes and degrees of adornment were modestly hidden away.

Ruby stood behind her counter, back straight, arms folded behind her back, watching the street through the glazed main door. Maybe she'd see Him again. She'd seen Him twice last week and once this week, on Monday. She guessed He was walking to catch a train as his steps were brisk and he looked ahead. She'd known it was Him from the very first sighting. He was a little taller than she remembered and darker-skinned than when he was young, but then all that time in a hot climate had left its mark. And she thought she detected the added distinction of a little thin moustache, making him look older than his twenty-five, nearly twenty-six years.

He hadn't had one the last time he kissed her, the very last time, after he'd completed his National Service training and before he was sent to Palestine. The Holy Land didn't make him very holy, did it, she thought. When he came back, it all went wrong. Five years ago, that was. But she still longed for him. She was prepared to forgive him, because she knew he had suffered and only she knew how to calm his nerves. She knew he was married now, but was he happy? Did his wife know about the horrors he'd seen and how they lurked in his dreams? And she imagined him in her arms every night in her cold single bed in that sparse room at the top of the pub.

She'd tried to forget him, really, she'd tried. There'd been Ray who worked at the printers. He didn't look after his teeth and would lose them all in a year or two. And Derek was a drinker and never had any spare cash, expecting Ruby to pay for herself when they went to the pictures. And none of the men who tried to interest her, and who she honestly tried to tell herself might replace Stevie, were right for her. She wanted the man who had promised her a doll's house when she was a girl, the man she had felt she knew through and through.

She glanced again towards the street and then she gave a little intake of breath. There He was again. Trilby hat, raincoat flapping, briefcase under his arm. For once he wasn't striding. No, he was slowing down, looking in the windows. Yes, he was looking in Bodgers' windows. Her heart was fluttering and she felt breathless, wondering if this would be the day when He would push open the door, when she'd hear it ring to announce his entrance and he would walk towards her counter, so then she could say, with a smile, 'Good morning. May I help you?'

But not today. After another minute or two he turned away and strode towards the station. Ruby clutched the edge of the counter.

It had been so close. If He came into the store, if He came to her section, if He spoke to her, He would see she was no longer a child, nor the tremulous teenager she had been when he had left, and certainly not the resentful, affronted girl who had run from his homecoming party. No, He would see a poised young woman with her curled hair, her powdered face, her red lips, her curvaceous figure, and He would want her again.

Chapter 43

10 April 1952

Well, Hello!

Miss Perkins was extra-sharp that morning. Sharp as lemon sherbets, she was. 'Don't think you can slack because of the bank holiday,' she said to Ruby and the new girl. 'You might be getting a day's holiday tomorrow because it's Good Friday and another on Monday, but I shall still expect you here on time on Saturday. Losing two days' trade won't help our sales figures.'

Ruby felt she rather wished bank holidays never happened. They weren't holidays at all as far as she was concerned. Aunt Ida expected her to 'help out' in the pub as they were always extra busy during these times. Bank holidays meant other people didn't have to work the following day and could spend all their money and all their free time in the pub, getting louder and drunker. But she would have to work at the store again after long hours gathering glasses, sweeping up fag ends and enduring coarse remarks from customers. 'You don't know what you're missing, love,' the warehousemen chorused when they 'accidentally' bumped into her as she made her way through the noisy throng in the smoggy public bar.

And this was the Easter bank holiday, which no longer held any pleasure for her. When she was a child, it had meant fragrant hot cross buns. It had been a time of celebration, as well as a time for two days in church, culminating in the presentation of a beautiful chocolate Easter egg decorated with sugar-paste flowers, almost too pretty to eat, although she always did. And when she had been evacuated to stay with Mrs Honey, there had been hard-boiled eggs with coloured shells, and Simnel cake. But since her parents had died, there had been no special eggs, boiled or chocolate. And no church service either, since Aunt Ida needed her to sweep the floors before the pub opened again. No, Easter no longer held any significance for Ruby.

And after the holiday, Bodgers always held its spring sale. Traditionally the preserve of the linen department, which assumed that housewives would want to replace sheets and pillowcases as part of a spring-cleaning purge, the sale had in recent years been extended to all departments. Miss Perkins took this very seriously and said lingerie would be marking down all undergarments, but not stockings, which were a regular best-seller. Ruby couldn't understand why anyone would want to buy extra knickers just because they were cheap. Surely you just replaced them as and when you needed new ones?

She busied herself, early on this Thursday morning, quickly tidying her section so she would be able to concentrate on looking for Him at the usual time, without any reprimands from Miss Perkins. At 9 a.m. precisely, the main door was unlocked, and at 9.05 or thereabouts, she saw Him. He wasn't rushing along as he normally did; he slowed his pace and looked in the windows. And then, she could hardly believe it, He pushed open the main door and entered the shop. She watched him veer right towards accessories, where she could see him come to a halt at handkerchiefs. The assistant produced a pale blue box, which Ruby knew contained lace-edged ladies' hankies. Delicate things, barely a wisp of cotton, more suited to dabbing a crumb from a cheek than blowing a nose in full flood.

He paid for his purchase and turned round, making for the street again, his head down as if he was going to assume his normal pace to the station. But he stopped, felt in his coat pockets and then, to Ruby's delight, he lifted his head and looked straight at her. He stood still, a frown creasing his brow, and then he slowly walked towards her.

Ruby gripped the edge of the counter. She had been longing for this moment, but what was she going to say, when the last time she had seen him he had been so unkind and she had been stricken with tears? But he advanced upon her and spoke in the deep velvet voice that had always stirred her below.

'Well, well, fancy seeing you here. And may I ask what you are responsible for in this lovely shop on this fine morning?'

'Ladies' underwear,' she managed to stammer. 'I'm a junior assistant now.'

'How very interesting. And you are in charge of this whole section, all on your own?'

'That's right. Would you like me to show you something?'

A smile creased his face, a smile she remembered and loved. 'I'd love you to show me some underwear,' he said in a low, confidential voice. 'But maybe not today.'

'There will be reductions after Easter. When the sale starts. If you are thinking of getting something for your wife, that is.'

'Maybe I will. I suppose you mean knickers will be coming down after the holiday?' And then he winked, turned away and left the shop.

Ruby nearly exploded with laughter at his cheek. If any of the customers in the pub had said anything half so outrageous, she'd have stuck her nose in the air and scuttled past them quick. But this was Stevie. This was the man she had loved – no, still loved and desired. So, did that make it alright?

For the rest of the day she couldn't help giggling every time she thought about what he had said. She couldn't laugh aloud, because of the decorous atmosphere of the shop and Miss Perkins' watchful eye, so she stifled her amusement and occasionally had to pretend she had a tickly throat and cough for a moment. 'Not coming down with a cold, I trust, Miss Morrison,' her manageress said with a disdainful glance at her. 'No, just a dry throat,' she whispered back.

He had seen her. He knew where she worked. Maybe he would return, she thought. And then he did. At the end of the day, just before closing time, as she and the other girls were tidying their sections and the cashier was totting up the day's takings, the front door pinged and he sauntered across to her counter.

'I couldn't go home without giving you this,' he said, placing a large paper bag in front of her. 'I remembered how much you said you used to like them, when we were young, so while I was in the shop I said to myself, I'll have to get one of these for Ruby. Go on, have a peep.' He glanced over his shoulder. 'Old Iron Drawers isn't looking right now. Have a quick shufti.'

She gently opened the bag and peered in. There, wrapped in cellophane with a yellow satin bow, was a large chocolate Easter egg, piped with sugar flowers in pink and green. 'Oh, it's beautiful,' she sighed, staring at the confection.

'I bet you've got loads waiting for you, from all your admirers,' he said. 'But I thought to myself, one more won't hurt my Ruby.'

My Ruby, he'd said My Ruby. Her neglected heart melted and called to him. 'Thank you. There aren't any others. And I don't have any admirers so thank you.'

'Enjoy it. Eat it all up and think of me when you've got chocolate all over your fingers.' Then he winked and turned to leave, but after only a couple of steps he looked back and said, 'I'll be back. After Easter. When the knickers come down.'

And this time, Ruby couldn't help herself. She started laughing. She tried hard not to, but delighted laughter poured out of her as if she hadn't laughed properly in years. He slipped through the front door before Miss Perkins could cross the floor, but as soon as she stood in front of Ruby, she said, 'I hope you're not going to be in the habit of associating with gentleman callers in my department, Miss Morrison.'

'Oh, that wasn't a gentleman, Miss Perkins. That was an old family friend,' Ruby said, thinking, but he's my gentleman. He may be married, but he's my gentleman and he just gave me the first chocolate Easter egg I've had in years.

When shall we be married,
Billy, my pretty lad?
We'll be married tomorrow,
If you think it good.
Shall we be married no sooner,
Billy, my pretty lad?
Would you be married tonight?
I think the girl is mad.

Chapter 44

July 1952

Promise Me

'I should never have done it,' Stevie said. 'You know that, don't you, Ruby? I should never have gone with Maureen. If I hadn't, I wouldn't be in this mess now. You were always the one for me, the only one. I know that now.'

Ruby looked into his eyes. It was still there, that sadness, that pain he struggled to shake off. He told her he still had nightmares. 'It's the blue shoe. Sometimes I pull at it and the whole leg comes away in my hands. And then this child's foot I found out in Palestine comes hopping across the rubble to join it. I'm wide awake then, remembering, sweating, I am. And Maureen says for Gawd's sake, you were screaming again. She says she's fed up of me waking the kids. Then she has to settle them down again.' Ruby had comforted him when she was younger and she could still comfort him now, help him chase away the dark memories.

She snuggled her head against his chest as they leant against the wall outside the back of the Odeon. In the dark alley no one could see them kiss and cuddle. The cinema's back row had been too packed for them to embrace properly. Outside wasn't comfortable and it was strewn with rubbish, but it was dark enough to hide their passion and she was happy to have his full attention. It wasn't his fault he'd had to marry Maureen. She must have led him on, so he had to do the honourable thing. Aunt Ida had delighted in telling her the news when it happened: 'You're well out of that one, my girl. I always knew he wasn't to be trusted.' And now there were two children and a baby. Maureen had him well and truly trapped. Yes, that was it, he was trapped when really, he was meant to be with his first love, his Ruby.

Since his kind gesture at Easter, Stevie had become more and more attentive, waiting for her to leave work, walking her back to the station and then, after a couple of weeks, persuading her to go to the cinema with him, 'Just like we did in the old days, Ruby, when we were young. You liked going with me, didn't you?' And she did like going with him, even when his hands began exploring her clothes and even when he encouraged her to make him happy by directing her hand to his urgent bulge. But he wasn't like the regulars in the pub. He only did it because he cared for her, because he really loved her.

'But once you leave her, we'll be together forever, won't we? I'm glad I've saved myself for you.'

'I've got to stay with her for now,' he said, 'for the sake of the kids. But I will do one day, Rube, it won't be long, I promise.' Stevie slipped his tongue into her mouth and his hand under her blouse, then undid his trousers a little, so her hand could find him. 'You're a doll. You know that, don't you, Rube?' It always ended like this, Ruby sticky and unsatisfied, Stevie red-faced and nervous in case they were caught.

'I wish we could go somewhere like a proper couple,' she said when he had finished and she had wiped her hand clean. 'We're grown-ups, we shouldn't have to lurk in a corner like this.'

'Maybe we can,' he said. 'My firm's sending me off round the country on some jobs. And guess where I'm going in August. Go on, guess.'

She laughed. He always made her laugh. 'I don't know. You tell me.'

'Somerset and Devon,' he said. 'They're short-staffed over the summer and the surveys still have to be done, so I'm filling in. To be honest, I'll be glad to be away from home. I said I'd come back at weekends, but I don't think Maureen would care if I didn't turn up once in a while. She prefers going over to see her mum, after all. I could say it's too far away to come home every weekend and then one time you and me could go and stay in some swanky hotel.' He looked at her, holding her around her tiny waist, then ran his fingers down the mother-of-pearl buttons at the front of her blouse. 'What do you say, Rube? Would you like that?'

'Oh, Stevie, I'd love that. Do you really think we could spend the night in a hotel together?'

'Course we could. And more than one night too. They'll think we're already married and couples do it all the time. You'd have to get some time off, mind. Old Prissy Perkins can't stop you having a bit of a holiday, can she?'

'No, she can't. I'm allowed a week off altogether, but there's never seemed any point in taking it till now.' Ruby preferred working in Bodgers to spending more time in the pub and the few times she had taken a day's holiday, she hadn't been left to herself as Aunt Ida always found jobs for her.

'We could go back to our favourite part of the world. See the rivers and the moors again. Breathe some fresh air away from all this dust and rubble.' Stevie held her hand as they started walking towards the street. The rebuilding of London had begun as soon as the war was over and it seemed as if every part of the city was under reconstruction, contributing noise and grit to the everyday grime.

'Fresh air would be nice. Apart from the park, and even that's not very nice these days, there's nowhere clean round here. By the time I've got off the train after work my hands are black and if I blow my nose, well, it's disgusting!' Ruby giggled and blushed. She would never want to seem less than ladylike to Stevie. She wanted him to think she was perfect.

'Bit of sea air would do you good. Set you up in case we get another bad pea-souper this winter. Last year weren't good and they say it's getting worse with all the buses running on diesel now.'

They reached the street and both stopped out of habit and looked up and down the road, checking they hadn't been seen together. Then Ruby glanced up at him. 'I'll have to book the holiday officially. I can't do it at the last minute. There's staff rotas to think about.'

'Of course, I know that. Let's say early August. Might get some lovely weather then.'

'How will we get there? Are you going to collect me?'

'I'll work it all out, don't you worry. Once I've checked my schedule, I'll give you a firm date and enough money for your train fare and so on. Then I'll pick you up at the other end. Does that sound alright to you?'

'But where do you think we'll be when we meet?' She frowned and bit her lip.

He paused to think, then said, 'Exeter perhaps, or Bristol maybe. One of the big stations that gets lots of fast trains. Then we'll drive somewhere nice and be together all day and all night.' He winked. 'You'll like that, won't you?'

She blushed again at the mention of nights. 'Don't forget then. I'll be waiting to hear.'

'I won't let you down, Ruby. Not this time.' His fingertips brushed against hers, lingering for a second before he began walking away. Then he turned back and blew her a kiss and Ruby glowed inside.

Sitting on the top deck of the bus taking her back to the sour smell of the pub and the even sourer jibes of her aunt, Ruby continued to hug herself with pleasure. He wanted to take her away from all this drabness. Somewhere they both loved, somewhere romantic. Then she began to imagine what he would think when he saw the shabby underpinnings beneath her everyday clothes. It had to be silk and satin, not grubby cotton and worn elastic. And maybe a new dress and shoes. Yes, definitely new shoes.

Chapter 45

At a Pinch

The Bodgers girls were never allowed much time for lunch. Supervisors and managers had forty-five minutes, but lowly assistants like Ruby had to make do with half an hour so she didn't usually bother to leave the store. Why walk to the station café and back when that was the same route she took to and from work? Why gobble a sandwich and only have fifteen minutes to window-shop? So most days Ruby sat in the staffroom, flicking through a tattered pile of magazines. If she was lucky, there might be a dog-eared copy of *The Lady*, making her long for an elegant home with sweeping lawns and a chic poodle. But mostly, it was a well-thumbed *Woman's Own* or *My Weekly* with its knitting patterns for tight ribbed sweaters, which she'd never dare wear in the pub with its far-too-appreciative public bar audience of scaffolders and plasterers.

Aunt Ida always took *Woman* magazine but only gave it to Ruby once she'd consumed every line, licking her finger as she turned the pages. She was obsessed with news about the forthcoming Coronation, now that Princess Elizabeth, as she had been, was the new queen since the death of the King. 'And we're gonna have one of them new television sets for it,' she told her husband. 'It'll bring in all the punters. They'll all want to come in here and see it. Nobody else in the street will have one. Make a fortune, we will.'

Uncle Reg took no notice of her. He liked the *Daily Mirror*, plus *Sporting Life* twice a week for racing tips. And they both fought to have first look at the weekly *Reveille*, which Ruby always tried to salvage before it was used to light the coal fire, because it was the best paper for photos of film stars and singers. Her cold attic bedroom walls were becoming quite papered with glamorous pictures she'd snipped out, hoping she could emulate a beguiling smile or a fashionable hairstyle.

But for the last two weeks, Ruby had been escaping from the store in her lunch break. If she took a couple of quick bites of her sandwich when she grabbed her handbag from her locker and another couple when she returned, she could use the time for herself, for shopping for her romantic getaway. She had been saving from her wages ever since Stevie had first mentioned the possibility of a short holiday, adding to the little stash she'd built up over the last couple of years in the hope of starting her life afresh one day. Many times she'd dreamed of going back to Devon, but she could never find the courage to tell Aunt Ida and buy a ticket. She just wasn't used to making big decisions on her own.

Once Stevie had been able to confirm the actual dates, she had booked the time off, even though Miss Perkins was not best pleased, frowning and saying, 'It's not really convenient. I had rather hoped we could do a stock check that week, Miss Morrison.'

She bought new underwear first. Not from Bodgers, as she didn't want any of the girls or Miss Perkins noticing or commenting. She went to a little lingerie shop in the middle of town and selected a peach satin bra and two pairs of matching knickers with cream lace trim. They were now hidden underneath her mattress. She didn't want Aunt Ida poking around in her chest of drawers, suspecting she might have a new boyfriend.

The full-skirted dress she bought in Bodgers was marked down after a customer returned it, complaining that it was poorly made. One button had worked loose and there was a small split under the arm, but it was easily mended and was priced well within Ruby's means. She'd hidden the dress under her winter coat and hung that behind a warm skirt and jacket in her wardrobe. She would have happily sewn herself a new dress and saved some pennies, but there was nowhere she could do that privately without her aunt asking questions. That pleasure had to be saved for the day when she and Stevie were finally married and had their own home.

And today, only a week before she could escape and be with him for four whole days, she was going to buy shoes. She'd spent the last two lunchtimes looking in shop windows, venturing in to shyly stroke the shiny leather, and now she'd finally decided. If they had them in her size – five and a half – she was going to buy the red leather court shoes she had fallen in love with in Lilley & Skinner. They were a little high, but they'd make her legs look longer and slimmer and would look just lovely with the new rose-printed dress now hidden on a hanger beneath her heavy woollen coat in the wardrobe.

Ruby crammed half her sandwich in her mouth and tried not to let Miss Perkins see she was still eating as she left the store. Chewing wasn't allowed and food was not permitted on the shop floor. And she was in luck: the court shoes were still in stock in the shoe shop. She dithered over both the dark green and the black ones on display, but the red looked so cheerful – she decided to have the red.

'I'm afraid we only have two pairs left in that style,' the shop assistant said, bringing out two boxes. 'And neither is quite your size.'

Ruby stared in deep disappointment at the glowing red leather held before her. 'But sizes do vary,' the girl said. 'Maybe try both of them on and see. Or I can get you a five and a half in the black.'

'No, I'll try these. I could stuff the toes of the larger size, perhaps.'

'Or try an insole,' the girl said.

Ruby stood up and tried a few steps. The large shoes slipped on her heels and she knew that even with an insole or heel-grip, they would trip as she walked, making her look like a little girl playing at dressing-up in her mother's high heels, rather than the elegant, mature figure she hoped to create. The smaller pair were much better. They were a snug fit, but then she'd been on her feet all morning running between brassieres and slips for a whole string of customers. 'I think these might be alright. I expect my feet are a bit swollen from standing for hours.'

'You'll soon break them in,' the girl said. 'Wear them with a thick sock and stuff them with rolled-up newspaper.'

Ruby stretched out her legs to admire the contrast between the red leather and her pale skin, shimmering in a recently acquired pair of nylon stockings. The shoes were very flattering. She stood and turned in front of the shop's low mirror, then walked towards the long looking glass so she could see her entire figure. The high heels enhanced the curve of her legs, her ankles looked more delicate than usual and the height encouraged a subtle sway of the hips. She thought she looked sophisticated and poised. Spinning round, she felt a sharp pinch on her little toes and the back of her right heel, but it wasn't that painful. Nothing she couldn't tolerate, she thought.

'They really suit you,' the shop girl said. 'Elegant, like Jane Russell.'

'I'll take them. They're perfect.'

The girl began to wrap them in tissue paper and place them back in the shoebox, but Ruby said, 'No, I don't need the box. I'll take them as they are.' The assistant looked surprised when Ruby paid for the shoes and then squeezed them into her handbag. She would wear them on the way to and from work for the next couple of days to try to stretch them. But she didn't want nosy Aunt Ida spotting the shoebox and drawing conclusions. No, she wasn't going to give her sarcastic prying aunt any clues as to what she was really about to do.

Chapter 46

13 August 1952

All Packed

It was typical of Aunt Ida to make her work late, sweeping the bar floors and polishing glasses. Usually she did those jobs first thing in the morning, before leaving for her job at the department store, but tomorrow she had an early start: Ruby had to catch her train for her romantic rendezvous.

'I don't call going back to Barnstaple a holiday,' Ida said. 'Southend's a holiday. Down the Kursaal, under the Dome, that's what I call a holiday, all them rides and flashing lights. You're not even right by the sea in Barnstaple.'

'It's not far to the coast. We might even go there one day. But that's not the point. I'm looking forward to seeing my friends in the village again. They were very kind to me when I was there. And I want to visit Mrs Honey's grave, given that I didn't know about the funeral. She was very good to us when we were there.'

'Huh, they did alright out of you. Got extra for taking in all those kids.' Ida sniffed and wiped her finger along the bar counter. 'This could do with a clean an' all. It's all very well for some, going off on holiday. I fancy a little trip to Southend myself when you get back from your gallivanting. I could do with some good fresh cockles and there's a place Reg and I always say does the best fish and chips. I had lovely skate with capers last time we went.'

Ruby ignored the jibes, finished cleaning and put the last glass back on the shelf. Once she was in her room she opened the window to let in a little air. It had been warm and humid with drizzly rain all day and her attic bedroom up in the eaves was hot and close. If the rain carried on like this, she'd have to wear her mac tomorrow. She sighed – she wouldn't look as elegant as she'd imagined, but she had to protect her lovely cotton dress.

She unwrapped her new nightdress from its tissue paper and held it out in front of her, admiring the shimmer of the cream satin and ecru lace. It was an extravagance, she knew, but she could hardly wear her old sprigged cotton nightie for the most important night of her life, her first night of real love in a bed with Stevie.

She refolded the garment and placed it inside her new blue weekend case. It wasn't really new, not brand-new, but when she had spotted it beneath the old clothes stall in Petticoat Lane, the pale blue leather had shone out in the dusty street and called to her. She had knelt down to examine the leather, scuffed on one corner, its clasps a little tarnished. 'Lovely, innit?' the stallholder said. 'Ten bob and it's yours.' Ruby had opened it, then bent her head to sniff the watered silk lining. It wasn't musty; it carried the faintest trace of perfume, Evening in Paris perhaps rather than the pungency of Tabu, which was Aunt Ida's new favourite, thanks to Arthur Cox and his dodgy sources.

As she hesitated, the trader made an offer she couldn't resist: 'Alright, love, eight shilling to you.' Ruby had paid her money, wondering how she was going to get a case, however small, past Aunt Ida. And she hugged it to herself all the way back, wondering who had used it before her and trying to put thoughts of it being found in a blitzed, ransacked home out of her mind. No, it had more likely accompanied its owner on a night at The Savoy, or maybe was part of a set of matching luggage that had cruised the Mediterranean every summer before the war.

Putting the case to one side, Ruby removed the underwear, also still folded in tissue, from beneath her mattress. She wondered whether to pack both sets and wear her old bra and knickers to travel, but as she caressed the satin she decided she couldn't resist. She had to be new and fresh from top to bottom tomorrow morning. Besides, he might be impatient; he'd been away two weeks now, he hadn't kissed her for nearly three – he might want to stroke her thighs and breasts in his car if they parked in a secluded place on the way to their hotel. She didn't want him uncovering greying cotton and frayed elastic when his fingers wriggled past the tops of her stockings.

And when they got to their hotel, they would do 'it' at last, Ruby thought. She was nervous, but excited too. So far, his fingers had probed her, sometimes pleasurably, other times less so. It couldn't be much more painful than fingers, could it? She bunched her own fingers together and felt the size of the rigid mass with her other hand. It felt smaller than when she was rubbing his cock, up and down, up and down, in some rubbish-strewn alleyway. Perhaps she should pack a couple of sanitary towels as well, in case there was blood. She wouldn't want to ruin her new silk knickers.

Sitting on the bed, Ruby kicked off her work shoes and picked up the shiny red court shoes. She pulled the balls of newspaper out of the toes and eased her feet into them, then stood up and took a few steps. They were still tight, despite her wearing them every day since she'd bought them a week ago and packing them with wads of paper every night. Her heels were sore and her big toes were pinched. But her feet weren't blistered and bleeding, just painful. And the shoes were lovely. Maybe she should wear her old ones for the journey, then change on the train, just before it pulled into the station, just before she fell into Stevie's arms.

He's so good to me, she sighed. Given me all this money. She knelt down by the bed and slipped her hand under the mattress again. There, in a small roll of notes, was enough for her fare across London to Paddington and then a return ticket to Weston-super-Mare. 'And not third-class neither,' he'd said, folding her hand around the cash. 'I'm sorry I can't give you enough to go first-class. Cos that's what you are for me, Ruby, a first-class sort of girl. But there's a bit extra for a meal on the train if you feel like it. Treat yourself.'

Maybe I should take a sandwich just in case, though, she thought. The dining car might be fully booked and I don't want to arrive half-starved. Stevie will want to drive straight to the hotel and won't want to waste time stopping off to find a tearoom. I'd better make myself something quick in the morning.

And lastly, she took the ring from her purse. He had given it to her the last time he'd kissed her. 'I'll get you a proper one eventually,' he said. 'When we get married properly. But this will look alright for the hotel.' He'd slipped it onto her ring finger. It was a little too big for her slender hand, but it looked like gold, a real gold wedding ring. Ruby held out her hand and admired it shining at her, a golden promise that they would be together forever one day. She slipped it off again and put it back in her purse. She'd wear it on the journey and practise behaving like a respectable married lady.

A few minutes later, lying in her hard, single bed, in her faded old nightdress, she imagined her first night in a double bed in Stevie's arms. After tomorrow night, she'd no longer be a virgin, she'd really be his lover, his mistress and then one day she'd be his wife. She promised herself she'd always put him first, always be there to listen to his woes, soothe him when the nightmares returned and never be too tired to comfort him. But during their first full night of sleeping together he'd be tender, because he'd know how to make love to her, being an experienced married man. He'd kiss her and run his hands over every inch of her body. And he'd tell he loved her more than ever now that they were united by the act of physical love.

My mother said that I never should
Play with the gypsies in the wood;
If I did, she would say,
Naughty little girl to disobey.

Chapter 47

14 August 1952

Chuff Chuff and Chocolate

The train was packed with holidaymakers. Of course it was. It was August, the middle of the school summer holidays, and hundreds of families were off to spend a week at the seaside, despite the rain. Weston-super-Mare was popular, with its long seafront and its pier for cheap entertainment. Ruby wished she had reserved a seat, but she hadn't been able to buy her ticket till she arrived at Paddington and then she had to fight her way aboard, along with all the married couples with their luggage and excited children.

Cramming her little blue valise into the netted luggage rack alongside the bulging cases, she squeezed into the only remaining seat she could find on the crowded train. She shouldn't have wasted time dashing into the Ladies, but she was desperate to spend a penny and she wanted to slip her ring on in there, rather than fumbling for it in her handbag on the train.

The husband and wife opposite her were unwrapping cheese and pickle sandwiches, accompanied by pickled onions. Ruby's provisions consisted of Fox's Glacier Mints and a small bar of chocolate bought from the station kiosk at the last minute. It reminded her of the paper bag of tuck she had clutched when she left home for the first time, as a child at the start of the war. She had meant to make herself a sandwich before she left the pub, but she heard Aunt Ida moving around in her room as she came downstairs and didn't want to face further questions, so she crept out with her case without making a packed lunch or saying goodbye.

As the train steamed out of the city, children knelt on seats, pressing their noses to the windows. There was little to see as they rattled along the line overlooking the increasingly suburban streets of west London, still pockmarked with bombed-out houses. Here and there she noticed rows of prefab single-storey houses, quickly erected for families who'd lost their homes in the Blitz. They look like toytown from up here, Ruby thought, looking down on the cream and white buildings with their uniform green paintwork on windows and doors. The gardens were neat, bordered with straight paths and wigwams of beanpoles. I could be happy in a little house like that. Me and Stevie don't need a big house. And anything's better than that horrible old pub.

She closed her eyes and tried to imagine having one of the neat little prefabs. She'd have green and white gingham curtains to match the outside and a neat kitchen with shining saucepans. Aunt Ida's kitchen was stacked with chipped enamel pans and burnt roasting tins, all beginning to rust. For one so keen on her personal appearance, always in a smart dress, always painting her nails, her housekeeping standards were surprisingly poor. There was no weekly wash like there had been in Mrs Honey's home. A bundle of sheets and shirts was only sent to the laundry once a month and Ruby had learnt from the start to wash her smalls herself in the little sink in her bedroom.

The deep kitchen sink was always filled with dirty cups and plates waiting for closing time and the wooden draining board was slimy with poorly rinsed glasses. The window looked out on a grim yard filled with dustbins, edged by a brick wall topped with broken glass, where a buddleia had sprouted and struggled to survive. No climbing roses and well-tended flowerbeds here. There were dead flies on the windowsill behind the sink and the grimy net curtain sagged from a drooping wire, tangled up in a sticky insect-strewn flypaper dangling from the window frame. In that dingy room, where silverfish darted down crevices, she could feel the domestic skills she'd learnt all those years ago from Mrs Honey in her warm, welcoming kitchen drifting away, unused, unappreciated. But one day she'd revive them, baking apple pies and simmering stews for Stevie and their well-scrubbed, well-behaved rosy children. And maybe they could be joined by his other children too and they'd all play together, like one big happy family.

With the trundling of the train and the surrounding chatter of families, and feeling the effect of her early start, Ruby began to doze off. She was nearly asleep when she felt something touching her knee. In her half-awake state, she thought she was being caressed by Stevie, but as she opened her eyes she saw a little girl gazing at her. Her curly blonde hair was swept up on either side of her head with pink hairslides in the shape of rabbits.

She smiled with pink gums and Ruby realised that her top front teeth had recently fallen out. 'I like your dreth,' she lisped, looking down at the flowery pattern.

'And I like yours too,' Ruby said. The child was wearing a plain blue dress with a white collar. 'And I really like your buttons. They're very special. Did your mummy knit your woolly for you?' Her pink cardigan bore buttons shaped like white daisies with a yellow centre. The girl shook her head vigorously, making her curls bounce. 'No, Nanny made it.' She turned and pointed. 'Over there.'

Ruby looked to see an older woman with an indulgent smile, watching them both. 'Push her away, if she's bothering you,' she said.

'It's alright,' Ruby said, 'she's very sweet.' She was. She was very sweet. Maybe one day, I'll have a little girl like this. I'd like girls, more than one. I'd brush their hair and plait it, just like my mother did once.

'What's your name?' the little girl asked.

'I'm Ruby. What's yours?'

'Barbwa.'

'Do you mean Barbara?'

'Yeth. Barbwa.'

'Well, Barbara, that's a lovely name.' It is, isn't it, Ruby thought. And my little girls will have first names and middle names; beautiful names because I am going to have beautiful children with Stevie.

And then she noticed that while the child had been resting her hands on Ruby's knee, her Fry's Five Boys chocolate bar, partially stripped of its wrapping, was melting in her chubby fingers and smearing Ruby's dress. 'Oh dear,' Ruby said, lifting up the child's hands and hastily wiping her skirt with her clean hankie. 'You'd better go back to your seat now. Ask your nanny to clean you up.'

Barbara looked shocked and almost began to cry as she tottered across the aisle to her grandmother. And looking around, Ruby began to realise that nearly every child in the long, crowded compartment, damp with rain-soaked clothes and hair, was already less tidy than when they had boarded the train. Chocolate was smeared around mouths and chins, noses ran and some children had tear-stained cheeks. Mothers and fathers looked more resigned and weary than at the start of their journey. 'How much longer?' was etched on all their faces as their little ones wailed and kicked and gobbled up everything to hand.

Ruby vowed not to make friends with any more children for the rest of the trip. Then shut her eyes to imagine a pristine house with her spotlessly clean daughters in white dresses with freshly plaited hair.

Chapter 48

November 2004

Little Monkey

Billie studies the old photograph, taken shortly after the school was evacuated to Devon at the start of the war. Some children looked serious, others smiled. Her father looked mischievous all those years ago and the young Joan already displayed the cheekbones and thick head of hair she'd have all her life. 'You'd never think all these kids had just been torn from their homes and families because of the war,' she said. 'Most of them look quite happy here.'

Joan takes the picture from her and frowns. 'This was taken very soon after we'd left home. In the first couple of weeks, I think. Lots were homesick in the beginning. Others thought it was quite an adventure. I think your dad thought it was going to be a bit of a laugh till he got into trouble.'

'You said something before about him not being with a nice family? On a farm?'

'Yes, it was just outside the village, so he could walk to school and come over to where I was staying with Ruby. He thought it would be fun at first, all working with animals and not having to mind his Ps and Qs, but it didn't quite work out like that.'

Billie has called in on Joan after another frustrating visit to the nursing home, where her father has made little progress since she last saw him. 'Well, tell me more, Joan. Dad's never talked about his childhood. The most we ever heard from him was his jokes about how young he was when he learnt to smoke. Oh, and picking up scrap metal on bombsites. I think he said Grandad was always looking out for parts. I feel it might help to know more about his past if I'm to understand what's bothering him. Whatever it is, I'm sure it's holding back his recovery.'

Joan switches on the kettle and fetches two mugs from the kitchen cupboard. 'I don't really know all the details of what happened. I just heard about it afterwards and your dad never talked about it.

'I remember it was our first Christmas after we evacuated. Your dad was coming to have dinner with us. He turned up at the last minute, looking very grubby and tired. He was famished as well. And then, when I helped him out of his wet things, his shirt slipped up and I suddenly saw these terrible red welts on his back. We reckoned that blasted farmer had given him a right walloping.'

Billie puts her hand over her mouth. 'But that's just awful. Poor Dad. Didn't anyone ever do anything about it?'

'I think Mrs Honey said she'd have a word with the farmer's wife. But he didn't want her interfering. Thought it would cause more trouble if she did. Said something about how it was all his fault as he'd had a bit of a barney with their son, I think.'

'But even so, that's just terrible.'

'I know it was. But you've got to remember, in those days it was quite normal for parents to smack their kids and it certainly wasn't unheard of for them to beat their children too, especially the boys. And in school, the teachers used a cane all the time. I know it's not the done thing now, but those were very different times back then.'

'But to leave noticeable marks on his back, the beating must have been really vicious.'

Joan shakes her head with regret. 'We reckoned the farmer used a belt. Nasty piece of work, he was.'

'But how could Dad put up with it? Was it just him there?'

'There was one other boy, Will, I think his name was, but he didn't seem to get in as much trouble. Your dad always was a bit of a monkey. Never could keep his mouth shut.'

'I can see that just looking at this photograph. He looks very cheeky.'

'Well, I expect that was half the trouble. He probably gave as good as he got. And in the end, he just couldn't take any more.' Joan pours the freshly made tea, then cuts slices of gingerbread. 'Have some, go on. I got it from the Women's Institute stall down the market. They always have good cakes.' Billie takes a piece while Joan continues, 'Anyway, he ran away from that farm, just before the snow came that winter. Lucky he went when he did, because we were snowed in for days on end, down in Devon.'

'I remember Dad telling us once about the bad winters when he was a kid. Me and Keith were complaining we never got much snow and Dad said we'd soon stop moaning if we had drifts like he'd seen when he was a boy.'

'It was certainly a winter to remember alright. But we were fine because Mrs Honey was so well organised. We never went without. There was always plenty to eat and the cottage was warm and cosy. Down there, we could almost forget there was a war, it was so safe and quiet.'

'So what happened to Dad? Where did he go?'

'He somehow got himself back to London. Hitched a lift just before the snow blew in. Your grandad wasn't best pleased at first. Tore Stevie off a strip for running away and not telling anyone. But then, when he realised what had been going on and just how badly he'd been treated, he kicked up a fuss and got the other boy, Will, taken away from that farm as well. I doubt they'd have been allowed to have any more evacuees after that.'

'Those poor little boys. How cruel. Just think, first he gets sent away from home and then he gets ill-treated like that. It doesn't bear thinking about.'

Joan sips her tea for a moment. 'I think it was probably worse than we ever knew, if the marks I saw were anything to go by. My dad told me, long after the war, that they took Stevie to the doctor the day after he came home. He suspected Stevie had a cracked rib and he also confirmed that he'd been thrashed with a belt. Nasty business.'

'Did Dad ever talk about it? Later on, I mean.'

'Not to me. But then he's always had this way of covering things up, hasn't he? Joking and swaggering, as if it's nothing to him. That's Stevie for you. During the Blitz he was apparently always out and about on his bike, running messages for the ARP. Mum said she worried about him but he always told her it was *Boy's Own* stuff. And he was finding scrap Dad could use as well. Mind you, I reckon he probably found a bob or two for himself, if the looters had left anything, that is. He thought it was all a big adventure.

Billie breaks her cake into little pieces and pops a bit in her mouth. 'Mmm, I know what you mean, he does make light of things. And talking of covering up, when we were kids, we always teased him for keeping his vest on in the garden and on the beach. But after what you've said, I'm wondering if he did that because of the marks you mentioned.'

'What, scars you mean? I suppose that's possible. But I've not seen him undressed since he was a kid.' Joan pauses, 'Scars can fade given time, but he might still have some faint marks. Though when you think about it, experiences like that, at a young age, likely scar the mind as well as the body. And maybe that's the kind of scar that never quite goes away.'

'Poor Dad. I'm beginning to see that life hasn't been that easy for him. As kids, we always thought he was so much fun, compared to Mum. Him with his racing, his fast cars and all that. But knowing what he saw out in Palestine and now this, I think he had quite a hard time of it really.'

'He always was good at putting a brave face on things,' Joan murmurs, 'but maybe now… now that he's knocked back, he can't keep it buried any longer.'

Rain, rain, go away,
Come again on April day,
Rain, rain, go to Spain,
Never show your face again!

Chapter 49

14 August 1952

Hill Starts

'Oh, Stevie, I've missed you so much,' Ruby squealed as she ran from the train and into his open arms.

He kissed her briefly, looking around as if he was worried he might see someone he knew on the platform. 'Come on. Got the car waiting for us,' he said. 'New one. Austin A40. Thought we'd need a decent car, going up and down those hills.' He slipped his arm around her shoulders and took her case with his free hand. Light rain was falling again as they left the station and she pulled her raincoat up over her head.

The car was very smart. Black with matching leather seats. As soon as Stevie had set her case on the back seat and sat in the car beside her, he leant over to kiss her properly and slid his hand under her skirt, running his fingers along the tops of her stockings. She soaked in the smell of his Imperial Leather shaving soap overlaid with Player's cigarettes and the scent of new leather seats. 'Careful, someone might see,' she said, breaking away from his kiss and peering through the window.

He laughed. 'Don't worry. Most of the passengers off your train are waiting for the bus, poor sods.' He was right. Very few of the travellers from London had cars waiting for them. The rain started falling more heavily and the car windows misted over. He pulled his hand away from her thigh. 'Better get going, before it gets any worse. We've got a bit of a drive ahead of us. About sixty miles, I reckon.'

Ruby regretted not using the toilet on the train, but she hadn't liked to wind her way down the corridor past all the sticky-fingered children. 'If it's that far, I think I'd better dash back inside quickly and spend a penny. Won't be a minute.' She opened the car door just as he was starting the engine and ran to the Ladies' waiting room in the station. Fumbling in her handbag for a penny, she felt herself trembling. Here she was at last, about to set off with Stevie and spend tonight and the next three nights with him in a hotel. After visiting the cold toilet, strewn with crumpled sheets of paper, she quickly rinsed her hands, checked her hair and lipstick in the speckled mirror, then pulled her coat over her head and ran back out through the rain to the car.

Stevie was sounding impatient. 'It's already half past three. We want to get there in time for dinner. We need to get going.'

'But if you go at sixty miles an hour we'll easily be there by teatime.'

'This car's a goer and I'll put my foot down, Rube, but the hills are gonna slow us down. You wait and see. Steepest hill in Britain we're going on. Got a gradient of 1 in 4 in places, it has.'

Ruby wasn't paying much attention. She was thinking whether she should change for dinner. What would be best? Stay in her creased dress or wear her skirt and blouse? Her dress was smarter, but it was rather crumpled after the train journey. Luckily the melted chocolate didn't really show as the pattern with its huge roses was so busy and vibrant. Maybe she should slip out of it and hang it up for a while. Some hotels have a maid service to press clothes, don't they? Or perhaps it would be a more modern hotel with an iron and ironing board in the room?

Stevie was still enthusing about the route they were taking. 'It's got really tight hairpin bends and climbs 1,300 feet in less than two miles.'

Then Ruby heard this last bit and burst out laughing. 'Honestly, Stevie, anyone would think you were more excited about driving your blessed new car than spending the weekend with me!'

He took his left hand off the steering wheel and caressed her thigh. 'Two thrills in one weekend. Aren't I a lucky boy?'

And he was right. It was a thrilling ride. Every time the car climbed the next section of hill, there was a bend and then a bit more to climb, until finally they had left Porlock village and were high up on the wilds of Exmoor. There were deep purple valleys on the left and to the right the road ran along the clifftop, with a sheer drop down to the dark green sea. Wild brown ponies were grazing among the heather, their manes blowing in the wind coming in from the sea. 'It's just beautiful,' Ruby gasped. Misty clouds hovered over the moorland and it felt as if they had floated right up to the top of the earth and into heaven. 'I'm so glad we've come back to Devon. Maybe we'll have time to go and visit the village where we went in the war. I'd love to see the cottage again and maybe take some flowers to Mrs Honey's grave.'

Stevie seemed not to hear her. 'Well, she didn't stall,' he said. 'We dropped down to nearly ten miles an hour at one point and I didn't fancy doing a hill start, I can tell you.' He drove on for a short while, rain spattering the windscreen, then said, 'You know what, I think we should pull over for a bit. Now I'm the one who needs to spend a penny.' He found a barren patch to the side of the road and turned the car towards the empty moors. Then he leant over and kissed her cheek. 'Won't be a sec, then I'll come back and get you in the mood, eh?'

Ruby watched him walk towards some scrubby bush. Maybe she'd suggest visiting Mrs Honey's old cottage again later, when he wasn't concentrating on driving. He ducked out of sight for a minute and then he was walking back to her with a big grin and she felt herself quiver down there. He always had that effect on her.

Chapter 50

14 August 1952

Is This It?

'Terrible summer we're having. What a pity your first visit to Lynmouth should be in such bad weather,' the receptionist said as Stevie signed the hotel register in the name of Mr and Mrs Matthews. 'And they say it's going to keep on raining.'

'Yeah well, we won't mind too much. It's our honeymoon, see.' And he turned to Ruby and winked, making her blush. She looked away, pretending to admire the plush maroon sofas in the spacious carpeted lobby. It being the height of summer, instead of a flickering fire in the marble fireplace, there was a large urn filled with erect white and pink gladioli.

'Then we must offer you our congratulations, sir and madam. We're delighted you've chosen to stay with us at the Tors Hotel.'

'Did you have to say that?' Ruby hissed at him as they followed the porter carrying the cases to their room.

'Well, why not? You never know, they might send up a free bottle of champagne.' He put his arm round her waist and squeezed her tight as they walked up the wide staircase.

Stevie tipped the porter who had carried their cases, then slipped out of his mackintosh and jacket while she walked over to the large French windows, opening onto a small balcony. Rain was blurring the view, but she could look down upon the whole town of Lynmouth curved around the harbour, nestled against towering cliffs, thick with trees. At the front, a row of houses with fretted wooden balconies reminded her of pictures of Tyrolean chalets.

Stevie rushed up behind her and threw her down on the bed, pushing her full skirt out of the way with his eager hands. 'I can't wait no longer, Rube,' he panted, pulling at her knickers and then his belt.

It was over so quickly, then he rolled over, lit a cigarette and lay back, saying, 'Won't be so quick next time, Rube. We'll take our time, eh?'

Ruby straightened her clothes, picked up her knickers and walked to the adjoining bathroom. Stevie had made a point of saying he'd booked a room with its own bathroom: 'We could have a bath together, Ruby. How about that, eh?'

She shut the door, then sat down on the toilet and mopped herself with toilet paper; soft paper it was, not the crisp shiny Izal Aunt Ida bought for the pub, which most people still used. There was no blood, just smeary stickiness. Her virginity must have been taken by his insistent probing fingers when they'd grappled with each other's bodies in dark doorways and alleyways over the last few months. But now they'd finally 'done it' properly, she couldn't help wondering: was this it? Was this what it was all about? She'd been so ready for him, so keen for the full lovemaking experience, but she felt empty, let down and somewhat disappointed.

She remembered how the girls in the staffroom at Bodgers teased her for her inexperience, sniggering behind their hands and saying, 'Ooh, she doesn't know what she's missing, does she? A bit of how's-yer-father does you good,' and then they would rock from side to side in waves of giggles. But Aunt Ida always presented a bleak alternative view, saying, 'Marriage is no bed of roses for women, mark my words.' She wondered if Uncle Reg had ever made love to his critical wife; they'd never had children. Then when Ruby picked up her lovely new silk knickers, she realised the lace was snagged and loose. She'd have to stitch it when she could.

She ran some warm water into the basin and unwrapped the little bar of scented soap on the glass shelf below the mirror. New soap too, not a cracked bar of brownish green coal tar used by many dirty hands before hers. She washed between her legs, then dried herself on a fresh white towel. Such luxury. Folded white towels. There was a bath towel, hand towel and a flannel, one for each of them, not just a skimpy threadbare striped towel like she had in her bedroom back at the pub. She held the towel to her face and breathed the smell of well-washed laundry and fresh air.

'Come on,' she heard Stevie calling from the bedroom. 'Let's go down and get a drink at the bar before dinner.'

Ruby joined him with a smile. 'I just need to touch up my lipstick and brush my hair.'

'You're gorgeous enough as it is,' he said, nuzzling her neck.

She gently pushed him away and sat down at the dressing table. In the mirror, she could see he didn't take his eyes off her. He must really love me, she thought, and smiled to herself.

Downstairs, he steered her towards a corner table in the lounge bar and clicked his fingers so the waiter came over to them immediately. 'Two gin and tonics,' Stevie said, without asking Ruby what she'd like to drink. She might have asked for a port and lemon, which was Aunt Ida's tipple, but maybe that wasn't sophisticated enough a drink for a lovely hotel like this. She hadn't ever drunk gin before, but Stevie knows what I like, she thought, so I'm sure it will be lovely.

The waiter returned with a tray bearing two cut-glass tumblers clinking with ice, two little bottles of Schweppes Indian Tonic Water and a small dish of Twiglets. As he left, Ruby leant forward to pour the tonic into her glass, but Stevie stopped her using the whole bottle. 'Don't drown it, love. You wanna taste the gin.' They clinked glasses and then sipped. It was strong and slightly bitter, making her throat tingle as it slithered down. But it was nice, all the same.

By the time they went through to the dining room, Ruby was feeling a little tipsy. She'd drunk two gins – doubles, Stevie called them. It made her giggle as she looked at the menu. 'Better order the fish,' Stevie said, 'as we're right on the coast here.' So she agreed and they both had the most expensive fish on the menu, the Dover sole. Stevie decided they should drink wine with their meal too. Ruby couldn't remember what he ordered but it wasn't really to her taste, even though she drank it to show her appreciation. It was sour, not at all like any wine she'd ever drunk before, but then she'd only ever had ginger wine or sweet sherry from time to time, never real wine poured by a smart waiter dressed in a black waistcoat over his crisp white shirt and striped trousers.

After the main course, Stevie tried to persuade her to have a dessert. 'You've got to have strawberries and clotted cream, Rube. Come all this way and not have clotted cream?'

'I'm feeling rather full and I've had such a lot to drink. But go on, you have pudding and I'll watch.'

But Stevie ordered for both of them anyway, so a big dollop of thick crusty yellow cream was placed in front of her, with a pile of glistening strawberries. It was delicious, but it was also making her feel so very full.

'I'll help you up the stairs,' Stevie said as they left the table and she wobbled getting up from her chair. He put his arm around her and guided her out of the dining room towards the staircase.

It's such an effort, Ruby thought, going up one step at a time. I feel wobbly and giggly all together. I'll have to flop on the bed when we get to our room. Maybe drink some water, then I'll be alright.

But when they reached the room and Stevie opened the door, he crowed with delight. 'There, told you. They've done us proud.' In a silver ice bucket there was a full bottle of champagne. Stevie opened it immediately and poured it into the two champagne saucers standing on the tray. 'Congratulations, Ruby! Here's to us!'

Stevie downed his glass almost in one, while Ruby sipped. It was quite refreshing, although the bubbles tickled her throat and nose. Stevie topped up her glass and then clinked it against his and said, 'Ain't this the life and no mistake?' and Ruby felt obliged to swig her champagne to share in his happiness.

Ruby's head pounded. Her mouth was dry. But how could she be thirsty, when she'd drunk so much last night? Opening her eyes, she saw the grey light of morning. It must still be raining as no sun streamed in through the gap in the curtains. She rolled to the edge of the bed and it was then that she realised she was completely naked. She wasn't wearing her rose-printed dress, her stockings or her silk knickers. She hadn't changed into her new satin nightdress either.

Stevie had his back to her and was snoring. He wasn't wearing pyjamas and she could see the livid scars that criss-crossed his shoulders. She winced at the thought of how he was beaten when he was only a boy. She wanted to stroke the weals, make them melt away, make all the bad memories of his ill-treatment disappear, like she always could when he sank into the bad times. But she didn't want to wake him.

She slipped from the bed and into the bathroom. As she sat down on the toilet and started to pass water she felt a burning pain. That whole area, and the innermost part of her thighs, felt bruised and sore. We must have done it again last night. And Stevie must have undressed me. But I don't remember. I can't remember anything after we left the dining room.

She opened the bathroom door a crack and peeked out. Stevie was still fast asleep. It was only seven o'clock. There was plenty of time for a bath; she could luxuriate with a plentiful supply of hot water, scented soap and those thick towels. At the pub there was never a constant supply of hot water. They boiled a kettle for washing up and usually had a daily strip wash. Aunt Ida only allowed a bath once a week and that was in just a couple of inches of tepid water supplied by the wall-mounted gas geyser. But here she could run hot water straight from the tap and have a deep bath right up to her neck. It was heaven.

Ruby was lying in the bath with her eyes closed, the back of her head resting on a folded hand towel, when Stevie burst in. 'I need a slash,' he said. 'Keep your eyes shut.' She heard him piss and flush the toilet and then, without asking, he stepped with a big splash into the bath. 'Budge up,' he said, fumbling between her legs. 'Oops, where's the soap gone now?'

She laughed along with him, but she couldn't stop herself thinking it would be nice to wait until she'd at least had a cup of tea before it started all over again. There was no stopping him though once they were both out of the bath and she winced as he forced himself inside her, making her kneel, wet and slippery, on the bath mat. 'Right, that's enough,' she said when he'd finished. 'No more. I'm getting dressed now.'

'You might change your mind after you've had a big fry-up,' he shouted back as she left the bathroom, wrapped in a big towel. 'A couple of sausages will get you going all over again, I bet.'

Ruby rubbed herself dry, wondering if all men were like this. Was this why Maureen had fallen for three kids in such quick succession? She pulled back the curtains. There was still no sun, just heavy rain. She'd have to wear her mac again, but at least her shoes were still dry. 'Look outside the door,' Stevie called. 'Should be a tray of tea for us out there.'

She tucked the towel tightly around her chest and opened the door, but as she bent to lift the tray, the towel fell, just as the couple opposite left their room. Ruby ducked back inside quickly. She hoped they hadn't noticed. Nobody had ever seen her adult naked body before, not until now and last night.

She quickly pulled on her underwear, skirt and blouse, then fetched the tray. No one saw her this time, but then there was nothing worth seeing now. She looked very plain in her ordinary clothes, without make-up.

Sipping the hot tea, she sat and looked at the damp and misty view from the French windows. The sea was grey, the wooded hills were dark grey and the town was grey and white. If it wasn't raining so heavily it would be wonderful. But it is wonderful here, she told herself. You're here with Stevie. It's what you've dreamed of. It's what you've always wanted, ever since you were a little girl when you were sent away to Devon and began to fall in love with him.

And then next minute, Stevie was standing behind her, a towel around his waist, leaning forward and fondling her breast. His towel dropped and she could feel his erection against her shoulder. He turned her head round and pushed his penis into her mouth, making her gag and pull away.

'Stop it, Stevie. I didn't say you could do that. It's not nice.'

'Come on, love. Don't be such a prude. You weren't so fussy last night.'

'What do you mean? I can't remember what happened last night.'

He laughed and turned away from her to pick up his clothes. 'You loved it. Right little raver, you were. Get you on the champers and there's no stopping you.'

She felt tears welling up. 'I don't remember anything. Are you saying you did that thing you did just now last night?'

He looked up as he pulled on his trousers. 'Ruby love, don't go getting upset. Everybody does it.' He grinned. 'There's other things I could teach you an' all, gel, things that'll get you really hot and bothered.' He finished buttoning his shirt. 'You're my little raver, Ruby, you are.' He bent to kiss her neck. 'I love my little raver, I do, more than ever.'

She blinked away her tears, smiled in the mirror and nodded. He loved her. He'd loved her before he'd ever taken her to bed and he loved her even more now. That made it alright then, whatever had happened last night. She was a real woman at last, giving her man what he needed and wanted.

'Right, I'm ready for a full English, aren't you, love? A big breakfast'll see you right, then we'll explore the town.' He held the bedroom door open and waved her through, bowing as she swept past him.

Just like a real gent, thought Ruby.

Chapter 51

November 2004

Cuttings and Cake

Will he ever be able to come home again, Billie wonders. Her father is shuffling with a walking frame from armchair to bed and from his bathroom to the care home's sitting room, but she can't see him climbing stairs, running a bath or cooking his own supper ever again. His hands tremble when he holds a cup, so she can't imagine how he could lift a boiling kettle and make his own hot drinks or even a sandwich.

She's talked to Keith and Pam and they agreed with her decision. It is best if he stays in Chigwell Care, where meals, entertainment and personal care can be provided. But was it the right thing to do? Does having power of attorney mean she could insist? Is this what he would have wanted?

She tries to remember the conversations she'd had with Mum on this very topic. 'Your dad and me, we wouldn't want you wearing yourselves out running over here all the time. You've got your own life to lead and we wouldn't want to interfere with that. We'd both be happier in a home when the time comes.'

And now that time has come and her father has settled into the home and seems happy, or at least as happy as he can appear to be with his still-limited speech and movement. Maybe inside he's seething with rage, wishing he could pick up that darned walking frame and throw it at me, Billie worries.

Keith and Pam had also left it to her to decide what personal possessions should be taken to the home. And so she has begun the task of sorting through a lifetime's gathered bits and bobs at her parents' house, where they lived and raised their children over more than fifty years. The birthday and Mother's Day cards her mother had always saved, the multiple tea sets that were never used, the old electrical plugs and bits of wire that 'might come in handy' in the garage and garden shed. Did everyone have such a collection of unnecessary, unidentified junk? Billie resolves to clear her own cluttered cupboards when she has a spare moment.

In the cubbyhole under the stairs, alongside the outmoded Ewbank carpet sweeper, which her mother had insisted on keeping despite the purchase of a Hoover (because electrics can go wrong), she finds a moth-eaten toy dog on wheels. It had helped her and her siblings learn to walk years ago, then her own children too, when they visited their grandparents as toddlers. Stained and threadbare, it has to be thrown out.

Upstairs, Billie packs up her father's good trousers and shirts. Those that are fraying and stained, she throws aside. He won't be gardening again. His golfing sweaters in their yellows, turquoise and raspberry pink she saves. She doesn't know whether he'll ever make it back to the golf course, but she loves seeing him in a bright colour, even though she'd always teased him about his love of clashing colours. She picks out his favourite ties from the selection hanging on the rail inside the door, plus a black one in case he has to attend a funeral. And tucked away at the back of the wardrobe, which smells of mothballs overlaid with her father's Imperial Leather shaving soap, she finds an old cardboard box. The black and orange Bear Brand box displays a friendly teddy bear gleefully waving a top hat. Bear Brand fine gauge stockings, it proclaims. Billie pulls it out, thinking, gosh how old is that? I've never heard of that make before. Mum must have bought those stockings years and years ago.

The box is battered and scuffed at the corners, but still sturdy and it's packed with photographs, postcards and scraps of newspaper. Billie tips them out on the bed and begins sorting through. These must be the rejects, she decides, after Mum stuck the best ones in the album. Tiny snaps, going back to her childhood, their first birthday cards too. And then at the bottom, she finds two postcards written by Dad, addressed to Mum, with cheery messages and love to her and 'the kids'. Both are dated around the middle of August 1952, about a week apart. One depicts the big pier full of amusements at Weston-super-Mare, while the other is a picture of the marketplace in Taunton.

Billie puts these to one side, then begins to examine the folded newspaper cuttings tucked underneath. Yellowed with age, they are all from around the same period of time, torn from national papers and also the *Bristol Evening Post* and the *Western Morning News*. And all carry dramatic headlines and shocking photographs reporting a disastrous flood in Lynmouth, in north Devon, on 15 August 1952. She glances through them, idly curious as to why they are here. Did Dad know someone who was affected by the flood there? Or maybe Mum had kept them for some reason?

When Billie arrives at the care home that afternoon, she goes straight to her father's room to put away the clean shirts and trousers she's brought. He is sitting in an armchair facing the television, with his eyes closed, but she's sure he isn't really asleep and so she says, 'Dad, I've brought some fresh clothes in for you. I'll take your others home to wash. I know they do all the laundry here, but I like to do what I can to help. And it means you're sure to get your own things back, not someone else's.'

He slowly raises his head to look at her. His watery eyes seem to be a paler, cloudier blue than they used to. A mumbled sound is the only acknowledgement she receives. She pulls a chair closer to him and sits down. 'I can stay here in your room if you like. We don't have to go in the main sitting room. I expect the tea trolley will come round soon. It usually turns up about three thirty, doesn't it? And what are you watching? You don't really like *A Place in the Sun*, do you?'

Billie chatters inanely for a minute or two, getting very little response. It's such hard work, she thinks. No wonder some people don't visit their relatives very often. She knows she is one of the few regular visitors, because she sees the names in the register that she signs every time she comes. She hasn't liked to ask him any more about Palestine since her visit to his old commanding officer. She's afraid he will react badly to any questions about that time.

And then she remembers the stocking box. She'd popped it into the holdall she'd used for the clothes. 'Oh, and I nearly forgot, Dad, I found another pile of old photos when I was clearing the wardrobe at home.' She takes the lid off the box and realises she hasn't put everything back the way she'd found it and the newspaper cuttings are on top. She'd folded them up again, but the first one displays the headline quite clearly. She picks it up and begins opening it out. 'Look, Dad, this is interesting. I wanted to ask you why you or Mum kept it all these years.'

And at that point, as she is unfolding the piece of paper to place it flat on his tray table, he finds the strength to swipe at it, tearing it down the middle, so she's left staring at him in astonishment, listening to his distressed cries.

'I'm so sorry, Dad. I didn't mean to upset you.' She puts the pieces of paper back in the box and hides them beneath the lid. 'Everything I do seems to upset you and I just can't work out why.'

Billie hugs her father, who is trembling and moaning. At that point a carer stops outside his room with the tea trolley. 'Is Mr Stevens alright?' she asks. 'Has something happened?'

'No, he's just a little upset, that's all. I brought in some old photos. Maybe I shouldn't have done that.'

'Well, I'll leave him his tea and a cake anyway. He usually likes his cakes. That'll make things seem better.'

Billie looks at the piece of iced chocolate cake. It looks tempting. Her stomach rumbles. But no, she mustn't take it. She's trying not to comfort-eat. His shaking hand reaches for his cup and she gently closes his fingers around the handle. 'I'll let you have a quiet rest now, Dad. I'll be back tomorrow and hope you feel better then.' But as she walks to her car, the realisation hits her: he isn't going to get better. And whatever it is that's unsettling him, it is still beyond her reach. She cannot see how she is ever going to help him.

Little Betty Blue
Lost her holiday shoe,
What can little Betty do?
Give her another
To match the other,
And then she may walk out in two.

Chapter 52

15 August 1952

Showers and a Show

Ruby didn't like to tell him she didn't want to go out that evening, although she was bothered about ruining her new shoes. If it hadn't been raining so much she would have enjoyed going out again. She liked walking and the river and the surrounding hills were so beautiful, but the blessed rain just wouldn't stop.

Earlier in the day she'd been soaked when they were waiting to go in the Victorian cliff railway up to the little town of Lynton, right at the top of the hill. 'Do we really have to go on this?' she said as they stood in line with other holidaymakers. She was wearing her raincoat and holding an umbrella, but her hair was getting flattened under the patterned scarf she had tied under her chin. She refused to wear a plastic rain hood, like many of the women in the queue; they looked so dowdy – but at least their hair was dry. Maybe she'd have to swallow her pride and wear one after all.

'Course we're going on it,' Stevie said, pulling his coat collar forward to light another cigarette with his Zippo. 'This railway's famous. Just like Lynmouth's famous. It's known as the Honeymooner's Paradise, I'll have you know. How about that, eh, Rube?' He bent down to kiss her under the shelter of her brolly and she hoped none of the other people queuing for the funicular railway heard his remark. She didn't want anyone, particularly the men, looking at her with knowing smiles, suggesting that they could imagine exactly what she had experienced over the last few hours.

As they rode to the top of the hill in the railway carriage, she did however admire the extensive view through the rain. The little horseshoe-shaped harbour with its fleet of fishing and sailing boats was indeed picturesque and she loved the cottages climbing the slopes of the wooded hills surrounding the village.

After wandering around the town at the top of the steep hill, they walked back down the winding paths through the sloping hillside gardens for a fish and chip lunch. 'You can't get fresher than this, can you?' Stevie said as they were presented with huge plates of crisply battered haddock. 'Better than you get round your way, by your aunt's pub, I bet.'

The food was good, but Ruby still felt full from the fried breakfast Stevie had encouraged her to order. She pushed half her chips onto his plate and when he tried to persuade her to take a large gherkin, she shook her head. He stabbed one with his fork and slid the whole pickle suggestively in and out of his mouth, saying, 'Sure you won't change your mind?' She knew what he was implying, but it made her feel uncomfortable and she couldn't finish the rest of her food.

After lunch they wandered arm in arm through the side streets, where the shops were full of souvenirs. Sheepskins, woollen scarves and coloured postcards filled the windows. 'Here,' said Stevie, 'this one does Devon Violet scent. That's what you need, Ruby. Then every time you smell it, you'll remember all about our time here.' And he insisted on buying a little bottle with a gold top and a picture of a nodding violet. 'It's just like you, a shy little flower.' That made her blush, but she liked him saying that. She liked him even more when he also bought her a hankie embroidered with a violet to match. Really, Stevie could be so sweet and thoughtful.

She made up her mind not to complain about the rain. She told herself she was very lucky. Stevie had paid for her train ticket all the way from Stepney, the overland train as well as the Underground. He had given her money for lunch on the train from Paddington to the West Country and then he had met her at Weston-super-Mare in his brand-new car. No, she mustn't complain. After all, when had she ever experienced such luxury before? She would never be able to afford a suite in a plush hotel and the Tors Hotel was certainly plush. Four nights they'd have altogether and the days were almost as passionate as the nights.

'Are you ready yet, darling?' he called. 'The concert party starts at half past five. We need to go in a minute.'

'Just coming,' she called back, checking her hair in the bathroom mirror. It was dry now, but still crumpled from that last tumble on the bed after their cream tea in the hotel lounge downstairs. She patted her dark curls, then reapplied her red lipstick. Her lips felt bruised from all the vigorous kissing, but not as bruised as her down-below parts. Would he always be this enthusiastic? She had no way of judging. Stevie was her first lover and as well as his wife, who she was sure no longer loved him or understood him, she guessed he must have experienced other women before he married.

A crack of thunder made her turn to look out through the bathroom window. Another rainstorm was teeming from the dark sky. She sighed. It was no good, she would have to tie that unflattering rain hood over her hair again. The stockings that she had hung on the towel rail to dry were still damp, so she put on a fresh pair. Then, taking the scrunched newspaper out of her wet shoes, she squeezed her feet back into them. They hadn't eased yet, even though the girl in Lilley & Skinner had said they were sure to stretch. Her toes were pinched and her heels were red and sore. They'd be sure to blister before the night was out from the chafing wet leather and all the walking.

Throwing open the bathroom door, she fixed a smile on her face so that before she had to wrap herself once more in a raincoat and plastic hood, he would see how pretty she was, however damp and bedraggled she looked by the time the evening was over. She was just about to open the little bottle of violet scent, but then she saw him. He was smoking another cigarette and staring out of the window with that moody expression he wore so often, where he seemed to slip away from the present day and into a miserable trough in the past.

'I'm ready now, darling,' she cried. 'All yours for an evening of adventure.' She picked up her damp raincoat and grabbed his hand. 'I know, let's sing all the way as we run to the Pavilion. Come on, let's sing "Singin' in the Rain".' Then he laughed, as she knew he would, and she felt sure she would always be able to make his dark clouds go away.

Chapter 53

15 August 1952

What a Night

'If I knew you were comin', I'd have baked a cake,' trilled the singer on the stage of the Lynmouth Pavilion, accompanied by three girls in full-skirted dresses wearing gingham aprons, swinging baskets as they sang and danced. Ruby's head nodded in time to the familiar tune, which she'd heard several Sundays running on the *Billy Cotton Band Show* on the radio. Aunt Ida loved Billy Cotton and always repeated the catchphrase that opened the programme: 'Wakey Wake... aaaaay!' she'd screech as the pub prepared for Sunday lunchtime service.

But when the Pavilion concert hall lights suddenly flickered and died, Ruby grabbed Stevie's hand. 'Oh no, I was enjoying that,' she said. 'What's happening?' It was the second half of the programme. They'd seen the pierrot, the juggler and the cheeky chappy, and despite the damp fug of the auditorium, filled with rain-soaked holidaymakers, were enjoying the entertainment and trying to forget how rain had poured all day long.

Torchlight glimmered in the aisles and on the stage, where the manager appeared and announced, 'Due to the power cut, I'm afraid we cannot continue with our show tonight. Take care leaving, everybody. It's a wild night out there.'

'Never mind,' Stevie said. 'We'll get a drink at one of the pubs then head back. We don't mind an early night, eh?'

Ruby's blushes couldn't be seen in the dark, lit only by the beams of the usherettes' torches. She clung to Stevie's arm as the audience shuffled from their seats and wondered if any of them would guess they weren't really married, bound not by vows but by their love of each other.

As people streamed down the stairs and into the street, there seemed to be some commotion ahead of them. And when they reached the main entrance to the Pavilion, Ruby could see why. Not only was it still raining heavily, but the road was awash with water and couples were clinging to each other as they struggled to walk through the stream rushing down the street.

'However are we going to get back to the hotel?' she said, standing back in the shelter of the theatre's porch and peering at the dark water and the unlit street.

'It's not that bad,' Stevie said. 'Look at those ladies, all arm in arm. If they can do it, we can.' Seven female holidaymakers had linked arms and were striding through the water, heads down into the wind, screaming with laughter, as if their seaside paddle had turned into a rough voyage. 'Come on, Rube. This is the quickest way back. We'll forget the pub and have a nice drink in the lounge bar back at the hotel.'

He pulled her from the safety of the entrance and she stepped down into the water. It was well past her ankles and as she began to walk, it splashed up past her knees. The floodwater was cold, but the rainy air was clammy and humid. She pulled the belt of her mac tight and tucked her head into the side of Stevie's arm. After a minute or two of sloshing along the street, she noticed people heading up a lane to the right, away from the flooded road. 'Shouldn't we be following them and go that way?' she said, seeing how the group was soon free of the streaming water.

Stevie held her tight and kept plunging forwards. 'No, that's the wrong way. We've got to keep going straight ahead to get over the bridge. Come on, it won't take us very long.' So on they strode, getting wetter and wetter, while the flood seemed to be getting deeper all the while. Ruby could feel the cold water splashing up

her thighs, soaking her stockings and knickers. Her poor dress was
a wet rag, its petticoats clinging limply to her legs.

She told herself they would soon be back in the hotel, safe and
dry, and that this was nothing to be afraid of. It was only water,
after all. But it wasn't gentle like the ripple of waves washing across
a sandy beach on a summer's day, it was tremendously powerful, a
mighty force that pushed and pulled at her, and with every step she
was afraid she might topple and fall into its depths. If she hadn't
been anchored to Stevie's strong arm, she was sure she'd have lost
her balance.

Ahead of them she could see the ladies who had left the Pavilion
just before them, still arm in arm, but above the rushing sound of
water and the crashing thuds of thunder, Ruby thought she could
tell their shrieks of laughter were turning to screams of terror. They
appeared to be slowing as the churning water rushed towards them
and, all at once, the woman nearest the riverbank screamed and fell.
Her companions were still striding forwards. They tried to turn back,
arms locked together, the nearest hand outstretched towards her,
but in seconds she'd vanished, torn away from them by the flood.

Ruby clung to Stevie. 'Did you see that?' she cried. 'That poor
lady. She's gone. She was swept off her feet.'

'Don't stop. We can't do anything to help her. Come on, we've
got to keep going.' He pulled her away, his body bent into the
storm, forcing himself through the gushing water. All around them
there was shouting from nearby shops and houses as the flood rose.
People were leaning out of open windows and pulling others in
from the street. Then an ambulance entered the road. As it tried to
turn, a woman was washed past it. But just in time, she managed
to grab one of the wheels, and was helped up by the driver.

'We can't keep going on in this,' Ruby cried. 'Why don't we
see if we can shelter in one of the shops like everyone else?' But
Stevie had a tight grip on her arm and kept pulling her forwards.
'We're nearly there,' he shouted back above the sound of the raging

flood, the thunder and the ominous creaking of stressed timbers in the nearby buildings.

As they neared the bridge leading to their hotel, he pulled her even harder. 'Look,' he said, as lightning flashed. 'We can still get across the river. And then it's uphill all the way, right out of the flood. We'll be fine.' They pushed through the raging water and Stevie clutched the parapet of the bridge. 'See, it's not even flooded in the middle. Look, it'll get easier from now on.'

Ruby felt so weary. All she could think of was reaching dry land, the hotel with its plush carpets, the bed with its candlewick bedspread and silky eiderdown. She wanted to lie down and sleep, not make love. As she dragged her feet from the water and stepped onto the brow of the bridge, she let her hold on Stevie's arm loosen and he strode forwards, moving more quickly now he was free of the hampering floodwater. 'Come on,' he called. 'Don't stop now.' But her feet hurt so. Her shoes were pinching terribly. And she knew they were ruined, her lovely new red shoes.

It was only a second, no more than that surely, but she paused and looked down at her shoes, wondering if she should take them off. Maybe she'd be quicker in her stockinged feet, but then she'd have to carry her shoes, her lovely new shoes. 'Come on,' Stevie called again, having reached the far side. 'We're almost there.' His voice drifted away on the wind, barely audible above the roaring, crashing water below them.

Ruby could hardly make him out in the dark of the rainy night. He was merely a voice, a shadow on the other side. His urgent words were fractured by the storm.

'I'm coming,' she shouted back. 'Wait for me.'

She tried to run towards him with her poor blistered feet, in her ruined red shoes. Limping, she slipped and fell against the side of the bridge. And surely it couldn't have been her fault, for she was so slight, she weighed nothing at all, but the bridge collapsed. The bridge fell into the torrent and she fell with it.

Chapter 54

November 2004

Mapping the Past

Billie loves Tuesdays. That's market day. It always has been, as far back as she can remember. She used to come here with Mum, who loved the market for its cheap plants and flowers.

Romford High Street is closed to traffic when the market sets up shop and Billie can take her time roaming the stalls with their piles of bird seed, leathery chews for dogs, cheap sweaters and bargain cuts of meat. She ignores the shrill cries from the fruit and vegetable stalls; Sainsbury's is cheaper and besides, she is due to start her shift at the library at ten and if she hurries, she can take another look at her research.

Spreading the Ordnance Survey map out on the table where the University of the Third Age group will shortly be meeting to continue working on their genealogy charts, she turns it over. She'd looked at it briefly the previous day, but had been rudely interrupted by a couple of boys from the local school muttering loudly in the medical section. They were only ten or eleven, so she knew what they were up to with their phones, and had to tell them to clear off if they weren't going to take out any books.

There are two halves, two sides to the big folded map. It opens up to show east Devon, but she needs the other side, west Devon. She smooths its creases and refolds the sections so she can pinpoint the area she's interested in. Then she takes the large envelope from her handbag. Two postcards, both dated August 1952, but a couple of days apart. Her finger traces the places named. Weston-super-Mare along the coast in the next county, Somerset, and Taunton, further inland. Barnstaple, where Joan had told her she and her brother were evacuated to, is also some distance inland and appears to still have a station. The other towns and villages are linked by winding country roads, marked with steep gradients across moorland, ringed with contours that she knows, from her geography lessons and walking holidays when she was young, mean steep rugged hills and valleys.

Then she unfolds the yellowed newspaper cutting from the *Daily Mail* that her father had almost torn in half with his fist. Dated 18 August 1952, the banner headline shouts, FLOOD DESTROYS HOLIDAY VILLAGE. Further down, she reads again the report of the devastating flood that had torn buildings to pieces in the popular holiday destination of Lynmouth, situated at the foot of a steep-sided valley. The neighbouring town of Lynton, high above it, was unscathed, while down below hotels, shops and homes were wrecked, cars tossed into the sea, bridges collapsed and people drowned. But how many died, how many were saved, and who were they?

Billie glances at the library clock. There's still ten minutes before she has to start work. She logs on to the computer and starts searching. The devastating flood is well documented. Days of torrential rain, followed by one night in which two swollen rivers joined forces, had nearly destroyed the town and claimed thirty-four lives.

A familiar voice interrupts her concentration. 'Researching your family tree, like everyone else, are you?' It's her fellow librarian Dan. He's always joking about the number of cardholders who only use the library to try to uncover their ancestry. 'Hoping they're really someone special,' he often adds, 'and trying to uncover a family inheritance, like *Heir Hunters*, that TV programme.'

'I was just reading about a flood a bit like the one there was in the summer in Boscastle. This one was in Lynmouth in 1952.'

'I've been there,' Dan says. 'Watersmeet. Means the two rivers come together. Only they came together rather too much that year. Tore the place apart apparently.'

'It sounds terrible. Lucky Boscastle wasn't that bad.'

'Well, it was bad back then, but times have changed, haven't they? People knew a flash flood was imminent and the emergency services were alerted before anyone drowned.'

'I suppose that's the difference. No mobile phones.'

'Not just that, no phones anywhere probably. My parents didn't have a phone at home when I was a kid. We had to use the phone box down the road. Anyway, why're you so interested all of a sudden? You planning a visit? It's great walking country.'

'Catch me walking these days.' Billie laughs. 'I did when I was younger. Cheap youth hostel holidays. But now I walk to Tesco and back, and that's me done.'

'You should try it again some time. Me and Pete love it. We're doing the rest of the Cornish coastal path in October, hopefully before the rain turns it into a mudbath. I don't fancy sliding down some of those steep sections, or climbing up them, for that matter.' Dan turns to the front desk and begins putting away the boxes of book club books awaiting collection.

'Youth hostels again?'

'Probably. Though Pete thinks we're getting too old for that now. We might think about pre-booking some B&Bs.'

Billie knows that Dan and Pete have been partners for ten years, life partners who are longing for the laws to change so their love for each other can be recognised.

'Maybe I will take a trip up there some time,' Billie says. 'Not for walking, but just to look around the area. I think my dad must have been near there fifty-odd years ago. I've found a couple of postcards he'd sent from Weston-super-Mare and Taunton. They're not that far away, over in Somerset.'

'I've just remembered,' Dan says. 'I'm sure there was a big article about that flood in one of the papers, back in the summer.'

'What, you mean the Boscastle flood?'

'No, the one years before that. You carry on sorting the books while I go online and try and look for it.'

Billie leaves Dan to skim over the keyboard while she checks which book clubs are due to collect their books and which have failed to return their loans on time.

After a few minutes, she hears Dan say, 'Yes, I've got it. Come and have a look at this.'

She leans over his shoulder and peers at the screen at a large illustrated newspaper article, dated 1 August of that year. THINK THE RAIN THIS WEEK IS BAD? runs the headline, above photos of Lynmouth in ruins, all those years ago. 'It looks dreadful,' Billie murmurs, trying to read the rest of the feature.

But Dan is scrolling down too quickly for her to take everything in and then he pauses and reads: '...*devastating floods killed 34 people... discovery of an unknown girl, a mysterious victim who to this day has never been identified.*' He scrolls further, then says, 'And this is the bit that really got my attention. Listen to this. "*And then there was 'Girl X', the body of a young woman who was never identified and still lies in an unmarked grave ...*"'

Dan rushes on, too quickly for Billie to read the paragraph for herself, then he reads out, '*Police found her body on the beach four days after the flood. The only poignant clues to her identity were that she was dark-haired, had "well-kept hands and wore shoes that were too tight for her"...*'

'I can't help wondering who she was. It's just like a murder mystery story, isn't it?'

But Billie says nothing. She holds her breath as she pictures the crumpled photograph, the picture that had obviously been tucked inside her father's wallet for many years, the image of a young woman with dark hair who had left home and was never heard of again.

Chapter 55

16 August 1952

Checking Out

As Stevie settled the hotel bill at seven in the morning, his hands trembled so much he could barely separate the notes. 'It's so dreadful down there, sir,' the receptionist sniffled, mopping the tears from her blotchy face with a sodden handkerchief. 'I can't blame you for wanting to leave and go home early. All those poor people and the whole village destroyed, just like that.'

'Yes, terrible business,' he muttered, taking his change. 'I must get going. My wife's waiting outside in the car.' The Tors Hotel reception hall was filled with anxious guests wanting to end their holiday and escape the horror of the disaster they could see from every window of the hotel and return to the safety of their homes.

Exhausted emergency workers, firemen, ambulance drivers and police slumped in the hotel's sofas and armchairs, grateful for the offer of hot drinks and breakfast. The lobby reeked of damp clothes and sweat. Many of them had worked through the night trying to help people to safety and now others were trying to work out how the village could be accessed from the eastern side of the valley, as the flood had destroyed all the bridges across the swollen river.

Stevie had been awake all night, pacing the bedroom, listening to the roar of the storm and the wailing sirens, frantically working out what he should do next. Poor, poor Ruby. There was nothing he could have done. He could never have saved her. She must have drowned. There was no way she could have survived that turbulent flood. He couldn't stay and report her missing; he'd be linked to her. He was a married man, an unfaithful married man with three children. He had to distance himself, get away as quickly as he could.

With the first grey light of dawn he'd stood at the bedroom window, looking down on what had been a model toy village yesterday, stamped on by an angry child and torn to pieces in just one night. It looked like a bombsite, a drenched, flooded bombsite, with the furious river still rushing down the valley and out into the harbour, bearing timber, rocks and bodies.

He tore himself away from that horrific view of disaster. He couldn't bear looking and he couldn't face walking down towards the town. He feared the bodies, the crushed bodies and parts of bodies. There could be no survivors from that torrent. He couldn't go looking for Ruby; he was too afraid he'd find her. He couldn't identify her. How could he look at her once-pretty nose, her sweet lips, crushed by debris, bloated by the sea? And her delicate feet, in her new high-heeled shoes.

He tried to push the images away, but he kept hearing her scream as she fell, saw her figure fall with the masonry from the bridge. The film frames jerked with the flashing lightning and the pouring rain, but his last glimpse of her was her shoes. They were red, weren't they? No, maybe they were blue. More blue shoes, like the blue shoe that held the foot, joined to the little ankle, that returned to his dreams, followed by the sandals clinging to the remains of Arab feet and the little brown foot he had once held in his hand, all of them running after him. He screamed and rushed to the bathroom to splash his face with cold water.

Stevie had seen too much death in his short life; shredded, burnt and blasted. But as long as he stayed at the hotel, high above the carnage, he wouldn't see the faces and the bodies. And what was worse? Flesh that was torn and scorched by a bomb blast and cooked further by the heat of the sun of the Middle East, or limbs that were bruised and broken by the rocks of the river bed and thrown into the sea to be nibbled by fishes? He couldn't cope with seeing or thinking about either. He had to leave immediately.

Stevie pushed his way through the melee in the reception hall and out to the hotel car park. His wife wasn't waiting for him in the car of course, she was at home with his three children. She wasn't expecting him back until the end of the following week, after he'd completed the various surveys he'd booked for the next few days. He was due in Taunton on Tuesday. It might be best if he drove straight there today and sent her a card. Make it look as if he'd stayed in Somerset, over the Devon border, all weekend.

Once he was on the Minehead road, he tried to think clearly. No one knew he was leaving the hotel without her. No one had seen him come back without her last night. The chaos created by the flood had caused pandemonium and anyone on the eastern side of the river, above the tumult of water, rocks, cars and debris, had been watching with horror as the village collapsed below them. No, nobody had taken any notice of him as he sneaked back into the hotel last night, or when he crept downstairs early this morning to put the cases in the car.

He drove on, barely conscious of the coaches, tractors and emergency vehicles passing him on the other side of the road, all heading for the disaster area, till he was high on the moors. 'Need to stop, must think,' he told himself. After passing a sign to a farm, he turned left and drove a little way along the lane until he reached an area of unfenced land and a nearby patch of woodland. Pulling over to the side of the track, he stopped the car and stepped out. It was raining again, not heavily but enough to make him duck his head and shield his eyes.

Stevie opened the car boot and pulled out his raincoat and hat, still damp from the previous night's storm. He grabbed the pale blue case sitting next to his brown valise, then slammed the boot shut. Tucking the little case beneath his coat, so it could not be seen, he began striding towards the woods. He was far from the main road, no farm buildings were visible and no one was around. If anyone saw him, they might think he was obeying a call of nature, seeing a man about a dog, as his dad always used to say.

As he walked over the squelching turf, fractured images of last night flashed in his brain, like a jerky Pathé News reel. Her scream as the bridge crumbled, his shouts when he saw her slip away in the water. His panic as he realised he couldn't save her. His instinctive reaction to run, to escape, to avoid questions and avoid seeing her mangled body.

Back in the hotel he'd rushed through the chaos in reception and up to his room, their room, their bed where they'd made love not long before leaving for the last time, not realising they'd never be together again. And he'd thrown himself onto that same bed and buried his face in the sheets scented with her. Biting the pillow till his cries subsided, he shivered, then forced himself to get up, change out of his wet clothes and think.

Who would know he'd stayed in this hotel? Who would know she'd been with him? How could she be identified and linked with him? Think, Stevie, think. What did she have with her and what could it prove? She had a handbag, yes, that's right, a handbag. Girls keep everything important in their handbags, don't they? Anything that could identify her would be in her bag. Her ration card probably and maybe letters? He hadn't sent her letters recently. They'd made all the arrangements for this trip by meeting face to face, so he could give her the cheap wedding ring and enough money for her fare. After that, they'd talked on the phone, with her waiting for his calls at an agreed time in the phone box at the station after she finished work each day. No, there'd be nothing in her bag or on her person that could possibly link her to him. And in any case, Ruby Morrison didn't come to the Tors Hotel for a weekend with her husband, Rita Matthews did, so who would ever think to associate the two?

Then Stevie set about gathering up the possessions scattered around the room. Her hairbrush and the unopened bottle of violet scent on the dressing table, her satin nightdress under the pillow, her stockings drying on the towel rail in the bathroom. He checked the drawers in the bedside cabinet, the chest of drawers and the dressing table, then peered in the wardrobe. There was no other sign she had ever been in the room. The rest of her clothes were still folded in the little pale blue case she had clutched so proudly when he had met her at Weston-super-Mare station. That was only two days ago. She had been so excited then, so happy to be with him again.

Beneath the trees in the little wood, leaves littered the floor. The rain still penetrated, but not as heavily as it did out on the open moor. Stevie tripped over fallen branches and twining brambles until he felt himself to be in the heart of the copse. He listened. There were no sounds other than the soft pitter-patter of raindrops and the occasional cry of a distant crow. He crouched down and opened the case. He was sure there was nothing inside that could identify Ruby, but he needed to check once more. No name tag tied to the handle, no label pasted inside, no letters slipped between the layers of silk and satin. Then, using her hairbrush like a trowel, he scraped at the woodland floor, through layers of recent and rotting leaves, till he revealed the mushroomy compost layer beneath and created a hole for each item: her knickers, her nightdress, her stockings. He gave each of her possessions a decent burial, finishing with the hairbrush. The case he ripped apart, pulling the lid off its hinges. Then he stamped on the pieces till they crumpled, and tucked them beneath some rotting branches. 'I'm sorry, Ruby!' he shouted. 'I'm sorry.'

And as he crept away from this woodland resting place, he thought how she would have liked it here, this quiet and peaceful wood, where the rain fell softly and a glimmer of sun was beginning to break through the clouds.

Chapter 56

November 2004

Can it Be?

'I wonder if I could have a word?' Fiona catches Billie when she's parked her car at the home.

'What's the matter?'

'Don't worry. It's nothing that serious, but I wanted to ask if anything happened yesterday?' Her long hair is ruffled by the breeze and she tightens the band gripping her ponytail. 'Your father had a very unsettled night and keeps trying to talk. He seems very bothered this morning as well. I don't think we can have our speech therapy session while he's like this.'

'Oh dear.' Billie's shoulders droop. 'It must be those pictures I showed him yesterday. I'm afraid I seem to have upset him all over again.'

'I'm sorry to hear that. Do you want to tell me about it? We can sit quietly in my office for a moment.'

Billie follows Fiona's slim figure, thinking that her slender limbs and hips haven't seen many Jaffa Cakes and gingerbread recently; her own skipped lunch was replaced by half a pack of chocolate digestives. 'I'd be glad of your advice actually. When we talked before, you said I shouldn't worry too much about him getting upset when we showed him those old photos. But I'm not happy about the way he's reacting. I don't think I should do it any more.'

'I'm sure it can't have done any permanent harm. Any kind of prompt to get him talking is good. But I must say, this recent distress does seem to be connected with an urgent need to communicate with us more. Have you been able to find out anything about the backstory to those photos that disturbed him the last time? The ones taken during his period of service abroad?'

'As a matter of fact, I have. I managed to trace his commanding officer and it turned out that Dad was involved in clearing up after a major bombing incident out in Jerusalem. It was pretty awful apparently, with a lot of fatalities. The man who told me all about it still seemed as if it had shaken him up badly too.'

Fiona jots a note on her pad. 'Interesting. I did wonder if there might be some deep-seated trauma.'

'I suppose in those days people just had to get on with it. There wouldn't have been any therapy or support back then, would there?'

Fiona shrugged. 'There's not always that much now either. I know ex-servicemen who are still struggling with their experiences. Bosnia, Iraq and now Afghanistan, they all have their horrors. Some can manage to work it out of their systems but others may carry a burden affecting them for the rest of their lives. That's not a criticism of them, it's just how different people react to extreme stress.'

'You think my father has been badly affected by something that happened all those years ago?' Billie thinks about how she has been pushing photos under his nose while he has been almost helpless with his limited movement and speech. 'Oh dear, now I feel just dreadful. And I thought I was helping him, but I can see I wasn't.'

'No, you mustn't blame yourself. I might be wrong in any case.' Fiona sits back in her chair, frowning. 'What do you know about his early years? Did he have a happy childhood?'

And Billie remembers what Joan had told her. 'I'd always thought he did. But recently, his older sister told me what a bad time he'd had when he was evacuated. He was about twelve, I think. He was very badly treated by the farmer he was lodged with for a few months. He was knocked about a bit, apparently.'

'Hmm, childhood trauma could be a factor.'

'Really? But I never knew about it until she told me. He's never mentioned it. If anything, he always made out what a nightmare he was as a kid. Cheeky, always in trouble, that sort of thing. He's even made jokes about helping out in the Blitz on bombsites and so on. Sounded like he quite enjoyed the war.'

'But that could just be bluff and bravado. Some people manage to bury the damage, but it can still break through. And sometimes trauma manifests itself in extreme behaviour.'

'Well, the only thing I can think of that's a bit over the top with Dad is his love of cars. He was a right one for a fast car and liked to push his luck too. He got a few speeding tickets in his time. Oh, and betting as well. Mum used to get rather cross with him. Thought it was frittering hard-earned money away. Down the drain, she always said.' Billie smiles, remembering her mother's weary sigh when her father came back from the pub with news of a successful win on the horses, or dangling the keys to yet another new car.

'Well, that doesn't sound too extreme,' Fiona says. 'Lots of men find solace in drinking and gambling, while others can't control their temper and some end up exhibiting serial infidelity. The worst-affected can crumble completely, but it sounds as if your father coped pretty well. After all, he built a successful career for himself and had a long and happy marriage.'

'I always thought they were happy,' Billie says with a sigh. 'In fact, I'm sure they were. And he's managed pretty well since Mum died too. So that's why the way he's reacting now is so hard to understand. I mean, I know he's not well, I know it's hard for him to communicate and do things for himself, but I keep feeling it's more than just frustration with him. I keep thinking there's something he can't tell us. His reaction to some of the photos is worrying me.'

'What exactly?' Fiona puts down her pen and sits back.

'You're going to think this is crazy. My imagination, honestly.' Billie pulls a wry face. 'Too much *Miss Marple*, I think.' She pauses, noticing the photos behind Fiona on her bookcase. Cats. She doesn't have children then.

Fiona laughs. 'Whatever it is, just tell me. Honestly, I don't mind.'

Billie clears her throat. 'Look, I know this is stupid, really I do. But I've got it into my head that my dad, my lovely dad, may have been responsible for someone's death years ago.'

'Whatever makes you think that?' Fiona pushes her box of tissues across the desk and Billie takes one, then blows her nose.

'It's this photo. The one I showed you before. A girl he once knew. She was his first girlfriend, I think, when he was young, before he did his National Service. Oh, I don't know... It seems improbable, but I just don't know what to make of it.'

'And why do you think this is significant?'

'He's kept the photo hidden all these years. I found it in his wallet. His sister knew who it was straight away and told me this girl was broken-hearted when my dad dumped her. But then I also found out that this same girl disappeared years and years ago. And no one knows what happened to her.'

'And why do you think that's got anything to do with him?'

'She hasn't been seen since the summer of 1952. And then I found some old newspaper cuttings at home. They were about this dreadful flood disaster in north Devon that very same year, in August. Then, when I showed them to Dad yesterday, that was when he became terribly distressed. And according to you, he hasn't got over it yet; he's still upset.'

'But I don't see what that's got to do with his old girlfriend?'

Billie takes a deep breath. 'One of the bodies from this awful flood was never identified. The papers called her Girl X. And judging from the little bit of information that was printed in the papers, I'm wondering if that woman and my dad's girlfriend are the same person.'

'But do you know if your dad was there then? Do you know if she was with him?'

Billie sniffs. 'Told you it was a crazy idea. No, I can't prove it, though I know he was in the next county around that time. But I can't work out why he's so upset about her photo and the flood. He can't tell me what's wrong, so I can only guess. And you're going to tell me I've put two and two together and made five, I know. But I can't help thinking perhaps they were both there during the flood.'

'And that means what…?'

'That she drowned and he didn't report it? Or worse, that there was some kind of accident? Or could he have killed her and made it look like she'd drowned, along with a lot of other people?' Billie bursts into tears.

'Well, it's a theory, but it's very far-fetched,' Fiona says in a reassuring tone. 'I know it happens all the time in *Midsomer Murders*, but it doesn't seem very likely, now, does it?'

'You're right. I know I'm being stupid. We're never going to know what's bothering him, are we?' She twists the sodden tissue in her hands. 'But I've decided I'm not going to show him any more photos from now on. I'll just have to stop thinking about it, if I can.'

'Mmm, best to give him a break from all this.' Fiona is thoughtful. 'But another reaction with PTSD, if that actually is what he's exhibiting, can be dissociation.'

'And what does that mean?'

'Well, I'm not an expert, but at its simplest, you could say it's irrational behaviour. So in this case, given the scenario you've sketched out here, a normal person would do everything they could to save someone's life and would certainly report them missing if there'd been an accident. But if someone is affected by PTSD, their instinct could be to deny the incident and flee the scene.' She slaps her knees and shakes her head. 'But we don't know if that is what happened. We don't know if these two people were involved in that disaster. You don't even know if they ever met up again years ago, so I suggest you put this idea to one side and try to forget all about it. Just enjoy the time you spend with your father. And try to keep him calm.'

'I will try,' Billie says, but as she walks away, tucking the soggy tissue in the pocket of her cardigan, she thinks she can't hide from the questions that are taunting her and that she suspects are also haunting her father.

Chapter 57

20 August 1952

Coming Home

Stevie sat outside the house in his car, gripping the steering wheel. Would he face awkward questions about why he'd come home early or would Maureen accept his excuse about the weather? He wasn't ready to face her or the clamour of the children just yet. The rain was still drizzling and as he gazed at his home he noticed how the grass had grown ragged in his absence. The roses were soggy bundles of brown petals. They didn't like the rain either. He was proud of his pebble-dashed semi-detached in a quiet cul-de-sac in Barkingside, built in a rash of post-war development, and he wasn't going to be forced to leave if she suspected anything. It was his house, bought with his hard-earned money. He couldn't lose his home and his family.

'I wasn't expecting you back till Friday night,' Maureen said, jiggling Keith on her hip to calm his grizzling. Little Pamela wobbled and clung to her mother's skirts, her thumb in her mouth, while Billie skipped and tugged at her father's raincoat, wanting him to scoop her up and onto his shoulders.

'The weather's been so bad, I had to cut it short. It's been impossible. Been soaked through every day.'

'I got your second postcard this morning. Lucky you weren't over in north Devon. You heard about the terrible flood up there, in Lynmouth?'

'Yeah, I saw in today's papers. Dreadful business.'

'Good thing you weren't caught up in anything like that. Loads of people have died there apparently and their homes and shops have all been destroyed. And one poor girl they found drowned hasn't even been identified yet.'

Stevie turned away, feeling sick. 'I'll just go and unpack. Need to get out of these clothes.' He hung his damp raincoat on the rack in the hall and went upstairs. He had seen the newspaper headlines and he'd bought copies every day, his heart thudding as he read the dramatic articles, turning the pages with a shaking hand to look at the photographs of how the picture-postcard village had been destroyed in a single night.

An unidentified girl had just been found. That had to be her, didn't it? And it said she was wearing shoes that were too tight for her. Tight shoes… poor Ruby, she couldn't keep up with him… damn those shoes. His breathing quickened. He couldn't stop his mind picturing the blue shoe, the white sock, the child's leg, the sandals, the little brown foot, Ruby's shoes… Everywhere he went, he was taunted by feet and shoes.

But what did unidentified mean? Was she no longer recognisable? Or did it mean nothing was found with the body that could identify her? He hated to think of her pretty face broken and bruised. But it must be Ruby. She wouldn't have been able to cling to her handbag in that swirling torrent and it could never have stayed with her or ended up near her body. Washed out to sea probably.

He sat down on the candlewick bedspread, his head in his hands. What else could he have done? He couldn't save her. She never had a chance, poor girl. No one could have survived those turbulent waters tossing cars and timber onto cruel rocks. He simply didn't have a choice.

'Are you alright, love?' Maureen hovered in the doorway, then placed a cup on the bedside cabinet. 'Not one of your turns, I hope. I've been getting a good night's sleep while you've been away most of the time, unless one of the kids wakes up.'

'Oh, I'm just tired. It's very tiring driving through the rain all the time. And it's such a long journey.'

'Of course. You just take it easy. I'm getting the children their tea now and we'll have ours once they've had their bath and gone to bed. Good thing I've got a couple of chops. I'd have got something special if I'd known you'd be back today. But the new car's alright?'

'Yeah' – he nodded, then reflected – 'but not the best for these long trips. I'm thinking of changing it for something faster. Then I might not have to be away quite so long each time.'

'You and your cars. Well, you know better than me what suits you.' And she closed the door as she left the room.

He closed his eyes, trying to shut out the images crowding his thoughts. The little blue shoe, Ruby's shoes, the sandals from the bazaar under a scorching sky. He could hear Maureen talking to the children downstairs, hear their occasional cries, their laughter, their chatter. He loved his children; he was a fool to risk losing them for the sake of a few nights of fun. Okay, he found domestic life with three small children tedious, tiring and stressful, but Maureen was a good wife and mother. She ironed his shirts and kept the house spotless and the kids were healthy and clean. Maybe his kicks lay elsewhere in safer territory. He'd had a near miss, he thought, and it might be better not to repeat it. Cars, they'd have to be his first love from now on.

Stevie drank his cooling tea, stripped off his shirt and fetched a clean one from the chest of drawers. It was crisp and smooth, smelling of fresh air and sunshine. It reminded him of his good fortune in having a wife who attended to all his needs. Then, as he hung up his jacket, he felt the pockets. He'd nearly forgotten he'd got a present for Maureen. She'd be pleased he'd taken the trouble to bring something back for her in spite of his difficult, tiring trip.

*

'Maureen, love, I got you a little souvenir.' He kissed her cheek as she popped the last spoonful of scrambled egg into Keith's bird-like mouth and slipped the little package into her apron pocket.

'Oh, you shouldn't have, love, you had enough to do with all this dreadful weather.' She leant across and kissed him. She wiped Keith's face and gave him half a Farley's rusk to chew with his emerging teeth, then unwrapped the present, a little bottle of scent and an embroidered hankie. Maureen spread the handkerchief out on her knee and held up the decorated bottle adorned with a gold stopper.

'Devon Violets, how lovely. Thank you.'

He put his arm around her shoulders and kissed the top of her head. 'Soon as I saw them, I thought of you, love.'

Chapter 58

Billie throws back her rain-spattered hood and bends to study the miniature model village of Lynmouth in the glass case. 'I wonder if I should bring Dad here?'

She and Joan are examining the scene recreated in the village's Flood Memorial Hall, where the names and ages of those who died that night, fifty-two years previously, are displayed on a large wooden plaque. From the youngest, a baby boy of only three months, to the oldest, a man of eighty years, it makes solemn reading. Below the list of known dead are the words, *One lady unidentified* and the names of four other people, under the heading 'Missing and Believed Drowned'. Around the walls are dramatic photographs of the devastated town, its shops and homes like splintered matchwood.

'And how on earth do you think that's going to help your father?' Joan says. 'It still takes him half an hour to drink a cup of tea, let alone dress himself and walk anywhere. He's in no fit state to be driven all the way up here.'

Billie has persuaded Joan to accompany her on this road trip to Lynmouth, promising stunning scenery, challenging walks and clotted cream. With a two-night stay at the Tors Hotel, she hopes she will be able to see everything that has roused her curiosity. Her father hasn't made much progress recently and Billie can't bear to upset him further by asking again about the photos and the newspaper cuttings.

But she can't let it lie. Her suspicions are eating away at her. Is it possible he knows what actually happened to Ruby Morrison? Is it linked to the disaster here so many years ago? And was he an unfaithful husband? So many questions are jumbled together in her head. She loves her father dearly and doesn't want to think ill of him, but are there ghosts in his past he must lay to rest?

'But if he could come here, maybe it would jolt his memory. I know he's been upset by the photos and the newspaper articles, but I keep feeling he wants me to know why. When he tries so hard to speak, I'm sure he's trying to tell me something important. And maybe then it would help me piece everything together.'

'It's not his memory that needs jolting, as his therapist keeps on telling you. It takes time to recover, you know that. It's all there, in his mind. He just can't grab hold of the right information and tell you about it.'

'Come on, I've seen enough. Let's get some lunch.'

After they've found a table in the café above the information centre, housed in the converted building that had once been the Pavilion concert hall, Billie says, 'Do you think Dad was always faithful to Mum or could he have had an affair? I keep wondering if he had something going on with Ruby and that's why he kept her photo all these years.'

'She looks very young in that picture you found. I expect she gave it to him when he went off to do his National Service. He was called up when he was eighteen, so she'd have only been about sixteen at the time. And then as I told you before, he didn't get back together with her when he came back from overseas.'

'But when I saw her aunt, Mrs Cherry, she said she thought Ruby was seeing someone before she went away. She used the term "fancy man". Could that have been Dad? Could they have met up again?'

'It's possible,' Joan says, laying down her knife and fork. 'Phew! I can't eat all these chips. Far too much for me, that is.'

Billie stops eating too. She could have happily eaten her plateful and the remains of Joan's on top of that, but thought better of it. Picking up the dessert menu and passing it to Joan, she says, 'What about some ice cream? Made with clotted cream, it says.'

'Clotted cream? Might be a bit rich for me.' Joan glances at the list, then says, 'I think the best ice cream ever was Rossi's. D'you remember it? Proper ice cream, it was. I wonder if they're still around?' She looks dreamy, picturing Italian ices in a parlour from the past. Then she lays down the menu. 'Funny that. I've just remembered something. You know how you do. That summer, 1952, I was expecting again. And I craved ice cream, in spite of the awful weather we had for weeks. Had a real thing about it, I did.'

'I craved tomatoes with all mine. Funny how you get these strange obsessions when you're up the duff. Go on.'

'Well, I've just remembered. I saw him when I'd popped into Rossi's, near Ilford station, late one afternoon. I'm sure it was just after I'd been to see Doctor Gilchrist, because of the headaches I was getting. I was feeling so hot and heavy, a right old hippo I was. I'd left the kids with Mum and I thought I'd like nothing more than an ice cream before catching the bus home. I knew that once I got back, I'd be caught up in their teas and bathtime so I thought I'd treat myself while I could.'

'Quite right, Joan. Got to grab any minute you can when your kids are off your hands. Precious moments, eh, and precious little of them.'

Joan pauses as the waitress removes their plates. 'Rossi's ice cream was the best, wasn't it? Anyway, I remember going in for an ice cream that day and seeing him go past.'

'You mean you saw Dad?'

'Yeah. I saw the back of him as I was sat in the ice cream parlour. I was feeling so hot and in need of a sit-down, so I decided to give myself a rest there. And he must have been on his way to the station. Same side of the road, so he must have walked right past me, but I only saw the back of him after he'd passed by.'

'So what was odd about that? He worked around there, didn't he?'

'I think his office was in Gants Hill then. And anyway, he travelled about a lot in those days. Used his car to drive himself all over the country.'

'But you're saying that he was in Ilford that day?'

'Yes, that particular day, I'm sure it was him in Ilford. I wasn't that surprised to see him there, but I was a little surprised at seeing him with a young woman. They were holding hands and seemed to be talking intently. You know, heads close together. Intimate, like.'

'And who do you think she was?'

'I don't know for certain. But I can tell you this much. It wasn't your mum. It definitely wasn't Maureen.'

'So could it have been Ruby Morrison?'

'Possibly. I don't remember it all that clearly. This is years ago, remember, and I hadn't seen her for two, maybe three years by then, I was so tied up with the kids and everything. But from what I can picture, height, build, dark hair, yes, it could have been.' Joan dabs her lips with a paper napkin, folds it neatly and places it on the table. 'I forgot all about it after that moment, because I was in hospital the next day. Pre-eclampsia. No wonder I'd been feeling so rotten.'

'I'm not surprised you didn't think any more about what he was up to that day. You had enough to worry about. Was that Jacky?'

'That's right. My youngest. The only time she ever gave me any trouble!' Joan laughs.

Billie picks up the menu again. 'They've got some lovely desserts. What do you fancy? More ice cream?'

'No, let's get on and see if we can find this cemetery you've read about. We can have a cream tea afterwards if we're peckish.'

Chapter 59

November 2004

A Murder of Crows

'It must be this one,' Billie says as they drive into the empty car park near the cemetery entrance. A chequerboard of grey and white gravestones stretches up the green hillside. 'I'm going to take a walk around, but you don't have to come if you've had enough.'

'I just don't understand why you want to come here if the unknown girl is meant to be buried in the churchyard.'

'Because we couldn't find her grave, that's why. It's unmarked. But other victims from the flood are buried here.' Billie shuts the car door and pulls up her hood. Icy rain is drifting in waves towards her. Not the warm rain of the flood year, but net curtains of bone-chilling drizzle floating down from the steep wooded hills all around.

She digs her hands deep into her pockets and starts up the grassy slope. Some of the neat graves dotted either side of the path have fresh flowers, others are adorned with drooping chrysanthemums. She takes some photos on her phone, then turns and looks back towards the car. Joan is plodding up the path, her head lowered because of the wet. Poor Joan, nearly eighty years old and dragged along on this wild goose chase.

Billie watches her force herself to keep going on the sloping path, slippery from the clouds of misty rain wafting from the wooded hillside on the other side of the graveyard. A clamour of rooks circles over the treetops. That's the librarian in me, Billie tells herself. Not a crowd, not a swarm, but a clamour. Oh well, better than a murder of crows at any rate. But the sharp calls of the rooks echo in the steep-sided valley, adding to the feeling of isolation.

'Have you found anything yet?' Joan puffs as she reaches her. 'We'll certainly have earned that cream tea soon. This is the second cemetery you've dragged me to this afternoon.' Earlier, they had stepped through a lychgate into the village's oldest graveyard, filled with elaborate memorials of cherubs and angels, as well as more modest stones, mossy and blanketed in autumn leaves.

They stand side by side, huddled close together, and Joan says, 'Do you think she'd rather be here than in that churchyard, so close to the river?'

Billie looks down on the green hillside, still so fresh though it is late in the year. The air smells of damp humus-deep woodland. 'I think if it was me, I'd want to be as far away as possible from the scene of my death. You can't escape the crashing of water over the rocks, down there in the valley. You'd be reminded of the flood every minute of the day and night. Up here it's quite peaceful, in spite of the rooks.'

They stumble further up the path, slipping here and there on fallen leaves and wet turf. When they step aside onto the grass to take a look at the inscriptions on some of the gravestones, Joan holds back. 'It's too steep and slippery for me. You go, I'll wait here.'

So Billie trudges up to the highest point, where there is a cluster of graves for the nuns from the nearby convent. A sisterhood, she thinks, or is there a better collective noun for nuns? She edges her way past a row of stones, trying to read the chiselled epitaphs, then turns back. 'I don't think there's anything I need to see here.'

They begin walking back down the path and then Joan suddenly stops and points to a large white mausoleum with a list of names. 'Oh, they're all victims of the flood,' Billie says and steps forward to take a closer look. 'How sad. They all drowned that same night. But at least here they're all together and not alone. Not missing, presumed drowned, or unidentified.'

Back in the car, Joan wipes the rain off her glasses. 'I just can't help wondering,' she says, 'this unknown girl, this Girl X, *why* was she never identified? If she was living or working here in either of the two villages, surely someone would have noticed she was missing and wondered if it was her? And on that list of the victims we saw in the Memorial Hall, there's names of people whose bodies were never found, but they were still reported missing, yet she wasn't. So why not? And who was she?'

'I've been thinking the same thing,' Billie says, opening a pack of Polo mints and offering one to Joan. 'Apparently it was incredibly busy here that year, just like every summer in a popular holiday resort, I suppose. In that exhibition it said the village normally had around four hundred and fifty full-time residents, but the population increased to twelve hundred during the holiday season.'

'So could she have come here just to work for the summer, maybe as a chambermaid or in a kitchen? Lots of hotels take on extra staff at busy times. But they'd still have noticed that she was missing. And that newspaper report you found said she had "well-kept hands". That doesn't sound to me like someone who had to work hard with their hands for a living.'

'I know, that's what I think as well. It's so strange. Why did no one miss her?' Billie sucks her mint and goes to turn on the ignition, then stops. 'Can you remember what kind of work Ruby did? I think her aunt said she was working in Bodgers, the old department store.'

'Yes, that's right, I think, over in Ilford. And I guess she was still working there when she left that summer.'

'Is Bodgers still there? I haven't been in that shop for years. I used to love that canister system the cashiers had on wires. Do you remember it? They whizzed backwards and forwards with the change. When I was a kid I used to love watching those things.'

But Joan isn't listening and she frowns as she tries to remember way, way back over the years. 'I'm pretty sure she was in the ladieswear section. Underwear, I think. She gave Mum some reduced stockings once when she was still going out with your dad.'

'So if she was a shop assistant handling lingerie, it's not very likely she'd have rough hands then, is it? She'd have to have well-kept hands. Nice nails and so on.' Billie spreads out her own hands with their short uneven nails and ragged cuticles. Maybe she should get one of those long-lasting gel manicures, like her daughters did sometimes.

'Well, I suppose she had to look the part, selling underwear and stockings all day. Though I think she had to work a bit in her aunt's pub as well, washing glasses and sweeping up.'

'Yes, her aunt told me she helped out.' Billie snorts, 'Or rather, the old bat moaned about how much she and her husband had been let down by Ruby's unexpected and inconvenient disappearance. She didn't seem at all concerned about her otherwise.'

They both sit silently for a moment, watching the rain, then Joan says, 'You've convinced yourself this unknown girl's Ruby, haven't you?'

'Well, what do you think? What could have happened to her? No one's heard from her in all these years, she knew this part of the country as a child, she was dark-haired, just like the description in the paper, and every time I show my dad anything about this village, the flood or her photo, he gets totally distraught. She disappeared the summer of the flood, when we know he was in the West Country for work. Yes, I'm beginning to think the girl in the unmarked grave that we can't even find could well be Ruby. Now, how do I tell my dad what I suspect? It would be like accusing him of killing her, wouldn't it?'

Joan doesn't reply. They sit in the car while the windows mist over with their silent wordless breath, the sky darkens and the curtains of rain turn to solid sheets. And all the while, the black rooks fly around the treetops, seeking their nests before nightfall.

Chapter 60

December 2004

Truly Sorry

Billie sits and strokes her father's hand. It is nearly four months since she found him collapsed in his favourite reclining chair in front of the flickering television. He is now able to walk in a shuffling, bumbling fashion with the help of a walking frame, he can drink from a mug with fewer spills and he is able to eat one-handed with a fork or a spoon. His face still droops on one side and his left arm is feeble, but Billie can see he has progressed to a degree, even though his speech is still largely incoherent.

'You're doing really well, Dad. Fiona said you joined in the singing yesterday and even had a go at dancing with one of the carers in the music session the other day. That's really good. Well done.' Billie knows these examples of his improvement are not that impressive. She has seen a carer grasp a seated inmate's hands and jig from side to side without them ever taking a step. It is well intentioned, but it is not a great leap forward.

Billie and her father are sitting apart from the other residents, who are watching *White Christmas* on the large flat-screen television. 'Why don't we go somewhere quieter?' Billie says, standing up. 'I can't hear myself think above all this.' Some members of the audience have joined in the songs, their fractured voices adding nothing of merit to the music.

Dick stands unsteadily and Billie puts a hand under his elbow, then they begin a slow walk to the empty dining room where lunch has been cleared away and tea will soon be served. There are flower arrangements on every table and some are set with places for supper, but her father is more settled if he takes his last meal of the day in the calm of his own private room.

After a member of staff has brought them cups of tea and cakes, Billie says, 'Joan sends her love. She said she'll be able to pop in and see you tomorrow.'

Dick tries to raise the teacup to his lips and Billie realises he is having difficulty grasping the tiny handle: 'Hang on, Dad, let me get you a proper mug.' She goes to the nearby kitchen and chooses a sturdy pottery mug, then half-fills it with fresh tea. 'There, that's better for you, isn't it?' She smiles as she sees him start sipping.

Billie peels the paper case off one of the iced fairy cakes and puts it in front of her father. Maybe I shouldn't do everything for him, she thinks with a sigh. Am I being too patronising? But it's difficult to take the paper off with only one hand. He puts down his mug, picks up the cake and takes a bite. Crumbs fall, but they drop on the plate rather than sticking to his sweater. He's wearing the yellow today, so cheerful. She takes his jumpers home to hand-wash, adding Vanish to the stains that are inevitable with the one-handed eating of sausage and mash, shepherd's pie and other soft foods that he can manage more easily.

'I've been meaning to tell you all about the little holiday Joan and I had the other week. Your big sister's such good company, Dad. We drove all the way across to north Devon. Such lovely countryside. I can't think why I've never been before, when we've done further south in Devon and been to north Cornwall too. Joan said it was near to where you both went when you were evacuated in the war.' Was it her imagination, or did he give a small gasp? He slowly puts the cake down on the plate, only half-eaten.

Billie wonders whether she should press on. She and Joan have already discussed this at length, over dinner in the Tors Hotel and all the way home on the M4 in the car. 'I'm not sure you should upset him any further,' Joan had said. 'Every time you show him that photo, he seems to get worse all over again.'

'But I feel I have to get to the bottom of this. If that unidentified girl really is Ruby, doesn't she deserve to have a grave marked by a proper stone bearing her real name? It's so sad that she's all forgotten, with no one caring about her and no flowers on her grave.'

'That's not strictly true. You know what it said in that book about the flood. Someone who looked after the churchyard planted bulbs on her grave because he felt sorry for her.'

'That's not the same as being known, though.' Billie sighed. 'If Dad was well, I'd force him to go there and see if I could drag the truth out of him.'

'Well, that's not going to happen. But I suppose I have to agree that it looks like she could actually be Ruby. The timings do all seem to fit together. But how you're going to prove it, I just don't know.'

So am I pushing him too hard? Billie pauses before going any further. *But what if he never gets any better? He might even take a turn for the worse and then we'd never know any more. I can't stop now, I have to carry on.*

'Dad, we had such a lovely time up there, all that beautiful moorland and hills. And we went to Lynmouth and stayed at the Tors Hotel, overlooking the village.'

And this time there is no mistake. He gasps and mumbles. His good hand bangs the table, his weak hand trembles and his mouth slackens, spilling cake crumbs moistened with saliva.

'We went to see the exhibition about the terrible flood there, more than fifty years ago.' Billie takes a deep breath. She is torturing him, she can see that she is. Whatever his connection to that place, that time, it is still full of painful significance for him.

'Such a shocking business, that flood, with so many people killed in just one night. And, do you know, what we both thought was so terribly sad was that one poor girl wasn't found till four days later. Four whole days, just imagine. They found her on the beach but she was never identified. No one knows who she is, not even to this day.'

Billie stops for a moment. Dare she continue, push on right to the end? She takes her eyes off him for a second, glances around the dining room, checking that no concerned carer sees his distress and leaps forward to insist that her father should be taken to lie down in his room.

'Joan and I thought that was so shocking. That no one ever reported her missing. It's like no one noticed she'd gone. No one even cared about her. She's buried in an unmarked grave, with nobody to visit her there. Don't you think that's awful, Dad?'

How much more can he take? His mouth is trembling and a thread of spittle dangles over his sweater. He's not forming coherent words, but he is trying to speak. And then Billie decides she must play her final hand, her trump card. She shows him the little crumpled snapshot again: 'I don't know if I'm right, Dad, but I've been wondering if this could be the girl in the grave. What do you think?'

He can't tell her; he can't say the words. But Billie has her answer. In his tears, now running down his cheeks, she has the answer she feared but wanted all the same. 'This is a picture of Ruby Morrison, isn't it? Joan told me. And Ruby went away just before the flood happened and has never been seen ever since.'

With his good left hand, he reaches for the photo. He holds it in tremulous fingers, while the tears continue to trickle. And finally, Billie understands what he is trying to say with his distorted utterances: 'Rooey... mm... orry.'

'Ruby, I'm sorry,' Billie whispers. 'You are sorry, aren't you, Dad?' She holds both his hands, the good one and the one still weak, trying to calm the shaking, trying to bring him some comfort. 'I'll see what I can do to put it right for you. It's never too late to say sorry and put things right.'

But is it? she asks herself, as she hugs him and kisses his bowed head.

Chapter 61

April 2005

The Flowers of Spring

'I can't go with you this time,' Joan says. 'My chest has been bad all this winter. Why don't you wait till the summer? It'll be much nicer then and maybe I'd feel like joining you.'

'But the traffic will be terrible then. It's much better to go out of season. I'll go on my own, or maybe Kevin will take a couple of days off and come with me.'

'But you've got nowhere with convincing anyone that the unknown girl is Ruby. You can't be a hundred per cent sure it's her so why do you want to go back?'

Billie has to reach for her tissues again. Dad's death has hit her hard. It was worse than when Mum went. But then Mum had made her peace with everyone. With Dad, it still feels like unfinished business. 'I have to go. I'm going for Dad's sake and because I feel so guilty. I keep thinking it's my fault, putting pressure on him. If I hadn't, he might have got better. I feel I made him worse and hastened his end.'

Joan sniffs. 'No, you didn't. It was the flu that did it. My little brother… Always did cause trouble. Loveable though.' She shakes her head. 'Off you go then. And once you've been back there, then you really must let it lie. Let that be the end of it, dear.'

'I will, Joan, I promise.' Billie gives her aunt a hug. 'I'm just tying up the loose ends.'

*

Two days later, all the way to Lynmouth she can't stop thinking. She drives alone with her unsettling thoughts and checks into a pub in Lynton, high above the seaside village below. The tearooms and guest rooms of both villages are busy with Easter holidaymakers, hill walkers and day visitors. The sun is shining and she can see why the area has always been such an attraction. She tries to imagine the scene before the flood, more than fifty years previously. Had Dad been unhappy in his marriage? Had he and Ruby continued the love affair that had started when they were both so young? Maybe they ran away together, hoping to start a new life, or was it just a dirty weekend that had ended in disaster?

I'm never going to know, Billie frets. And even though Dad's distress was convincing, even though I thought he tried to say her name, tried to say he was sorry, it wasn't enough in the end to prove conclusively that Ruby died here. None of the authorities I contacted thought it was enough to warrant further investigation. 'If you had the missing lady's hairbrush, there might be something we could do with DNA,' one supercilious representative from the coroner's office said, 'but we can't go disinterring a body with so little evidence and without good reason.'

No, that's true, Billie thinks. But I can honour the memory of someone my father clearly cared about in my own way. I will never know if my theory is correct, but I do know that she meant something to him and that it has a link to this place.

She walks all the way through the town above the harbour and out to the new cemetery. This time there is no rain; there is warm spring sunshine and the hillside scattered with tombs is also thick with primroses, their scent gathered by a soft breeze. Billie follows the path up the slope and stands looking back down the hill towards the tall trees on the opposite side above the busy car park. The rooks are quiet today. She guesses they must be hatching eggs in their nests. In place of their raucous shrieks she hears the twittering of small birds in the hawthorn that edges the cemetery.

Billie walks between the graves and picks primroses from the clumps dotted beneath the hedges. Then she strolls down to the mausoleum for other victims of the flood and lays a bunch of flowers on the plinth. After a moment in contemplation, she begins her walk back into town. She hums as she walks, her nose buried in the posy of flowers she still carries.

When she reaches St John's Church near the river, she walks all around the churchyard, checking under the dark shrubs of yew and viburnum, trying to convince herself that she may yet locate the unmarked grave. But it's fruitless. She stands for a moment, looking at the flowers she had intended leaving, and then she knows what she must now do.

She enters the church, which like the Memorial Hall displays a wooden plaque bearing a list of the names of those who died in the flood. Near the bottom right-hand corner are the familiar words she's read before, *One lady unidentified*. Billie lays her flowers beneath this inscription, bows her head, then leaves the church and walks across the car park to the low stone wall bordering the fast-flowing river.

Even on a bright spring day the race is turbulent, tumbling over rocks, rushing headlong to the ocean. Steps lead right down to the water's edge, wet mossy steps, so she grips the handrail for safety. And as she reaches the sodden grass at the very bottom, she holds her final primrose over the river, saying, 'This is for you, Dad. This is the end. This is where you finally say goodbye to Ruby.' Her fingers part and the flower falls into the rushing torrent and is swiftly swept away, down to the waves of the sea.

Jenny Wren got well,
And stood upon her feet;
And told Robin plainly,
She loved him not a bit.

Chapter 62

It's Raining, It's Pouring

Damn this rain. I wanted to work in the garden all afternoon, but the rain is getting heavier so I think I'll make an early start on dinner. If the rain lets up, I can pop outside later to finish deadheading the roses. They'll be sodden by then. Remind me never to plant Bourbon roses again. Heavy rain turns them into brown balls of cotton wool.

We're having cold chicken tonight, with salad. Always an easy dinner when there's so much gardening to do. Who wants to spend hours cooking when you can be outside? I throw the new potatoes into a pan of cold water. They're easier to scrape if they have a good soak first.

After filling up the kettle, I put the television on. It's a bit of an indulgence having a set in the kitchen, but I might as well treat myself to a sit-down and a cup of tea. I don't usually watch anything at this time, but *Ground Force* might be on, or a property programme. But it's nothing gentle like that. It's news. A flood. I clutch the worktop to steady myself. No, it can't be. I feel cold, I'm shaking, dizzy, terrified. My heart is jumping, thumping. Terrible news, no more, not all over again. Where is this? Is it now? It can't be then, but how can the flood be happening again?

There's rushing water, the force of the torrent throwing rocks, cars and branches against buildings and the collapsing bridge. I know what that feels like. You can't understand the sheer power of water unless you've been there, felt its weight, its ability to carry anything, from a car to a chair, a child to a fully-grown adult.

I can't bear to watch it a second longer. I switch off the television and sit down. My head is thumping and my hands are shaking. Tea, I need tea. I force myself to stand up and make a pot. Jim will be back from the allotment soon. He usually has a cup of tea there and a chat with the others when they've done enough digging and picking. Peas have done well this year and we've already had some lovely potatoes. Early Rocket variety, I think he said they were, and there's plenty more to come, beans through till October, and raspberries. Dear Jim, he's always worked so hard, he's been a good provider, maybe I should have been more honest with him, but I just wanted to put it all behind me.

I look out onto the garden. The hydrangeas are doing well, with big heads of blowsy flowers. In fact, all the garden is doing well, apart from those darned roses, with the amount of rain we've been having this summer. The year I bought the hens, thinking how much I'd enjoyed collecting the eggs when I was a child with Mrs Honey, I made the mistake of letting them free-range for a couple of weeks. I soon realised, when they started turning my flowerbeds into dust baths. Now they're secure in a run at the bottom of the garden and I give them weeds and grass cuttings.

And then, as I stand gazing out through the kitchen window, I can see it all over again. The churning rush of the water. I feel the cold splash of it against my thighs as we rushed back and then the sickening crash as the bridge collapsed. We'd been so near to safety, so close. The hotel was only a few hundred yards up the hill. Its lights glimmered through the sheets of rain, warning us to hurry.

It all happened in seconds. One minute I was limping towards him, calling for him to wait for me, the next I was falling into the torrent. After that I don't remember a thing. I must have screamed, I'm sure, but I've no idea whether he called after me, whether he ran back down the road trying to help, because the crashing sound of the raging flood was so overwhelming. Did he just stand by the collapsed bridge in horror, watching how I was torn away from him and thrown over the rocks? And at what point did he give up and abandon me?

Chapter 63

16 August 1952

The Ruddy Shoes

'You've had a lucky escape, love,' the fireman said when he found me. I didn't know what he meant. I was soaked, bruised and broken. I didn't know where I was, although I could hear water. Lots of rushing water.

'That fallen tree there saved you. Caught up on it, you were.'

I think it was early morning when he reached me. Everything looked grey. I could hear the gulls whirling above the grey water in a grey sky. My rescuer must have clambered and slipped over rocks, branches and timber from the houses ripped out of the village. I couldn't move and I could barely speak, my mouth was so battered. Some teeth were missing, my lips were bleeding, as was my head, my hands, my whole body.

'What's your name, love?' he'd said. And I couldn't even whisper it. He stayed with me, holding my hand I don't know how long for. I must have drifted off some of the time. I think he put a blanket over me or was it his coat? I was shivering. He said it was the shock, but I think it didn't help that I was almost naked.

The river had torn all the clothes from my body. My awful old mac I didn't care about, but my lovely summer dress with the roses and net petticoats was torn in half. The skirt was ripped away. I think the bodice was just about still there, barely covering my breasts. And I don't know about my silk knickers. They were probably in shreds.

The only bits of clothing left intact were those wretched tight shoes, still clinging to my bloodied feet. Those ruddy shoes. I should have pulled them off and run for my life before the bridge crashed into the water. It might never have happened if I'd worn sensible shoes. If only I hadn't been so vain. Maybe in proper walking shoes I could have kept up with him.

They took me to the hospital in Barnstaple, so I did go back there in the end. And I stayed a long time, while my pelvis, my legs and my arms set, my mouth mended, and my memory cleared. I remember drinking through a straw. Everyone was so kind to me there. And while I healed, I realised how very alone I was, more alone than I had ever been before. I didn't have visitors. No parents, no aunt and uncle, no Mrs Honey and no more Stevie.

My poor face was so bashed, with a fractured jaw and broken nose, I couldn't speak properly for several days and even then, my speech was slurred because of all the drugs they were giving me for the pain. I tried to speak. I tried to ask if Stevie had been to the hospital. 'Has anyone been asking for me?' I tried saying, again and again.

I knew I couldn't give them my real name. Because Stevie had said, hadn't he, 'Now don't forget, Ruby. If anyone asks, you're Rita Matthews now. We don't want them thinking we're not married, do we?' And I'd enjoyed playing the part and wearing the cheap ring he bought for me, but that too was lost. I'd always known it was too loose.

I knew I had to keep pretending and let them think I couldn't remember. And when they found me that morning by the river, there was nothing on me to say who I really was. No handbag, no ration card, nothing. All gone, torn from my hand, washed away, down, down to the very bottom of the sea. Not even a wedding ring, to suggest I was a married woman.

I must have been in the hospital for weeks when that lady came from the welfare department. I was able to talk a little by then, so I asked her to check the hotel. She wanted to know my name and where I lived and I couldn't tell her, could I? Not if I wasn't really me. At first, I said I couldn't remember. It was all mixed up in my head. Then I had an idea. I said, or rather mumbled with my bruised mouth and broken teeth, 'The Tors Hotel. I'm from the Tors Hotel.'

'Oh, right,' she said. 'Were you working there or were you a guest? I can make enquiries there and they may have some records that will help you remember your name.'

I let her think that. She was kind and she was doing her best. But she didn't come back to me. I suppose that's because they couldn't tell her anything. And then I knew the only thing that would help me was if he'd come to find me. I did wonder for a while if he hadn't made it back to the hotel either. Maybe he'd rushed back to where I'd fallen from the bridge. Maybe he jumped in to try and save me. It would have been nice if he'd tried. If he'd sacrificed himself for me.

He should have done the decent thing and reported me missing too. That was the least he could have done. The Missing Persons Bureau was in Barnstaple, so near and yet so far. I know that because the BBC announced it several times on the radio, when we listened to it on the ward. So he must have heard about that. He must have known he should have told them I'd fallen into the flooded river. But eventually I knew he didn't lift a finger to try and save me or find me. He didn't stay and do the decent thing. He ran away, too scared to admit that he, a married man, had been having an affair with a young girl. Too haunted too, I suppose, by the demons I knew he fought in his dreams, the demons I'd thought I could help him conquer.

I found out the truth for myself in the end. Once I was well enough to walk a bit, weeks after I'd been found, I limped painfully and slowly down the corridor to the phone box in the hospital. One of the WRVS ladies who came round the wards with a trolley of sweets and magazines kindly gave me coins for the phone call, once I'd looked up the right number in the telephone directory.

So I called the Tors Hotel and spoke to the receptionist. 'I was staying at the hotel with my husband, the night of the dreadful flood,' I said. 'And I think I may have left my weekend case behind by mistake. The name is Matthews. Mr and Mrs Richard Matthews.' The woman had mumbled about holding on a minute while she was checking. I put more coins in and eventually she came back and said, 'Oh yes. You checked out the day after it happened. A lot of our guests finished their holidays early after that terrible night.'

'And is my case still with you? Pale blue? In lost property perhaps?' I heard rustling and whispering and then she said, 'I'm afraid not, madam. I've double-checked, but according to our records, no property was left in the room at that time. I'm so sorry we can't help.'

I replaced the receiver and leant against the wall, feeling so lost for a moment. Then, despite the plaster of Paris on my legs, the crutches I needed to walk, the stitches in my arms and the teeth I had lost, I realised I felt strong. Before, I'd been little more than a child but now I was a woman. I may have been on my own, but it was up to me to decide what happened next. I could suddenly see my future ahead of me. I didn't have to be Ruby Morrison who lived with her unkind aunt and worked in Bodgers any longer. Nor was I Rita Matthews. I could be whoever I wanted to be so I decided I wanted to be Grace Williams.

I worked it all out as I hobbled back to my bed on the ward. Poor Grace, one of my best friends from school. Her mother had been too scared to let her go away when we were all evacuated. More fool her. They'd all died the same night as my mum.

So when the social lady came back again and I told her my memory had all come back to me and I remembered my name and address, she said, 'Well, Grace, as you unfortunately lost everything in the flood, I am going to be able to give you a new ration card.

And as soon as you are better, you should visit the local register office and ask for a replacement birth certificate. That's a very important document and you'll need it if you want to get married or apply for a passport. You just have to tell them when and where you were born.'

Well, I knew that alright. I knew the birthdays of both my best friends. Joyce and Grace, both born at home in Ilford, neither of whom I'd ever seen again after that bus had pulled away at the start of the war, with us all on our way to the station. I hadn't thought about them in years. They were ten when they died, but I went away, came back and was still alive. I could have chosen to be Joyce Wall, but I'd always liked the name Grace. Simple and elegant. Grace Williams, that's who I was now.

But did I want to go back to London? No, I can stay in Barnstaple, I thought. I'd always liked Barnstaple and the villages around. I could stay here. No one knew me in the town and dear Mrs Honey was sadly gone. She'd never have recognised me anyway, as I was only eleven when I left to go back to London. I was sorry she'd died and I decided I would visit her grave when I was well enough. But her departure made it easier for me in a way. If no one here knew me, I realised I could start a completely new life. No more sweeping out the public bar, no more knickers in Bodgers, no more Miss Perkins and her pursed-lipped disapproval, no more coarse remarks from the regulars in the pub, but also no more Stevie. I was a bit sad about that, but then I thought he couldn't care for me as much as I'd imagined. He'd never have left without trying to find me or giving the authorities my name if he really loved me.

And when I was well enough, I left the hospital on my own. No one came to meet me and help me walk down the steps. I didn't have a beautiful pale blue case or silk underwear, but the WRVS ladies gave me a set of decent clothes and a pair of shoes. My red shoes had been saved and kept in my hospital locker, but I couldn't bear to look at them, let alone wear them. They were badly scuffed and the leather was brittle and hard from the floodwater.

The volunteers also helped me find somewhere to stay. I rented a room over a hardware shop and I got a job in the bakers along the high street. I've always liked bread and cakes. Rather too much, some might say. But that didn't put Jim off. He likes something to get his hands on, he's always said. And he liked the burnt pasties and sausage rolls we sold off cheap when he came in every day for his dinner. He worked across the street in the bank.

Solid, reliable Jim. We made a go of it. Three kids, two grandchildren so far and a good pension for him and security for me. That's how I learnt at last about real love. It's not the sweet nothings, a posh hotel and the passionate kisses that really matter. It's loyalty, kindness and companionship that makes a marriage. I hadn't known that when I was young. There was no one to teach me about real love. Dad was gone, Mum went too and Aunt Ida didn't care for anyone but herself. Joan, Mrs Honey and Doreen were kind, but they couldn't help me the way a mother could have done.

Jim asked me once in the beginning about my family. 'All gone in the Blitz, sadly,' I said. 'I recovered from my injuries, but the others didn't. But I came here as a child and loved it and promised myself that if I could, I'd come back to live here one day. And I did.'

'And if you hadn't, we'd never have met. I'm so glad you came back, Grace.'

'So am I,' I said. And it's true. I am glad. And here he is now, with a box of veg from the allotment. His trousers are muddy, his fingernails are black, but he is smiling as he sees me and I smile back.

'Terrible news about the flood up at Boscastle,' he says. 'But thank heaven no casualties.' He stands back and looks at me. 'You're shivering, love. You're not coming down with something, are you?'

I shake my head. 'It's this blessed rain. I got a bit chilly.' And I kiss him and put the kettle on again. And while I wait for it to boil, I remember those lost at Lynmouth and wonder if Stevie ever saw that list of names. Thirty-three names in all, followed by the words, *One lady unidentified*. I've often wondered who she was and whether she was trying to leave a life that didn't suit her, like me.

I read about her in the papers, that 'Girl X'. They said she was dark-haired and had well-kept hands, just like me. And then they added a crucial detail, saying 'she wore shoes that were too tight for her'. I've always been glad they added that tiny extra clue to her identity. I hope he read that and assumed that poor girl was me. I hope he remembers how I hobbled and how I couldn't keep up with him. And I hope he is truly sorry and ashamed that he didn't try to help.

But I'm not sorry, though of course I pity the poor unknown girl. I know the flood took many lives, which is terribly tragic, but it gave me the chance of a new life, a better life, and I'll always be grateful for that. But I haven't been back there. I can't even bear to go near a river any more. My life is here now. I have a good life and I've found real and enduring love.

Mrs Honey's Christmas Pudding Recipe

Makes five 1-pint basins

1lb currants
1lb raisins
1lb sultanas

1lb chopped beef suet
4oz plain flour
12oz white breadcrumbs
1lb 12oz brown sugar
2oz mixed candied peel
1.5 teaspoons allspice
0.25 teaspoon nutmeg
0.5 teaspoon salt
2lb cooking apples
6 eggs
Quarter-pint brandy
Butter to grease

1 Put dry ingredients and apples together in a large bowl and mix together. Apples should be peeled and finely chopped. Dried fruit should be washed.
2 Beat eggs and add to mixture. Stir until everything is mixed in properly. Add brandy.
3 Divide mixture evenly between greased basins. Cover securely with greaseproof paper then a pudding cloth and steam for

five hours each. Water should come only halfway up basin and should not boil dry.

4 Puddings will keep in a cool dark place for one year. To reheat, steam for approximately one hour.

Mrs Honey's Mincemeat Recipe

1lb cooking apples
1lb raisins
1lb sultanas
1lb currants
8oz mixed candied peel
1lb chopped beef suet
2oz almonds
1 teaspoon mixed spice
1lb brown sugar
Grated rind and juice of 1 lemon
Quarter-pint brandy

1 Peel and chop apples finely.
2 Mix all dried fruit, suet, almonds and peel together in a large
   bowl until black.
3 Add spices, sugar, lemon rind, juice and brandy.
4 Mix thoroughly.
5 Pack closely in dry sterilised jars.
6 Cover with wax-tissue paper dipped in brandy and then tie
   parchment over the top.
7 Make at least one month before using. Will keep for one year
   in a cool dark place.

Mrs Honey's Pancake Recipe

4oz plain flour
pinch of salt
1 large fresh egg
½ pint milk
Oil or lard for frying
Lemon and caster sugar to serve

1 Add the salt to the flour in a large basin.
2 Make a well in the flour and break the egg into the well.
3 Begin mixing the egg into the flour, then add a little milk.
4 Keep beating the milk into the flour until you have a smooth creamy batter.
5 Grease a frying pan with a little cooking oil or lard and heat on the hob.
6 The pan should not be pooling grease, just smeared.
7 When the pan is hot but nowhere near smoking, pour a large spoonful of batter into the pan.
8 Quickly swirl the pan around so the batter spreads out over the pan surface.
9 Keep the pan on the heat until the pancake shifts when you jerk the pan. The sound of rustling will tell you it is cooked underneath.
10 Toss or turn the pancake to cook the other side for about a minute.

11 Serve on a warm plate with lemon and sugar. Or make a batch of pancakes and store, interleaved with greaseproof paper. Pancakes can be kept and reheated or wrapped in paper and foil, then frozen.

WW2 Rations 1940: per one person (adult)

Butter: 50g (2oz)

Bacon or ham: 100g (4oz)

Margarine: 100g (4oz)

Cooking fat/lard: 100g (4oz)

Sugar: 225g (8oz)

Meat: To the value of 1/2d and sometimes 1/10d – about 450g (1lb) to 350g (12oz)

Milk: 1800ml (3 pints) occasionally dropping to 1200ml (2 pints)

Cheese: 50g (2oz) rising to 225g (8oz)

Eggs: 1 fresh egg a week

Tea: 50g (2oz)

Jam: 450g (1lb) every two months

Dried eggs: 1 packet (12 eggs) every four weeks

Sweets & Chocolate: 350g (12oz) every four weeks

A LETTER FROM SUZANNE

Thank you so much for reading *The Girl Without a Name*. I hope you found the story of the unnamed girl as sad and intriguing as I do. If you enjoyed this book and want to keep up to date with my latest releases, just sign up at the following link. Your email address will never be shared and you can unsubscribe at any time.

www.bookouture.com/suzanne-goldring

I hope you have enjoyed reading *The Girl Without a Name* and if you did, I'd be very grateful if you could write a review. I'd love to hear what you think and it makes such a difference helping new readers discover one of my books for the first time.

I love hearing from my readers – you can get in touch through my Facebook page, Twitter or my Wordpress website.

@suzannegoldringauthor

@suzannegoldring

www.suzannegoldring.wordpress.com

BACKGROUND TO THE BOOK

I first became aware of the Lynmouth flood disaster in my early teens, when I stayed there with my parents about twenty years after that dreadful time. In such a beautiful location, filled with carefree summer holidaymakers, it was hard to picture the destruction that had occurred not so very long before, and the rushing sound of the river was no longer ominous. But when I returned as an adult years later, I became more interested in the catastrophe and immensely curious about the possible history of the unidentified young woman, named Girl X by the newspapers.

And the more I thought about who she could have been and why her absence was not reported, the more I began to think about the state of mind of people who might have been in the village in 1952, not so very long after the end of the war. Every adult who was there that dreadful night would have lived through the years of the Second World War and its aftermath. Some would have come through the war inconvenienced but relatively unscathed, while others may have been damaged by experiences that left deep scars, influencing their behaviour and relationships for the rest of their lives.

For answers to questions about the impact of trauma on an individual, I turned to The Ripple Pond, a support network for the adult family members of British service personnel and veterans. This charity's important work gave me insights into late-onset Post-Traumatic Stress Disorder and emotional numbing, helping me develop the story you have just read.

Thinking about the lives of young adults in 1952, young people who may have been wartime evacuees, may have had to leave bombed-out homes, may have lost friends and family, made me think about the consequences of disrupted lives and inevitably led me to think about my own parents. References to the war often cropped up in conversation, but not in detail.

My father, to whom this book is dedicated, was an only child and was evacuated at the age of twelve to Street in Somerset. He wrote home complaining about the food and conditions there and returned to the outskirts of east London for the rest of the war, running messages for the fire service. When he was called up to do his National Service he was sent to Palestine, where as far as I can remember, he enjoyed his time there, even though it coincided with the bombing in Jerusalem of the King David Hotel. Luckily, he was not involved in the search for victims there.

We may never know who Girl X was, never know why she wasn't reported missing, never know why she wasn't identified. The explanation I have explored here is just one possibility, but nearly seventy years after she drowned, it is increasingly unlikely that her identity will ever come to light. But if you go to the wilds of north Devon, I urge you to visit the Flood Memorial Hall, which graphically conveys the devastation of 1952. The twin villages of Lynton and Lynmouth are still picturesque, the surrounding scenery is dramatic, the cliff railway still trundles up and down the steep hill, the river still tumbles over the rocks and you can still eat your fill of fish and chips and cream teas. On a summer's day it is hard to believe that all this was shattered nearly seventy years ago. But stand on the riverbank and listen to the rushing thunder of the water and you will understand the power of this mighty flow and maybe feel a shiver at the thought that this beautiful river once destroyed lives and homes.

The Valency River that runs through Boscastle on the north Cornwall coast caused similar devastation on 16 August 2004, eerily fifty-two years almost to the day after the Lynmouth flood. Yet this time emergency services were alerted rapidly and arrived promptly to prevent loss of life. When you visit this village in its deep valley, you will hear the river rushing down to the sea and wonder how something so clean and clear can be so destructive. And it was not hard for me to imagine how news of the Boscastle flood could revive disturbing memories for anyone who had experienced the floodwaters in Devon years before, giving me my starting point for this novel.

RESEARCH

Because Ruby and Stevie were only children when they were affected by the long-lasting impact of their experiences during the Second World War, I decided that it would be appropriate to use children's rhymes to mark the various sections of the book. All the rhymes and street songs marking these divisions were found in the collections documented by the famous folklorists, Iona and Peter Opie.

I also referred frequently to the definitive account of the Lynmouth flood, written by Eric Delderfield. First published in May 1953, not even a year after the disaster, and reprinted nineteen times since then, it contains many eyewitness accounts of that terrible night. It was here that I found the description of seven lady holidaymakers who linked arms to wade through flooded Lynmouth Street after attending the concert party at the Pavilion. One member of their group was nearest to the crumbling riverbank and was washed away by the swollen river. That was fifty-six-year-old Elsie Cherry from Highgate in London. Her body was found in Clovelly, along the Devon coast, many weeks later. I hope she and her friends would not be offended by me immortalising her charming surname. I am sure the original Miss Cherry was a much nicer person than Aunt Ida.

Further reading:

National Service, Peter Doyle and Paul Evans
The Blitz, Juliet Gardiner
The British Army in Palestine, National Army Museum

The Lore and Language of Schoolchildren, Iona and Peter Opie
The Lynmouth Flood Disaster, Eric Delderfield
The Oxford Dictionary of Nursery Rhymes, Iona and Peter Opie
Wanderings in North Devon, Revd. John Chanter
Wartime Childhood, Mike Brown
https://www.africanstudies.northwestern.edu/docs/publications-research/special-publications/wilks-8-3-11.pdf

ACKNOWLEDGEMENTS

I am immensely grateful for the encouragement of writer friends in three writing groups where we share our work, our successes and our struggles: the Vesta girls, Carol, Denise and Gail; the Ark Writers, Helen, Katrina, Jenny, Di, Mark and Jenni; the Elstead Writers Group, Stella, Jacqui, Richard, Paul, Chris, John and Martin.

I am also very fortunate in having the enthusiastic support of my very understanding editor, Lydia Vassar-Smith, and the calming voice of my literary agent, Heather Holden-Brown.

And finally, my immense thanks to Sue Hawkins, co-founder of The Ripple Pond, and her colleague, Tracy Carter, for their sound advice and for reading this novel before publication.

THE RIPPLE POND
Statement from Lynne Wigmore, Manager of The Ripple Pond:

We offer a support network for the adult family members of British service personnel and veterans. Feelings of isolation and loneliness can be utterly overwhelming. By putting members in touch both face to face and virtually, The Ripple Pond facilitates genuine and confidential support in a safe place. Our members tell us that this peer support, together with informative signposting, helps them face daily challenges. Building their self-esteem and confidence results in a more positive state of mental health. Finally, they begin to take control of their lives once more.